MW01231773

# BEFORE THE STREET LIGHTS COME ON

*A Friendsmas Story*

BY

## ASHLEY ANTOINETTE

www.asharmy.com
Designed By Destiny Darcel
Edited by LaMia Ashley
ISBN: 978-1-963400-01-4

Distributed by Ashley Antoinette Inc.
Submit Wholesale Orders to:
owl.aac@gmail.com

# DEDICATION

This book is dedicated to all the women who understand the value of other women. May you know a good friend. May you be a good friend. May you inspire, uplift, and protect every woman in your reach. This one is for the girl's girls. Ash Army, this book is for you. Thank you for finding me. Thank you for choosing me. Thank you for connecting with me. Thank you for empowering me. Thank you for allowing me to be Ash, the woman, and seeing beyond the brand. Thank you for knowing my heart and accepting my flaws. Thank you for loving me and every woman next to me. Thank you for finding yourself on my pages. I am so thankful for this girl tribe. This is sisterhood. Wow, the power of words, the purpose of God, and a Black girl with an imagination and a dream brought us all to this very page in this fictional story and in the stories of our lives. I hope this chapter is the one we can't wait to read aloud. I love y'all.

-xoxo-

Ash

In honor of

## Sequoia Murphy

"Our forever butterfly."

#asharmy

*For my Day 1s*

*Khloe*
*Vee*
*Shonda*
*Char*

*Whatever you lack, borrow it from my soul. I love y'all 'til they drop me.*

*For my Day 2's*

*Tiffanie*
*Telebah*
*Bianca*
*Tamesia*
*Alexis*
*Latrise*
*Carmen*
*Iesha*

*You are proof that friendship has no prerequisite. All it requires is loyalty & love.*

*To My Babies*

*Syd*
*Tori*
*Imani*
*Jessica*
*Jada*
*Shay*

*Thank you for believing in me first. You taught me how to be a leader of girls before we became women. My first and forever babies. I know y'all grown now, but hush.*

*To the Women Who Shaped Me*

*Jacqueline*
*Tammy*
*Raven*

*I can build a village of loyal women because I was raised in one.*
*Thank you. I love you.*

# CHAPTER 1

**December 17th**

I really don't understand why Shy is so damn extra when it comes to Christmas. I mean, the themes and the dress codes, and the freaking minimum spends. Like, be fucking for real. I've got two kids to buy gifts for. I'm suddenly remembering why I haven't been home to visit for Christmas in years. It's too much damn pressure." Elliot Campbell walked around her bedroom, putting clothes into the open suitcase that sat on her bed as she complained endlessly. Christmas break was a season she welcomed. The two weeks off work and the extended reprieve from her kids' school schedules felt like heaven, but the thought of packing her entire family up and making their way to Michigan to spend time with friends and family gave her an anxiety she hadn't anticipated.

"You know Nashyla wouldn't be Nashyla if she wasn't a little extra. She has a whole Friendsmas itinerary," Sloan replied.

"Wait, what? I thought it was just dinner! I'm not trying to follow a schedule my whole break. I have other people to visit besides y'all bitches. And I already know every event has a different dress code."

"Yeah, girl, you already know. Check the group chat. She dropped the itinerary last night, but I can't lie, it looks like a whole vibe. It's gonna be a good time. We've got ice skating on the rocks, girls' night in, we're going to the Christmas Tree Farm, and some other shit, but it's a dope week," Sloan informed.

"Sounds like I'ma need a vacation after vacation," Elliot mumbled. The groan she let out only made Sloan chuckle harder.

"Ellie, just get your ass on that plane and stop complaining. You haven't come home for Christmas in four years. Everybody misses you, and I want to see my Goddaughters."

"Fine," Ellie sighed. "Let me get off this phone and finish getting my life together. I'll see you hoes tomorrow. Love you."

"Love you too, girl. Safe travels," Sloan answered.

Ellie sighed and hung up the line. She hated this feeling of displacement. The thought of going home terrified her. The longer she stayed away, the more her anxiety grew, and it was a shame because the little city that had made her was one she took so much pride in. Flint, Michigan, had been a glorious place when she was growing up. Poverty had eroded the place over the years, leaving more boarded-up houses than family homes behind, but still, it was home. All her memories of ripping and running the streets with her girls were made on those city blocks. She hadn't grown up with much. She and her brother, Cassidy, were raised by their mom and dad. They hadn't been rich, but they survived. Her father had worked endlessly to make sure he took care of his family. There wasn't much room for extras like the Tommy Hilfiger and $150 tennis shoes girls used to wear. Ellie knew her family was tight for money, and she never tried to keep up with the other girls her age. She was grateful for everything, even when her parents could give her nothing, but it made her an outlier at school. She was teased endlessly about her Payless shoes and cheap, hand-me-down clothes. Before she met Sloan and started borrowing her clothes, Ellie was the girl everyone ignored. In fact, she was the girl Sloan blazed. One fight with Sloan in the 7th grade had landed them both Saturday detention for a month, and the pair went from enemies to fast friends. Sloan was the most popular girl in school, so with that one friendship, sisterhood followed, and her homegirls never left her uncovered. There were four of them. Ellie, Sloan, Shy, and Courtney. She would rotate in and out of their closets so much that she had a full wardrobe. From old-school Baby Phat velour suits to fresh Saucony sneakers, whatever they had, they shared, and Ellie was grateful. She was able to feel like more than the busted-down girl from the projects. She reached for the picture of the four of them that sat on her vanity, and she smiled. Most girls didn't learn the value of true friendship until they were older. Ellie had learned it early. They had supported her through every single phase of her life. She was 40 years old, and she had been through some things that had shaken her to her core. She had experienced days so dark that she'd never thought the sun would rise again. Her heart had been used and abused, leaving her empty and fearful of a life without love. Loneliness was impossible, however, because her friends had been right there, every single time, without judgment and always coming with wine. Lots and lots of wine. She sighed and placed the picture back as a knock at the door jarred her from her thoughts. An interruption. When you were a mother of two, there was always someone needing something. Her time was not her own to spend. Some days, it overwhelmed her. The lack of peace of it all. Most days, she welcomed the chaos of having daughters. Today, she was tired.

"Hey, Mommy, can I get money for Robux?"

The sweetest little face stood in front of her, gripping an iPad to her chest.

"No, baby, you've already spent your allowance for the week. If you want more Robux, you'll have to wait until you earn your next allowance," Ellie said. "You can come give me a hug, though." She bent down so that she was at eye level with her baby and reached out her arms. The most fulfilling sense of peace filled her every time she hugged her kids. Her oldest daughter, Brooklyn, gave hugs out like winning lottery tickets. It was a long shot that she would get one from her attitude-filled teenager these days, but this little one, she gave them out for free. It was a remedy for an ailment that children didn't know their mothers had.

Tessa was a doll. Ellie often got lost in her youngest daughter's dreamy eyes. She wished she could say her beauty came from her, but she honestly had no idea where it came from. The adoption had been closed, and she hadn't been privileged to meet Tessa's birth mother. From the moment she laid eyes on the three-month-old little girl, Ellie had fallen in love. They both had. Ellie and Cairo had adopted this beautiful girl together four years ago, and she was almost positive that it was the decision that had ruined them. She had traded motherhood for her marriage, and although she would never regret this little light in her life, she had been heartbroken ever since. It was one of many reasons she hadn't been home in so long. Her husband had moved back to Michigan and started a whole new life, and Ellie was humiliated. They weren't even technically divorced, and he had completely replaced her. In the blink of an eye, she had gone from a kept housewife to a single mother. Life had been hard. Life had been unfair, but the little arms wrapping around her neck so lovingly were worth it.

"That's my big girl. I love you, baby," Ellie said. "Did Brook help you pack?"

"No, she said I had to pack myself," Tessa said. "I'm finished already."

Ellie stood and took Tessa's hand. "Come on, let's see what you have in your suitcase," Ellie said. They walked through her three-bedroom townhome until she reached Tessa's room. As soon as she saw the suitcase lying wide open, she smiled. It was all toys, electronics, her favorite pajamas, and two shirts. "You did a great job, Tess," Ellie encouraged. "Why don't you climb in bed? I'll give you one show before it's lights out. We have an early flight in the morning."

"Okay. I can't wait!" Tessa exclaimed.

"Me too, baby," Ellie said softly. She turned off the overhead light and clicked the night light by the bed as Tessa clicked into the YouTube app on the TV. *These damn new school kids are a different breed. I'll never understand the desire to watch kids play with the same toys you let sit inside your closet,* Ellie thought playfully. Ellie was halfway out the door when Tessa's sweet voice halted her.

"Mommy, will we get to see Daddy when we get to Michigan? That's where he lives, right?"

The question took her breath away. There were these moments, these triggers, that just punched her in the gut and made the pain of Cairo's desertion feel fresh. It was those moments that she had to soldier past. It was shit just like this that felt like the heaviest weight God had ever made. Having to be a mother while she was hurting at the hands of the man who had vowed to love her was a masquerade she was underdressed for. She tightened her core and blinked away the sting in her eyes. "We'll see, baby. Get some rest and spend a little time with God before you close your eyes."

Ellie narrowed her sights on the closed bedroom door at the end of the hallway and then went to check on her oldest child. She curved her pointer finger and knocked softly on the door. It was only a courtesy knock because she was already jiggling the door handle.

"Brooklyn, open this door! What I tell you about locking doors in my house?" she fussed.

She heard rustling and hurried movements behind the door.

"You've got three seconds to open this door…"

"Mama, I was just studying," Brooklynn squealed in exasperation as she snatched open the door. Brown skin. Oh, how she loved her baby's brown skin and those black eyes and those pretty, pouty lips where her lies lived. Brooklyn was a replica of Cairo. She was the one thing they had gotten right, a beautiful creation that came from their love.

"Girl, you must really think I'm dumb. Don't insult my intelligence. Studying what? The semester ended today, so what the hell you studying, Brook?" Ellie fussed. She hated this new, sneaky version of her daughter. It was like, as soon as Brooklyn hit sixteen, all hell broke loose.

"I was just reading." Brooklyn would feign innocence until she was blue in the face.

"Is that weed I smell?" Ellie asked, walking past her daughter, and stepping fully into the room.

"Mama, no! You're tripping!" Brooklyn denied.

Ellie followed her nose to the adjoining bathroom and pushed open the door. Sure enough, there was evidence of ashes floating in the toilet. Ellie hit the lever. "You got to flush twice to get rid of evidence, genius! You think you're too smart for your own good. Where'd you get the weed from?"

"I was just holding it for a friend! It's not even mine!" Brooklyn cried out.

"Brooklyn, I'm fed up to here with you," Ellie said, saluting her forehead. "What is going on with you? You don't do drugs. We don't do drugs! Do you know how many kids out here dying behind these drugs? This shit could be laced with anything! Have you ever heard of Fentanyl!? You don't smoke anything! Don't take anything! Not even a Tylenol, Brook! We've talked about this!"

"I wasn't, Ma!" Brooklyn wailed. Her pretty, perfect daughter was a bold-faced liar, and it broke her heart. It shouldn't have. She remembered her own lying phase through her teenage years, but being on the parental side felt horrible. She was losing control of her little girl, and it didn't feel good at all.

Ellie snapped her fingers closed right in front of Brooklyn's lips. "Stop talking, just stop lying. Your eyes are red, Brook. You're high! Don't do that. Don't lie to me. Telling the truth is a sign of respect and love. I can't protect you if you lie to me about your actions. We'll deal with the truth. But don't look in my face and tell me lies. Love me better than that. You don't lie to people you love, and we can't come to common ground if I can't trust you. You grown enough to smoke in my house, be grown enough to admit it."

Ellie took a deep breath and calmed herself because she didn't want to be the screaming mom. She wanted to be the mom that her daughters felt like they could come to about anything. Frustration was making her handle this poorly, and she didn't want to push Brooklyn away. Brooklyn stood frozen, like a deer in headlights, and she knew that her child was too afraid of punishment to deliver the truth to her in this moment. It disappointed her, but she knew accountability wouldn't be learned tonight. She sighed. "I'ma let your father deal with it. Please just finish packing and get some sleep. We have an early flight." Ellie was defeated. "And keep this door open."

"Okay now, Miss Mamas. I need you to keep this baby in here for a couple more weeks. We want baby's lungs to develop a little more before he makes his arrival," Sloan said as she withdrew the ultrasound wand from her patient, Monica. She snapped off her gloves and then stepped over to the sink to wash her hands before turning back to face the mother-to-be.

"I'm sorry. I just panicked. I felt that contraction and saw the blood in my panties and just rushed here," the woman replied. "We've been waiting so long for this to happen. I just don't want to take any chances."

"Me either. I've seen you guys through from the tears of thinking you couldn't get pregnant to hearing this little nugget's heartbeat. I'm invested, and I'ma see it through all the way until this baby is in your arms."

"Still, I feel bad. I didn't mean to call you into the ER in the middle of the night."

"Don't worry about it," Sloan said, smiling. "And everything looks fine. It's just Braxton Hicks and a little spotting, but your cervix looks good. Don't hesitate to come back if you have any concerns. The nurses know to call me when any of my patients hit this door, it doesn't matter the time," Sloan said.

"You're the best," Monica replied.

"Remember that when you're in labor and I'm asking you to push," Sloan answered with a chuckle. "The nurses will get your discharge papers. I'll see you after Christmas break."

Sloan exited the room and hurried to the doctor's lounge. She was exhausted. She had delivered three babies in a 24-hour period, and as soon as she had clocked out, one of her mother's to-be had come into the emergency room. She loved her job, but the demand was taxing. It left little time for a personal life. She had sacrificed so much to get where she was in life. While most of her friends had partied their way through their twenties, Sloan had pursued a career. School had filled her days, and work had filled her nights. She had been so focused on becoming a doctor that she missed out on a part of her life that she couldn't quite recapture. She was a reputable and highly successful OBGYN, but she wasn't sure the trade-off was worth it. All her friends had families or serious relationships— at the very least. Sloan had no one. There was no man waiting for dinner at home. There was no mess to clean up from kids destroying their rooms all day. There was no confidante to confide in about the ups and downs of her day. It was just her. She was one of one, and sometimes the silence could be loud. Her entire life was predictable and routine, down to her drive home. There were no kids to pick up along the way. There were no prescriptions to grab for her needy spouse. There was just her. She drove the same route, day in and day out, by herself. Her life was designed for one, and she was incredibly lonely. Today was no different. When she crossed the threshold of her five-bedroom home, she sighed. She didn't even know why she had purchased such a large place. She had thought she would grow into it one day, but it was only a reminder of her solitude. A pair of shoes sat by the door. One place setting was arranged on her dining room table. Being alone wasn't her choice. She tried to date, but it seemed she had waited too long. At 39 years old, any eligible bachelor now came with baggage. Men her age had children, bad credit, and bitter baby mamas. She brought so much to the table that it was hard to find a man who matched her contribution. Dating was a joke, and even when she did make time, men often lost interest in her because her availability was limited. She immediately grabbed a bottle of wine from her collection, poured herself a glass, and kept it pushing to her bedroom. Her master bathroom was her favorite room in the house. It was her personal spa. The clawfoot tub called her name after standing on her feet all day. She peeled off her clothes and then turned on the faucet. Epsom salt and lavender bubble bath felt like luxury as she poured each into the stream of running water. She sipped from her glass, almost gulping until half the glass was gone, then she turned on the shower. She swirled the red wine in her glass once more and measured it by eye. "Definitely a whole bottle type of night," she mumbled. Hurried feet carried her right back to the kitchen. "The one perk of living alone is I can walk around this bitch naked," she huffed. She grabbed the bottle and ran back to her bathroom. She showered first, to get the germs of the day off her body, before submerging into the bubble bath to soak. The bottle came with her, fuck the glass. Every part of her body ached, even her fingertips. Pulling babies from ten-centimeter wombs all day had exhausted her. She was too spent to even order dinner. The half-eaten bag of veggie straws she had in the kitchen would have to sustain her until morning. She wished there were someone there with her to help make this house a home. She didn't even need a man to do much. Make his own money, change a light bulb or two, and just order her some dinner on her way home from work. The luxury of having someone to cuddle next to and ask about her day would be a bonus. Instead, Pinot Noir kept her company every night. She soaked until her skin wrinkled and then climbed out. Her routine was almost too routine. There was no spontaneity, no warmth, no love inside these walls. She had skipped so many seasons of her young adulthood to guarantee success, and she wasn't sure if it was worth it. She was almost out of child-rearing years, with no man in sight. It was a scary realization that she had possibly missed her window to start a family. It was a heavy reality to face. She had taken a week off to celebrate Christmas, and she couldn't even remember the last time she had used her PTO. She was married to her work. She had vacation time stockpiled, and still, there was anxiety about being away from her expectant moms while she spent time with her friends. Tomorrow, the festivities would kick off with or without her, however, and she didn't want to miss out, especially since her best friend,

Ellie, was coming home. It would be a holiday to remember, and she was determined to clock out of work mode and tap into girl time. She felt like the friend who was constantly dropping the ball, and she didn't mean to be that girl. She wanted her girls to know that their moments were important to her, too. Sloan hadn't purposefully neglected them, but she knew she hadn't been as available to them as they had been to her. She would need to spend the next week making up for lost time. She felt like their friend group only existed in text messages. They sent memes and social media posts back and forth to each other all day, but they hadn't all been together in so long. Sloan spoke to Ellie the most, which was insane, considering Courtney and Shy lived less than thirty minutes away. Life had simply been busy, and she had done a bad job of maintaining her bonds. She prayed there were no bad vibes once they all got together. Too much time and distance between friends could be tricky. The last thing she wanted to do was spend her long-anticipated days off wrapped up in negative and awkward energy.

# CHAPTER 2

**December 18<sup>th</sup>**

I know these hoes better come with some good gifts," Shy said as she watched her assistant wrap the luxury items she had purchased.

"You said the limit was $200 per person, right? That should be enough to get some amazing gifts," Lola responded. "I exchange Amazon and Starbucks gift cards with my friends for Christmas, so this is out of my league."

Nashyla smiled at her assistant. "At 25, I was buying Starbucks gift cards, too, girl. People think your 20s are the best years of your life. They're shitty. You're just cute and broke. You don't know yourself, you let people handle you any kind of way. You ain't got no kind of code, no standards. You share hotel rooms on vacations. Those are your struggle years, low-key."

"Not you just read my entire life down," Lola responded, shocked but amused.

"Your 30s get better, but I'm pushing 40, babyyyy, and I feel like I'm in my prime. Heels high, pockets high, boundaries higher. So, yeah, anything under $200 won't cut it for this Friendsmas. Speaking of, did you clear your calendar? I need you here for set up."

"I did. I wouldn't miss it," Lola said.

"You're the best." Shy beamed as she sat in the makeup chair while her team danced around her. She had built a life for herself that people dreamed of.

"Oh, don't forget to book the videographer. I need to make sure I capture the content. My gifts were sponsored, so I must post the girls' reactions when they open each one and make a recap video for socials."

"Do I need to get photo releases from your friends so they can be posted?" Lola asked.

"Umm… they better not fucking ask me for no photo release. All these damn luxury gifts I'm bringing. I'm way over the $200 limit. They better let me get my content in peace," Shy joked.

Lola nodded and took notes for accuracy.

Shy was so excited. She was an events type of girl. She did everything with excellence. The best caterer had been hired, the itinerary had been set, and the dress code had been established. She even had backup outfits in case somebody came out of alignment. She could not wait to enjoy the next few days with her homegirls. Her life was one big party. This was nothing new to her. Being a self-made brand came with perks and a fast life that almost mimicked celebrity, but she didn't always get to enjoy those perks with her real friends. She was always on the scene with other influencers and brand girlies. This would be the first time in a long time that she got to turn up with her besties. She was sure she had gotten carried away with the planning, but it was only because she was excited. Shy didn't know when they would all be together again, so they were about to make up for lost motherfucking time.

Her phone rang as her makeup artist was applying her eye shadow.

"Can you get that for me, Lola?" she asked. "Who is it?"

"It's Courtney," Lola announced.

"Put her on speaker," Shy said. "Hey, Court!"

"Hey, girl," Courtney's tone was all Shy needed to hear to know that something was about to damper her plans.

"What's wrong? Why you sound like that?" Shy asked.

"Girl, James gotta work, and I can't find a sitter for the baby, so I'ma have to miss some of the events this week," Courtney informed.

"What? Noooo! Courtney!" Shy protested. "We've been talking about this for months! Your mama can't watch the baby?" she asked.

"Girl, you know I don't like to ask people for shit. I'ma just have to sit out. When I can make it, I will, but mom duty comes first."

"This sucks so bad," Shy groaned. "You can bring the baby with you. Maybe ask Ellie if Brooklyn can babysit."

"Sis, I have a four-month-old. Brooklyn is a teenage girl. She don't know how to care for a newborn," Courtney said. "It's cool. I'll just have to get in where I fit in."

"Okay, boo. I'm sorry. I feel so bad." Shy's sympathy was real. Out of them all, she was sure Courtney deserved this week the most. She was laid off from the shop, following taking maternity leave after having her most recent baby, and she was hardly ever available for girl time anymore. Shy hated it for her girl. Everything had always been hard for Courtney, for as long as Shy had known her. She had been the first one to have a baby out of the gang. Court had gotten pregnant at 16 and had dropped out of high school shortly after to get her GED so that she could work full time. Courtney had been working ever since. Life had been an uphill climb from there.

"Don't feel bad for me, girl. Everybody can't live the soft life," Courtney said.

Shy didn't miss the resentment in Courtney's tone.

"You deserve the soft life too, Court," Shy replied.

A beat of silence filled the line, and Shy's heart ached for her friend.

"I got to go, Shy. I know Ellie gets in tomorrow, but I'ma probably miss the welcome home thing at her dad's. Y'all have fun. Take a shot for me."

Courtney hung up the phone and sat there, dazed, as her stomach churned in discomfort. She didn't know how her life had come to this. Something as simple as linking up with her childhood friends over Christmas break had become problematic. She stood and walked into of the room where her child's father sat. He sat, legs wide, a beer balanced on his knee, before pulling it to his mouth for one long swig. So much tension filled the space between them that she was almost hesitant to speak.

"I told them I wasn't coming," Courtney announced.

"I ain't ask you to do that. Don't put that on me," James shot back. His eyes never left the television.

He was right. He hadn't blatantly forbidden her, but the moment she brought it up, the interrogation had begun.

Where were they going? Would any niggas be there? When would she be home? Why did she need hair and makeup? Why was one of the events overnight? Was she sharing a room with anyone? She had told him about Friendsmas months ago, and still, when the time came, his insecurities sprouted. She knew what they would lead to. She would be defending unreasonable accusations for weeks if she moved in any way that felt suspicious to him. He would ask her the same question, rewording it strategically to try to get her to give a different answer. She had to tiptoe around the details of a perfectly innocent experience just to make sure she didn't incite mistrust. She always felt cornered and defensive. The truth wasn't even true enough for him when his jealousy reared its ugly head. It was like he wanted to catch her up in a lie just so he could release whatever anger he harbored. It was exhausting, and it filled her with so much anxiety that she would just rather stay home.

"I didn't say you did. I just told them you had to work," Courtney said. It wasn't a lie. He did have shifts to cover. He worked construction and those hours were long and hard, especially in the winter. Forty-hour weeks didn't come along

19

easily in the dead of winter, so taking off wasn't the best idea. Hanging out with her girls just complicated shit. She would rather disappoint them than shake up shit in her home. James' jealousy could lead to dark places, and she wasn't willing to risk that. Things had been good. She wanted them to stay that way. If that meant she had to stay home with the baby, then so be it.

"You're a mother anyway. You can't bop around with your single friends looking for trouble. I don't know why you was even trying to," he mumbled.

A fire ignited in her chest because she hated it when he did this. She was already salty about having to sit out of the celebration with her friends. He had gotten his way. She was going to be inside. *Nigga just got to talk shit and pour salt in the wound*, she thought. Her pride just wouldn't allow her to keep quiet.

"What does them being single have to do with me going out? What does me being a mother have to do with it?" Courtney asked, folding her arms across her chest.

"You can't relate to them. Y'all ain't on the same shit no more. Or are y'all?" he challenged, finally turning from the TV.

"Every time you leave up out of here with your single homeboys, I can assume you on bullshit?"

"How we get on me? We talking about you and them bops you run with," James said. "Sound like you deflecting cuz you were trying to be on some ho shit." She heard his anger building, but he was pouring gasoline on hers as well.

"Nigga, I'm 39 years old! What another woman does with her pussy has nothing to do with what I do with mine. We are grown-ass women. My friends ain't got shit to do with me."

"So, you admit they out here wild?" James shot back. Here he was, putting words in her mouth.

"They're grown! I don't even know what they doing it like these days because I haven't seen them! I'm here, stuck in the house with your stupid ass!" she shouted. "You got your mouth poked out every time I leave the house!"

"You talking real slick, defending your fucking ghetto-ass friends. You act like I'm talking about you or something," he accused. "If you had sat your ass down and mothered Quan, maybe he would still be here right now! You were out, shaking ass with these same bitches!"

His words snatched the air from her lungs. He stood and stormed past her. "Let me get out of here before I slap the shit out you," he mumbled. She couldn't even muster up a response. The sting of the memories that rushed her threatened to unravel her. Their first son, Devin, had been gunned down when he was 14 years old while she was out celebrating her 30th birthday with her girls. It had been nine years, and nothing had been the same since that fated day. Her life had gone to shit in the blink of an eye. James had always been a little controlling. She met him in high school when she was 14. He was ten years older than her, so the control had always been present, but after their son was killed, he had become downright mean, and she knew it was because he blamed her. She didn't need his punishment. She blamed herself.

She was grateful when her son's cries wailed through the house. The sound was like an alarm that snapped her out of a bad dream. Shaken and draped in sorrow, she went to her son's crib. He was so little, such a gift. She had thought new life would make them happier, would make James less resentful, less angry, but it had done none of those things. It had just cemented her into the relationship further. Baby Christian had become the reason why she couldn't leave James. She had contemplated not having him. She had been on the brink of leaving the relationship altogether when she found out she was pregnant. Now, she was here. Now, she was stuck. Courtney picked Christian up, and the guilt she felt was immeasurable. She regretted having this baby, but damn it, she still loved him so much. "Mommy's so sorry," she whispered as she nuzzled his ear. "You deserve so much better." Christian's first Christmas would be spent in a tense home with parents who were disconnected and full of antipathy. Perhaps, if she stayed home and focused on her family, things would get better. *I just gave this nigga another baby. This has to get better.*

# CHAPTER 3

**December 18th**
**Day 2**

As soon as the wheels of the plane hit the tarmac, Ellie felt the tension rise in her chest. "Lord, please let this week be good for me and my girls," she whispered as she anxiously began to gather her things. The plane rolled to a stop at the gate, and as soon as the pilot clicked off the seatbelt sign, she stood. Thankfully, she had been upgraded to first class so she and her girls would be among the first to get off the plane.

"Brooklyn, get your sister. I'll get our carry-ons," Ellie instructed.

Wasn't shit harder than juggling kids in the airport for a single mother. She carried Tessa's backpack, Brooklyn's tote, and her purse plus a wheeled carry-on. She was overheating before she even made it to the baggage claim.

"Is Daddy picking us up?" Brooklyn asked.

"He should be here," Ellie responded.

She pulled out her phone and turned off airplane mode, before sending her estranged husband a text.

*We landed. Are you here?*

Maneuvering her way through the airport was hell. Funky bathrooms, impatient passengers, and crowded gates made it feel like she was navigating a maze. When she found her way to the baggage claim, she was relieved to see that the carousel was already spinning.

"Do you see your dad?" Ellie asked. She was grateful that he had agreed to pick them up. They barely had cordial conversation, but she knew he would want to see his children while they were in town.

"No, maybe he's waiting in the car. You want me to try his phone?" Brooklyn asked.

"Yeah, I see our bags. I'm going to grab them. Come with me, baby," she said, grabbing Tessa's hand. She lugged the heavy bags off the conveyor belt with one hand as she held on tightly to Tessa with the other. All it took was a split second for her adventurous daughter to get into mischief, so she always made sure she kept a watchful eye. "Okay, my girl. Up here," Ellie said, blowing out an exasperated breath as she lifted Tessa on top of the largest suitcase so she could straddle it for a ride.

Her eyes searched the crowd for Cairo, and she frowned as she went to Brooklyn. "Did you reach him?" Ellie asked impatiently.

"He says he can't come. He got caught up at work," Brooklyn informed.

"At work?" Ellie repeated skeptically. "If he knew he was working, why wouldn't he just say that?" she fussed. She wheeled the baggage over to a bench. "Here, you guys, sit here. Let me make some calls."

Ellie didn't want to call an Uber. It was an hour drive to her parents' home and an Uber would charge her an arm and a leg. She could have made other arrangements if she had known Cairo was going to leave her stuck. She blamed herself for even leaning on him for support. As much as he had dropped the ball lately, she should have lowered her expectations. Hoping to receive the best of someone who had already revealed the worst to her was a trait she needed to rid herself of. She broke her own heart by believing in a man who was full of false promises. She was almost ashamed to make the phone call for help, but she didn't have another choice. Ellie sighed as she scrolled through her call log and found the number. It was to someone who had always had her back, but she knew that with this call, she would also have to offer an explanation, and she had been avoiding explaining her situation to her family for years. She took a deep breath and placed the call.

"Yo, Loyal, I really appreciate ya support, man. You really came through for this Christmas giveaway," Cassidy stated as he sat across from his new business partner.

"Not a lot of niggas come out the joint and land on their feet the way you have. This is commendable, bruh. Happy to be a part of it," Loyal replied.

Cassidy nodded and lifted his cognac-filled tumbler in the air, and Loyal followed suit before they each swallowed it down.

"It's crazy because I went in at 19. Had my whole life ahead of me. Hoop scholarship and all. One bad decision took me down the wrong path for 23 years. I come out and the whole city done changed. It died, man. The shit decayed while I was gone. I just want to bring a little life back to it," Cassidy said.

"I feel that," Loyal responded. "I guess that's why I haven't moved on from investing in a city that they say isn't worth my time. The construction contracts are bigger in the bigger cities, of course. Detroit, Novi, and all that, but the shit here feels personal."

"Rebuilding the block," Cassidy stated.

"These blocks raised us, dawg. I made my first hundred grand on these streets and never looked back. I can't abandon them now that I'm on," Loyal stated. "It's good to have you out here with me, doing the work. The cigar lounge is smooth. It's a real grown vibe, and the giveaways you doing for Christmas for the community is commendable. I can respect that. Most niggas just think about profit. They don't think about pouring back into the people that support them."

"That's how you stop the wolves from entering the den, my nigga," Cassidy answered. Cassidy had known when he decided to open a business on the north side of the city that being robbed was a possibility, so he quickly aligned with the community. He made money, and he gave money back. It made niggas think twice about tearing his efforts down. He had only been open six months, but he had invested a lot in community outreach. He was apparently doing something right because Loyal now wanted to invest.

"Real shit," Loyal confirmed.

The ringing of his cell phone interrupted them, and Cassidy noticeably brightened at the name that illuminated his screen.

"Damn, bruh, must be nice. A woman ain't never brightened a nigga day like that," Loyal quipped, sporting a rare smile as he finessed his goatee.

"Mine either, this baby sis," Cassidy chuckled as he answered the call. "What's up, E?"

He paused as Ellie's fussing practically bled through the phone.

"So much for brightening that day," Loyal said, amused as he heard the woman cussing and fussing on the other end of Cassidy's line. He couldn't make out what she was saying, but he knew she wasn't happy. Cassidy signaled for the waitress.

"Don't worry about it. I'm not too far from you. I'm downtown Detroit. I'll be there in thirty," Cassidy stated.

He hung up and Loyal stood. "I take it we gon' have to settle the rest of this business later," Loyal assumed.

"Yeah, apologies. My sister just flew in, and she needs a ride from the airport," Cassidy informed. "My pops is cooking a welcome home dinner. Why don't you slide later, and we can finish chopping it up? It's kind of the kickoff to Christmas season for our family."

"Nah, I don't want to intrude. We can pick it up after the holidays," Loyal responded.

"No pressure, my nigga, but you know how that fiscal shit go. We need to wrap this business before the year end," Cassidy stated.

Loyal nodded. "True that."

"The whole neighborhood ends up at the house when the old man gets to cooking. Trust me. It's not an intimate thing at all. I'll text you the address. Pull up, get some food, and we can finish this up."

"Yeah, a'ight. I'll pull up for a minute," Loyal answered.

"Better not keep your sister waiting. She sounds like she got a little bite behind that bark. I got the tab."

"Next one's on me," Cassidy stated. They slapped hands the way gentlemen from the streets usually do, and Cassidy made his exit.

Cassidy emerged from the restaurant and handed the valet his ticket. Ellie couldn't have called at a more inopportune time, but there would never be a day she rang his line that he wouldn't fly to her rescue. He hoped he hadn't fucked up business by putting family first. Loyal owned the biggest commercial construction company in the state, and he wanted to invest in his cigar lounge, Sigaro's. In fact, he wanted to expand and open more locations. They hadn't even scratched the surface of the conversation when Ellie had called.

He pushed the old-school Cutlass to the max until he pulled up to arrivals at Detroit Metro and then pulled out his phone to call her. He got out as she emerged from the glass doors, lugging bags behind her.

"Uncle Cass!" Brooklyn shouted as she ran to him.

"Wow, look at you. Man, where my shotgun at?" he asked as he wrapped her in a hug. "My little boss ain't so little no more."

Brooklyn laughed at the nickname he had given her long ago. Ellie would take her to visit him, during his bid, and every time he would see her, he would tell her that she was the little boss. She beamed at the title back then, and even still, she wore it with pride. It had been a while since Ellie had visited the prison, and he hadn't seen her since he'd gotten released. This reunion was long overdue. He hadn't even met Tessa formally yet.

"And you must be Tessa," he said, bending so that he was at eye level with the little angel before him. Her soft hair was styled in locs and decorated with sporadic seashells, and her skin was the warmest shade of brown he had ever seen. "You're a princess, aren't you?"

"I don't think so," Tessa giggled.

"Yeah, you are. You just don't know it yet. Your mom is a queen, which means you're the princess, baby girl. I'm your uncle, Cass. It's so nice to finally meet you," he said. He held out his hand for her, and she placed her little hand in his. He kissed her knuckles and then stood to finally receive his sister.

"They're beautiful, E. Come over here," he said. Ellie placed the bags down and rushed into Cassidy's arms. "What took you so long to come home, huh? Your big bro been free almost a year, and I'm just now wrapping my arms around you."

It was freezing outside, but the duo didn't care. It had been decades since they had been able to hug one another. He felt Ellie shudder and heard the soft cries she was stifling, and he held her tighter.

"No tears, E. I'm home now," Cassidy comforted.

She nodded and squeezed her brother tightly before pushing him hard. "For being stupid!" she shouted.

Cassidy frowned and held out his hands innocently. "You been wanting to do that for 23 years, haven't you?"

"Yes, jackass," she teased. Her daughters laughed, and Ellie wiped her eyes. "You're good, though? Like, really good? Nothing happened to you in there? Your mind is good?"

"Lots of shit happened in there, but your brother a G. I ain't fold, and I promise you, I'm good," he said seriously and in a low tone so that his nieces didn't overhear.

"You promise?" she asked.

"On me," Cassidy stated, placing a hand over his heart. "Let's get y'all to the house. Papa can't wait to see y'all."

"How is he?" Ellie asked.

"If you ask him, he'll say he's fine. He's def missing mama, though," Cassidy stated.

"Aren't we all," Ellie shot back. It had been four years since their mother had been called home. It had happened two weeks before Christmas. It was the last time Ellie had been home.

"Get in, I got the bags," Cassidy said.

"Why do you still have this car?!" Ellie asked. "This shit is ancient! I'ma need you to take some of that lounge money and go to the dealership, because no. Nobody's pushing old schools anymore." She lifted the front seat so her girls could squeeze in.

"It's kind of cool," Brooklyn chimed in.

"It smells like gas!" Tessa added.

"It's a classic," Cassidy stated. "Remodeled classic. Classic shit never goes out of style."

"Sounding just like an old head who went to jail and ain't up on the times," Ellie teased. "I bet you still rocking them Fubu jerseys too, ain't you?"

"You got jokes, I see," Cassidy said, taking them in jest. "Papa is throwing you a welcome home dinner, just a heads up."

"Wait, what?" Sheer terror shot through her. "Why does it feel like I'm about to walk into an ambush? Who is coming, Cass?"

"You know the regulars. Auntie Lisa, probably some of the church members, a few neighbors. You know Uncle Joe and his kids coming with their kids. You know your daddy."

"It sounds fun, Mommy," Tessa said. "Will Daddy be there?"

"Umm, no, baby. Daddy had to work. I'm going to take you guys to him tomorrow," Ellie said. "Okay?"

"Yeah, okay," Tessa said.

Her tone wasn't to be missed. "When's the last time they saw him?" Cassidy asked.

"Don't," Ellie whispered.

They rode the rest of the way in silence as Ellie took in the sights outside her window. There was just something about Christmastime in Michigan that made her feel festive. It was the only time of the year when she didn't mind the frigid temperatures or the mountains of snow. Christmas lights decorated everything, from the businesses they passed, to the houses, to the highway overpasses. It made her heart leap in excitement, even though she had no idea what was in store for her time here. It was the season of joy, and she felt it bouncing around inside her. Christmastime just brought the little girl out in her. When they finally made it to her childhood home, she climbed out of the car, freeing her daughters from the back. Her dad was out on the porch before she could even announce herself.

"My girl!" he shouted. He didn't have on coat the first, and he didn't care as he made his way down the porch stairs and accepted her into his arms.

"Oh, Papa, you're going to freeze," she said.

"I'm an ox, girl," he said, growling in her ear as he held her close. "I missed you, Ellie. It's good to have my baby girl home."

His health hadn't allowed him to make the trip to go visit her since her mother had passed. This was his first time seeing Tessa face-to-face, but they were far from strangers. Her father made sure to FaceTime her twice a week, and he spent an hour on the phone with each of them. It was a ritual that he never broke. He only released her to open the circle as Brooklyn and Tessa crowded him for a hug.

"Papa!" Tessa cried out in excitement. "Can we go sledding on the hill you were telling me about? Can we please, please, please?"

"You damn right we can! Papa gon' show y'all how to do Christmas the right way!"

"A'ight, old man, let's get everybody in the house," Cassidy instructed.

Ellie reached for a bag, and Papa removed it from her grasp. "You know better. Get them girls in the house and check on that spaghetti that's in the oven," he said. "I'ma drop the fish in the fryer in the backyard as folks come. Don't nobody like cold fish."

Ellie snickered and did as she was told. The man could cook his ass off. She never remembered her mother having to lift a finger in the kitchen. It was always her dad. His Louisiana roots had been a blessing to their family coming up. Breakfast and dinner were always on the table, waiting for them like clockwork. She could smell the love he put into the food as soon as she stepped through the door.

"Brook, take Tessa upstairs, and y'all get out them airplane clothes. All your cousins will be pulling up soon, so don't take long," Ellie said.

"Yes, ma'am," Brooklyn responded as she disappeared with Tessa in tow.

Ellie looked at the fresh fish that had been gutted and cleaned then seasoned in the stainless-steel sink.

"Papa, your blood pressure gon' be through the roof!" she scolded as she picked up the seasonings and looked at them.

"You preaching to the choir, Ellie; just leave it alone," Cassidy stated as he bypassed the kitchen with her bags and headed for the stairs. "I'ma get y'all set up upstairs, then I'ma head to the liquor store. You want something back?"

"Casamigos," Ellie said.

Cassidy nodded. "What about you, old man?"

"He don't need no liquor plus all this salty food. His pressure!" Ellie protested.

"My pressure's fine. The doctor's been on it, and I don't eat like this every day," Papa defended. She opened the oven and saw three different types of dishes.

"Meat and pasta, seafood spaghetti, and cheese cannelloni. I know the youngest baby don't eat meat."

Ellie scoffed and turned to hug her old man one more time. She never had to ask for his consideration. He made decisions that were best for his entire family without having to be told or scolded. She loved him dearly, and she hadn't realized how badly she had missed this house until this very minute.

"Welcome home, baby," he said, eyes glossing because he, too, had missed her. He sniffed away his emotion. "It's a celebration. Let me celebrate!"

"Okay, Cass, go'n and make your liquor run." Ellie removed her coat and pushed her sleeves up to her elbows. "Homemade garlic bread coming up," she announced.

"Bitchhhhh, did I hear homemade garlic bread? Don't get started without me! I been trying to learn that recipe for fifteen years!"

"Aghhhh!" Ellie couldn't even contain the squeal that erupted from her when Shy barged into the house. She had been letting herself in since they were teenagers, and today was no different. The two old friends ran to each other, screaming and talking over each other in their excitement.

"Oh my god, it's so good to see youuuuu!" Ellie shouted. "Girl! You look good!"

Ellie hadn't missed the enhancements. If she knew her friend like she thought she knew her friend, the new body hadn't come from the gym.

"You know what they say. Hoes ain't ugly, girl, they just be broke," Shy joked as she did a spin for Ellie. Ellie shook her head and smiled because nobody brought energy to a room like Shy. She was loud, bold, and unapologetic. She was all the things that Ellie was not, and it was the reason why they had become such good girlfriends. They were yin and yang. It just worked for them. "Hey, Cass," Shy greeted.

Cass nodded her way and made his exit.

"Mr. Whitlock! I brought wine," Shy said as she walked into the kitchen and planted a kiss on Papa's cheek. She reached into her Birkin bag and pulled out a small bottle of Paul Masson. "And I got a little nip for you, too," she whispered.

"Alright now. That's my girl. Y'all get in this kitchen and keep an old man company while I set up this food. You know how to chop vegetables for a salad, or you too pretty to get your hands dirty?"

"You're the only man I'd get in the kitchen for, Papa. I got your back. Come on," Shy replied.

"You gon' kick off them heels?" he asked.

"Now, I didn't say I was gon' turn down my sexy while I was doing it, Papa. Come on, now, keep up." Shy's banter brought so much laughter and lightheartedness to the room. She had always been a good time.

Ellie shook her head as she began to prep the homemade dough. Her aunt, Lisa, walked through the door next, and behind her came cousins and family members she hadn't seen since her mother's funeral.

"Are the girls coming?" Ellie asked.

"Court is home with the baby and, girl, Sloan ass be…"

"Working, heffa! Sloan's ass be working!" Sloan finished the sentence for Shy as she snuck into the kitchen.

"Best frienddddd!" Ellie shouted. Instantly, they both teared up as they hugged. They swayed from side to side as their emotions got the best of them. They had always been this way. The closest of the bunch. Ellie and Sloan were more like sisters than friends, and time, life, and distance had made them miss each other terribly. Sloan pulled a bottle of tequila from inside her coat jacket as if they were still teenage girls and Papa wasn't supposed to see it. She blew air kisses at Shy and then set the bottle on the kitchen island. "Is it shot o'clock or what?"

"You ain't said nothing but a word, sis," Shy countered. "Let me play bartender real quick. Ellie, go get my nieces so I can say hi before I take these shots. They not about to call me the drunk auntie. Where they at?"

"Girl, they're around here somewhere with their cousins. Knowing Tess, she's convinced Brook to take her sledding down that hill in the backyard," Ellie said, shaking her head. She picked up her phone to FaceTime Brooklyn and, sure enough, when she answered, Ellie saw the large pine tree that marked the top of the sledding hill.

36

"We're out back, Ma! Come outside!" Brooklyn shouted.

"Okay, baby, here I come," Ellie called back. It was the most innocent she had heard her teenage daughter sound in months and Ellie loved it.

"Oh, if I'm going outside, I'm definitely taking a shot first," Shy said.

"Did you bring anything besides those high-heeled boots?" Sloan asked, frowning.

"No, but I'ma just sit on the patio. These are Fendi. Besides, I'm not trudging up that hill to play with them kids," Shy answered.

Ellie snickered as Shy found red cups and set up six shots. There were three of them, and their routine was to always run it back. They each grabbed a cup and held it up.

"To us being together again. Y'all bitches mean everything to me. I'm so glad you came home, Ellie. To Friendsmas," Shy toasted.

"To Friendsmas!" they all joined in. They tapped the cup on the edge of the counter before taking it, then picked up the second cup and took that round to the head, too. Ellie grimaced, and Sloan frowned in disgust.

"My shot days are few and far between. This is terrible," Sloan complained.

"Who are y'all?" Shy laughed. "Y'all know the rules. See a shot, take a shot. This is the energy I need all week." As if she had jogged her own memory, she held up a finger to get them to wait. "Oooh, speaking of, you know we must start the festivities off in a benevolent spirit, so we're going to choose a charity and volunteer at one of their events tomorrow. I didn't want to choose the charity by myself, so I sent a list to your emails," Shy said.

Cassidy walked back in the front door carrying two large brown paper bags. The family that was gathered in the living room all stopped him along his way to the kitchen.

"But wait, Cass is hosting a toy drive at his cigar lounge. Can we just support that?" Ellie asked.

"Sounds good to me," Shy said.

"You good with that, Sloan?" Shy asked.

Sloan's eyes followed Cassidy through the house.

"Nigga fine as fuck, ain't he?" Shy asked, snickering. Ellie shook her head. She remembered her friends and their crushes on her brother back in the day.

"Don't start, y'all," Ellie warned, gagging playfully. "Hey, Cass! Come here for a second!"

Ellie poured a hefty shot for Cassidy and handed it to him.

"You remember Sloan," Ellie said. It had been 23 years since he had seen her, but there was no way he couldn't remember her.

"Of course; how you doing?" Cassidy greeted.

"I'm good," Sloan replied with a short smile. "It's good to see you." Ellie frowned because she knew her friend. She was always pretty demure with men, but she couldn't even look Cassidy in the eyes.

"So, you know we have a week of Friendsmas events planned, and one of the tasks includes supporting a local charity event. We want to pull up to yours tomorrow. How can we help? You need toys? Need us to serve food? Like, what you need? We got you."

"That's love," Cassidy replied. "I appreciate you ladies. I think we're set on the donations but just come by. We could always use the extra hands on deck. I'm sure I can put you to work somehow."

"It's a date," Sloan replied. She grimaced and then tried to correct herself. "I mean, not a date. I don't know why I said that. I meant..."

"It's a date," Cassidy confirmed, smiling graciously, relieving the foot from her mouth. "Here are your bottles. Y'all don't get too tore up, a'ight?"

"Nigga, you ain't nobody daddy, go'n about your business," Ellie dismissed, waving him off and pushing him out the back door. "Go check on your nieces and make sure Tessa keeps her hat and gloves on, please!"

"I got you. Have fun with your girls," he said.

"Bitch, not jail did a body fucking good! They don't even make niggas like that on the outside!" Shy hissed.

"Eww, stop," Ellie groaned. "Help me with this food and pour some more shots."

"You and my mommy were best friends in high school?" Tessa asked.

"We were. Your mom is my favorite person in the whole world," Sloan answered as she held the little girl in her lap while they warmed up in front of the fireplace.

"I wish I had a best friend," Tessa said, sadly.

"You don't? What about kids at school?" Sloan asked curiously.

"They're mean to me. They call me ugly," Tessa revealed. "One day, Mommy and Brook came to school for family day, and they said I don't look like them. They said I'm the ugly one."

"Tessa, baby, you're beautiful. Those eyes and that beautiful nose. Your skin. Your locs. Don't listen to those kids. Kids are mean when they're hurting inside. Somebody hurt them and it makes them feel better to hurt other people too. Don't let them. You heal hurt people with love. Okay?" Sloan schooled. Her heart ached for this little girl. Kids could be so mean. "And whenever you need a reminder of how beautiful you are, you have your mom call Auntie Sloan, okay?"

Tessa nodded. "Can you be my best friend too?"

"I sure can. I'll be your best friend forever, baby doll," Sloan agreed.

"And you tell them kids at your school that your uncle don't play. I'll fuck their daddies up since they can't control their mean-ass kids."

Sloan turned to find Cassidy leaning against the door frame. Tessa jumped up from Sloan's lap and ran to Cassidy. He scooped her effortlessly and tossed her in the air before slamming her softly on the plush couch. It all looked so rough to Sloan, but Tessa loved it. She giggled endlessly. "You better head out and get a couple more turns on that sled before the kids leave," Cassidy said. Tessa went racing out the door.

"You're good with her," Sloan complimented. Cassidy took a seat on the floor next to Sloan and wrapped his arms around his knees before clasping one hand around the opposite wrist. "You have kids?" she asked.

"Nah, no kids. I got locked up before that could happen for me," he said.

"I guess this is kind of a welcome home party for you, too. I remember when all that went down," Sloan said.

"It wasn't my finest hour," he admitted.

Sloan was almost afraid to look at him. He was a felon, a drug dealer and convicted murderer. Being around him made her feel anxious. She didn't know what to say to a man who could take the life of another human being. He made her nervous, and the butterflies dancing in her stomach were from fear, not attraction.

"Have you changed?" she asked.

"That's a big question," he countered.

"After two decades in prison for murder, it shouldn't be hard to answer." She didn't mean to be so direct. She instantly regretted the words because they felt aggressive. She had no right to be questioning this man, but oddly, she really wanted to know. "I'm sorry. That was out of line."

"I'm used to it," he said.

"Used to what?" she asked.

"People judging me. Niggas' preconceived notions. People being afraid of me," Cassidy answered.

"I'm not afraid of you," Sloan lied.

"So, you just make it a habit of looking at the floor and spinning that ring on your finger when everybody talks?" he asked.

Sloan stopped spinning the ring.

"Instead of being afraid of me, just ask me whatever it takes to put your mind at ease," Cassidy said.

Sloan took a deep breath and turned her body so that she was facing him.

"Is that better?" she asked.

"Much," he countered. She took him in. Shy was right; prison had built him up damn good. He was tall, and his body was defined. The prison tattoos told a story of grit that she was sure was terrifying. His honey hue was a little light for her taste, but his energy was as dark as night. He was the type of man who carried his hood resume everywhere with him just from his demeanor. He couldn't turn it off. Even if he was dressed in the finest suit, his aura repped a set he couldn't erase. He was born and bred in the streets, and he had been cemented in the penitentiary. A man like that was dangerous, and he intimidated Sloan. "So, shoot."

"I used to come here all the time. You used to be around me all the time, Cassidy. I don't know how the boy I used to crush on... My best friend's cool-ass, fine-ass, older brother became what you became."

"What did I become?" Cassidy asked.

Sloan shook her head in disgust. "You beat that old man to death with a pole. They ran the crime scene photos on the front page of The Flint Journal for a week. We sat in that courtroom, waiting for you to apologize. You didn't shed one tear, showed no remorse. How could you do something like that with your bare hands? That's barbaric. It's psychotic. That man didn't hurt anybody. You went there for what? To try to rob him? You could have left that old man with his life."

"I guess you know everything then, Sloan," Cassidy replied sarcastically.

"I know enough to know that you're capable of snapping out and that people should fear you," Sloan replied, standing to her feet. Cassidy didn't rush to join her. "Ellie and Papa Whitlock seem happy that you're home, and I'm happy for them because I know what they went through when you got locked up. Ellie was a wreck. Your mom was heartbroken, but you deserved every year they gave you, Cassidy. A man that's capable of losing control like that, for no reason at all besides his own selfish plans to take something he didn't earn..." Sloan scoffed. "Yeah, I'm afraid of a man like that."

"Is everything okay in here?" Ellie's voice interrupted them, and Sloan was grateful for the intermission.

"Yeah, E, everything's good," Cassidy lied as he stood to his feet. "I'ma head out. I've got a big day tomorrow. I'll see you at the toy drive," he said. "Mama's car is in the garage. The keys are in her jewelry box. Good seeing you, Sloan."

Sloan didn't respond, and Cassidy brushed by her and off into the night.

Ellie looked at Sloan in exasperation.

"What the hell was that about?" Ellie asked.

Sloan shook her head. "Nothing, girl. I'ma call it too. I'll see you tomorrow. Welcome back."

# CHAPTER 4

### December 19

**M**a, why do we have to come to this? Papa said he was going to take us Christmas shopping today," Brooklyn huffed as she got out of the car. "And Daddy is supposed to pick us up."

"Because y'all need to learn about giving and not just receiving, baby. Come on," Ellie said as she let Tessa out of the backseat. The event didn't start for another hour, and there was already a line of people around the block. She made her way to the door.

"I'm Ellie, Cassidy's sister. My girls and I are here to volunteer," she said to the woman at the check-in desk. They let her in without a fuss, and she entered the lounge.

"Wow," she said. She was impressed. This wasn't just a cigar lounge; it was a luxury spot with a full kitchen, bar, and televisions throughout. There was a stage for a live band and all. Christmas décor was being set up throughout. She spotted Cassidy, and she made her way over to him.

"I want you to meet my partner, Loyal Brier; this is my sister, Elliot Campbell," Cassidy introduced.

"Nice to meet you," Ellie said, smiling. "These are my daughters, Brooklyn and Tess. Where y'all need us? All the girls are coming to help out as well."

"My nieces can come with me," Cassidy said. "We've got activity stations set up all throughout the back parking lot to keep the families occupied. United Way is here, Big Brothers Big Sisters, a few local businesses, all types of vendors. You can kind of just hang out, get in where you fit in. Go have a drink at the bar, grab some food. You and your girls start a tab and just chill."

"Get in where I fit in?" she repeated as she watched Cassidy whisk her kids away. "Okayyy," she sighed. "So does that mean my help ain't wanted?"

A hint of amusement played on Loyal's face, and Ellie focused on him for the first time. He was mysterious. He was casual enough in denim, a hoodie, and a pea coat. Only a keen eye would notice that the casual wear was really designer, and he was wearing over ten thousand dollars in clothing. The watch wasn't bust down, so it wasn't flashy, but she clocked another $60,000 just on his wrist. She appreciated that he wasn't dripped in chains, but the Cartier shades were another few thousand— easily. He was fine, and he was paid.

"I think we got enough help here, honestly. He told me you're in town for the holidays. I think he just wants you to enjoy yourself while you're here," Loyal said. "Let the workers work."

"Well, what are you going to do?" she asked.

"I'ma secure my investment," he stated. "North side of Flint, huge crowd. We got to make sure it stays peaceful out here. It's Christmas; everybody wanna make it home."

She frowned, looking at him curiously. "So, how exactly are you involved with my brother? What do you do?"

"She's suspicious," he noted.

"She's protective," Ellie corrected. "Cass just got home, so if you're some street nigga who thinks he's about to clean drug money through my brother's legit business, it's not happening. He can't afford to slip up, and nobody's sending him back to jail."

"That's not what this is, but as loud as you are, you're going to have people thinking otherwise," Loyal said. "Have a drink with me." It wasn't a question. It was a command. He pulled out one of the bar stools behind her, and she reluctantly sat as he took his place next to her. He didn't face the bar. He half faced her, and half faced the door.

"What can I get you, boss?" the bartender asked.

"Boss?" Ellie asked, looking at him skeptically. "Investor equates to boss, now? I think I'd like to see the agreement between you and Cass."

"And you're the little sister?" Loyal asked.

"The little sister who has an MBA in business. I'm well versed in contract law," she informed. Ellie hadn't used that degree in over ten years. When Cairo had convinced her to become a full-time, stay-at-home mom, he had promised to take care of her. She was out of practice and out of work all because she had believed in love. His salary had been

47

more than enough to provide them with an opulent life. When he left, she was so far behind her colleagues that jumping back into the workforce felt foolish. She would be starting over, working her way up from the bottom with college graduates who were almost half her age. Still, she wasn't so rusty that she couldn't make sure Cassidy wasn't being screwed.

"I can see that," Loyal said. "I'd be happy to send it over to your office after the holiday, but for now, I just want to have a drink and celebrate the way Cassidy is pouring back into the city with this event. The way people remember his name will change with events like this. This is a good day. Care to join me?"

"Sure," she said skeptically.

"Sure," he repeated, chuckling. "A sure is better than a no. You like to give a nigga a hard time, I see."

"I live for it," she said, smiling.

"I see, I see." He finally turned to the bartender. "I'll take Henny on the rocks, and the lady will have…"

"Lychee martini, please, with a sugar rim," she finished for him.

"Sugar rim," he said, finessing the hair on his sharply lined chin. Everything about him was precise. From his line-up to his manicured nails, he was well-groomed. Not so much where she thought he was sassy, but just enough to recognize he was polished. A clean-ass man with some home training but sharp edges. "I bet you eat all flats when you order wings too."

She laughed because it was incredibly accurate.

"I do love a good five-piece, fried hard, all flats, with bleu cheese and buffalo on the side," she said.

"Sounds about right," he snickered. "Can't trust a broad who eat bleu cheese, though."

"What?" she laughed. "What kind of logic is that?"

"That's some stank-ass cheese," Loyal shot back, laughing. The bartender delivered their libations, and she sipped hers.

"I see that husband of yours got his hands full?" he commented, looking at the shiny rock on her finger.

Her smile dwindled. "Hmm," she answered, shrugging. "That's a very complicated story."

"If you were my wife, I'd need you to make the story short and sweet. I'm married, the end, type shit. Got to make it plain for niggas," he shot back.

"If I were your wife, I think you would have made it plain for niggas without me having to say a word," she countered. "That's the type of man you are, right? Or am I sizing you up wrong?"

He smirked and almost blushed, and she felt a sense of accomplishment.

"Cassidy's sister," he said, almost in disbelief as he rubbed a hand to the back of his neck. "Cassidy's married fucking sister."

"Hey, baby, there you are! I've been looking for you."

The sweet voice that interrupted the moment was like a needle scratching a record the wrong way. The woman was gorgeous. Tall and dark, with legs that seemed to go on for miles as they disappeared under the short dress she wore.

She had to be freezing in that thing, but apparently, it was worth the attention she garnered. She was reminiscent of some 80s supermodel. Naomi or Iman. Ellie's eyes went to the ring on the girl's finger.

"Wow," Ellie nodded as if she was reaching an understanding. She was shocked, but then again, she wasn't. Niggas would be niggas on every day of every week. "Seems like I was the one asking the wrong questions." She stood, grabbed her drink, and then sashayed out of the way. "Here, sis, you can have my seat. It was nice to meet you, Loyal."

She went to walk away, but he grabbed her elbow, standing from his seat as he pulled her back. He took her phone from her hand and held it out for her. This was a bold move in front of someone who was obviously his girl.

"Open it," he instructed. She was curious as to how far he was going to take this, so she did as he said. He typed his number into the phone.

"So we can review that contract," he stated.

She scoffed. "Are you really this guy?" she huffed.

"Don't start sizing me up wrong all of a sudden, Elliot," he stated. He held out her phone and accepted it before walking away. She wanted to glance back so badly but she didn't . She didn't even know where she was headed; she just wanted to get away from him.

Ellie breathed a sigh of relief when she saw Shy, Sloan, and Courtney enter the building.

"Court!" she screamed happily. "I thought you weren't coming!" Her friend was beautiful. She wore no makeup at all, but she was beaming. She nodded to the stroller.

"I didn't want to miss it. Sloan said it was kid-friendly, so I packed Christian up, and here we are," Courtney said.

"You look so good!" Ellie complimented.

"Girl, bye, don't lie. This size 14 ain't it," Courtney replied insecurely as she pulled on her shirt.

"No, sis. I promise. I'm not blowing smoke. Motherhood suits you. Hair long, nails long, skin dewy, you look amazing," Ellie insisted. "How's James?"

"Girl, let's not even go there. I just want to enjoy my time out the house and catch up with my girls," Courtney stated.

"Enough said," Ellie stated. "Y'all go ahead and find a booth. Cassidy already told me we don't have to work. So, grab a seat. I'ma head to the little girls' room and be right back. Order me another lychee because I got to tell y'all about this lying-ass nigga I just met," Ellie said.

"I'm going to walk around for a bit. Go live and show everyone what's going on, bring some attention to the cause, and try to get some more people down here. Where Cass? Does he have a Cash App set up for this event? I can get some online donors, too," Shy stated.

"I'll go find him. I kind of owe him an apology," Sloan stated.

Ellie paused. "Apology for what?"

Sloan shook her head. "Nothing, girl. I just put my foot in my mouth yesterday about him finally getting out of prison, and I just want to make sure we're good."

"Well, he's out back with the girls," Ellie said, pointing to the rear exit sign. "Meet us at the table when you're done."

Ellie hurried to the bathroom and then joined Courtney at the booth.

"Let me seeeee himmm, Court," she cooed as she reached for baby Christian. "Oh, my goodness. He's so precious."

Courtney gave a flat smile, but Ellie didn't miss that it didn't reach her eyes.

"You feeling okay? No postpartum or anything?" Ellie asked.

"I feel fine," Courtney answered. "Exhausted, of course. He isn't sleeping through the night yet, but that's normal."

"I think they're giving away formula and diapers. You want to grab some?" Ellie asked.

"I don't need a handout, Ellie," Courtney stated firmly. Her tone made Ellie look up from her adorable nephew.

"I didn't say you did, Court. It's free shit. You have a newborn baby. You better take some of this shit home," Ellie teased.

"We're good," Courtney insisted.

"Okay," Ellie replied. Ellie knew not to press the issue, but Courtney's defensiveness was a red flag that things were, indeed, not good. She texted Sloan and told her to get in line to get the items for Courtney anyway. Even if they had to sneak the items into Courtney's backseat, Ellie was determined to make sure her friend went home fully stocked. She knew Courtney well enough to know that something was wrong, and until she felt comfortable advocating for herself, Ellie would make sure she kept a close eye on her friend.

"Auntie Sloan!" Tessa shouted.

"Hey, niece!" Sloan greeted picking her up. "Hey, big girl," she extended to Brooklyn.

"Hey, Auntie," Brooklyn greeted with a hug. "We're about to ice skate. You want to come?"

"Ummm, I prefer my skates to have wheels," Sloan said, skeptically. "How about your uncle, Cass, and I go get y'all some hot chocolate and watch from the sidelines."

Brooklyn snickered. "Deal," she said. "Extra chocolate syrup and marshmallows in mine, please," Brooklyn added.

"Extra hot in mine!" Tessa shouted after them.

"Got it," Sloan promised, laughing at Tessa's request. She turned to Cassidy, who hadn't spoken at all. "How about it? Walk with me?"

He scratched the top of his head and nodded. "Yeah, a'ight."

"You don't have to sound so miserable about it," she joked.

They strolled through the sea of people as an awkward energy settled between them. "Look, I'm sorry for how I came at you last night," Sloan said.

"You said how you feel. Ain't no apology needed for that," Cassidy stated.

"It was fucked up," Sloan admitted. "I just. I have my own history with murder, you know. With my mom. It's just..."

"I get it," Cassidy said. "But I'm not like the nigga that took your mom away. The circumstances were different."

"How?" Sloan asked. Cassidy sighed.

"It's not the time or place," Cassidy replied.

"You know what? You're right. I just wanted to apologize. I couldn't even sleep last night after I left," Sloan confessed.

"Yeah, a nigga ain't get much sleep either," Cassidy responded. He stepped up to the Hot Chocolate counter.

"What you need, Cass?" the man working the booth asked. "Let me get three large hot chocolates, extra chocolate and marshmallows on one, extra hot on the other," he repeated.

Sloan laughed. "You know extra hot isn't a thing, right?"

"Listen, I'm just following directions," Cassidy stated. "Whatever they want, they can get from me. I've missed too much to ever tell them no."

He passed her a cup, and then he carried his nieces' as they walked back to the skating rink. He took a seat on the bench and placed their cups on the ledge. Sloan took a seat next to him.

"Oh, Shy wanted to know if you have a company Cash App. She's going live and wants to have her followers donate to the cause digitally," Sloan said.

"Yeah, it's $sigaro," he said. "She's really internet famous out here, huh?"

"She likes to think so," Sloan laughed. She pulled out her phone and sent the Cash App name to their group chat.

"What are you up to these days, Sloan? Besides judging niggas," he stated. She could tell he was still in his feelings about their misunderstanding, and she couldn't say she blamed him.

"I'm a doctor. I deliver babies for a living," she informed. "Forever a bridesmaid, never a bride."

"I'm sure that's by choice," he replied.

"Umm, yeah, I guess you could say that. My choices have led me here. I just never have time to date, let alone to invest the amount of effort it takes to get serious enough to make a baby," Sloan said. "Now, I'm forty and my eggs are crusty and although I did freeze some when I turned 33, I don't know if I want to fertilize them alone. It just seems so desperate to choose some stranger who went to a sperm bank."

His brows hiked in confusion. "I don't know what to say to that, except, I think you should do whatever is going to make you happy, Sloan," Cassidy responded.

"Sorry. Don't mean to be talking about reproductive issues in the middle of your event. Which is great, by the way. This is amazing. It's something to be proud of," Sloan acknowledged. "Where did you get the seed money for this place?"

"It wasn't drug money if that's what you're thinking," he said.

Her silence gave away her guilt.

"Damn, a nigga just ain't shit in your book, huh?" Cassidy asked.

"I don't know, Cass. I just don't know adult you. I only know the boy who got locked up before he even had a chance to live," Sloan said.

"I'm not that kid anymore. I saved some kid in lockup from getting his ass beat during his seven-year bid. His dad owed me. He was getting ready to sell this place when I got out, and we came to an arrangement. I'm paying it off out of a percentage of sales over five years. It's all legit, Sloan."

"Good for you," Sloan said. "I mean that. This is quite a footprint you're leaving on the neighborhood. Look at all these people. Some of these families wouldn't have gifts for their kids, Christmas trees, or Christmas hams if it wasn't for you. Maybe you are different now."

"I'm just trying to make it out here, man. A nigga name burnt. Can't get no regular job, trying not to go back to what I know and walk a straight line. Being an entrepreneur is the only way I can survive, and I ain't never been no bottom feeder. I was always going to be a millionaire, Sloan. Whether it was by hook or crook. I only know how to go big."

"Well, look at you, Cass. This is neither hook nor crook. It's legitimate, and it suits you," Sloan said, smiling.

He smiled at that, too, nodding his head bashfully and then looking out at the ice where Brooklyn was calling him.

"I better get back to the girls," Sloan said, standing.

"Thanks, Sloan. A nigga will sleep a lot better tonight."

"Me too," she agreed. She stood and took a few steps before turning back. "Oh, and I hate to ask, but is it possible to get a few extra cases of diapers and formula for Courtney? She has a newborn, and she could really use that stuff."

"Yeah, of course, say less," Cass stated. "I'll drop it off personally later tonight."

Sloan beamed. "Thank you."

"Don't mention it."

Sloan walked away, but a large part of her wanted to stay right there in the cold with him. She had entered the conversation with so much anxiety, but she was walking away with peace. He was a good listener, and she hated that she couldn't just keep talking to him. She glanced back once more before going inside, and she smiled as she watched Brooklyn and Tessa fawn all over him. She was glad that they had been able to clear the air because he felt like a friend in the making. An unexpected friend that she didn't see coming.

# CHAPTER 5

irl, get your ass off that live!" Courtney snapped.

"Okay, y'all, I've got to go because my girls are waiting for me, but it's not too late to come support this amazing event. If you can't make it or want to support from afar, don't forget to hit that Cash App. The money will go to a great cause. Love y'all, byeeee." Shy signed off the live and put her phone in her bag.

"Okay, bitch, now catch up, you two shots down," Ellie said. "Your ass, too," she added as Sloan walked up.

Courtney laughed as Sloan and Shy took their shots like champs.

"This feels so good. It's been so long since we've all been together. So, today was charity; what's tomorrow's Friendsmas activity?" she asked.

"We're going to pick out and chop down Christmas trees tomorrow," Shy informed.

"Oh, the girls would have loved that, but they're going to be with their dad. Cairo is picking them up from here," Ellie whined.

"That's okay, girl. Bring Papa if you want. Invite Cass. Bring the baby and James. Like, it's a family thing," Shy informed.

"I'm going to bring my assistant, Lola. She's great with kids. She can even watch the baby if you ever need her to, Court," Shy offered.

"Thanks, Shy, but he's still so young, and I don't know her like that," Courtney stated.

"Well, Brooklyn can watch him for a few hours whenever you need her to. She loves babies, and she's good with them. She can do it right at your house so you're comfortable," Ellie volunteered.

"Yeah, that sounds like a better option, honestly. If I need her, I'll let you know," Courtney said.

"Don't hesitate," Ellie added. "Even if you just need a break or need a nap or an extra set of hands while we're in town. It's no big deal. We're here to help." Ellie's phone rang, and she rolled her eyes when Cairo's name popped onto the screen.

"Cairo is here for the girls. I'll be right back," Ellie said as she slid out of the booth.

He met her at the door, and Ellie's feet stopped moving when she saw his girlfriend enter behind him. The disrespect it took to bring her inside was astounding.

"Where's Brook? I told her to be waiting out front for me," Cairo stated.

"Hello to you too, Cai," Ellie spoke. "How dare you bring her in here. And the bitch don't got no manners. She can't speak?"

"This is why I didn't want to agree to do this because you can't handle it," Cairo stated.

"I can't handle it? I've sent you divorce papers how many times? I'm not the one dragging my feet on making this official. That's you. You can't trap me into staying married and then flaunt this bitch at the same time," Ellie hissed.

"I'm just here for my daughter," Cairo stated.

"Daughter?" Ellie questioned.

"Yes, I'm only taking Brook. She's my blood. I don't owe the rest of y'all nothing," Cairo stated.

"Over my dead fucking body," Ellie whispered harshly. Their body language spoke volumes, and Cairo towered over Ellie's small frame menacingly. It felt too much like a threat, and the tension in the air had the entire building on edge. Loyal came to her side.

"You good over here?" Loyal asked, stepping in between them, staring Cairo down with intention. If looks could kill.

"Who the fuck is this?" Cairo asked, elevating his voice.

"I'ma be a problem if you don't lower your voice in this bitch," Loyal said calmly, flicking the tip of his nose in annoyance while clasping both hands in front of his body. He covered Ellie with his stature. The message was clear. Cairo would have to go through Loyal to get to her. Ellie didn't know if Loyal was making things better or worse, but she couldn't deny that she felt protected.

"I'm fine," Ellie whispered to Loyal as she grabbed his elbow.

"I know you're fine because nobody's calling the play but you tonight," Loyal said as he burned a hole through Cairo.

"I promise, I'm fine, Loyal." Ellie wished that were true, but she couldn't hide how hurt she was. Her voice shook, and Loyal saw her eyes prickling with raw emotion. Truth was, she was grateful for Loyal's presence. It gave her the courage to stand up to Cairo. It was something she hadn't done since he had abandoned her.

"You will not treat our daughter like she's less than. We adopted her together, Cai! We chose her! You cannot take Brooklyn and leave Tessa behind. She's not trash! You can't just throw her away!"

"Enough of the dramatics, Ellie. You wanted that baby," Cairo said.

"You asked me for another baby, Cai!" Ellie hissed in exasperation.

"And you couldn't give me one! You had to go and find some substitute because you couldn't do your fucking job! I wanted you to have my child. I wanted my blood to flow through their veins. Not some mutt you brought in off the streets from some junkie."

The slap that came next echoed through the building, and Ellie swung with so much might that she busted the inside of his lip. He lunged for her, but Loyal met Cairo with a discreet burner to his midsection, pulling Cairo in by the back of the neck.

"I don't want to leave you leaking out here in front of your daughters, my nigga, but that's gon' be they last memory if you take another step," Loyal whispered.

"Daddy!" Tessa's voice broke through the entire building as she entered the room and spotted Cairo.

"Alright, alright," Cairo mumbled, lifting his hands, conceding as he took a slow step back. Loyal holstered his gun and stepped back so that Ellie's daughters could greet their father.

"Dad!" Brooklyn joined the excitement and rushed to hug him.

"Please," Ellie pleaded through gritted teeth. Ellie couldn't believe Cairo would play so dirty. She didn't expect much from him regarding her, but to purposefully hurt a child, their child, was a new low for him. It was a cruelty she didn't even know he was capable of.

"Are we going with Daddy?" Tessa asked.

"Ma?" Brooklyn asked, frowning as she finally picked up on the awkward energy in the room. "Daddy, we're coming with you, right?"

Ellie held her breath as she waited for Cairo to make his next move, but before he could, Loyal spoke. "There's been a change of plans. You guys aren't going tonight. I surprised your mom with floor seats for everyone to the Pistons game tonight. So, your dad is going to have to come back for you in the morning. Ain't that right, my guy?"

Cairo looked down at Tessa and then over to Brooklyn, and he nodded.

"Yeah, I'm going to let you go to the game with your mom tonight. I'll call, and we'll try again tomorrow," Cairo stated. "Let's go," he said to his girlfriend.

"Come on, baby," Ellie said, pulling Tessa away from Cairo. "Let's find your uncle and say bye so we can head to the game. Brook, take Tessa and go tell Uncle Cass bye."

"But, Ma, I was going to walk Dad out," Brooklyn protested.

"Brooklyn, do what I said," Ellie said sternly.

"This isn't fair, though! We always get to see you! We never get to see Daddy!" Brooklyn protested.

Ellie felt like she couldn't win. She was fighting Cairo and now Brooklyn.

"Brooklyn! Just listen sometimes! Take your sister and find Uncle Cass, now!" Ellie shouted. Her tone was harsh, but it had nothing to do with Brooklyn. It was hatred and frustration boiled over from Cairo. She was a mother trying to shield her cubs, and Brooklyn's protests were making it harder.

Brooklyn sucked her teeth and stormed by Ellie. "I hate you," Brooklyn mumbled. Ellie closed her eyes, and tears fell down her cheeks.

"Don't do this here," Loyal said, stepping in front of her so she could hide her face in his chest. Loyal nodded to one of his men in the room. "Clear everybody out. Party's over."

"I'll be back for Brooklyn tomorrow," Cairo said. "It'll be easier for everybody if Tess wasn't there."

"You're a fucking coward, Cairo, and I'm disgusted that I ever married you," Ellie shouted after him.

"Look at me," Loyal commanded. Ellie lifted teary eyes to his. "That nigga ain't worth your energy." He cupped her face and cleared her tears with his thumbs.

"I'm a mess," she countered.

"You're gorgeous," Loyal said. It was the way he said it that made her open her eyes. His stare was so intense. Nothing about his touch felt new. Nothing about his protection felt foreign. It was like he had known her for years, and it hadn't even been hours. She could see herself fucking, and fussing, and fighting with this man for years to come.

She frowned as he cleared more tears.

"People are watching, Loyal," Ellie whispered.

"Let them," Loyal replied.

"Your girlfriend," Ellie protested.

"Doesn't  matter," Loyal stated. He said it so plainly like her concern was invalid.

She hadn't come home for this. She couldn't afford more messy situations in her life.

"I can't handle anything else that's complicated, and you are giving off nothing but red flags."

Loyal's sigh revealed his frustration with her.

"Just come to the game with me and my people. Your girls are in for enough disappointment with their father. At least let me be a man of my word. I'll show y'all a good time and get you back home safe. You can even bring your friends if you like. After tonight, we can leave it where it is. Okay?"

Ellie knew she couldn't renege on the game. If she did, her daughters would force the issue of going with Cairo tonight.

"Okay," she reluctantly agreed.

"I'ma have a talk with Cairo tomorrow, E. I'll hurt that nigga over you," Cassidy said as he sat in the booth across from his sister.

"Hey," Sloan said, jarring his attention. Sloan sat next to Ellie, consoling her, but her eyes were on Cassidy. He stared at Sloan. "No," she said simply.

"You expect me to sit back while he treats my sister and nieces like shit?" Cassidy asked. "I will lay a nigga to rest so easily over them. Without thinking twice. Like it's a part of my everyday routine."

"Right, of course, you will, Cass," Sloan stated. "Excuse me," she said. Cassidy watched Sloan walk out of the booth, and Ellie watched in confusion as Cassidy went after her.

"What is that about?" Ellie asked.

"Chile, I don't know, but if they fucking, Sloan better tell me every fucking detail," Shy added. Courtney snickered.

"They're not fucking," Ellie stated with certainty.

"Well, bitch, who is? Because it's a whole lot of energy in this room. Who is that nigga that stepped over you?" Courtney asked.

"And more importantly, who is that bitch he over there walking to the door?" Shy threw in.

"I don't even know him. He's Cassidy's business partner. I met him today," Ellie stated.

"And he fell in love at first sight, bitch, because what the entire fuck? What kind of man even inserts himself like that without having a dog in the fight? I thought he was going to slap fire from Cairo's ass!" Shy stated.

"And he wouldn't have been wrong," Courtney chimed in.

"This is all just too much," Ellie said. "My baby is going to be heartbroken when Cairo refuses to take her. How can he do this to her?"

"He ain't shit, Ellie. A nigga character don't really come out until you're on bad terms with him. He's trash, and you don't deserve this. I'm so sorry, but I think the news will land softer if it comes from you than if it comes from the rejection that little girl gon' feel when her daddy leaves her behind," Courtney stated.

"I agree, but tonight, take your daughters to the game and let that fine-ass man knock the bottom out that pussy." Leave it to Shy to lighten such a heavy mood. The girls exchanged high-fives as they cackled in agreement while Ellie shook her head at their antics.

"He has a girlfriend," Ellie protested.

"Do he know that? Cuz I can't tell. He's tall, dark, handsome, paid, and clearly aggressive. He was ready to blick something over you and he barely knows you. If he has a girlfriend, then he's a dog, but, bitch, dogs are meant to be taken on a walk," Shy said as she eye fucked Loyal from across the room.

"Walk that nigga around the block like Jill Scott," Courtney agreed.

"After dark, around the clock, or whatever her poetic ass said," Shy added on.

The duo burst out into song, singing the classic lyrics, and Ellie fell into a fit of laughter. This is what her soul missed. The presence of good girlfriends made life bearable. Even through the chaos men caused, good friends pulled you out of the darkness.

"Thanks, y'all. I guess I'll call y'all tomorrow," Ellie stated.

Courtney and Shy slid out of the booth and headed out the door. "Let me know when y'all make it home."

"We will! Love you!" both girls chanted in unison.

Loyal re-entered the building as the girls made their exit, and Ellie didn't miss the fact that he grabbed baby Christian's car seat from Courtney and followed her to her car. She went to stand in the doorway and watched as he walked both her friends to their respective cars before he turned back toward the building.

They stood in between the space that separated the inside from the outside.

"We gon' head back in?" he asked.

"Not yet," she said, lowering her head in disgrace.

She suddenly leaned her head back and lifted her eyes to the ceiling. "Shit can't ever just be easy, can it?" she asked. "What am I going to do?"

"Explain this to your daughters. That's all you can do. You can't take accountability for another person's actions. You can prepare them, though," Loyal said.

"That's what my friends said, too," she admitted.

"Smart friends."

"I can't figure you out," she said.

"It's just day one. You're not supposed to yet," he replied. "You ready for the game?" he asked. She nodded, and he took her hand to lead her back inside to grab her children. The Pistons game would be a good distraction for them all before having to deal with heartbreak in the morning.

"You want to talk about it?" Cassidy asked.

"Not with you." Sloan's words were like a sledgehammer to his chest. He could decipher the disappointment in her tone. She was a beautiful woman. Her West Indian and Creole features fused into a masterpiece. Her skin was a shade of cinnamon that made him feel like she was blushing all the time, and those eyes could break a man. On the rare instance she found the courage to look at him, he felt like she was begging him to man up, begging him to be better. Her stature and station in life were so elevated that even when she lent him her time, he felt like he had to earn it. She was so beautiful that she was intimidating, and Cassidy wasn't a man who rattled easily, nor did he have a problem attracting women. He sat next to her on the bench, removing his coat so that he could put it over her arms. They were silent as he leaned forward onto his knees, rubbing his hands together to generate some heat. Her long, curly hair blew in the sharp winter winds. He smelled whatever perfume she had sprayed in it. He had never smelled it before, but it was the loveliest fragrance he had ever encountered, and it fit her perfectly.

"You want me to be a better man than I am," Cassidy admitted. "There's always been a consequence behind disrespecting people I love. Especially, E."

"And do you even think about the consequence behind that? You're on parole, Cass. Even if you don't kill Cairo. Let's just say you rough him up a bit, and he hits you with charges. Then what?"

"Why do you care?" Cassidy asked.

"I don't," she said.

"You storming out says otherwise," Cassidy said.

Sloan sighed. "Maybe, I do, shit, I don't know. Black men just be wasting their lives. Like, it's already a shortage of you niggas who actually like Black women, cuz let's be real, most of y'all live to humble us. Then, there is you. You have all the potential to be great, all the potential to love a woman right. You were raised right. You were shown love. You saw a Black man loving a Black woman growing up. You went to church, and I know you did, cuz your mama used to make me wake my Black ass up every Sunday I spent the night at y'all's house, and you were right there with me and Ellie, sleepy but present. You come out of prison, after over twenty years, and you jump into the community, and you're getting money with ease, but you're ready to self-sabotage already. You could be a king, Cassidy, but you'd rather be a stereotype."

"Asking me to let a nigga play in my sister's face…"

"She chose that man," Sloan shouted. "She saw Cairo and saw the little red nose, saw the big-ass red shoes, hell, even saw the balloon he was carrying, and she joined that nigga's circus, willingly. We all warned her about him. He was a womanizer dressed up as a good guy, disguising his bullshit with money, and Ellie still chose him. She's grown. She knows how to handle her situation, and you have to let her handle it. I'm not saying let him whoop her ass because, at that point, you'll be defending us all because I would be right there with her fighting that man, but risking your freedom over some machismo bullshit is stupid. The one thing Ellie wants more than being defended by you is for you to be free."

"Yeah, I hear you," Cassidy grumbled. He knew she was right, but it was hard to accept the realization that his baby sister was a grown woman and that she didn't need him anymore. "I'ma fall back, within reason. You might have saved a nigga life tonight."

"I did," she shot back. "Yours."

The crunch of snow announced Ellie's presence as she emerged from the back door. "Hey! Is everything okay out here?" she asked.

"Yeah, we're good, E," Cassidy stated.

"Well, we're about to head out for the game. Are you guys coming? Loyal says he has enough tickets for everyone."

Cassidy looked at Sloan. A crowded game wasn't really the place he wanted to be right now— not with her.

"Nah, I'ma pass, E, I've got a lot to do here tonight," Cassidy declined. "And about Cairo…"

"I can handle Cairo, Cass. I love you enough not to get you involved," Ellie said.

Cassidy glanced at Sloan and scoffed because she indeed knew her best friend.

"You let me know if the nigga loses his mind or something. Anything that feels even close to intimidation, and you gon' call your muscle off the bench. I'm never going to let any nigga make you feel unsafe," Cassidy said. "I'll crash out over you."

"I know," Ellie said. "And what about you, Sloan? You in or out?"

"I'ma call it a night," Sloan said. "I got to rest up for Christmas tree chopping tomorrow, remember?"

Ellie laughed. "Shy and this damn itinerary," Ellie cracked. She backpedaled toward the building. "Okay, get home safe. Love y'all."

"Love you!" Sloan shouted back.

Before Ellie disappeared, Cassidy shouted, "Oh, and E!"

Ellie turned back to him. "Loyal's a good nigga."

"I figured. You wouldn't be letting me and the girls go anywhere with him if he wasn't," Ellie snickered. "Alright, I'll see y'all."

Cassidy turned back to Sloan. "Let's get back inside before I freeze out here."

She stood and slid his coat off her shoulders. He didn't bother putting it back on. He simply led her to the building and back into the heat.

"You want a drink, or you have to get out of here?" Cassidy asked.

Sloan thought about going to her empty house, and she shrugged. "I guess I can stay for one drink," she complied.

"Shots aren't your thing, right?" he asked.

"God, please no," she protested. He gave a lazy smile and pulled out the Kahlua, rum, and a few other ingredients.

"I'ma make you a gingerbread martini," he said.

"I love gingerbread anything. I wanted to make a gingerbread house, but it was too crowded at that station," she said as she watched him prepare the drink.

He whipped up the drink and set a napkin out in front of her before placing it down.

"None for you?" she asked.

"I'm simple. McCallan over ice works fine for me," Cassidy

stated. "Give me a second. I'll be right back." He went to the kitchen and dug through the pantry before emerging with a gingerbread kit in his hands. "I knew we had extras in the back."

Sloan smiled and sipped her drink. "This is hella good," she said. "Okay, bartender!" She praised, raising her glass to salute him.

"I've had to work the bar plenty of times over the last few months when we got busy. This place is growing faster than I thought it would. I need to hire more help," he explained.

"That's a good thing. I'm proud of you for the way you're attacking life," Sloan said.

"Making up for lost time. I got to go full speed, you know?"

Sloan opened the kit and laid the items in front of them. He watched as she began to put the house together. "Christmas is your favorite holiday?" he asked.

"Yeah, you can tell?" she laughed.

"This little house lit your whole face up," Cassidy observed.

"I used to do these with my mom every year on Christmas Eve," Sloan stated. She picked up one of the gummy candies and popped it into her mouth. "The trick is to make sure you put extra icing on the corners of the walls, otherwise, it's just going to fall apart."

She was so meticulous about each placement of every little candy piece.

"You eating more candy than you decorating with," Cassidy joked. Her laughter professed her guilt.

"That's why the back of my house always blank. Mind your business if you not gon' help," Sloan chastised.

"I'ma let you do your thing," he said, admiring her.

"Whatever happened to that nigga you were so in love with back in the day?" Cassidy asked.

"Deyontae Cook?" Sloan knew exactly who Cassidy was talking about.

"Yeah, that nigga," Cassidy said with distaste. "Old-ass nigga, dating your young ass."

"He was only a senior," Sloan defended.

"And you were in 8th grade," Cassidy stated. "Matter fact, you were in the 7th grade when he first started sniffing around. Chester-ass nigga. That's why I beat that nigga ass. Ho-ass nigga."

"Times were different back then," Sloan stated, laughing. "It was like a badge of honor to pull an older boy. When I look back, it was hella creepy."

"You used to love his bitch ass, too," Cassidy judged.

"Yeah, until he went to college and broke my heart," Sloan informed. "We lasted a few years. His junior year I got on BlackPlanet and found out he was in another girl's top five. Turns out he was her boyfriend at Michigan State. As I was starting my senior year, I was nursing my first real heartbreak."

"That top five was treacherous back in the day. I remember three different girls had me in their top five, caught my ass up," he said, reminiscing as they shared a laugh.

"Who came after him?" Cassidy asked.

Sloan frowned. "Are you checking my ho fax?"

Cassidy bellowed at that. He sipped his drink and came around the bar, pulling up the stool next to hers.

"I'm trying to figure out why a woman like you doesn't have a man," Cassidy pried.

"Men don't like alpha women, Cass. I make my own money, so impressing me with money isn't a sure win for them. Then the ones who aren't in my tax bracket think I'm stuck-up. I work all the time, so I don't have hours to spend on the phone with someone. I don't respond to texts right away. I can't hang out at all times of night. Men lose interest in me fast," Sloan admitted. "Being too accomplished is a thing for women."

"Seems like a trivial thing to overlook a woman like you for," Cassidy answered.

"Until you're the man on the other side of 60-hour workweeks, and I'm too tired to have sex at night," Sloan said. "The men I've dated aren't wrong. I get it."

"I don't," he said as he watched her closely. Everything about Sloan was feminine. From her dainty, almond-shaped, French set, to the way she sat cross-legged on the bar stool. "Niggas have made you think you're not the prize just because you're hard to catch."

He watched her place the final piece of candy on the gingerbread roof, and then she dusted off her hands.

"There," she beamed with a smile. "All done." She cracked off a piece of the roof.

"All that work just to destroy it," he chuckled. She bit into the gooey treat, laughing.

"Yup. You want to try?" she asked. She held it to his mouth, and he bit a piece of the snack. They were one drink in, and the temperature in the room was rising. Their eyes met, and she quickly looked away. "I should go," she said.

Cassidy finished his drink and then set the tumbler on the countertop. He knocked on the wood before standing. "Okay," he said. "I'ma wrap-up here. You should head home before it gets too late. I'ma make sure I drop the diapers and shit off to Courtney like you asked."

She stood, gathered her bag, and dug her keys out . "You remembered," she smiled.

"I know a honey-do list when I hear one," Cassidy snickered.

"A what?" Sloan asked.

"Papa told me to always respect a woman's honey-do list. My mama used to give him all these tasks to get done at the beginning of the day. Didn't matter how small they were. Sometimes it was simple shit, but he never missed one thing. He said it was the way he built trust with my mama. Showing up, fulfilling her needs, never breaking his word, and fulfilling that damn list. Didn't matter how big or small. She never needed to nag him because he prided himself on never forgetting," Cassidy schooled.

"Papa knows something about women," Sloan smiled. "That's incredibly sweet."

"I never saw a man love a woman better than that man loved my mama," Cassidy stated.

"Is that how you love women?" Sloan asked.

"I haven't had the chance yet," Cassidy said shamefully. "Prison took away a lot. When I find the one, I hope to get it half as right as my parents did."

Sloan felt like she was listening to a fairy tale. Her hand

rested underneath her chin, and she gazed at him with dreamy eyes while he spoke.

"Little badass Cassidy has grown up to be quite a man," she complimented.

He grimaced and rubbed the back of his neck. "Was I that bad?"

"Kind of. Jail wasn't too far off-brand for you."

"That's fucked up," he shot back. She laughed so hard that she snorted. "I'm glad you find my imprisonment so entertaining." He couldn't blame her, though. He had been on a bad path as a teenager and a young man. If the law hadn't sat him down, the streets would have laid him down. He was lucky to have a second chance.

"You seem to have learned something from it, Cass. Good for you," she said, getting serious. "Walk me to my car?" she asked.

"That was happening, anyway, don't insult me," Cassidy stated seriously.

He followed her outside and walked over to her G-Wagon. "Little Sloan, pushing big toys these days," he complimented.

She shrugged. "I wanted it until I got it and realized how much gas it sucks up and how rough it rides," she snickered.

He opened the door for her and held out his hand to help her step up and into the truck.

"Be careful out here. Let me know when you make it home," he said.

"Is that your slick way of asking for my number?" Sloan asked.

"It wasn't, but that was smooth as hell," Cassidy admitted, scratching his temple. Sloan pulled out her phone. "What's your number?"

"810-785-1325," Cassidy said. "Have a good night."

He closed her door and then trudged through the snow back to his lounge as she drove away.

# CHAPTER 6

These seats are so cool! I can't believe I'm sitting courtside at a professional game! Ma, can you take my picture?" Brooklyn squealed as she turned in her seat and posed with duck lips and a peace sign.

"It comes with a suite, too, if y'all want to switch and watch it from the box at halftime," Loyal stated, chuckling at Brooklyn's excitement.

"This is unreal! I'm trying to go live, but I get like no bars in here. Is there WiFi?" Brooklyn asked.

"Yeah, let me get you right," Loyal said. He took her phone and connected the WiFi, and then passed the phone back. "Go ahead and flex all you want."

Loyal motioned for an older couple, who sat on the end of the row.

"Ellie, this is my stepdad, Robert, and my mom, Tracy," Loyal shouted the introduction, in an attempt to be heard over the crowd. "These are her girls, Brooklyn and Tessa."

Ellie leaned in and shook their hands. "It's nice to meet you!"

"Come on! That's a foul!" Robert screamed, keeping one

eye on the game as he shook her hand. "Basketball is serious business in our family," the old man explained. "It's nice to meet you, beautiful."

"Nah, man, don't start; this one's off-limits," Loyal said, snickering.

Tracy laughed and slapped Loyal's knee before reaching a long arm out to Ellie to squeeze her hand. "She's pretty, son."

Ellie blushed and took her seat.

"Old man always running game on every girl I bring home. He been doing that since I was fifteen," Loyal said, clueing her in. She smiled in amusement. "Nigga always flirting, and Ma, you just be encouraging him."

"Kind of sounds like you're a chip off the old block," Ellie teased. "I'm just saying, considering I just met you, and somehow, you've convinced me and my kids to go on a date with you."

"This ain't a date. I'ma do this much differently when you allow me to take you out for real," he whispered in her ear. "This is..."

"Pity?" she asked, frowning.

"Grace," he replied. "And us getting to know each other."

She nodded because she could accept that.

"Mommy, can I get popcorn and soda?" Tessa asked.

"No soda, my love, but yeah, we can get you some popcorn," Ellie said. "Brook, do you want to take your sister to the concession stand?"

"There's a waiter for front row," Loyal informed.

"That's okay. Tess is an explorer. She only wants the

popcorn because she wants to walk to see what she can find along the way," Ellie explained.

"But, Mom, I'm on live!" Brooklyn protested.

"This girl and this damn live. She's not even watching the game," Ellie fussed. "Most girls who sit front row ain't sitting front row to watch the game. It's about the look, not the game."

Ellie shook her head. "I guess," she responded.

"Come on, little one, let's go explore," Loyal said, standing and leading the way up the long staircase that led to the concessions.

Ellie was winded by the time they got to the top. Loyal seemed to be a regular face at the games. Several people stopped to speak to him as they made their way.

When they got to the concession booth, Loyal picked Tessa up and put her on his shoulders so she could see the menu.

"You can get whatever you want," he said.

"Not whatever you want, Tess. Baby, be polite and choose two things," Ellie said, placing limits before her daughter got out of hand. Loyal turned to Ellie, noticing how uptight she was. She wore her day all in her body language. Her arms were crossed, and her brow was bent. Her shoulders were so tight that she looked like she was stuck in a permanent shrug. The confrontation with Cairo had stressed her out.

"Hey," he said, grabbing her attention. "She's fine. Relax. Let that shit go, and let me show you and your girls a good time."

She sighed and nodded. "And there's no limit with me," he added. "You want anything?"

"A margarita, please," she said, smiling. "I'm sorry. I'm just in my head about facing all this tomorrow."

"Don't apologize," Loyal responded. "You dealing with some shit you shouldn't be. It's some sucker-ass shit." He freed one hand from holding Tess and pulled her closer so he could whisper in her ear. "I'm sorry you're going through that."

His understanding somehow made her chest feel lighter.

Tess ordered up the menu. She ordered so much stuff that Loyal had to tip the workers to deliver it to their seats.

"These seats really are crazy," Ellie shouted over the roaring crowd.

"I'm glad you like 'em," Loyal stated. "I figured your kids would like the action. I normally chill in the box instead." He pointed to the hallway where the players access the locker room. There's an elevator that takes you up to the suite floor.

Ellie ducked as a loose ball flew her way. "Yeah, the box suite sounds like more my speed," she said, laughing as she picked up the ball and threw it back to the referee.

"Ma, you're on the Jumbotron!" Brooklyn shouted.

Ellie looked up and waved shyly as the camera focused on her and Loyal. He gave a quick smile to the camera and slapped hands with one of the players on the bench before focusing back on Ellie.

"You're so much cooler than me," Ellie laughed. "Everybody knows you here."

He chuckled and shook his head. "They just showing love because I'm a season ticket holder. My old man used to buy season tickets every year. He would work double and triple time, just to scrape up enough money to afford that little luxury. We'd be so high up you couldn't even see the players. They looked like ants way up in the nosebleeds. Now, I gift him floor seats every year."

"That's really sweet," Ellie said. She glanced down at Robert. "He clearly loves it."

Loyal nodded. "He does," he chuckled.

The whistle blew, and another loose ball came rolling their way, knocking over Ellie's drink.

She leaned down to clean up the mess.

"Don't worry about it, they'll get it," Loyal said, flagging over the wait staff.

Ellie looked over to her girls who were having the time of their young lives. "You guys want to maybe go up to the suite for the rest of the game?"

"No way!" Brooklyn said.

"It's so much fun down here! Can we stay? Pleaseee!" Tessa begged.

Tracy waved a hand at Ellie. "You two go on up; they can hang out down here with us. We'll meet you at the top when it's over," Tracy offered.

"Oh, no, I couldn't ask you to do that," Ellie stated.

"They're fine, hun. We've raised plenty of kids. Go ahead," Tracy insisted.

"Ma, you're being a helicopter mom. I'm a teenager. We're fine," Brooklyn added.

"Okay, okay," Ellie sang as she reluctantly lifted out of her seat. "Do you want me to take you to the bathroom before I go?"

"No, Mommy, I don't have to go," Tessa insisted.

"I'll take her at halftime, Ma," Brooklyn promised.

Ellie looked around unsurely but followed Loyal as he took her hand and led her up to the suite. It was empty and pure luxury.

"Now, this is how I prefer to attend a sporting event," she said as she stepped inside. A buffet was set, bottles of liquor awaited them, and television screens lined the wall.

"I figured you'd be more comfortable up here," Loyal snickered. He grabbed a bottle and carried it to the leather sofa. "Grab two glasses for me?" he asked.

She did and then joined him on the couch.

"Thank you for this, by the way," she said. "And thank you for standing up for me."

"Don't mention it," Loyal stated.

"Why did you? If you don't mind me asking." Ellie hadn't been able to take her mind off the encounter.

"You looked like a deer in headlights," Loyal said. "You were confident and assertive when I met you at the bar. As soon as he walked into the room, you shrank. It felt like he had bullied you before. I ain't mean to overstep, because I know I did, but I ain't like that shit at all."

"I really appreciate you standing up for me. I haven't had someone do that in so long. I guess that's what I've been searching for since my brother got locked up. Cassidy was always my muscle. He was always my protector. People knew not to fuck with me because they would have to answer to him. When he went away, I went through a few niggas just searching for that feeling, that loyalty. There was an unconditional love that suddenly was missing in my life."

"And your husband gave you that?" Loyal asked.

"I don't think he did. When I look back, it's crystal clear that he was never man enough to fulfill such a big duty. He almost love-bombed me, coming with my first big wow moment for everything. He was the one who bought me my first Louis; he took me on my first little Caribbean vacation. He did basic shit like make me call off work but give me the money I'd make in a day. Hair money. Nail money. Little girl shit. I fell too fast, too hard, and next thing I know, we were married," Ellie whispered.

"Do you still love him?" Loyal asked.

"He up and left me four years ago after we adopted Tess. No warning. No explanation. Just left. He refuses to give me a divorce to avoid paying me alimony. He's holding my life hostage, and now he wants to break my baby girl's heart. I loathe that man," Ellie admitted. She cleared her throat and reached for the bottle in front of them. She poured two shots.

"They say you aren't supposed to tell a man how the man before him broke your heart. It's a playbook for them to manipulate you," Ellie stated.

"Manipulation isn't my game," Loyal replied. "I don't lie to women. Ain't shit playa about a nigga that got to lie. I live in my truth and let women choose what they're okay with and what they want to walk away from."

"Like you having a girlfriend," Ellie interjected. "Or was that an engagement ring I saw on that girl's finger? She's gorgeous, by the way."

"She's beautiful," he replied. "She also fucked my potnah in Miami three months ago, which is why she's my ex."

"Yikes," Ellie stated, gritting her teeth. "Why is she still around?"

"I think she's hoping we can fix it," Loyal admitted.

"Can you?" Ellie asked.

"I been with her since college," Loyal stated. "She's the mother of my son, so I'ma always make sure she's good, but I can't see myself moving backwards."

"Hmm," Ellie said as she stared curiously at him. "Men like you scare me." She sipped her drink and grimaced as it burned on the way down.

He smirked and went to retrieve the bucket of ice and a bottle of cranberry juice. He mixed her a more enjoyable drink, and she graciously accepted.

"The last thing I want to do is scare you, Miss Elliot," he answered. "I don't quite know what I want to do with you yet, honestly. I didn't see you coming."

He moved a tendril of her hair out of her face, and she giggled.

"I have butterflies in my stomach like I'm a schoolgirl," she admitted.

"I don't want to make you feel that. That's anxiety. That's uncertainty mixed with a little adrenaline," he explained.

"What do you want me to feel when I'm with you?" she asked.

"Safe."

His answer shocked her, and her eyes widened in surprise. "Okay, yup, we gon' call it a night," she said, standing.

He frowned in confusion. "Did I say something wrong?"

Ellie shook her head and swept her short bob behind both ears.

"No, but that answer isn't typical. That's not casual. A man who answers like that is a man that will eventually get what he wants from me. I'm going to get in over my head with you. The way you moved about me earlier wasn't casual. You stepped like you knew me, like you had love for me, and you don't even know my middle name. What's going to happen when we get attached? It's already so intense. I'm here for a week. Literally, six more days. My life is a mess. Your situation is all over the place. We live in two different states. This doesn't even make sense. Let's just not do this. We can make a choice right now to walk away. We just met. We don't have to even go down this road."

"I'm already a quarter mile down that road, E," Loyal said.

She sighed and rested her back against the wall as he stood. He walked over to her and placed his hands against the wall, creating a fortress around her and forcing eye contact.

"I'm married, Loyal," Ellie stressed.

"Do you want to stay married?" Loyal asked.

"He will contest a divorce," Ellie argued.

"That's not what I asked," Loyal said. He was so close to her that she could smell the alcohol on his breath. His cologne infiltrated her senses, making her dizzy, or maybe it was the liquor, but if she were a betting woman, she'd put it all on his aura. She had known this man less than six hours, and already, she was spellbound. Ellie wasn't even a fall in love, be swept off her feet type. She was practical and smart, but Loyal had her wishing that she had met him at a different time in a different way. She wasn't healed enough to handle a man of his magnitude. "Do you want to remain married to that nigga, Elliot?"

"No," she whispered.

"And is that the sole reason why you're in your head about fucking with me? If you weren't married, would my tongue be here by now?" he asked, running a hand up her thigh and resting it on the face of her pussy. Ellie was sure she had lost her mind because she was letting this man drive 100 mph with her in the passenger seat. They didn't have a GPS, weren't any seat belts, no nothing, just risky fucking business. She had to slow it down. Her brain wasn't processing this shit right because the wrong answer was on the tip of her tongue. If she wasn't married, would she be getting her pussy ate in the box suite at the Pistons game right now?

"Yes," she panted.

"So, let's make you a widow."

Loyal said the shit like he was discussing the score of the game, and it was then that she knew he was more than an entrepreneur. He may have been into construction and real estate, but she'd bet her bottom dollar his riches were built on top of bodies and bricks.

He stepped back and walked over to the railing as he overlooked the ball game. Ellie was shaking; her adrenaline was running so high.

He was a man who saw something in the store, and he was being told he couldn't buy it. He was willing to rob the whole joint to get it.

Ellie joined him and eased her way in front of him. His hands naturally wrapped around her waist, and he pulled her into his body.

"Loyal, feelings are visitors. You can be infatuated with me today and disinterested tomorrow. Let them visit, let them leave, because I go home in six days," she whispered. "Let's just have fun while we have this moment. You know very little about me. I might not be worth all this trouble you're signing up for."

He stared down the bridge of his nose at her. "I'm attracted to you, E. I ain't trying to do no visiting. I'm trying to settle in."

"Do you always move this fast?" she asked, chuckling.

"What's your middle name?" he asked.

"What?" she asked, confused.

"You said I didn't know it. I'd like to know it," he said, licking his lips.

"Marie," she whispered.

"No, I don't normally move this fast, Elliot Marie Brier." His answer blew her mind.

"Brier?" she asked.

"It's gon' be your last name one day, might as well try it on," he stated. "See if it fits." She waited for the laugh. It never happened.

"Loyal!" she said, frowning as she gripped the bottom of his chin. He moved his head out of her grasp.

"I got money on this game, E," he said as he tried to see around her.

"Are you completely insane?" she asked.

"A little bit," he answered truthfully. "Over you, I'ma lose my mu'fucking mind. I can already see it." She didn't even know what to say. It had been a long time since her husband had made her feel like he was attracted to her, and he had never given her the impression that she was irreplaceable. This feeling of obsession, of power over this man's focus, was magnifying. She felt like she was that bitch, and she was in awe of how firm he was in his position regarding her.

"Don't look surprised. You know you got it," he complimented, smirking as he licked his lips while still observing the game. She blushed, and he pulled her closer, allowing her to rest the side of her face on his chest. Elliot was too damn old to find this attractive, but damn it; his toxicity was exactly her type. Rich nigga. Hood nigga. Or whatever the song said. She was so intrigued. She was flattered, and most of all, she was turned the fuck on. Their natural chemistry was insane.

"I know nothing about you, and you know very little about me," she reasoned.

"So, let's learn," he proposed. He finally gave her his attention and stared down the bridge of his nose at her. "Can I kiss you, E?"

She loved that he called her E. Only her brother called her that, and now him.

"Out of all the liberties You've taken over my life in the past six hours, a kiss is what you ask permission for?" she asked, snickering. It seemed like the smallest request.

"It's your body. I'll always ask permission before assuming it's okay to touch a woman," he whispered.

She stood on her tiptoes and wrapped her arms around his neck.

"You have your phone?" she asked.

He squinted in confusion and pulled it out of his back pocket. "It's right here. Why, what up?"

"What's the date?" she asked.

"December 19th," he answered. His furrowed brow expressed his confusion.

"I want you to remember the date of our first kiss," she swooned.

"Oh, you one of those women," he snickered.

"I'm absolutely one of those women," she assured. "If we fall in love, you need to remember the important dates."

"No ifs, E, only when," he replied. Her attraction to this man was unreal. It was his confidence and his assertiveness that won her over most, but she saw so many qualities in this man that were lacking in her last relationship. She initiated the kiss, caressing the sides of his face as she started with slow pecks to his lips. When his tongue parted her lips, she shuddered because he filled her mouth so deliciously. His lips were soft, and his tongue sweet. One hand gripped her ass, pulling her into his body while the other gently pinched her chin. He moaned as he explored her mouth.

"Knock! Knock! Someone wanted to come see the suite!"

Ellie was grateful for the announcement. It gave her time to unravel herself from this man's arms before her daughters busted them. She went to greet them, and he held onto her hand until the natural distance of her steps separated them.

She looked back at him, and he winked at her, causing her to smile as she walked back inside the suite.

"Oh, it's lit up here too, Ma," Brooklyn stated.

"I know, right!" Ellie exclaimed. She glanced back at Loyal as he intently watched the game, and she wondered if she could handle this. He made her feel like a twenty-year-old girl again, and she wasn't sure if that was a good thing. After their kiss, she was certain that she wanted more. If he kissed her lips like that, she could only imagine the expertise with which he would handle the rest of her body. They watched the rest of the game as a family, and by the time it was over, Tessa was spent. Loyal had to carry her all the way to the car.

"It was so nice meeting you guys," Ellie said.

"You too, honey. I'm sure we'll be seeing you soon," Tracy said. Ellie smiled and hugged the woman and then hugged his father as well.

They all climbed into Loyal's Porsche and rode in silence all the way to her parents' home. He gripped her thigh the entire way. She wondered if he knew he was setting her ablaze or if he was just naturally dominant. When they arrived, he exited the car and pulled Tessa from the backseat.

"Oh, no, I've got her. Trust me, you are not ready to meet my daddy," Ellie said.

They all turned to the house as the porch light flickered on, and Brooklyn said, "Looks like he ain't got no choice."

Ellie bit her bottom lip. "You want to come in?" she asked.

Her daddy stepped out on the porch with a shotgun resting at his side.

"Daddy, put the gun down," Ellie said. "I'm a grown woman." She was so embarrassed. She turned to Loyal with an apologetic grimace on her face. "I'm so sorry."

"He just protecting what's his, E. I respect it," Loyal said. He stepped up on the porch carrying Tessa. "I'm Loyal Brier, sir. It's nice to meet you." Loyal extended his hand while balancing her child with his other arm.

"Bishop Whitlock," her father returned. "Come on in and get my grandbaby down to bed," he ordered.

"He was just leaving, Papa," Ellie said, trying to intervene.

"Nah, he dropping my daughter off after midnight, he gon' come in here and have a nightcap," Papa replied.

"Oh my god," Ellie mumbled, mortified. "Come on, I'll show you where to put her."

Loyal followed her up the stairs and into the bedroom, where her girls were sleeping. He laid Tessa down on the bed. "I'll be down. I just need to get her ready for bed. I'm so sorry about this in advance. He's never not grilled a boy I've brought home."

Loyal licked his lips and then bit his bottom lip as he nodded. "Don't worry about it," Loyal stated. "I can handle it."

As he walked out, Brooklyn entered the room.

"Good meeting you, Brooklyn," Loyal said, holding his fist out for a pound. She giggled. "Oh my god, you're so old," she critiqued, but she offered her fist for a pound.

"They don't do that no more?" Loyal asked.

"Not at all," Brooklyn smiled. "But you're still pretty cool. Thanks for the tickets."

"Anytime," Loyal said, leaving the room.

"Papa just might shoot him," Brooklyn giggled.

Ellie laughed as she began to undress Tessa.

"Is he your boyfriend?" Brooklyn asked.

"No, baby. He's just a friend. I barely know him. He's your uncle's business partner," Ellie stated.

"But he likes you, Mom. Like a lot," Brooklyn stated.

Ellie didn't know why that made her blush, and Brooklyn got hyped at her mother's response. "You like him too, don't you?!" she squealed loudly in excitement.

"Shh! Shh!" Ellie hushed.

"I mean, he is fine for an old head," Brooklyn mumbled.

Ellie turned on Brooklyn so quick, Brooklyn caught whiplash. "Girl, get your ass in that shower and get to bed. Talking about he fine."

Ellie put Tessa in the bath, waking her up briefly so that she could get her clean and changed, then she said her prayers with her daughters before returning down to the living room.

She was anticipating a full-on grill session, but instead, she found Loyal sitting at the kitchen table with a drink in his hand as they sat over a domino game.

"Well, what do we have here?" she asked, amused.

"I'm tapping this young boy's ass, is what we have here," Papa gloated. One thing about her daddy, he was going to talk shit while he won. Hell, when he was losing, too. Spades, dominos, and tunk were like Olympic games in this house, and there was always money on the floor.

Ellie couldn't help but grin. She walked over to her dad and stood over his shoulders, massaging them as she stared at Loyal. This was as lighthearted as she had seen him all day. The laughs, banter, and smiles the men exchanged were reminiscent of a father and son. Loyal was comfortable with her father, and more importantly, her father was comfortable with Loyal. It was the relationship she had hoped her husband would have with her dad, but it had fallen flat.

"Thank you," she mouthed at Loyal.

He simply nodded and kept his attention on her dad. She loved when a man showed interest in the people she loved. Cairo had never made the effort to get to know her father or any of her friends. He only wanted to isolate her, which is why he had moved her away from Michigan in the first place. Her own relationship with her loved ones had suffered because of the distance.

"Well, I'm going to head to bed," she announced.

They barely heard her as they continued their conversation. She thought she was in the clear until Loyal called her name. She secretly loved that he noticed when her presence was diminished in the room.

"Yo, E," he said.

She turned back to him and waited.

"Hey, Bishop, I don't mean no disrespect in your house, but I'd very much like to kiss your daughter good night if that's okay with you," Loyal said.

Papa huffed and waved his hand. "Go'n about it then, li'l nigga," Papa stated.

Ellie melted when Loyal crossed the room and commanded her chin and kissed her softly on the lips. No tongue for the sake of her daddy's watchful eyes. The forehead kiss that followed made her heart flutter.

It felt undone, like an "I love you" was supposed to come after affection like this, but she wasn't delusional. They barely knew one another.

They stood there, forehead to forehead, for a full thirty seconds. Thank God for her daddy being there because Ellie would have fucked this man on the first night.

Papa cleared his throat, and Ellie couldn't contain her grin as she said, "Goodnight, Loyal."

"That ain't what you wanted to say, but I'm a patient man. I can wait for it," he said.

"I have no idea what you talking about. You got something you want to say?" she asked.

"Yo, Bishop, you ever heard of meeting somebody and knowing right away that they belong to you?" Loyal asked.

Ellie's eyes bugged in astonishment. This man was pulling her daddy into his antics.

"Mmm hmm; I felt that way about her mother. Told her she was going to be my wife the day I met her," Papa said.

"Sound like history repeating itself to me," Loyal stated.

"Papa, don't hype him up," Ellie grinned.

"Ain't nothing wrong with a man knowing what he wants. She got a husband, though. Got to get rid of that one first," Bishop chastised.

"Yeah, I'm on top of that too. We gon' hold a funeral before the wedding. How that sound?" Loyal asked, amused at the horror on Ellie's face.

"Baby girl, I like this nigga here. He about his business. That's what I'm talking about," Papa championed.

"Oh my god. You're fucking horrible," Ellie whispered. "Don't listen to him, Papa," she said aloud.

"Enough of that, now. Quit delaying this ass-whooping, young man. Go'n upstairs, baby girl, and let the men handle business."

Loyal returned to the table, and she made her way slowly up to her old room.

She rushed inside and put her back against the door as she heaved breathlessly.

"That nigga is a problem," she whispered. She liked him too much. The intensity of him almost scared her. She pulled out her phone and hit her group chat.

*Bitches, I got a 911. Wake the fuck up!*

# CHAPTER 7

ourtney lay in bed with Christian beside her as she snickered at the group text thread she was engaged in with her girls. It felt so good to see her friends. She hadn't realized how much she missed them until they were all in the same room. She heard the front door open, and she looked at the time. It was a little after midnight. He was home early. She hated the tension that filled her home when he walked through the door. He filled her with instant anxiety, and she didn't know when their dynamic had become this toxic exchange.

She listened to his every movement as he made his way through the house. The way her body braced itself for bullshit was alarming. Her eyes misted because she realized somewhere in the history of their relationship, she had begun to fear this man. She didn't even know when or how it had occurred.

His shadow appeared in the bedroom door, and he flicked on the light without regard.

"Can you turn out the light?" she asked. "The baby's asleep." It was insensitive habits like this that made him selfish. He only considered himself in their existence.

"My bad," he said. He turned out the light and undressed in the dark, coming out of his clothes and leaving them in the middle of the floor.

"I thought you were working a double tonight?" she asked.

"They shut down construction for the night due to the snow we're expecting," he explained. "What you been doing all day?"

"Not much," she said. "Ran a few errands."

He had just gotten home and had already earned two strikes on her shit list. He never picked up after himself. He just assumed she was going to come behind him and take care of it. It was like she had two kids to take care of.

"I thought you were going to clean up today?" he asked.

"I didn't have time," she answered. "I'll get to it tomorrow."

"How is it possible that you sit at home all day but don't have time to clean this house? Did you cook?" he asked.

That, she had done. She had put a roast in the Crock-Pot before she met up with her girls.

"Yeah, there's a plate in the oven for you," she informed.

That seemed to be enough to stop him from talking shit. He walked into the adjoining bathroom and closed the door. She sighed in relief when she heard the shower come on. Her phone buzzed, and she picked it up to continue her conversation with her friends when she noticed Ellie had hit her on the side.

### Ellie
*Hey! Cass just pulled up to your house. He has diapers and formula for you.*

"Shit," she mumbled as she scrambled from the bed, making sure to push Christian to the middle of the mattress as she hurried to the door before Cassidy rang the bell.

She opened the door just as he was coming up the stairs.

"Hey, Court. How you doing, baby?" Cassidy asked. "My fault about stopping by so late. It took me a minute to wrap things up. I put this stuff to the side for you. I thought you could use it for the baby."

"Oh, umm, I told Ellie we didn't need charity, Cass," Courtney stated.

Cass placed the boxes down on the porch and stood, hiking up his pants as he stared Courtney in the eyes.

"No charity, Court. This is just extras. If you don't take it, I have to give it back to the sponsors. I'd rather gift it to the baby, you know?"

Courtney heard Christian begin to whine, and she glanced back inside the house.

"I'm sorry, the baby just woke up. Give me a second," she stammered. She rushed back into the bedroom, slipped into her satin kimono robe, and then scooped Christian from the bed. She rushed back to the door.

"You can... umm... just place the stuff right here by the closet. Thank you, Cass. This really wasn't necessary," she said.

"No problem, Court. You're family," he said. "Man, he's little. Handsome, too," Cassidy complimented.

Courtney smiled as she bounced Christian in her arms while rubbing his back.

"Thanks, Cass," she smiled and kissed her baby's cheeks.

"I'll get this stuff inside and get out your hair," he said. He began to carry the cases of diapers inside. There were over twenty cases, and over thirty cans of formula that he had pulled aside for her. "This should last you for a while. If you ever need anything else, you know I'm just a phone call away, right?"

"What's all this?" James asked as he emerged from the bedroom.

Courtney stiffened, and panic filled her because she knew James and his pride would take Cassidy's kindness as offensive.

"This is Ellie's brother. We went to support his charity event today," Courtney explained.

"Cassidy." Cass stuck out his hand to greet James.

"It's kind of late, ain't it?" James held suspicion in his tone and reluctantly shook Cassidy's hand.

"Yeah, man, my bad. I just wanted to make sure I got this to Court."

"We ain't in need of no handouts, my man. We appreciate the gesture, though," James stated.

She sucked in air because she knew he would take this the wrong way.

Cassidy frowned. "It ain't like that, man. She's my sister's friend. I'm just looking out."

"Yeah, nah, we're good, fam," James stated sternly. "Take the baby in the back and get him to sleep."

Cassidy's frown deepened, and he squared his stance defensively. He turned his attention to Courtney.

"Yo, you good?" Cassidy asked.

Courtney looked at James nervously and then back to Cassidy. "Yeah, Cass. Thanks for thinking of us, but we're good. I promise. It's late. I do need to get this one down," she said, tripping over her words as her heart went haywire in her chest. She could see James' temper raging just from the look in his eyes. She knew he was piecing together a puzzle in his head and overthinking.

"Look, man, I ain't got the room in my truck to pack all this back in there. If you really don't want it, I'll send somebody by to pick it up tomorrow before we go tree chopping," Cassidy stated. "You coming to that, right?" Cassidy's question was for Courtney.

"Umm, I..." she was going to try to make it after James went to work, but she had no plans of telling James.

"It's a part of Friendsmas," Courtney said, adding context for James.

"I thought Friendsmas was all girls," James stated with no nicety in his tone. There was accusation in his tone, like Courtney had been caught in a lie. She was so embarrassed and unnerved that her eyes watered.

"Yeah, well, they gon' need some help binding them trees and loading 'em up and all that. Ellie volunteered my services. You should come, man. Make it a family affair," Cassidy stated. Courtney appreciated Cassidy trying to make James comfortable. She recognized an olive branch when she saw one, but she was mortified that he was witnessing her toxic relationship in person. She knew he would tell Ellie.

"Yeah, we'll see," James stated dryly.

Cassidy was trying to smooth an awkward situation over, but James wasn't giving him much effort in return. Cassidy stared James down, and Courtney knew he was deciding whether he needed to check James. She prayed he didn't .

"Thanks for stopping by, Cass," she said softly. Her eyes said, "Please, just go."

"A'ight," Cassidy said skeptically, never taking his eyes off James. "I'll see you around, Court."

As soon as James shut the door, she braced herself for the argument to come.

"So, you thought I was working a double shift and had a nigga pulling up to my house in the middle of the night?" James accused.

"Here we go," Courtney sighed. "He was just being nice. Nobody wants Ellie's brother."

"You ain't say shit about going to no charity event. That's why this house wasn't clean," James stated. "I bust my ass for you, and you out here fucking with niggas." James practically growled the words as he pointed two fingers at her face, mushing her and then pushing her toward the bedroom. "You ain't coming up off no pussy, but fucking on another nigga in my house?"

Courtney pushed him off her. "I'm not fucking anybody!" she shouted. Christian's screams erupted as he yoked Courtney up. Her eyes widened in horror as she held on tight to their son. It wasn't until he was in her face that she smelled the alcohol on his breath. She lifted her foot and kicked him in the balls, taking the wind out of him long enough for her to rush into the bedroom. "What the hell is wrong with you?! I'm holding our son!" she shouted through the door. James' jealousy was out of control. She couldn't even pick up her phone without him thinking she was secretly texting someone. She was livid. She put her son in his crib and then grabbed the baseball bat she kept under the bed before pulling open the door. "Nigga, you got me fucked up!" she shouted. She kept her distance but pointed the bat at him.

"You think you slick. All that slick shit gon' catch up to your ass one day," James stated. "I thought I told you that Friendsmas shit was dead."

"It was just a charity event! I haven't seen Ellie in four years! I couldn't just skip everything!"

"But you can skip work, though? You said your mental state wasn't right. You taking a leave of absence from your fucking job; got me picking up all these overtime hours to compensate for you sitting at home on your ass all day, but you feel good enough to link up with your friends," he accused.

"It's not like that. I was only there for a little while," she defended.

"When I asked you what you did today, you ain't mention shit about no charity event. You fucking with that nigga?" he asked. He was on the attack, looking to discredit anything she was saying, and Courtney felt cornered.

"No!" Courtney shouted.

"What other niggas were there?" James demanded. His mind was fixated on assigning guilt when there was none for her to claim.

"Oh my god! I don't know! I was there with my girls! It was for the community, so all types of people were there! Damn! You can't be that insecure!" she shouted. She made the mistake of lowering the bat and never saw the slap coming.

"Got a nigga showing up to my door like I ain't taking care of what's mine." He was seething. "You keep playing with me, and I'ma put your ass out on the streets. Simple ass."

Her feelings were on the floor as she felt the sting of his hand. Her lip quivered uncontrollably as she sobbed. He had never flown off the handle like this before. He would yoke her up and bark down on her when his jealousy was in overdrive, but he had never struck her. She was in a state of disbelief. She had met this man when she was in high school. He was ten years older than her. He was all she knew. She was terrified to leave but also sick of staying. He was becoming intolerable, and Courtney didn't know how much more she could take.

Ellie fell asleep in the middle of her group chat and to the sound of Loyal and her dad playing dominos downstairs. The only thing that woke her up was the tapping sound on her windowpane.

"What the hell?" she groaned. She kicked off the comforter and scrambled to her window to find Loyal standing outside in the middle of the front yard. He tossed the pebbles he had in his hand and held his arms out wide. This fine-ass man was in her parents' front yard in the middle of the night like a love-struck teenager, and she was smitten. The smile that spread across her face was infectious. She felt the warmth from his attraction spread through her entire body. Loyal Brier was awakening parts of her that age had dulled. The belief in happiness. The belief in love at first sight. The belief in a man when he said he was feeling a woman. Disappointment and heartbreak had clouded her judgment, making her doubt men before they even opened their mouths. This man was doing something different with her psyche. He was unapologetically pursuing her. She knew he had his pick of women, and the fact that he saw this middle-aged woman, with her two children, and complicated situation and didn't run the other way, made her feel like she was still worth something. If she was honest, she had accepted crumbs from Cairo because she thought her best days were behind her. Loyal made her feel like her best days just may be to come.

She checked the time and lifted her window.

"It's 3 am!" she hissed. "Where is my papa?"

"He's on the couch asleep. The nigga hustled me out of every dollar in my pocket, and I keep at least ten bands on me," Loyal said, smiling boyishly as he rubbed his wavy head. "School took everything, even the lint in my pockets. That's a slick-ass old man, E." Loyal's lighthearted tone told her that he had enjoyed the evening with her dad, and that warmed her.

Ellie climbed out onto the snowy roof, stifling laughter

because she knew he wasn't lying. She had seen her father run a con before. He would lose a few hands purposefully, before pretending to be desperate and increasing his bet, only to later win every round. Sneaking out onto this roof was pure nostalgia. She hadn't done this since she was a teenager.

"It's freezing out here, Loyal," she shivered. "Go home!"

"Come with me," he invited.

"What?" she gasped, shocked.

"Climb down the ladder and come home with me, E." Loyal said it plainly, like it made perfect sense. "I got a big, warm bed waiting for you."

"Have you lost your mind? How many games did you lose?" She knew the rules when playing dominos with her daddy. Loser took shots, and Papa drank the strong shit.

"I won a few," he snickered, trying to save his pride. He had a beautiful smile with dimples that sank into his dark skin. She noticed that he didn't smile often, but when he did, it was a masterpiece. Nothing was more attractive than seeing a Black man smile.

"You lost a few more," she laughed. "Just wait right there. I'm coming out."

"Just climb down," Loyal suggested.

"Boy, me and that ladder ain't been friends since I was a teenager," she said, laughing. "I'd bust my ass trying to climb down that thing. I'm coming. One sec." She climbed back inside her window. "Shit!" she whispered as she nursed frozen toes. She knew he shouldn't drive. She wasn't crazy enough to invite him to sleep under her daddy's roof. She slipped into sweatpants and a sweatshirt, threw on her daughter's Ugg boots, and grabbed her purse, then her phone, before she tiptoed down the stairs. Ellie paused as the old house creaked beneath her feet, and her daddy grumbled, readjusting on the couch. She waited a full minute before continuing.

She felt like she was sixteen again as she snuck out the front door. She ran down the porch stairs right into Loyal's arms.

"There she go," he said proudly as he drowned his face in the crook of her neck.

"You're cold," she whispered. She smelled the Paul Masson on his breath. *Yeah, Papa beat this nigga real bad*, she thought, fully amused. "And you're drunk. Give me your keys," she said.

"I'm not fucked up, E, I can drive," he replied.

She held out her hand and didn't say another word. He dug in his pocket, handing over the keys. They got into his car, warming up.

"I'm going to call you an Uber," she stated.

"Or you could just come home with me. I'll bring you back in the morning before your girls wake up," he offered.

"I can't stay the night with you, Loyal," she protested.

"It's gon' be your fucking house sooner or later anyway, E," he said, frowning. "Might as well come home with a nigga."

"You see our whole lives already, huh?" she asked, yawning.

"You do too, you just too scared to admit it; same way you were biting your fucking tongue in the house," he accused.

"I'm being cautious," she corrected. "And smart. We aren't

kids, and relationships like my parents' don't happen these days. I have two kids, Loyal, and you have…" she paused. "I don't even know how many kids you have. I don't even know you."

"You're being pussy," he shot back.

"Are you trying to bait me into saying I love you," she chuckled. "You're really fucking drunk."

He placed one hand behind her seat and stared across the car at her. "Hey."

The seriousness of his tone caught her attention, and he commanded her gaze. "These are sober thoughts. You make me feel some shit I never felt before, E. Before you said one word, my entire body reacted to you when Cass introduced us."

She looked down at her hand at the ring that adorned her left finger. She didn't even know why she still wore her wedding ring.

"You make me feel seen," she whispered. "Yesterday, you were a total stranger. Today, you're…"

"A man who trying to change your life."

She turned in her seat to face him. "I didn't even know my heart was half beating before yesterday."

"Can't have that." He opened his palm, inviting her to place her hand in his, and then he closed his grip before lifting their conjoined fists to his lips. "I don't know what this is, E, but I'm fucking with it."

"Time will tell us what this is," she whispered skeptically.

"Only niggas scared of time is niggas who plan on wasting it," he replied. "Go get some rest. I'm good to drive," he assured.

"Are you sure?" she asked. He heard the worry in her.

"I'll tell you a story; I'll never tell you a lie. Trust me." She pulled out his keys and placed them in the cup holder. "When you make it inside, I'll pull off."

She didn't know why watching this man leave was so hard. She had felt the same devastating sinkhole form in her chest earlier when she had gone upstairs. Now, she couldn't even bring herself to pull her door handle. When would she see him again? She needed firm plans in place to ease her mind.

"Tomorrow, I'm going Christmas tree shopping for Friendsmas..."

"What the fuck is Friendsmas?" he asked.

"It's like Christmas, but with friends. We have all these events planned. It's a whole annual thing that me and my girls do," she explained. "Would you want to come?"

"I'll try to fall through. Send me the details," he replied.

"Can you do more than try?" she asked.

"I'll be there," he promised. "Have a good night."

"You too," she answered.

# CHAPTER 8

t's about time you made the time to get in here. I swear doctors make the worst patients."

Sloan clenched her teeth as her OBGYN probed her uterus. "I know. I'm always taking care of my own patients. I can't remember the last time I took a personal day to take care of myself," she said.

"Well, everything looks functional. Ovaries look good. Fallopian tubes are healthy. I do see a cyst," she informed.

Sloan came up on her elbows, trying to see the monitor.

"There, you see the circumference?" Dr. Adams asked.

"Will I need surgery?" she asked. "I can clear my schedule to take care of it immediately..."

"You're the patient. I'm the doctor," Dr. Adams reminded her, chuckling. "If you're thinking about transferring embryos, I'm not super enthusiastic to cut and disrupt your uterus. We'll monitor it and see if the body re-absorbs the fluid. You can come back in a few weeks, and we'll see what the body does naturally. If it grows, then we'll begin to talk about surgery. I'll perform the pap and do the breast exam, and you should be good," Dr. Adams said.

"How much of a window do I have to utilize the eggs we extracted?" Sloan asked.

Dr. Adams withdrew her probe and rolled away from the exam table, turning to wash her hands while Sloan sat up.

"Well, you froze your eggs early enough to give yourself a great chance to have a successful pregnancy. I will say that pregnancy is hard at your age, but science is truly advancing to where women in their 40s, and even into their late 40s, are having success bringing a baby to term. It's my personal belief that it's much easier on the body, and safer for you, if we figure this out over the next two years."

Sloan felt so much pressure.

"This would be so much easier if there was a man in my life who wanted to do this with me. How do you balance your career with your family? You were lucky, Dana. You met your husband in medical school. I want a baby so bad. I can't see myself not experiencing motherhood, but I'm not even dating anyone."

"There are other options, Sloan. There are plenty of sperm donors," Dr. Adams advised sympathetically.

"That feels unnatural. It already feels like a science experiment, but not knowing my child's father? Not being able to tell my child where they come from or having a co-parent to lean on? It just doesn't feel right," she said. Her voice broke as she became lost in overwhelm. "I just waited too late to think about love and children. What if it never happens for me?" she cried.

"There are all types of families. Families aren't just nuclear anymore. Stop subscribing to some tradition in your head. If you want a baby, have one. I can recommend a place that has a higher percentage of Black donors if that's important to you," Dr. Adams said.

Sloan nodded.

"I'll think about it."

Dr. Adams handed her some brochures on In vitro fertilization and gave her a reassuring smile.

"Let me know. I'm here to help. The nurse at the front will get you checked out."

Sloan cleaned up and made her way to her car. She wasn't in the mood to be around anyone, but she had a full day ahead of her. They were driving an hour north to go to the Christmas Tree Farm. They were meeting at Shy's house, and she was already running behind. Thank God she was already dressed for the occasion in the outfit Shy had demanded they all buy. She prayed the gold foil Moncler ski jacket, Louis Vuitton winter boots, and black tights kept her warm. Sloan was cute as fuck, but she feared they would freeze while traipsing through the snow. She took the hour's drive to Shy's house. When she pulled up, she marveled at the opulence of the mini-mansion in front of her. She hadn't been to Shy's home since she had purchased it a few months ago. Shy had insisted on waiting until her housewarming to show it off. She climbed out of her truck, noticing that everyone else had already arrived.

Sloan grabbed her gloves, the bottle of tequila she had been tasked to bring, and her handbag, then rushed up the walkway.

She rang the doorbell and could hear the jovial noise inside, but no one came to the door. She picked up her phone and called Shy, but the voicemail picked up. After trying Ellie and Courtney to no avail, she turned the doorknob and eased her way inside.

"Damn, influencer money must be good," she whispered in awe as she admired the home.

"Umm, hellloooo?" she called out as she walked inside and peeled off her coat. "So ain't nobody hear the doorbell, huh?"

When she rounded the corner, she paused, shocked that there were cameras rolling and a room full of people. She had thought it would be just the girls, but a full social media crew was present, as well as everyone's families.

"Heyyy! Bring your late ass over here, girl! We got to get this content!" Shy said, waving her over.

"Not y'all got a full photoshoot going on right now," Sloan said. "I'll let y'all have it." Sloan went around the room, greeting everyone.

"Hey, Papa," she greeted Ellie's dad. She kissed both of Ellie's girls and spotted Cassidy. She frowned when she noticed the young girl he was talking to but didn't bother interrupting.

"No, bitch, you hopping your fine ass in this picture. When we old and gray, memories are all we'll have," Shy stated.

"Okay, okay," Sloan said as she walked over to the 15-foot Christmas tree. "Shy, this house is fucking everything. It's huge! You not scared up in here by yourself?" she asked.

"Girl, no, my ass be in here naked with my wine glass and my music cranked to ten, enjoying the fruits of my labor,"

Shy bragged.

"Girllll, what labor?" Ellie exclaimed, cackling. "You take pictures all day."

"It's harder than it looks," Shy teased, sticking out her tongue. "Ain't that right, Lola?" Shy motioned for her assistant. "Oh, Sloan, this is Lola, my assistant. If you need anything, just ask her. She'll take care of it."

"Aww, baby girl, poor you," Sloan snickered as she realized the girl who had Cassidy's attention was on Shy's payroll.

"Bitch, I pay my assistant good. She ain't complaining!" Shy defended.

"I'm happy to help, y'all," Lola said, laughing.

"Girl, blink twice if you need help," Ellie joked. Shy even had to laugh at that one.

Shy pointed a finger at Lola. "You better not bat an eye!"

The crew was on ten, and it felt like old times when they would talk shit all night at a Friday night sleepover. Only now, they were grown women with much bigger problems than boys and hating opponents.

"Where's Court?" Sloan asked. "I thought for sure I was gon' be the one holding us up."

"Her phone's going to voicemail. Her house is on the way. The sprinter can just hop off at her exit, and we'll pick her up," Shy stated. "Let's finish getting these photos, though."

Sloan posed for a good ten pictures before she grew tired of the attention.

"Okay, that's enough for me, I'm pouring wine. Shy, where you keep your bottles?"

"In the pantry," Shy stated.

Sloan went to the pantry to retrieve a bottle. She was present, but at the same time, she wasn't. Her mind was still on the information she had been given at her doctor's appointment. She poured herself a full glass of Pinot Noir and then took a seat at the island as she opened her phone. Her browser was already open to articles about In vitro fertilization. It was all she could think about lately. She sipped from her glass and tapped her short fingernails on the side of the cup as she read the article.

"Is everybody good on drinks? I used to bartend. I can make anything you like," Lola said.

Everyone put their drink orders in except Cassidy, and Lola sashayed over to him. "What about you? Can I do anything for you?" Lola asked.

"Nah, I'm good," Cassidy stated.

"Are you sure? I literally make the best drinks," Lola persisted.

Sloan glanced up from her phone and rolled her eyes. "Oh my god," she mumbled under her breath. She understood Lola's attraction. Cassidy was the type of man you noticed at first glance. He couldn't be missed, and masculinity floated in the air around him. He was humble yet confident all at the same time, but he was also a grown-ass man. Lola was barely legal, and it showed.

"I guess I'll take a drink. Something dark," he said. "You can make mine neat. Remy XO if she has it."

"I got you, handsome," Lola said. She was eager to serve him, and as bad as Sloan wanted to hate, she couldn't. She would serve that nigga, too, if she was Lola. Lola walked into the kitchen and Sloan surveyed her from head to toe. She was a stunning girl. Titties sitting. Her body was young and tight. She had the naïveté of a girl exactly her age. She was young and dumb, and Sloan's old ass felt ancient next to her.

"I'm making drinks. Would you like anything?" Lola asked.

*Lawd, why she got to be nice*, Sloan thought. She gave Lola a fake smile.

"No, I'm good with my wine, thanks."

She watched as Lola poured Cassidy's drink, and when she was done, Sloan said, "I think he likes it with a little Coke. Shy usually keeps a case in the garage. "You want me to go grab one?"

"Oh, no, you're a guest. I got it. Thanks," Lola said. Sloan waited until Lola was out of sight before she took Cassidy's drink to the pantry and grabbed the vinegar she had seen inside. She added it to his drink and returned it to the countertop before returning to her own drink. Since he wanted to be sweet to this young-ass girl, she was going to spoil all that shit. She didn't even know why she was hating. She just was, and she was unapologetic about it.

She set his drink back where Lola had left it and scrolled inconspicuously through her phone as Lola pranced back into the room.

Lola carried a case of Coca-Cola with her, and she finished mixing the drink before proudly carrying it back to Cassidy.

"Here you go," Lola delivered proudly. She sat next to Cassidy and handed him the drink. His attraction was in his body language. He paid attention to this girl when she spoke. It was surface level, she could tell. Men were visual creatures, and Lola gave a good fucking aesthetic, but it still turned Sloan's stomach. She couldn't hear the conversation taking place, but the hand he placed on Lola's knee burned her. When Cassidy reached for the spiked drink, she felt a bit of triumph. She expected him to have a huge reaction, but he was so fucking cool that when he sipped the tainted drink, he didn't even react. She watched him take a tattooed hand to his beard as his brow dipped in confusion. He picked up his phone and held up a finger for her, indicating that he had a sudden call, and then he stepped out on the back patio. Sloan put one manicured hand over her mouth to contain her amusement, but she couldn't stop her laughter. She was so fucking tickled. It was like she was laughing at an inside joke.

"Bitch, what the fuck you over there giggling at?" Shy asked.

"Nothing," Sloan answered, holding up her hand to wave them off. But she was so damn amused as she glanced outside and watched him pour the drink into the snow. She hollered, holding her stomach as tears came to her eyes.

"What is so funny?" Ellie asked.

Sloan excused herself to the bathroom and enjoyed her practical joke. She dabbed at her eyes as her laughter subsided, fixing her makeup, and reapplying her lipstick. She admired herself. Forty really was the new 20. Sloan kept her body up, nourished her skin and hair, stayed prayed up and stress free. She accepted her imperfections and loved every inch of herself. Body and mind. She was beautiful, yet she was still alone. Young girls like Lola had the right sentiments. They hooked 'em early, secured a bag, and rotated these niggas at their convenience. Sloan had chased accomplishments, not men, and now she had a bunch of trophies and no dick, no badass kids. It looked like freedom. It masqueraded as peace, but it was a mental jail cell that made her feel like she would never find the one her heart belonged to.

She dabbed at the corners of her eyes, and then re-emerged from the bathroom and was surprised when Cassidy blocked her path. He backed her into the bathroom, closing the door behind him. She burst into laughter at the sight of his annoyance.

"That's cold, man," he said. She was expecting anger, but when he leaned into her and laughed too, she had to cover her mouth to stop from making too much noise. "That's fucked up, yo."

"It was just vinegar. It's not gon' kill you," she said, amused. "Shouldn't have been being friendly." She shrugged unapologetically. "She's like five years old, anyway, nigga."

"You want me to be rude to the girl?" Cassidy asked.

"Absolutely. That's the expectation," she said stubbornly, mugging him and gritting her teeth in irritation.

"She's not who I'm focused on," he replied. "But a nigga out of his depths, Dr. Martin."

"You didn't even speak to me when I got here," she scoffed.

"You didn't use the number, Sloan. I'm trying to read the room. I know my past makes you uncomfortable," Cassidy admitted. "You're a fucking doctor."

"So that means you don't speak?" she questioned. "You acted like you didn't even see me."

"I saw you," he shot back. "You're art, Sloan. How could I not see you?" The compliment made her feel so good. Her entire body warmed.

"Where you even learn how to game women so well? You been in jail a hundred years, negro," she fussed, feeling flustered and upset all at the same time. "I'm surprised you could see anything with that young-ass girl in your face," she demanded. "Stop flirting before I punch that bitch."

"Wow. That's diabolical," he stated, laughing.

"I'm old enough to be that girl's mom," she whispered. "Stop making me jealous of fucking college co-eds."

"She's 25, Sloan, you ain't that old," he said.

"If I was fast like Courtney's ass, she could be my daughter," Sloan fussed.

"I don't mean to change the subject, but have you spoken to your girl?" Cassidy asked.

"Who? Court?" she asked. It was an odd question coming from Cassidy.

"Yeah, I dropped off the stuff you asked me to for her last night, and her dude gave me real weird vibes. She almost seemed scared of that nigga," Cassidy stated.

"Wait, what?" Sloan's worry was evident.

"She said everything was fine, but it just ain't feel right, you know what I mean? I ain't want to overstep, but you should check on your friend," Cassidy stated. "And if the situation need some straightening, you don't go nowhere near it. None of y'all. You make one phone call and I'ma handle it. I hope I'm wrong."

"I'm gonna call her now," Sloan said, concerned as she

pushed past him and rushed to her purse.

"Hey, sprinter's here. You ready to…" Shy paused when she saw Sloan's face.

"Whoa," Shy said. "What's wrong?"

"Nothing. Let's stop by and check on Court. It doesn't feel right doing this Friendsmas thing without her," Sloan said. She didn't want to ring the alarm if Cassidy were wrong, but there was no way she could avoid checking on her friend.

"Yeah, we were doing that anyway. What are you not saying?" Shy asked.

"Let's just stop and check."

The luxury Mercedes Sprinter was tense. Nobody knew why except Sloan and Cassidy, but Shy had her suspicions. She rode in silence, as the city streets passed her by, and she dialed Courtney's number every few minutes. The automatic voicemail was killing her. Either her phone was dead or on Do Not Disturb. This was not the vibe she had planned for Friendsmas, but she realized that so much time had passed since they had all been together that they hardly knew what was going on with each other. Shy glanced over at Sloan, who sat next to Cassidy. She didn't miss the intimacy that existed between them. Sloan was worried, so she was also dialing Courtney back-to-back, but the way Cassidy was rubbing the back of her neck to ease the tension in her shoulders was telling. If she weren't so worried, she would be ready to spill the tea, but Courtney had her shook.

When the driver arrived at Courtney's address, Sloan stood. "I'ma go get her. I'll be right back."

Sloan gave Shy a weary look, but it wasn't one that Ellie missed.

"What's going on?" Ellie asked. She immediately knew something was aloof.

"Nothing," Shy said.

"Try again with your lying ass," Ellie stated. "What the fuck is going on?"

"Look, E, I stopped by here last night to deliver some diapers and shit and shit just felt off," Cassidy said.

"Off how?" Ellie asked.

"I don't know, man. Shit seemed tense. She was timid, almost. Her old man was in his body about me coming by so late," Cassidy stated.

"Like he was gon' do something to her?" Ellie asked, alarmed.

"I didn't say that. It just felt off, like he thought I was a nigga she was messing with or some shit," Cassidy replied. "Look, y'all stay here, and I'ma go knock on the door," Cassidy said.

"If James thinks you're her side nigga, you going to the door is just going to make a bad situation worse," Sloan said. I'll go see if she's coming or not. James is an asshole, but they've been together forever. They lost a kid. They got this new baby. They've been through a lot. They probably just hit a rough patch."

Cassidy climbed out of the sprinter and held out his hand to help her down.

"I'ma walk you to the door," Cassidy stated.

"I don't think that..."

"I wasn't asking," Cassidy stated as he grabbed her hand and helped her navigate the icy path to the door.

Shy glanced over at Ellie.

"Bitch, are you seeing what I'm seeing?" Shy asked under her breath.

Ellie glanced up at Sloan and Cassidy as they stood side by side.

"He's just being protective," Ellie stated. "Sloan wouldn't go there with my brother. We know what type of men she likes. That's my girl, but she's a snob."

"Girl, jailhouse dick will turn her saditty ass inside out," Shy snickered.

Sloan rang the bell, and James pulled open the door.

"Hey, James, is Court here? She's supposed to come to the Christmas Tree Farm with us, but she isn't answering the phone," Sloan greeted.

"Yeah, she's here," James answered unenthusiastically. He pushed open the screen door and stepped back as Sloan and Cassidy walked inside.

"What up, bruh, you a'ight?" Cassidy asked.

"Trying to make it, man," James said. "My bad about last night. It was late, and you caught me by surprise."

"It's all good as long as shit's good, you feel me," Cassidy responded.

"Court, your friend here!" James shouted.

Sloan looked around the house. It was a mess.

"Sorry for the chaos, man. The new baby got me pulling doubles, and Court ain't had a chance to clean up. The baby kicking both our asses, dawg," James said. Sloan could hear the heaviness in his tone.

Courtney emerged from the back room, holding her son, and Sloan looked her over.

"Are you okay? You aren't answering your phone," Sloan said, worried. Courtney was dressed, but she looked tired, like she had been up, crying all night.

"Oh, yeah, I'm good. The baby didn't sleep well last night so I was up all night with him. I must have forgotten to put my phone on the charger," Courtney said.

"Did you forget about the Friendsmas plans today?" Sloan asked.

Courtney looked at James.

"It's a lot to do around here, Sloan. I really need to get my house together, and it's too cold to have Christian outside like this, plus it's James' first day off in months. We kind of need the time together," Courtney stated. Sloan knew her friend. Courtney was giving her every excuse in the book, and they were viable reasons, but Sloan just didn't feel right leaving her behind. She searched for signs of distress, but there was no evidence of the conflict that lived in this home. The slap had hurt, but it hadn't left a bruise, and there was nothing to show for the emptiness Courtney felt inside.

A knock at the door announced Ellie's presence.

"Hey, Court," Ellie stated as she steered Tessa inside. "Hey,

James. Can we use your bathroom?"

Tessa squirmed uncomfortably. Courtney reached out one hand. "Come on. I'll take you."

Ellie noticed the messy house instantly as she followed behind her friend and daughter.

"I might as well go too before we hit the road," Sloan insisted. "I'll be right back."

James sighed and motioned for Cassidy to follow him to the kitchen.

"You want a beer or something, man?" he asked.

"Yeah, he'll take one! We might be a minute!" Sloan shouted.

Courtney led them to the guest bedroom, and Ellie waited until Tessa was in the bathroom to turn to her friends.

"What the fuck is going on, Court?" Ellie grilled.

"Nothing, y'all. It's just not a good time. I'm going through something," Courtney's eyes watered. Sloan could read the signs of postpartum depression. She saw it every day in her line of work.

"Okay. Here's what we're going to do," Sloan said. "We're going to reschedule the Christmas tree thing and stay here and help you out. We'll get this house together, get all this laundry caught up, and cook some meals for you to freeze, so you'll have a jump-start on your week."

"Y'all don't have to do that. I've got it under control," Courtney said.

"No, you don't, babe," Ellie whispered. "And we're not leaving you off Bad and Boujee."

Courtney laughed to keep from crying as her friends

hugged her, forming a small circle.

"Okay, good thing is, we got enough liquor in the sprinter for a whole party," Ellie said.

"Let me go tell Shy to send her motherfucking content team home. Can you help your niece wash her hands?"

Courtney nodded. "Yeah, I got her."

"Make sure she sends that thirsty-ass assistant home too," Sloan added.

"Girl, nah, that's who we sending to the store for the shit we need!" Ellie protested. "We need her!"

Sloan walked back out to the living room and over to the kitchen table where Cassidy sat, chopping it up with James. The two seemed to have broken the ice, and Sloan was appreciative because she knew Cassidy wasn't friendly.

"So, slight change of plans. We're going to need y'all to go do some man stuff for a while," Sloan said.

James scratched his head skeptically. "I know y'all don't know each other, but it's Friendsmas, and we can't leave our girl out. So 'tis the season to make new fucking friends, mmkay?" Sloan proposed. She saw their resistance, but before either of them could answer, she settled the matter. "Okay. Now, me and my girls are going to get this house together, cook some food, and prepare some bomb drinks. While the fellas are going to take the sprinter and take the kids to find a Christmas tree for this house. doesn't have to be real. We need a nine-foot tree and all the accessories. Can y'all handle that?"

"Doesn't sound like we have a choice," James grumbled.

"Don't be the Grinch that stole Christmas, James. Go get your coat," Sloan snickered, patting his shoulder as he walked away.

Cassidy scratched his temple and met her eyes. She closed the space between them.

"Please do this," she whispered. "I need to know what's fully going on with my friend, and I don't feel safe leaving her here with him."

He sighed.

"Yeah, okay," he submitted. "I'ma have to learn how to tell you no."

"Now, why would you do that?" she teased.

"Spoiled ass," he whispered, biting his bottom lip. Her breath hitched, he was so close, and an anxiety filled her that she couldn't explain. She was so conflicted when it came to him. Cassidy was a felon. He had a history of extreme violence, and she didn't believe in rehabilitation, but he presented something so different than what she expected a man fresh out of prison to be.

He saw her sudden apprehension, and he took a step back.

"We'll be back."

When Ellie walked back inside, she looked like she had seen a ghost.

"What's wrong?" Sloan asked.

"Brooklyn wants to go with her dad since the plans have changed," Ellie said.

"He says he'll pick us up," Brooklyn stated.

Cassidy stopped at the door.

"Do I need to stick around for that?" he asked.

"No, I can handle Cairo," Ellie said. James emerged from the back of the house, and the men headed out.

SWV set the soundtrack for the cleaning session as Ellie, Sloan, Courtney, Shy, and Lola went to work. They sang in four-part harmony like they used to when they were in middle school.

*You're the One* was their shit back in the day, and they swore they were going to be the next big girl group. It didn't matter that Shy could barely hold a tune, she had a big ol' booty and a cute little waist, and she could dance her ass off.

"Girl, this song wild as hell. We were singing about being side chicks back in the day and ain't even know it," Courtney joked.

"No, for real!" Shy laughed. "I been a side chick a time or two. It's a little lit. All the dick and none of the drama," She shrugged, and Ellie tossed a sponge at her.

"Girl!" Ellie shouted, nodding to her daughters who were posted on the couch. They were hypnotized by their devices, thankfully. Brooklyn never took her headphones off her head, so she hadn't heard the banter, and Tessa was in heaven playing her Nintendo Switch.

Sloan hollered.

"Girl, they not worried about us."

"How long have you guys been friends?" Lola asked as she loaded the dishwasher.

"Since these bitches tried to beat me up in middle school," Ellie snapped.

"You love bringing up old shit," Sloan dismissed, shaking her head.

Courtney smiled as she looked around her house.

"I really appreciate this, y'all. You have no idea. Shit has just been hard. I just don't feel like myself, and things have just been bad between James and me," Courtney admitted.

"How bad?" Sloan asked. "Cass felt like the nigga was kind of aggressive when he came to the door last night."

Courtney's lip quivered as she remembered the slap. She was lucky he hadn't left a bruise behind, but the side of her face was still sore. "Usually, we just argue, but last night was the worst it's gotten. Losing a kid changed him. It changed us both," Courtney admitted.

"Do you need a safe place to go? You don't have to stay here," Shy interjected. Courtney shook her head.

"I just feel like we can get back on track. I just can't pull myself together enough to try. I'm tired all the time. I'm disinterested in everything, and he thinks it's because of another nigga, so it makes him jealous and crazy, but I don't know what it is. I just don't feel like myself," Courtney cried.

"That sounds like depression, Courtney. Probably postpartum, and you both sound like you have some PTSD from Dev's death. You need help and so does he, but if he's flying off the handle and being possessive and insecure and jealous, then you need to get help separately until you're both well enough to come together," Sloan said softly, using a tone she typically reserved for her patients. "It's okay to reach for your own oxygen mask first, friend. All you got to do is say the word. Nod your head, and we'll pack a bag and get you up out of here."

Courtney felt herself breaking down, and she stifled her sobs because her nieces and Lola were in the room. She simply wiped the tears from her face and nodded her head.

Sloan looked to Shy, and Shy knew what to do without instruction.

"I'ma get your shit," Shy stated.

Suddenly, Brooklyn jumped up.

"Daddy's here," she announced. Ellie's heart sank as she stood from the table.

"I've got her," Sloan said. "Go handle your business."

Ellie felt her chest constrict. She could no longer avoid the inevitable.

"Give me a second, Brook. I need to speak with your dad," Ellie stated.

"You got this?" Shy asked. "Cuz we can jump his ass like we jumped you back in the day."

Ellie appreciated her girl, lightening the mood. Everyone laughed, even Courtney. Shy really was the friend who you couldn't live without.

Ellie pushed out a deep breath.

"Listen out for the hootie hoo, bitch. If you hear that, come running, because this man be testing my patience."

She walked out onto the porch and folded her arms to try to keep out the bitter wind as Cairo approached.

"Have you come to your senses or you still acting crazy?" Ellie asked.

"She's not my daughter, Ellie," Cairo sighed.

"If you break my little girl's heart like this, I'ma make your life hell, Cairo. This easy, little, quiet separation that

I've given you is going to become a messy and complicated divorce. I don't want conflict, but I won't let you get away with mistreating my child. I can't stop you from taking Brooklyn, but if you do this, I promise you I'm coming for everything you owe me plus tax. Including child support. Including spousal support. Including that nice little house you got that trifling-ass girlfriend living in. Half of your savings, half of your investments, half of your retirement. Or you can do the right thing, and I'll walk away from it all empty-handed."

"That's tough talk, but I know you better than that. You're not tough," Cairo said.

"When it came to protecting myself, maybe not. When it comes to protecting my kids, I'm not the same bitch," Ellie warned.

"You could have avoided this a long time ago if you had told that little girl she was adopted. You're pretending to be her mother."

"I am her mother!"

Brooklyn opened the screen door, and Tessa ran out onto the porch in excitement.

"Daddy!" she screamed.

Cairo didn't even bend down to hug Tessa. Ellie didn't know how she had ever been attracted to this man. Everything about him disgusted her.

"You're going to stay with your mom, sweetheart," he told Tessa. "Brooklyn, let's go."

"Why can't Tess come?" Brooklyn asked.

"It's complicated, baby girl, but it's between me and your mom. Let's go," Cairo said, summoning her off the porch.

"That's not fair! I want to come with you, too!" Tessa pleaded. Ellie couldn't stop her tears as she made her way down the stairs to pick Tessa up.

"It's okay, big girl. You can stay here with Mommy. Daddy has some big girl things planned for Brooklyn."

"Stop lying to her, Ellie! Damn it! Stop telling her I'm her dad! I'm not her fucking father!" Cairo snapped.

The sound of Tessa's cries cracked Ellie's heart in two.

"Daddy!" Brooklyn shouted in shock.

"Get in the car, Brooklyn!" Cairo shouted.

Ellie could see the conflict in her oldest child. She wanted to check on her sister, but she also hadn't seen her father in such a long time. Ellie pressed Tessa's face into her shoulder and consoled her as Brooklyn stood there, distraught.

"It's okay, baby, go with your father. It's okay," Ellie said, reassuring Brooklyn.

"But Mom…" Brooklyn's voice was so broken that she reminded Ellie of the little girl she used to be before the lying and the smoking and the teenage growing pains.

"It's okay, baby. I'll see you when you get back to Papa's in a few days. It's okay," Ellie soothed. "I've got Tess."

Brooklyn reluctantly went to her father's car, and Cairo stood there staring at Ellie.

"Leave," Ellie said in disgust.

Cairo looked remorseful, and even that pissed her off because his guilt didn't erase the hurt he had just inflicted. He got in his car and drove away, leaving wounds that Ellie knew Tessa would be nursing for the rest of her life.

# CHAPTER 9

Ellie sat in the front row of the sprinter as they rode back to Shy's house to retrieve their cars. The night had been ruined. Ellie was numb. Her heart hurt so much that she felt nothing. Tessa had cried herself to sleep. As she laid her head in Ellie's lap, Ellie stroked her hair softly. If Ellie could carry this pain for her baby, she would, but life didn't work that way. Her phone rang, and she scoffed when she saw Loyal's name pop up on her screen. She couldn't even think about a man right now. In fact, she hated all men just off the strength of Cairo being on the same team. *Bitch-ass nigga*, she thought. She regretted coming home. If she had stayed away from Michigan, like she had planned, her daughter's heart would still be whole.

*Friendsmas is a joke*, she thought. There wasn't a bit of Christmas cheer in sight. The entire van had been silent. No one spoke and she was sure it was because they didn't know what to say. Her life was a spectacle and if these weren't her closest friends, she would be certain that the gossip would be all in the streets by now. She was mortified. It was this exact feeling that she had avoided all these years. She hadn't wanted witnesses to the unraveling of her marriage, but now her loved ones had front-row seats.

Sloan sat in the back of the van, tucked away in the corner as she rested her head on Cassidy's shoulder. He lifted his arm, and she leaned into him, exhaling as he rubbed circles into her shoulder.

Her heart was so tender at the thought of Ellie's situation.

"I got her," Cassidy whispered in her ear. She looked at him, trying to make out his features in the dark to no avail. He lifted a hand to her cheek and caressed the side of her face reassuringly, and Sloan sighed. She lifted her feet onto the empty seats beside her and laid her head in his lap as he kneaded the tips of his fingers into her scalp. There was such comfort in his touch, so much gentleness, and caring that she had no choice but to hand her anxiety over to him. She sighed as she closed her eyes. She was asleep before she knew it.

The hour-long drive passed by in what felt like the blink of an eye, and when Sloan felt Cassidy shift, she was aroused from her rest.

"That's a wrap, everybody," Shy said dryly, standing and getting out of the sprinter first. "Court, come on, girl, let's get you settled."

"Good night, everybody," Court said, giving Ellie a reassuring squeeze on her shoulder before she exited the sprinter. One by one they got off and Cassidy picked Tessa up from Ellie's lap.

"I got her, E," he said. Ellie nodded and then Sloan grabbed Ellie's hand and led her off the sprinter.

"Do you two want to stay the night with me tonight?" Sloan asked as they followed Cassidy to Ellie's car.

Ellie shook her head. "No, I just want to get home. How am I going to explain this shit to my baby, sis? He's the only father she knows. He is her father, Sloan."

Sloan nodded her head in support. "He is. All daddy's ain't made equal, unfortunately. Cairo has turned into such a bitch-ass nigga, but your baby has so much love, Ellie." Sloan glanced at Cassidy who was placing his niece gently in the backseat. He grabbed the snow brush from the trunk and began to clear Ellie's windshield. "She will be okay eventually and we're all here for y'all. Whatever extra support you need. We got you."

Ellie swiped away a renegade tear and sniffed away her frail emotions, as she blew hot air into her cold hands. She couldn't allow her own feelings to take over because she knew once Tessa awoke, she would have to be strong for her. Tessa would have questions and Ellie had to be able to answer them without breaking down. "Thanks, Sloan. I love you. I'm going to head home."

Sloan nodded and hugged her friend long and tight. "Okay. Text the group chat when you make it. I love you. If you need anything, call me."

Ellie walked to her car and hugged Cassidy next before getting inside and driving away.

"Let me get you on your way, too," Cassidy offered, walking beside her. "You got a scraper?" he asked as she unlocked the doors.

"Yeah, it's in the back."

She opened her door and hopped inside as she watched him stomp through the snow as he rounded her car, cleaning off the windows. His nose was red by the time he finished.

"Be careful out here on these roads," he warned. "None of that lead foot shit. You still drive like you racing everybody on the road?"

"Boy, I drive just fine, thank you very much," she defended. "You tried to teach me to drive one time. You can't hold that against me my whole life."

He chuckled, rubbed his hands together, and blew hot air into them, before stuffing them in his coat pockets.

"I really hate this for Ellie," Sloan said as she started her truck and turned sideways so that she faced him. "I hate this for Courtney too. Friendsmas isn't feeling so festive this year."

What should have been an epic reunion was turning into a week filled with hurtful memories. She couldn't say it was all bad. As she stood in front of Cassidy, she saw a silver lining, standing right in front of her.

"Yeah, I'ma swing by and check on Tessa in the morning. She'll need to know she has a man in her life that she can count on. That nigga doing some damage, man," Cassidy stated. He clenched his jaw tightly, grinding his teeth so hard that his temple pulsed.

"The best thing you can do for them is fill in the gap," Sloan advised. "He's still Brooklyn's dad. There's only so much straightening you can do to him."

Cassidy struggled with falling back when it came to this, and she could see it.

"Bye, guys!" Lola shouted as she walked by Sloan's truck. "Cassidy, I'm headed to this lounge I know. Live music, good food. It's a vibe. Drinks on me if you're interested."

Cassidy's brow lifted at her boldness. She was on his radar. He hadn't missed the flirting Lola had engaged in all day. She was young and uncomplicated, and she wanted him to know it. Sloan shook her head and awaited his reply.

"I'm good, man. I'ma call it," Cassidy said, letting her down gently.

"I swear these young hoes don't have no home training," Sloan stated in disbelief.

Cassidy laughed and licked his lips before stuffing his cold hands in his jacket pockets.

"She's harmless," he laughed and looked down at his feet.

"Harmless my ass. She's throwing pussy at you and you eating the shit up. You whole ass blushing right now!" Sloan shot back, rolling her eyes.

"Ain't nobody thinking about that girl, man," he denied. "I'm a little preoccupied with somebody else. Can't figure out how to get around all her walls, though."

Sloan hadn't expected him to be so honest. Her stomach hollowed as he stepped closer, occupying the space between her body and the door.

"You're in my head, Sloan," he admitted as he placed a hand to the side of her face. He leaned into her and rested his forehead against hers. He didn't know if she was trembling because she was cold or if she was terrified.

"I can't," she whispered as she snapped her eyes closed and pulled back. She was running.

"Why do you do that?" Cassidy asked. "It doesn't feel good to know you're afraid to get close to a nigga. I heard you the other day. I did my dirt, but I paid for it too, Sloan. I'm not that kid anymore. I'm not a bad man."

"I know you're not," Sloan sighed.

"Then what is it?" Cassidy asked. Sloan looked off, and she began to fidget as anxiety filled her body.

"It's nothing," Sloan insisted. He had the deepest eyes. She could only imagine what they had seen. When he stared at her, she felt transparent, like he could see right through her to the center of her soul, where she hid her secrets. "Please stop looking at me like that. I can't go there with you. We don't match. You don't check any of my boxes, Cass, and yes, you served your time, but you still took a life, Cassidy. That's not a small thing you're asking me to overlook."

Cassidy scoffed and took a step back, nodding his head in frustration as he closed her door. "Say less, Dr. Martin." She had offended him, and now he was walking away. Her head was spinning because she was relieved and horrified by his departure all at the same time. She hopped out of the car and stormed after him.

"That's it!?" she yelled.

Cassidy spun on her suddenly. "Fuck you mean is that it? Should there be more?" Cassidy asked, annoyed and face bent in confusion.

This woman was his sister's best friend. She was a puzzle he couldn't quite crack, but damn if he didn't want to crack that bitch. He knew she had her reservations. He could see her battling with herself every time they were in the same room. He was trying to respect her boundaries, but Cassidy wanted Sloan in the most addictive way.

"Could there be more?" she shot back.

"How much truth can you handle?" Cassidy asked.

"That's all I ever want to hear from you. The minute you lie to me, we no longer communicate," Sloan said.

"I want to fuck you, Sloan," Cassidy admitted. Sloan sucked in air and held it, forgetting to breathe as her lashes fluttered in shock. He was going there. No detour, no scenic route. He was getting straight to it. "I knew it the minute I saw you again. I want you in my bed, legs wrapped around my waist. Not on no quick shit. Not on no one-time shit. I want access. I want to eat your pussy whenever I feel like it. I want to watch my dick slide down your throat. I want to swallow your tongue while I beat it slow, real fucking slow because I know that shit good, and probably gon' have a nigga ready to bust as soon as he in it. I want it bad as fuck. I want it so bad my dick gets hard at the thought of you, and I ain't starved for no pussy. I called up pussy last night just to get you and your judgmental ass out my head, but you were still there. I pictured your face as I made love to another woman, Sloan. She called my name, and I heard you. That's how bad I want you, but you're afraid of a nigga so I can't pursue you. You're my sister's friend, and I'm trying to be respectful, but you're everywhere. You're everywhere she is, and every time I see you, I'm in my head wondering what this beautiful fucking woman feels like. I know it's tight cuz you stingy with it. You sitting on it, and niggas ain't patient enough to work for it. I know she wet because I smell it, Sloan. Right now, I can smell how sweet it is. And I know that's some bold shit to say, but a nigga been locked up for a long time; I know what wet pussy smell like, and you always wet around me. I think about you all the time and I ain't gone be able to get it off my mind until I've wrapped my lips around your clit. There's some truth for your uppity ass. A nigga too gutter for you, though."

Sloan's pussy was soaked, and her mouth was slightly agape as her clit throbbed to the cadence of his voice. She felt shock waves ripple through her clit as she came from fantasy alone. The way he painted this picture. The yearning she heard in his voice. She wondered how many times he had reached for his dick when she crossed his mind. If any other man had come at her this boldly, she would have been disgusted, but Cassidy's truth intrigued her. He masturbated to her fantasy. How many times had he fucked another woman while running her face in the background of his mind? The thought turned her the fuck on to the point where her nipples screamed for attention. Sloan had never lusted for any man. Men usually lusted for her, but this feeling was mutual, but he was right, she was afraid of so many things. She didn't even know what to say.

"Get in your truck and go home. It's cold out here," he said, unable to hide his frustration and irritation. Sloan reached up and grabbed the sides of his skull cap and pulled his entire face toward her as she kissed him. He backed her up to the side of her truck and kissed her so deeply that her nipples hardened. She had never been kissed with such passion. He took her chin in the U of one hand and finessed her lips with expertise. Neither wanted to pull away, but they couldn't stay here forever. Or could they? This wasn't just a kiss. This was a full-blown make-out session. This man was sucking on her entire tongue. She moaned from the pure torture of arousal alone. She was so wet that she felt her leggings soak. She wanted everything he wanted. The clothes between them were torture. Fifteen whole minutes of indulging in this man's lips made her legs shake. Neither cared that it was freezing outside. She stood in the cold, clasping his forearms as she tried to clear her head.

"I can't do this, Cass," she whispered, eyes burning with tears because she knew he wouldn't understand.

The disappointment in his eyes gutted her, and he nodded, wiping the taste of her off his lips as he backpedaled to his car. She climbed into her truck and gripped the steering wheel as she lowered her head and cried. She heard him start his car and speed off in frustration. She wished she could go after him, but she also knew that lust wasn't enough reason to break her own rules. Her mother had lost her life to a violent man, to a repeated ex-con, who had claimed to be a changed man. Her mother had trusted a man at his word, and in the end, she had paid that mistake with her life. So, no, Sloan couldn't take this further. She would just have to keep her distance to make sure that whatever this attraction was didn't grow.

**Knock! Knock!**

Courtney turned toward the bedroom door as Shy peeked her head inside. "Hey! You okay?" Shy asked.

"Yeah, I'm fine, girl. James just keeps blowing up my phone. We're in a whole text battle right now," Courtney stated. "He says he's sorry. Wants us to come home."

"Do you want to go home, Court?"

Courtney thought about all the anxiety that dwelled in her chest when she was within the walls of her own home. She felt on edge every second of every day. She walked around on eggshells because she had lost track of his triggers. She couldn't really tell what would sour his mood. After Devin had been killed, he had developed a disdain for her, and it had grown stronger over the years. Now, they felt so far apart from one another. Sex was routine, a chore even, and the only emotions that she felt were negative ones. She knew she loved him. They had been together for too long not to love him, but she had also hated what their life had become. Her heart used to skip beats when he would walk in the room, and now, it filled with panic. It wasn't always bad, but the good was so few and far between because they were both drowning in grief.

"No, I don't think I do. Not right now. Our demons are battling one another for space in that house. The house is too small for that much misery." Courtney's confession was chilling. It was the first time she was able to truly pinpoint the problem. They were battling themselves, which stopped them from being able to consider one another. "It's wild because when I first met him, I was rushing to be grown. I did everything before it was time because I was trying to keep up with his pace. He was a grown man, doing grown shit to me, putting grown woman expectations on my body and my mind, and I let him have so much control. I let him shape who I became instead of knowing that he needed to adjust to who I naturally grew into, or risk me outgrowing him altogether. Now, I just feel stuck. I feel damaged. I feel like he customized me for him and like I wasted all my good years with a man who now doesn't even like me. I'm in the middle of a mid-life crisis, bitch. Nigga stress me out so bad I got a whole streak of gray hair under this damn wig," Courtney complained.

"Bitch, I got gray pussy hair. How about that?" Shy said.

"Oooh, bitch, no you don't!" Courtney hollered, laughing so loudly that baby Christian stirred in his sleep. She covered her mouth but couldn't stop.

"Swear to God. A bitch about died when my esthetician pointed it out," Shy said, shaking her head.

"Thank you, Shy," Courtney said sincerely. "For welcoming me without thinking twice, for even making the time to come by to check on me when you knew something wasn't right. I know I go months without picking up the phone sometimes, but it's never because love is lost. I'm just lost right now. Everybody else is thriving, and I feel like the friend who ain't got shit and didn't do shit with her life."

"You're the friend who prays for us. You're the friend who cooks for us. You're the friend who looks at the glass half full. You're the one who forces us to work our shit out when we get to being petty with each other. You're the friend who hypes us up when we're afraid. You're the friend who will tell us when we're wrong. I can go on and on about you, Court. We notice when your energy is missing from our circle. You aren't the underachiever. You're a grown woman, and life has been unkind to you, but you get back up and you keep fighting. You've just been fighting in silence. Now that we know what's going on, we're fighting with you," Shy encouraged. "I'm not even saying James is a bad guy, but if he loves you and he loves his son, he'll get some help for that grief and stop taking the shit out on you. You deserve him at his best, and if he can't give you that, it's time to wrap this shit up."

Courtney nodded. "You're right. I can't even say anything because you're speaking facts."

Shy stood. "I want to give you one of your Christmas gifts early," she said.

"Oh, Shy, please, don't. I'm not going to lie. My gifts to y'all aren't that expensive. I couldn't afford a lot this year, and I know how you shop. I'm really not comfortable..."

"Girl, shut up! I'll be back," Shy said, rushing from the room. Courtney felt the pressure of matching the value of her gifts. That was another reason why she hadn't wanted to be super present for the Friendsmas festivities. She didn't have the same means as her girls. It was easy for them to blow bags on one another. Courtney had to choose between a halfway decent gift for them and paying her light bill. Shy returned after a few minutes, and she held a jewelry box in her hands.

Courtney opened the box, and she gasped when she saw the beautiful strand of pearls inside. "These are your nana's, Shy. She left these to you in her will. I can't accept this," Courtney said.

"You can and you will," Shy stated. "My grandmother was from Louisiana, girl, and she didn't pass these down to me because they're expensive. Her great, great-grandmother gave them to her. She blessed them in the backwoods of Bastrop. You probably ain't even never heard of it. Those pearls protected every woman in my family from any man who ever wanted to do her harm, starting with the slave master she originally made them because of. Swear to God, last nigga who tried to plot on me teeth fell out his mouth, and the nigga went bald, and his dick stopped working."

Courtney went from tears to gut-hurting laughter.

"I promise youuuu!" Shy hollered. "Now, they yours, so James can play if he wanna. Nigga gon' fuck with them ancestors, and they ain't never playing about whoever wearing that necklace. Voodoo the fuck out his ass!"

Courtney rushed Shy and hugged her tightly as she released pent-up emotion, crying on her shoulder.

Shy closed her eyes and held her back. "Merry Christmas, boo. You're going to be okay. We promise you, sis."

Sloan tossed and turned for hours as she tried to force her mind to shut off. She was worried about so many things. She and Ellie had spoken for over an hour after she got home. Ellie was so hurt, and all Sloan could do was pray with her and be a listening ear. Courtney's situation weighed heavily on her as well. She had already gone online and started a new bank account in Courtney's name. Luckily, she had Court's social security number from her medical records, since she was Courtney's OBGYN as well. She had put aside ten thousand dollars in emergency money, just in case Courtney ever felt the need to escape permanently. She knew it took time to leave, and that Courtney would likely end up back at home. Sloan didn't like the idea of her friend being trapped in a situation due to lack of finances. It wouldn't happen on her watch. It seemed like Shy was the only one who didn't have a pressing problem to fix, and she was grateful for that. Then, there was the looming heartache hovering over her bed like a storm cloud. She felt like she had been gutted right down the center. She may not share her problems with her friends, but she had them. She had a lot of them, but she was the strong friend. She was the one they went to for support. She couldn't show weakness and reciprocate a need because who would hold their circle down? She lay in bed in anguish. Cassidy had blindsided her. She could still feel his touch. She could still taste his lips. She wanted to call him, but it just wasn't appropriate. What would she tell people? They didn't have a shot at anything real. She couldn't claim him publicly. She was in a predominantly white and very corporate profession.

The medical field was elitist. She had worked very hard to be respected in the healthcare community and to be an advocate for Black maternal medicine. She couldn't let a man with a record a mile long claim her. She could never introduce him to anyone. As soon as they looked him up, her entire career would be discredited. She knew it was wrong, but it was life. It was how the world worked. He hadn't been a part of the world in a long time, so he was naïve if he thought otherwise. He could call her uppity all he wanted. She was a realist, and even though she felt such ease in his presence, she knew he was a very temporary visitor in her life. He could never stay. Her history, mixed with his history, was a recipe for disaster anyway. Even if she could get past the professional stain it would cause, the things that traumatized her from her childhood were triggered by his story, and she couldn't shake that, no matter how hard she tried. Her tears were so natural that she didn't even realize they were falling until her pillow was soaked. They just leaked out the corners of her eyes as she stared at the wall. She had never felt a connection like the one she felt when she was around Cassidy. It didn't matter if they were in agreement or at odds, the energy exchange was electrifying. Some days, she went through her routine simply because she had done it so many times before. She knew what to do, when to do it, and what to say, like clockwork. She just switched the day of the week and the color of the scrubs. When she was near him, days felt lived. They felt unique. She felt every second. He ignited jealousy, anger, excitement, intrigue, confusion, allure, infatuation, seduction. She felt alive, but the one emotion that she didn't want to feel was also present. He triggered a dark place. A fear that he hadn't put in her was also reignited in his presence, and it was strong enough to halt her in her tracks. Still, being away from him, especially after knowingly hurting him, felt like torture. She remembered meeting him for the first time. He was just as fine then as he was now, and she had been enamored by him. He was the most geared-up boy on his block. He sold dope just to be able to afford his signature Tommy Hilfiger and Jordan sneakers. She wondered if he remembered the day she had become infatuated with him. Sloan was a regular fixture in the Whitlock household, and one Saturday night she couldn't sleep. She knew she needed to because Mama Whitlock had a strict rule. If you spent the night at their house on Saturday, you were waking your butt up for church Sunday morning, and she wasn't letting you miss Sunday school either. But Sloan couldn't shut her mind down. She was in the 9th grade when he walked in on her, eating ice cream at the kitchen table by herself. He was sneaking into the house at two o'clock in the morning, and he hadn't expected to find her sitting in the dark. It was the night he had asked her about Deyontae Cook. She was so proud to have an older boyfriend that she ignored his warnings, but they stayed up all night, eating ice cream and talking about their dreams. He had planned to go to college and pledge a frat. She had wanted to become a doctor. He told her he would show her around if she ended up where he was. He insisted on her ending up where he was, in fact, and she had agreed. She remembered it like it was yesterday. She still recalled the feeling of laughing with him on that living room floor. Telling him all her goals. Him telling her what type of businessman he was going to become. He had kissed her that night. He didn't know that it had been her first real kiss, or he probably would have remembered. She remembered, however, and although she had a boyfriend, she had planned to meet him at Howard University one day. Only he never made it. She watched him drift farther and farther into the streets until the night of his arrest. All their lives had changed that day. Sloan remembered the sick feeling of devastation that had crippled her for months after the police had taken him. She wondered if he knew that she had held onto that one night... those plans, she had taken them seriously, and he had broken her heart. He had chosen a different path, and she went on to fulfill everything she had told him she would.

"Fuck this," she whispered as she climbed out of bed and abandoned the room, bare feet carrying her to the kitchen. She poured herself a glass of Cabernet. The silence in this beautiful home was ugly. To be this successful, yet this unaccomplished all at the same time was nasty fucking work. Where were her children? Where was her man? Where were the wedding pictures that were supposed to be sitting on the mantle? The home was sterile, barren— like her womb. She picked up her phone, and her thumb lingered over his name. She swallowed down the whole damn glass of wine. Liquid courage. She surrendered her burden to the ceiling as she let her head fall back on the couch pillow in despair. "Don't call this man," she whispered. She reached for the bottle on her living room table and poured another glass. How she could clear an entire bottle of wine, by having only two glasses should be studied. A bitch was sulking, and wine was the remedy. She wondered if they had wine drinking contests, like those stupid-ass hot dog eating contests. She scoffed at the ridiculousness of her own mind. She was that fucking bored. That lonely. She had nothing better to do but think about stupid-ass shit because she had done some stupid-ass shit and let some phenomenal-ass dick slip through her fingers tonight. She was a smart girl, but clearly, she lacked common sense. "Know damn well prison niggas got good dick," she scolded herself.

She swallowed her pride and centered herself Indian-style on the couch. She had rejected Cassidy earlier. She was nervous that he would push her away. She pressed his name anyway. She braced herself as the phone rang. She was so damn anxious, and her worst fears were realized when the voicemail picked up. Fear crippled her as she wondered if he was with another woman. Maybe the woman who had borrowed her face the other night. He didn't have to do that tonight. No need to fantasize. He could have the real thing. All he had to do was answer the phone. Sloan didn't know if she was chasing something that was bad for her or avoiding something that was good for her. Her discernment was off; she just knew she needed something from him. There would either be a consequence or a blessing at the end of this decision. She was prepared for either. Or maybe the Sauvignon was convincing her that she could handle this.

"Answer the fucking phone, boy!" she shouted into his voicemail.

Her doorbell rang, and panic struck her. Hurried feet and white-painted toenails ran across the hardwood floors, and she pulled the curtain aside to peer outside. It was two o'clock in the morning, and it looked like a blizzard outside, and he was standing on her doorstep. She unlocked the door, and her chest heaved, and her brow wrinkled. Her entire body was revolting. A stampede of soldiers marching on behalf of love charged forward inside her chest. She didn't even know how he knew where she lived. She really didn't care. He could have stalked her ass, and she would have given him a gold star for ingenuity at this point. He stepped inside, and she shut the door. He was in different clothes, so she knew he had gone home first before coming there. He smelled like he knew he was about to make love to a woman. The Tom Ford cologne infected her air as soon as he crossed the threshold of her home. She never wanted to forget that smell. She wanted him to move in and spray that shit all over the place, to make her home, his home, to turn her scent to his scent. How long had he been outside her house? Was the conflict between them weighing on him the way it was with her? Was the distance between them torture for him, too?

"Why does this feel like this?" she panted.

"Because life made us wait," he answered. Her eyes misted, and she held her breath as he closed the space between them. "It's two decades of anticipation between us," he said, as he stared at her. She nodded and lowered her head. She was so emotional and a little drunk. He lifted her chin. "I know why you're mad. I know where the resentment comes from. I know why you're holding back. I hate that you've been lonely, Sloan, but I'm so fucking grateful it ain't a nigga in the way. Almost like you saved it for me," Cassidy said. She had so many things to say before he arrived, but now, she couldn't find words. Only tears. Only fears. He was gentle in the way he kissed her collarbone. She pinched her eyes closed, and she felt her chin fall victim to the trap between his fingers as he kissed her and then scooped her off her feet. She dropped the wine glass, not caring that it shattered on her floor. Frantic hands pushed his jacket off his shoulders as he carried her into the living room. He placed her on the oversized, plush, ivory couch, and she unwrapped her package, removing his hoodie, then his t-shirt, as they kissed slowly. The Nike Tech joggers came next. She knew what to expect at the end. She had felt it when they had kissed earlier in the day, but seeing all of him was mind-blowing. She hadn't had dick like this before, especially dick that was making up for lost time. She was afraid she may not be able to take it, but damn it, she was going to try. He pulled her thighs to the edge of the couch and lowered to his knees. Her powder blue silk teddy and short kimono robe allowed easy access, and he hoisted her hips up in the palms of his hands like he was prepared to eat watermelon on a hot summer day. "Damn," he whispered as he dove in. Her clit was paying attention. She was so ready and wanting that it was swollen and glistening in a pond of desire. It was so fat and pretty that Cassidy licked his lips and took a preliminary taste just to sample it first.

"Mmm," he appreciated. He immediately went back in. Her stomach caved in as he sucked on her whole pussy. Clit, labia, perineum, ass, he ate it all. She thought she might have to coach him, that she would have to tell him what she liked. Sloan didn't have to say shit. He was a man deprived, and she was a woman in supply of everything he needed.

"Cassidy!" she shouted. "Oh my god!"

It had been so long since she had been touched by a man. Nobody had ever eaten her pussy like this. She folded. Literally, he folded her in half, pushing her legs back and ravishing her. Some men were too rough with a woman. They sucked too hard or used too much spit, or not enough, or they licked the cat wrong like they were scared to get their faces wet. Cassidy did every motherfucking thing right, EVERYTHING. She Didn't know if it was because he had been constrained from a woman for so long or if the nigga was just a beast, but he slurped on her pussy like it was his job; like she was his parole officer, and he was trying to seduce his way out of a drug test; like it was his last meal before execution. He had, indeed, fantasized about her; she could tell just from the way he handled her. There was so much appreciation in his touch, so much gratefulness in every suckle of her clit. He was in distress, and her clit was pacifying him. He didn't rush. He went through seven courses, and Sloan was losing her mind.

"Is it good, baby?" she whispered as she stared between her legs, mouth slightly ajar as she witnessed his exquisite work. She was amazed.

"Mmm," he groaned.

"Cass," she panted. "Cass, please don't make me cum yet. I won't be able to cum again if you don't slow down."

He paused, and she sat up on her elbows, winded as he worked around her clit, placing teasing kisses on her inner thigh.

"Please. I want to last with you. I can't orgasm more than once," she admitted. "I don't know why. It just doesn't happen that way."

"Yeah, you can, baby," he whispered confidently. "Let me show you." He inserted three fingers inside her and pumped them slowly as he massaged her clit with his free thumb. Her eyes rolled in the back of her head. A guttural sound escaped her as he covered her clit with full lips and applied pressure, then circled it with his tongue. "I'm about to nut. Cassssss."

"I can taste it," he assured her. "Good fucking girl."

He stood, and his dick was completely hard. His skin stretched so beautifully over those eight, thick inches that she didn't dare ask him to cover it. She knew fucking better too. She taught sex education classes, and still, logic was snatched from her brain at the sight of that good dick. He could see her weighing the consequences of some deadly disease in her mind. The doctor in her was overthinking. Not really because she was a grown-ass woman and she was thinking on point, but she was in her head and about to ruin the moment. "Trust me," he whispered. He knew he used condoms with other women; she didn't, but the fact that she let him proceed spoke volumes for him.

He slid his girth up her wet slit, coating himself in her first and teasing her sensitive clit even more before finally entering with ease. He slid all the way inside until his balls touched her ass, and then he rested there for a minute. That pussy was tight, warm, and soaked. She hummed around him. Pussy would talk to a man if he were doing his job and hers was speaking in French. He pulsated inside her. His dick was begging him for a little release. Precum was oozing out of him as he rested inside her for a few seconds. He was hitting a spot so tender that she reached down to grab his wrists.

"I ain't gon' take nothing you don't want to give, baby. I'm in the right spot. You give me how much you want me to have," he coached. She rolled her hips slowly, adjusting to his size and whimpering with every movement she made. She was timid, and he knew it was because someone had hit her with sex that had hurt or caused discomfort before.

"Can I take care of you?" he asked. She knew what he was asking. He wanted control over this night, over her body. He was about to deliver some good dick, and he needed her to trust him. He hit her with one slow stroke, and he felt her get wetter. She nodded, and he continued. His body was incredible. He used every muscle to control the pace and was careful not to weigh her down as he tensed into her depths. Missionary with him wasn't boring. It was the position for lovers. She had never felt this connected with a man before. He placed kisses of adulation all over her body as he stroked. His favorite spot to kiss was her lips, but he gave every part of her a little time. Her ears, her chin, the valley at the base of her neck that sank in every time she cried his name. Each perfect brown nipple, her fingers that he made her dip into her juices so he could taste her more, and even her toes.

"That's two," he counted as he watched her cream on his dick. She was coating him, and Cassidy had to stop stroking and change positions to stop his nut.

He climbed on the couch, sitting on his knees. "Turn around, baby. Sit on it," he instructed. She used the back of the couch to hold onto as she rode him in reverse. Sloan was a fit woman. She did Pilates every morning to make sure she stayed in shape, and it showed in her stamina. The way her ass moved as she rode him was a vision, and the stretch marks that covered it was art in human form.

"You riding it so good. You waited for me, didn't you?" he asked.

"Yes," she moaned. "God, Cass, yes." Good dick would make a bitch say anything. She had taken plenty of dick before him, but she loved a man who talked her through it, and Cassidy was playing into a fantasy that had been in both their minds for years. This was the most passionate dick she had ever had, and he was the one she was pining for now, so he got the prize as the best. A woman always hyped a nigga dick game when she liked him, but surprisingly, Cassidy wasn't coming to play. She felt her orgasm building everywhere, and there wasn't one reservation in her mind about submitting sexually to him. Whatever he wanted to do, whatever he wanted her to try, no matter how deep or fast or hard he wanted to fuck, she would go there with him. It felt that good. She never wanted this to end.

"Is it mine, Sloan?" he asked as he fell victim to the rhythm of her riding him. The way his dick disappeared between her ass cheeks every time she bounced on it, he couldn't contain himself. He gripped her waist tighter as he matched her strokes. Thick-ass dick made her legs shake. "Tell me it's mine."

"It's yours!" she whimpered.

"Can I put my name on it?" he asked. He had never even considered dropping off his last name inside a woman, but he knew he wasn't pulling out. They would have to worry about the consequences in the morning.

Sloan couldn't even answer; all she could do was cry out in pleasure as she came. "That's three," he counted. She was too tired to position herself, so he moved her entire body, facing her in the correct position to ride him from the front.

"My clit is so sensitive," she whimpered as he eased his dick in and out of her. She was spent. She couldn't move, but she felt every inch of dick he pumped into her as he did the work for them both. Thank God he was strong. He was fucking her back, lifting her hips, and annihilating her pussy. Her clit was overstimulated. Mini orgasms shot through her body like aftershocks with every stroke. In all her years, her pussy had never been beaten up. Cassidy was going for the knockout. It was the most overindulgent, sensitive, gluttonous, erotic, nasty, pleasurable thing she had ever experienced with a man. She felt his dick contracting as he released. She hadn't done shit in a whole thirteen minutes, and still, she felt like the champ for taking him down.

"Fuck," he whispered as he finished, breathing hard. "Oh fuckkk." She loved a vocal man. She hated guessing if a man was enjoying her or not. He fucked her slowly through his entire nut, and the pressure of his dick sliding against her clit milked her of one last orgasm. Her clit was throbbing it was so aroused. She convulsed even at the pressure of his body, and she felt another orgasm slide out of her effortlessly. She was overstimulated at this point. A connoisseur for him. She didn't even tell him about that one because this was greed at this point. She was done. She rested her head on his shoulder, and he sat there with the mess he had made in his lap. He kissed her shoulder so gently, so proudly. It felt like he was giving her a gold star. She wanted to take that bitch to the playground and show it off to her homegirls. She had never been satisfied like this.

"I've thought about this for a long time," he admitted. "Thank you, baby." She smiled, blushing at his level of comfort with her. She was *baby* now. Might as well change her whole name. This moment felt intimate in a way that was reserved for lovers.

She rested on his chest, and his hold was so tight that she wanted to stay there forever. So much pent-up emotion filled her. It was overflowing, and she had an overwhelming urge to let it out. Her heart pounded as silent tears rolled down her cheeks. He would have never known she was emotional if he didn't feel them wet his chest.

"Why are you crying?" he asked as he stroked her hair softly.

"I'm just glad you're home," she whispered. "I never thought you would make it home. I didn't even know you remembered that night."

"I never forgot," he answered. She craned her neck to look up into his eyes. He reached down under her armpits to pull her closer to his face. Her lips were his to try whenever he pleased. "If they ever take me away again, at least..."

He hadn't realized how much his bid had affected her until he heard her sob at the notion. He hadn't even finished his sentence. He cleared her curly hair from her face, and he could see a storm of emotion in her. There weren't words he could say to erase whatever she had faced during the time he was gone, so he would have to show her. He had lived with the weight of disappointing his father and being away from his sister and mother. He had no idea there was one more person who had felt the consequences of his choices.

"Come here," he whispered. He adjusted, getting comfortable on the couch, and she tucked herself under him and pulled the throw blanket over them.

"I don't want to talk about that," she cried.

"Okay," he soothed. "We won't." He kissed the top of her head and rubbed her back until she calmed. "I'm not going anywhere." That seemed to reassure her, and he felt her breathing slow. They lay there in silence, overthinking.

"How we gon' hide this from Ellie?" Sloan mumbled, half asleep.

"Shh... go to sleep," Cassidy said. "Everybody and everything else don't exist until tomorrow."

# CHAPTER 10

Sloan was in a love story. She had to be because that was the only time men behaved like this. She woke up to the softest kisses, and she moaned as she readjusted into his body. Cassidy reached around her body, gripping her ass, and pulling her closer.

"Good morning," he whispered.

Sloan couldn't even open her eyes. "Not yet," she whispered back. The sun wasn't even out yet. She wasn't ready to face reality.

"I've got to go, Sloan," he said regretfully. "I've got to meet Loyal about some business."

She opened her eyes, and he was there, staring at her. She had been in love with this man since he was a boy, and she wanted to say those three words so badly. She wouldn't, though. It would only make him want more than she could realistically give, and that wasn't fair to him. She wanted to ask him to stay. They had waited for this moment for two decades, and one night hadn't been enough. It was passing them by already, and she desperately wanted more, but she knew there was no amount of time that would be enough except for forever. So, he was right. She needed to accept it for what it was— a fantasy fulfilled. Logic told her that his departure made sense, but she couldn't convince her heart to understand. Her eyes were already fucking watering.

He kissed her, and she closed her eyes as he turned her on her back. Those kisses went from her lips to her breasts, down her stomach, until he captured his prize.

He ate breakfast quickly, pulling that morning tension right out of her body and leaving her quivering. He rested his head on her stomach, kissing her skin as she rubbed the top of his head.

"You scare me, Cass," she whispered. She felt him tense, and she knew her words affected him. "After you went away, my mom…" Sloan's voice was shaking, and she had to massage her hands to stop them from trembling. She could still see her mother's battered body in her mind. "She was killed…" Sloan paused as the trauma of that day seized her entire body. "… by her boyfriend. He was someone who was supposed to love her. I saw him dote over her. Day in and day out, until one day, I came home and found her in her bedroom, beat up until she wasn't even recognizable. He strangled her to death, Cass, and when they finally caught him, I found out he had done the same thing to another woman before. He was on parole for assault and attempted murder of another woman ten years before that. He was violent, and he went away for it. He paid for his crime and convinced everybody he was a changed man, only to do it

164

again. I don't date violent men. I don't trust rehabilitated men. You beat that man to death, Cassidy." She cried because she knew he wouldn't be an exception to that rule. "As gentle as you were with me last night, how can you hurt someone the way you did? How do you even have that in you?"

Morning had brought logic back to their situation, and the moment was sobering. He sat up, and so did she. They were no longer living in their fantasy. This was reality, and he swiped one hand down his face before leaning forward on his knees and bowing his head.

"I would never hurt you, Sloan," he said, clearing his throat because it was knotted in emotion from the fact that he knew her fear of him was real.

"That's what he told her, too, until he did," she whispered. She looked off, unable to be accountable to his stare. He was silently pleading with her to trust him, to believe him. She wanted to, but what was her mother's death for if not to teach her a lesson? If she refused to learn it, she was destined to repeat it. Men in jail were con artists. They were masters at manipulation and concealing. They learned how to be better deceivers in prison, and she just couldn't be sure that Cassidy was truly different, or if he was just masquerading.

"I don't know how to do anything except live in my truth," Cassidy said. "I can tell you, and I will tell you, every day, that I'll never hurt you, but it's my actions that matter."

"I just can't reconcile the 'you now' versus the you that did that," Sloan cried. "The trial, Cassidy. You sat up there and didn't show an ounce of remorse. I came to your trial every day. I skipped school to make sure I was there next to Ellie every fucking day until the day they put you on the stand and showed the crime scene photos."

"I remember the shit, Sloan. I don't need you to play it back for me," he stated in frustration. It had been the worst time of his life. "I looked for you after that. I searched every face in that crowd for you until I realized you weren't coming back. I was scared out my mind and I used to focus on you. I thought you were the prettiest girl I'd ever seen, man." He nodded his head in understanding as he concluded that this wasn't going to happen for them. "I'm sorry I can't be who you need. It kills me every time I feel your fear creep into your mind when I'm around. Because I would fucking never..." He shook his head and reached for his clothes because there wasn't even a point in continuing. The fact that she thought he would lay a finger on her put a pain in him he couldn't quite shake. "I don't want you to be anywhere you don't feel safe, Sloan. Last night was..."

"Perfect," she whispered, pushing a tear off her face as she watched him dress.

"A mistake, Sloan," he said, snatching up his shirt. "I would have never taken advantage of you if I knew..."

"I don't feel taken advantage of," she protested. "That's not what I'm saying!"

"Did you feel like you couldn't say no? Like I ambushed you by coming here? I been trying to not press you, trying to not see you, not be attracted to you, Sloan, but you're everywhere. You and Ellie attached at the fucking hip. My baby sister's best friend, and I'm in love with you. I been on that type of time with you, Sloan. I put your fucking picture up in my jail cell because I was proud of you, and seeing you gave me hope."

She gasped. His vulnerability was rare, and she felt like if she made the wrong move it would flee.

"What picture?" she asked.

"It was a medical journal article; some shit you wrote. They took your picture, and Ellie sent it to me. Your face made me feel safe for 23 years, and I get out and you tell me I fucking scare you," he muttered, scoffing. "Life is a mu'fucka, yo. You have no idea how long it took me to get to you." Hopelessness. Her fear discouraged him, and then the vulnerability was gone. She saw him harden right before her eyes as he said, "Maybe I am the monster you think I am."

"No!" she denied. "No, Cass, baby, no!" She approached him and held his face in her hands. He was disappointed, dejected even as he pulled his face away. His body was tense. His shame was high.

"Ellie gave me your address. I told her you left something in the sprinter. I should have never come here without being invited," he stated. "Scared of me hurting you? That's wild, man," He shook his head. She had offended him. She was hurting him. *I'm the bad guy,* she thought. She didn't mean to tear him down with her truth. She knew she cared too much because his disappointment filled her with agony, too. "I'ma respect your boundaries, Sloan." He kissed her forehead and made his way for the door.

"Cassidy!" she shouted, crying. He stopped at the door.

"If you gon' call it, Sloan, just call it. Let's wrap this shit up and let another twenty go by. I had no plans to contact you when I got out. You walked into the house the other day, and I thought we might be able to recapture time. Let yourself find a man that fits in your perfect picture. Somebody you feel secure with and let me find someone that's okay with my past."

The idea of that was sickening. Her fight or flight was going haywire. "I don't want that," she cried.

"What do you want?" he shot back. "What you see me as? A nigga that's perfect to call up when you want a little thug in your life? When you want your pussy ate or that attitude adjusted? You want dick? I'm already doing that with a few bitches, Sloan, I don't need to do that with you."

She recoiled. This was as harshly as he had ever handled her. Her feelings were in her stomach.

"Wow, Cass," she scoffed, offended. "If I knew being honest was going to lead to this, I would have never said anything. So much for never hurting me." She laughed and shook her head at her own foolishness. Sometimes, you had to just laugh to keep from crying. She held onto her stomach because she couldn't calm that ache. "I knew better. I'm so fucking stupid. Those few bitches you got in rotation can have you."

# CHAPTER 11

L oyal pulled up to the construction site of the new hotel his team was building downtown. He was glad the sun was shining. Michigan winters were rough, and the temperatures had dropped into the negative, which had shut his project down for a few days. They were back up and running, which meant money was flowing. His project manager handed him a helmet as soon as he stepped out of his Cybertruck.

"Thanks, man. My potnah, Cass, should be pulling up any minute. You got those site plans drawn out for me on the new lounge?" Loyal asked.

"Yes, sir," the man said, holding up a long cardboard cylinder that contained the architectural designs.

"Perfect," Loyal said, taking the designs. "You ready for the company Christmas party?" Loyal asked.

"Yeah, the wife is real excited about it. It's the only time we get to dress up and go out on the town," the man answered. Loyal smiled and patted the man on the shoulder.

"It'll be a good time," Loyal stated. "Look forward to seeing her tomorrow. I'll be in my trailer. Send Cass in when he arrives."

Loyal kept his stride as he looked down at his phone. He had called Ellie once since the basketball game, and she hadn't answered. He didn't know if he should read that as disinterest or not, but he knew that the burden to return the call was on her. He didn't have these types of problems. Women didn't normally make him wait. She had said she was only in town for a week. Perhaps her schedule was too busy to squeeze him in. He knew she had a lot going on, so he wasn't tripping, but he hoped to see her before she left town. He Didn't know what it was about this woman, but he hadn't stopped thinking about her. He had hoped to invite her to his company party, but instead, he opted for his child's mother. He couldn't show up alone, and Ellie was MIA.

The knock at the door caused him to glance up as one of the construction workers stepped inside.

"Mr. Brier, I don't mean to pop up on you or nothing, but I was wondering if I could get a minute of your time," the man said. "I'm James."

"Yeah, man, have a seat," Loyal stated. He walked around the desk and sat down. "What can I do for you, my man?"

"I've been working for the company for a while, and I'm grateful for the opportunity. I'm wondering if there's room for another general foreman."

"You want a promotion?" Loyal asked.

"Yeah, my girl she just had a baby and she's not working. I'm not union, so I don't have the insurance package. I got some shit going on, man. I need benefits. I'm trying to get some help, but I can't afford the sessions out of pocket, but the benefit package for the general foreman will allow me to get what I need," James explained.

Loyal hadn't been paying much attention at first because he didn't need another foreman, but when James's voice cracked, Loyal tuned in. It took a lot for a grown man to swallow his pride and ask for help.

"Sessions," Loyal repeated. "Like, mental health session?" he asked.

James took his hard hat off and held it between his shaky hands. He was visibly upset. Loyal noticed his red eyes and the weathered look on the man's face.

"I lost my son four years ago. Feels like my mind been going slowly ever since. My girl is fed up. She took my son and moved out. Said if I don't get some help for my anger, she wasn't coming back," James said.

Loyal was shocked at the level of honesty.

"I know it's a long shot, but I just need to catch a break," James stated. "I'll even keep my same pay, but if you can throw in the benefits, man…" James cleared his throat again and pinched the bridge of his nose to compose himself.

"There's no shame in asking for work," Loyal said. James's struggle hit home. "I wish more men would have the courage to do what you just did." His own father struggled with mental health issues, so Loyal understood. The second knock at the door signaled Cassidy's arrival.

"Stick around, man. I'ma see what I can do. I might have an opportunity for you," Loyal said.

Cassidy entered the trailer, and Loyal stood to greet him.

"My nigga, welcome," Loyal stated as they embraced like gangsters.

"What you doing here, man?" Cassidy asked as he took a seat beside James.

"I work here," James stated.

"Small world," Cassidy replied. "You doing a'ight?"

"Making it," James stated.

There was some tension in the air, and Loyal sat back to read the room.

"How y'all know each other?" Loyal asked.

"My sister is best friends with his girl," Cassidy stated.

Loyal identified the conflict immediately. "Got it," Loyal stated. "Well, woman business aside, we need a foreman on the building of the new lounge. How you feel about James heading that up?"

"I ain't got no problems with that," Cassidy stated. "Unless that's a problem for you?" Cassidy asked, leaning onto his knees, and turning his head to the side to make eye contact with James.

"Better pay, benefits, vacation time," Loyal listed off. "Shouldn't be no issues."

"Nah, man, I'm cool. Grateful for the opportunity. Thank you. Thank you both," James said.

"Go see H.R., and we'll start making the transition effective immediately. New benefits will be active January 1st," Loyal informed. James had renewed energy as he got up from the chair. Cassidy sat back and kicked out one leg as James headed for the door. "Yo, man, the company Christmas party is tomorrow. Get a suit, get your girl a dress, and invite her out. Might help you get back in her good graces."

James nodded. "Will do. Appreciate it, man."

James exited the office, and Loyal and Cassidy squared off.

"What's that about?" Loyal asked.

"Too much to get into, bruh, let's see these plans," Cassidy stated.

Loyal took the designs out of the tube and rolled them out across his desk.

"I'm thinking expand the capacity on the second lounge and have a members' only section on the second floor. Create some exclusivity," Loyal explained as he pointed to the paper and walked Cassidy through the floor plan. "Construction should take less than four months if we can get it on schedule as soon as spring starts. We could be open by Thanksgiving next year," Loyal stated.

"And the split?" Cassidy asked.

"60/30/10, your way," Loyal stated. "I'm a man of my word."

"What's the three-way split?" Cassidy asked. "We discussed 60/40. Who's the third entity?"

"Your sister," Loyal stated.

Cassidy sat up in shock.

"You talked to her about this?" he asked.

"It's her Christmas gift; I don't need to," Loyal informed.

"Wait," Cassidy stated. "Nigga, what?"

"I fuck with your sister heavy, Cass. She don't know it yet cuz she refuse to call a nigga back, but she's going to be my wife one day," Loyal said.

Cassidy chuckled and scratched the back of his neck.

"Yeah, nigga, you don't know E at all," he snickered. "I'ma sign this shit just to see what the fuck gon' happen. You a wild boy. Ellie is a lot of things, but she ain't for sale. She gon' take your head off for this one."

"I'm not trying to buy her, bruh. That ain't my intention. I don't mean no disrespect," Loyal stated.

"I don't think you do; otherwise, we wouldn't be signing anything. I think you need to get to know a woman you claim to want to marry. E ain't gon' accept this," Cassidy stated.

"She's still married, my nigga. You know that, right? She in the middle of some bullshit with this nigga, and you putting this much pressure on her just gon' make her run the other way."

"What bullshit?" Loyal asked, nose flaring slightly in irritation.

"Man, you know the shit that happened at the lounge. It's hard on her and my niece," Cassidy said. "Still, she's too independent for a handout, and I know you saying it ain't one, but that's how she gon' take it. You ain't even took her out yet, bruh, slow down."

Cassidy snickered as Loyal poured two glasses of Louis XIII.

"She leaves town soon. I only got the holidays. A nigga can only go so slow," Loyal stated, chuckling. "How about inviting her to the Christmas party? That's something she can say yes to without feeling like she's selling her soul."

"That's a start, my nigga. A much slower start than giving her ten percent. We can put the ten in escrow for her after you've discussed it with her."

"Yeah, that sounds good," Loyal stated. He held up his glass and Cassidy tapped it with his own. "We're going to make a lot of fucking money off this chain. We open one a year, and follow this same floor plan, but move down I-75 into Metro Detroit. We talking tens of millions per year. How's that for proving niggas wrong?"

"I ain't really trying to prove shit to nobody at this point," Cassidy stated. "I'm just trying to get my paper and rebuild my life, man. "I'm learning it don't matter how much a nigga change. Once people see you at your lowest, they can only remember you there. So, I'm looking forward, not back."

"To looking forward then," Loyal toasted.

# CHAPTER 12

**E**llie pulled Tessa's locs up into a ponytail and then took a toothbrush and gel to her edges. Her little face had been overcast with sadness all morning. Ellie was infected with her woe. Whenever either of her children was in pain, she would always feel the same symptoms. It didn't matter what it was. She was so in tune with them that her body mimicked whatever ailed them. Ellie sat in the chair across from Tessa. It was Christmas Shopping Day on Shy's Friendsmas itinerary, and they were supposed to meet at the mall, but Ellie just wasn't in the Christmas spirit, and the forlorn look on Tessa's face said the same.

"I know you feel sad, baby. I'm so sorry your daddy hurt your feelings," Ellie stated.

"He says he's not my daddy," Tessa stated.

Ellie had a lot to explain. These were big concepts to a four-year-old.

"So, you know how I always told you that you were the biggest gift I ever got?" Ellie asked.

Tessa nodded and looked up at her with emotion-filled eyes. They were so glossy from the tears threatening to fall.

"Someone else grew you in their tummy, Tess, and that person wasn't supposed to be a mommy, but God knew that I needed another daughter, so he chose me to be your mommy. I took one look at you, and I fell in love. I knew you were supposed to be mine, baby."

"You're not my real mommy?" Tessa asked.

Ellie had to turn her head away from Tessa to stop her sobbing. "I'm not the woman who birthed you, but I am your mother. I will always be your mother. I adopted you, Tess, which means I chose to have you as my daughter forever. Nothing will ever make that change, and I love you the same as I love Brooklyn."

"Did Brooklyn grow in your tummy?" she asked.

Ellie hated the question because she knew that it automatically created a hierarchy.

"She did, baby, but you are just as much mine as she is."

"So why am I not Daddy's too?" Tessa asked.

"Your dad is wrong, Tessa," Ellie said. "Your dad didn't leave just you. He left me. He left me, and he signed up to take care of me forever, too, but that's okay. I know God is watching, and God will straighten him out in His own time for not keeping his promises. But even when a man breaks his promise, know that does not mean you are to blame. That does not mean you are not worth loving. You are made of love, and I will always be here to give you love and to take all the love you have to give me. I'm sorry this hurts you, but I'm here to hold your hand always. I'm here to answer any questions you have, always. I'm here for you and you live inside my heart, even though you never lived inside my tummy. My heart is what counts, and you and Brooklyn own the whole thing. You have one half, and she has the other half, equally. Nobody has a bigger piece. Okay?"

"So where is the woman who grew me in her belly?" Tessa asked.

"I don't know, baby, but when you get older, if you ever want to know her, I will help you find her, and even then, nobody can change the fact that you are my daughter, and I am your mother. Forever and ever. Right?"

Tessa nodded, and Ellie sighed. Nothing felt settled. She was so unnerved. She knew she would be for a while until she was sure that Tessa was okay. Her father walked into the room. "You've got a visitor," he said.

"I'm not expecting anybody," Ellie stated. She stood and went to the kitchen window.

"I don't know anybody who has a Cybertruck, Papa," she said, frowning because the car was like a damn spaceship. She couldn't see through the windows. When Loyal climbed out of the car, she shook her head. It was a different car than the one he had been driving the other night. She looked down at her outfit. She was in mom mode. Jeans and a sweater that hung loosely down one shoulder. She didn't even have on makeup or her contacts. She wore her glasses.

"Tell him I'm not here," Ellie stated.

"Tell who?" Tessa asked.

"Nobody, baby," she said. "Keep quiet." Ellie put her finger to her lips to hush Tessa.

"Why we avoiding him?" Papa asked. "Do he need some straightening?"

Ellie smiled and shook her head. "No, Papa Bear, he didn't do anything wrong. I just have a lot going on right now. I can't focus on him right now. And I'm not dressed."

Papa walked up to her and gave her a kiss on the cheek then bent down to kiss Tessa. "You beautiful, baby," Papa stated. "But I'll get rid of the li'l nigga. Unless my nigga trying to run it back, then you gon' have to suck it up because that's my boy."

Ellie wanted to protest, but Papa was already headed to the door, and she would have to raise her voice too much to get his attention.

"Well, if it ain't the man who turned my pockets inside out," Loyal greeted with a laugh so genuine Ellie had to stop herself from giggling.

"How you doing, son?" Bishop greeted.

"I'd be doing better if your daughter would throw a nigga some rhythm," Loyal stated.

"She difficult like her mama was," Bishop said. "Told me to tell you she wasn't here, but I got to throw my guy a bone. She don't know what's good for her, anyway. Come on in."

Ellie scrunched her face in embarrassment as Loyal came walking into the house behind her traitorous-ass father. "Really, Papa?" she confronted.

` "The man needed to see his woman. Who am I to keep a man from his lady?" Bishop asked.

Ellie shook her head and sighed.

"Hi, Loyal!" Tessa's voice was full of excitement, and Ellie looked down, surprised because her mood had been somber all day. She was grateful for that much.

"What's up, Tess?" Loyal greeted. "So, I've got an idea, baby girl, and I need you to tell me if it's a good idea or not."

"What is it?" she shouted.

He still hadn't spoken to Ellie, and she stood there, arms crossed in front of her.

"So, you not speaking?" Ellie asked.

Loyal glanced at her, and the finger he put up to halt her made Ellie cock her neck back.

"This serious business right here, E, hold up," Loyal stated.

"I was thinking, it's only four days until Christmas, and I didn't see a tree the last time I came here," Loyal stated.

"We were supposed to get one yesterday at the Christmas Tree Farm, but the day was ruined," Tessa said, her voice dripping in sadness at the sudden reminder.

Loyal bent down so that he was at eye level with Tessa. "Yeah, I heard about that. I know a thing or two about being adopted," Loyal stated. "Did you just learn that you were yesterday?"

Ellie's stomach sank. "Loyal."

"Serious business, E," he said, but without looking at her this time.

"No, like five minutes ago!" Tessa said.

"That's a pretty big surprise. I remember when my mom told me that the only dad I knew adopted me."

Ellie gripped the counter as her eyes widened. She didn't know how to stop this. She knew she should, but Tessa was fully tuned in. Loyal pulled a kitchen chair out and took a seat while pulling a chair out for Tessa.

"You're dopted too?" Tessa asked.

He nodded, smirking because she left the 'a' off the word. "Yeah, a lot of kids are. You see, sometimes, mommies and daddies don't know how to be good mommies and daddies. My real dad, he can't take care of me with his whole heart, so he had to let somebody else who could, make sure I had all the love I needed. So, God sent me a man who would love my mother really good, and he was so good and loved her so much, that he loved me even more. He adopted me and has been the best thing to ever happen in my life. The man you met at the basketball game the other day, he's my stepdad, but I call him my bonus dad because he chose me."

"But my daddy married my mommy, and he only wants Brook. He doesn't want me," Tessa said, eyes filling with tears. Ellie's filled with tears, too.

"Look at me, Tessa," Loyal whispered. "When people leave you, God replaces that love by a thousand. God didn't choose Brook's daddy for you. That's why he can't stay. God chose you and Brook to share your amazing mom. She's beautiful, and she loves you beautifully, and a mother's love is so strong, you really don't need anything else. Anybody can leave you, but as long as you have your mom, you'll always be okay."

"But when will God send a daddy to pick me? Like your dad step picked you?" Tessa asked.

Ellie's chest ached because he was riding a fine line. Ellie couldn't take anymore disappointment, and they didn't know each other well enough for him to make her child any promises.

"It's stepdad, and God's getting him ready for you, baby girl, and he's healing your mommy's heart so that she's ready for him too," Loyal said. "And he gon' love you so much that it ain't gon' be no step nothing. Just a daddy to take care of you, your mother, and your sister. Until then, you have a bunch of people who love you. Your aunts, your granddad, even though he a cheater at dominos…"

"At Go Fish, too!" Tessa exclaimed, giggling.

"Then, there's your uncle, Cass. Your sister," Loyal named. "And me, Tess. Until I can get your mama to answer my calls, just know I'm a friend, and I'm here for you whenever you need anything, even if it's just someone to convince your mommy to let you get more than two snacks," Loyal said with a wink.

Ellie turned toward the sink and concealed her tears as Tessa lunged for Loyal, wrapping her arms around his neck.

"Never let anybody take away that pretty smile," Loyal said. "Now, about this Christmas tree. I think we still got time to put one up in here. What you think? You down for a trip to the Christmas Tree Farm?"

"Yeah!" Tessa shouted. Her joy had returned, and Ellie was a mess.

"Bet, go tell your papa the plan and see if he wants to come," Loyal instructed. Tessa took off.

Ellie turned around with fire in her eyes. "Garage! Now," she stated, as she stormed by him.

Loyal followed behind her, and she made sure the door was closed before she went the fuck off.

"Don't ever do that with my child again," she warned, pointing a finger as tears streamed down her face.

"She was heartbroken, E," Loyal said.

BEFORE THE STREET LIGHTS COME ON

"And that's not your job to fix! What's going to happen when we leave in a few days? When you disappear from her life? You just told my daughter that God sent you to be her daddy! She already has one father who isn't sticking around! Now, when you leave, she'll feel like she's not good enough for a father to stay! How dare you?!"

"E, you..."

"This is my life!" She shouted, cutting him off. He had the patience of Job because he just stood there calmly and let her get her shit off. He didn't feed into the argument, he didn't match her energy, he didn't take offense. He was a man who knew how to let a woman release without being reactionary. "I don't know if I feel like a challenge to you or you want to conquer me! Or you just used to motherfuckers bending to your will because of your status and your money, but if you ever make my daughters a promise you have no intention of keeping again, I will take my father's shotgun and blow your Goddamn head off your shoulders!"

Ellie held her stomach in excruciation as she sobbed. "Why would he just abandon her like this?" she cried. She covered her mouth with one hand and reached out and leaned against her mother's car as she sobbed. Her words weren't even meant for him; her frustration was toward the bitch-ass nigga who had put her in this position. She hoped Loyal knew. These were stray bullets not meant for him.

He walked up to her and pulled her into his arms, and Ellie hid beneath his tall body.

"You swear like a sailor, E," he whispered. "I swear you Bishop's daughter like a mu'fucka. I mean, damn, you just cursed me smooth out. I ain't even know somebody so pretty could talk so ugly."

She went from tears to laughter in the blink of an eye and then back to tears as he palmed the back of her head, massaging her scalp as he allowed her to get it out.

"I don't say shit I don't mean, Elliot," he said as she leaned back and looked up at him. "I don't promise shit to kids and then fall through. Only person don't believe that Daddy's coming home is you."

She both loved and hated his finesse because it felt so good, but it also came with red flags, because how could he promise these things without knowing her?

"This is irresponsible, Loyal. It's dangerous," she whispered. "It was fun when you were just playing with my head, but you're playing with my kids. I'm terrified of this."

"I'm sorry," he stated. "It's going to take you a little longer to accept what I already know. I'll let you set the pace, but we gon' end up in the same place, E. Trust me. Fight against whatever guards that nigga made you build to let me love you. If you want me to prove it, then I'm willing to do that."

"What happens when I leave?" she asked.

"You're not leaving," he replied. "This is your home. This is where your friends are. Your family. Your mother's memory. Your man," he said, lifting her chin and nudging her face with his.

She closed her eyes and rested her head against his chest, and he said, "The days of you doing everything alone and being filled with panic are over for you, E. Whatever you need, whenever you need it, that's on me. Life is about to get real soft for you. Trust that."

"How do you handle me so well? How did you handle that conversation with Tess so well? You're like medicine, Loyal. My every interaction with you feels unnatural; like, it's not real. Like, it's a dream. I've been fighting for peace for four years since that man left us, and you come along, and you just feel like rest. You give me the same feeling I get when I take off my bra after a long day or when I pull my feet out of five-inch heels after suffering all night. You just feel like relief. I don't even know you, and a simple hello in my brother's lounge feels like it's about to change my life. Sometimes, you don't know what to do with peace when you've become used to war for so long. Why are you applying so much pressure when you can clearly pick an easier woman with an easier circumstance? It feels like you're gaming me."

"Niggas done fucked up so much with women that chemistry feels like game. You're defensive and mean and bitter and broken, and I ain't scared of none of that shit," Loyal stated.

"Can we please just be careful about what we pull our kids into? Pull me into the deep end, go ahead, but there are kids involved, Loyal. Yours included, which we haven't even talked about yet. Please, just consider that this is complicated," she whispered.

"Know that I'm a man that considers everything, but okay. I hear you," he responded.

He kissed her lips, lingering long enough to leave her

reeling before pulling away. He grabbed her hand and led her back into the house.

"Told you she wasn't going to shoot him, Papa," Tessa giggled as soon as they stepped back inside the house.

"Shit, your grandmama would have shot me," Papa stated. Loyal snickered, and Ellie shook her head.

"Be nice to him, Mommy," Tessa said as Ellie bent down to pick up her daughter. Tessa hugged her neck so tightly.

"I will, baby," Ellie promised. "Okay, time for Christmas tree shopping."

"Y'all go ahead, I'ma rest these old bones. I'll be here when you get back with some hot chili and homemade cornbread," Papa stated. "Vegetable chili for you, baby girl."

Papa kissed Ellie's cheek and shook Loyal's hand, and then Ellie led the way out of the house.

Sloan's heart beat out of her chest as she stared down at the medication in her hands. She knew she wasn't in the mental space to make this type of decision, but a decision had to be made. She only had 24 hours to decide, and the clock was ticking. She had yearned to hear from Cassidy all day. She desperately wished for him to call her or to send flowers or to even just text her phone or like a picture on her Instagram, but all she received was silence. She had spent years enjoying her own company. She had never needed a man to make her feel fulfilled, but after one night of indulging in him, she now felt like she couldn't breathe without him. She wondered if their lovemaking was reminiscent of what it would be like if they could be together. Was the spectacular show a normal occurrence, or did he give her his all because deep down in his bones he knew that it wouldn't happen again. She hated this extreme dopamine high that came with loving him because whenever he wasn't around, there was a feeling of depravity. Now that they were at odds and hurtful things had been said, she felt like she was dying. She wished this was a simple fight between two stubborn people who were avoiding an easy answer, but it was deeper than that. If she had known it would end up like this, she would have never crossed the line with Cassidy.

"Sloan, what the hell is taking you so long? You told us to come over here and ride with you, but we could have met your slow ass at the mall," Shy fussed as she knocked on Sloan's bedroom door.

"Come in," Sloan called out.

Shy opened the door, and Sloan stood like a deer in headlights.

"Bitch, is that a Plan B pill?" Shy whispered. "Bitch! You fucked Cass, didn't you? Spill all the motherfucking tea. You dirty ho! We all said whoever fucked him first would share the details! Why didn't you call me?!!!!" It was a pact they had made behind Ellie's back in high school. It had been just schoolgirl crushes back then. Her circumstance today was much more serious.

Sloan wished she wasn't a doctor at this moment. She wished that she could pretend that last night hadn't happened and pop up with a positive pregnancy test and then claim naïveté. But she couldn't. This was her field of expertise, and she knew exactly how the female body worked. She and Cassidy had made love without protection while she was ovulating. There was a damn good chance she could get pregnant.

"I did," Sloan answered.

"Oh, Ellie gon' kill your ass. You know her rules about her brother. She used to beat bitches up who tried to get close to her just to shoot they shot at Cassidy back in the day. She wouldn't even let us stay the night too often because she knew I was gon' fuck that nigga if I ever came across him in the bathroom in the middle of the night," Shy laughed. "Be brushing my teeth and accidentally let him put the tip in."

"This isn't funny, Shy," Sloan snapped, torn on what she should do.

"You let him hit raw?" Shy asked. "All that condom talk you be giving us, and you let a jailbird hit you without wrapping up?"

"Don't call him that," Sloan whispered. It was insane how she was defending him to others but villainizing him for the exact same thing.

"I mean, I love Cassidy. He's family, but he is very much so institutionalized," Shy said. "How could he not be? He spent half his life locked in a cell."

"Ughhh!" Sloan groaned as she paced the room. Shy's assessment wasn't making her feel any better. "How did I let this happen?"

"Girl, when did this start?" Shy asked.

"When did what start?" Courtney interrupted as she walked into the room, carrying her son.

Shy pursed her lips and shook her head. "It ain't my business to tell," she said.

"Bitch, you gon' tell her anyway as soon as y'all out of my earshot," Sloan fussed.

"She's fucking Cassidy, and now she got to decide if she wants to take a Plan B," Shy spilled.

"Hmm," Courtney stated.

Sloan frowned. It wasn't the response she was expecting.

"What's that? What's that hmm? What does that mean?" Sloan asked.

"I mean, I'm not that surprised. You've always kind of been in love with him. Ever since we were kids," Courtney stammered, shrugging like it was no big deal.

"We all had our eyes on Cass as teenagers. That doesn't count," Sloan dismissed.

"No, Sloan. Our shit was hormones. The way you looked at him was different. All that time you used to spend at Ellie's wasn't just because of her. He was kind of your first love; y'all just never admitted that y'all was feeling one another. Anytime he would come around us, it was you he teased, you he wrapped an arm around, you he brought shit back from the corner store. He made you smoke with him and him only when he found out you were smoking weed. And he hated that nigga, Deyontae! He beat the nigga up over you, Sloan."

"That beef was not over me!" Sloan defended. She was lying

through her teeth because Cassidy had already confirmed that it was, but they didn't need to know that.

"Girl, be fucking for real," Shy moaned, rolling her eyes. "The truth is Ellie made you choose. You loved her friendship more than you loved a boy. You never put niggas over your girls, and you never will. You chose Ellie over Cass back then."

"If he hadn't gone to jail, I always thought y'all would have ended up together," Courtney admitted.

"Girl, they mama used to call you her daughter-in-law!" Shy exclaimed. "Why are you playing dumb?"

Sloan's eyes betrayed her.

"Whoa, is this serious with you and Cass?" Courtney asked.

"No, we're done," Sloan said. "We just can't be together. It will never work."

"Then why are you hesitating to take that pill?" Shy asked.

"Because I'm almost forty years old and I don't have a kid yet. I don't even have a man to help produce a kid. I haven't had a man in two years. I don't date. I might as well be celibate. I have no one, and I really want to be a mom. I froze my eggs, and I was preparing to find a donor to fertilize one and start the process of having a baby alone," Sloan admitted as she flopped down on her king-sized bed. "But now this. I don't know what to do."

"Oh, sis," Courtney whispered, sympathetically. "Maybe talk to Cassidy. He doesn't have kids. What if y'all want the same thing?"

"He won't. Not with me," Sloan feared.

"That man loves you," Courtney said. "I can tell. Whenever you're around, his eyes are on you. He like secures your space or something. I can't explain it, but I've noticed it. It's like he's looking at everything within ten feet of you that could bring you harm and trying to figure out how to prevent it. I know because I don't have that, and I admire what you have with him. And you don't even appreciate it. He would step in front of a bullet for you."

Sloan had never noticed that before. She just thought he looked out for her off the strength of Ellie.

"Girl, we don't even know if you will actually get pregnant. You're panicking about the possibility, and if you do, you do. Keep it, and don't tell him," Shy said. "You don't owe anybody any explanations about what's happening with your body."

"That's not an option," Sloan stated. That was the only thing she was sure of. She respected Cassidy too much to deceive him so maliciously. "There's just so much to consider. I can take this pill and just get rid of the possibility altogether. But what if I'm wasting my only chance to get pregnant the natural way and to know the father of my child? But if I do get pregnant naturally, it will be with 39-year-old eggs. I froze my embryos at 33, so they're much healthier. At 39, these eggs are stale, chile. A baby is more likely to not make it to term or to be born with health defects or abnormalities. There's so much science behind this shit."

"Girl, you losing me," Shy stated.

"My heart is in shambles, and I feel like I'm not in the right state of mind to even be deciding this right now," Sloan cried.

"Why are you deciding this by yourself? What happened between y'all?" Courtney asked.

"Prison happened," Sloan whispered. "But I think I love him, y'all. Like, I think I'm madly in love with that man, and my heart is broken because there is no solution to the things that are keeping us apart."

"Which is what, bitch? Because I'm bored. This feels self-inflicted like a mu'fucka," Shy snapped. "Because if you say some shit like you're too good to be with a felon…"

"I mean, that's part of it, and not that I'm too good. I'm not saying that. I just worked too hard to let a man taint my respectability. We all know he will," Sloan argued.

"Well then, bitch, cry," Shy said bluntly. "Because if you are letting what other people think stop you from loving him, that's on you. Fuck what people think!"

"It's not just that, though, is it?" Courtney asked.

Sloan buried her face in her hands and cried from her soul. Her girls wrapped their arms around her. They had never seen her like this before. The last time she had been brought to tears over a boy was when Cassidy had gotten locked up. She had taken it extremely hard, almost as hard as Ellie. Now, it made sense.

"I'm afraid of him," Sloan sobbed. "Of what he's capable of doing."

"Because of what happened to your mom," Courtney said, putting the story together in her head.

"Cassidy is not like that nigga that took your mom," Shy whispered passionately.

"A part of me wants to trust that, but the part of me that

never dealt with my mother's death, and the part that has to go in front of that parole board every six or so years and advocate why they should never free that man, is telling me to run the other way. What do you do when your heart and your mind disagree? My mind has never failed me. My heart, on the other hand," she cried. "I just can't."

"It's going to be okay," Courtney said. "I've known you a long time, and you believe in love, Sloan. Yes, doing In vitro and getting a sperm donor is possible, but if there is the possibility of having a baby with a man you love and who loves you, regardless if y'all end up together or not, every time you look at that child, you'll remember the love they came from. You have your reasons for not being able to choose him, but at least you'll always have a piece of the love you're depriving yourself of if you end up pregnant by him."

"And if you don't end up pregnant, you still have the embryos as a backup," Shy said.

Sloan nodded and wiped her runny nose with the back of her hand. She stood. "Okay, give me a minute, please. We can go shopping. I need some retail therapy. I just need to clean myself up. I'm sorry if I'm ruining the day."

"You're not," Courtney reassured. "We'll be out front when you're ready."

Sloan waited until she was alone and opened the Plan B pill. She looked in the mirror. She prayed she didn't make a decision she was going to later regret.

"Just do it," she said to herself.

# CHAPTER 13

**M**ommy, can we get this one?" Tessa shouted in excitement as she pointed to the biggest tree on the property.

"Baby, that won't fit in Papa's house," Ellie said. "It's at least 18 feet tall!"

"But I don't want a little tree," Tessa pouted.

"What about this one over here?" Ellie asked as she led the way to a seven-foot Spruce.

"That's a baby tree," Tessa whined.

"Come over here, Tess," Loyal said, motioning down one of the rows. "Now, what about this?" he asked. "It's not super tall, but it's nice, right? Look how big it is around. Plenty of room for the fat man to leave toys underneath."

Tessa put her hands over her mouth in shock as she laughed. "You can't call Santa that! He won't bring you any presents!"

Ellie laughed, and Loyal placed a hand to his heart. "You right. Can't offend Santa," Loyal stated.

"Loyal…"

"Umm, let's call him Mr. Brier," Ellie interrupted.

"Mr. Brier is my stepdad," Loyal said, frowning.

"Well, she can't call you by your first name. Where's the respect? She's a kid," Ellie frowned. "What do you want her to call you?"

"If you would quit bullshitting and take that ring off your finger, I could replace it and put a real title on it," Loyal said, smirking as he picked up the ax. Ellie gave him a warning look. "I know, I know. Your pace. But come here."

She begrudgingly obliged, dragging her feet slowly as she made her way to him. He pulled his gloves off and then lifted her left hand. "You stop me if I'm crossing a line," he said as he took her ring off her finger. It felt like her hand was lighter, and she squeezed her fist closed.

"You want to keep it?" he asked.

She thought about it for a beat before shaking her head. "No." Loyal threw that bitch clear across the field, and she gasped before laughing.

"I can't believe you just did that!" she said.

"On to bigger and better," he stated. "Now, back to our business, li'l mama." He focused back on Tessa. "Can I be your OG?" he asked.

Ellie's heart melted. *The way he uses his words is incredible*, she thought, in awe of him. His love language had to be words of affirmation because he made her feel so loved every time he spoke. Even her daughter felt at ease when he spoke to her. He was so passionate and intentional with what he said. The nickname was simple enough, but she knew the significance it held in their culture. It was respectful and meaningful without trying to fill the place of the word daddy. It was perfect.

"What is an OG?" Tessa asked.

"It's somebody in your life who's older than you, who you respect. Somebody you can trust. Someone who has lived and experienced a lot, so they give good advice. Somebody who protects you. Somebody who you can go to for anything. Somebody who loves you no matter what. And this is the most important one of all; somebody who is very, very, very, handsome, and who your mommy loves enough to let them be a part of your life," he explained. "Don't forget the very handsome part."

Tessa giggled.

"Does that sound like anybody you know?" Loyal asked.

"You're my OG, and Brooklyn's OG, and mama's OG too?" Tessa asked.

"I want your mama to call me something else one day, but I got to work real hard on that one. You gon' help me?" Loyal asked.

Her Chiclet-sized teeth beamed as she nodded her head in excitement. "A'ight, that's a bet," Loyal stated.

"How are you this good with her?" Ellie asked.

"It's easy to be good to people you want in your life," Loyal stated. "A'ight, y'all, step back. You still want this tree, right?"

"Yes! That one is perfect!" Tessa shouted.

"A'ight then, OG gon' get you this tree," he said. He wielded the axe in both hands, and then swung it again and again, until the thick trunk threatened to break. "Come on and use those muscles to chop down this tree," he said, letting Tessa take the final swing. He had done all the hard work, so when he let her help with the last swing, the tree fell.

"I did it! I did it!"

Her glee was contagious, and Ellie was appreciative. She recognized his effort. He was out here in Timberland wheats and expensive everything, chopping down trees for her and her child, just to make up for the failures of another man.

The attendant came and helped Loyal strap the tree to the roof of his Cybertruck and then Loyal paid and they headed to get hot chocolate before departing.

"Mommy, Mommy, can I go play on the sleds with the other kids?" Tessa asked as soon as they sat down at the picnic table. Ellie eyed the mini activity station that was set up for kids and assessed in seconds that it was low risk.

"Sure, baby," Ellie said. "Finish your hot chocolate first so you warm up a bit."

Tessa was so excited she couldn't contain herself. She took a few sips, then she jumped up and down, spinning around in circles before coming back to take a few more sips. She drank it all, then darted off.

Loyal smiled.

"She wearing a nigga out," he chuckled.

Ellie sipped her hot chocolate.

"She likes you."

"Yeah, she's a cool kid," he replied.

"If I choose to stay here in Michigan, what does that look like for you?" she asked.

"It looks like I'd move you in-"

"Unt uh," Ellie interjected, stopping him before he even got started.

"I have two girls. I can't just move in with you. This has to happen progressively. We need to date. We can't skip steps. They need to get to know you. I need to get to know you."

"I'd put you up in a place of your choosing, fully furnish it, cover all expenses to relocate, and whatever else you need me to do," Loyal responded.

"What's the catch? Because I keep waiting for the other foot to drop with you. Anything that seems too good to be true normally is."

"There's no catch. I do have a requirement, though."

"And that is?" Her brow lifted.

"I need to have a conversation with Brooklyn's father, and you need to push forward with that divorce. I'll pay for whatever attorney is necessary," Loyal stated.

"And what about you? Your situation? Your baby mama? Your son?" She wasn't a fool. She knew that there was unfinished business there. If she was considering uprooting her entire life and giving him a chance, he needed to uproot his as well.

"That situation will never reach you," he assured.

"What does that mean? Because it doesn't sound like you're ending it. Just because it doesn't reach me doesn't mean it's not present. I don't do side bitches well," Ellie stated. "I don't have time for anything that I have to second-guess."

"I told you; my game isn't manipulation. I like to tell the truth and let a woman choose her own experience," Loyal stated.

"Loyal, be straight up with me. What am I getting into with you?"

"I know you in some shit right now that has left you fucked up, E. I can't predict the future. I can only tell you I ain't coming into this with bad intentions," he said. "Some people you just meet, and you know. It don't take a man years to know when they've met their one."

"I can't handle more drama," she said. "It just feels like we both have situations that are too complicated for us to entertain anything with each other right now. There is a such thing as meeting the right person at the wrong time. You know the fucked-up shit I have going on, but I'm going in dark. Like, what's the arrangement with your son's mom? Is it clear you're ready to move on? Is she still attached? Are you still fucking her?" There was so much mystery around this man.

"We just met, E. I ain't ironed out the details yet, and I don't want to lie to you. I was with Tisa for a minute. She's familiar, so yeah, I have been fucking with her," Loyal stated. "But I have no problem making it clear. I ain't have a reason to do that before now, so I was just letting it be whatever I needed it to be." His brow furrowed as he looked at her sincerely.

She didn't know why it hurt her feelings to know that this man, who she had just become acquainted with, was out here doing shit that men did. Of course, he was sleeping with his baby mama. She couldn't be angry at him because he hadn't done anything wrong.

"How do men do that? Just check out of one relationship and jump into the next?" she asked. "I don't want to be the woman who stepped over another woman to snag a man."

"You aren't the reason for the demise of that relationship, E. It's been dead, we just holding on to what's familiar at this point. I'll always make sure she's good because she has my son, but my heart ain't there. My loyalty was there because I got her pregnant, and I'm a man who takes care of the people on my team. We have a lifelong attachment. If me providing is going to be an issue, then this might be hard for you. I'll respect it if it ain't for you, but I'm not in love with her, and there will be no baby mama drama aimed at the woman I'm with. Niggas who allow shit like that don't have control over their situation. I do."

*Sounds good until that damn girl stalking me on social media and keying your car,* she thought.

"I wouldn't give you up easily if I were her," Ellie admitted. He moved around the table so that he was sitting next to her.

"Trust me not to get you into no bullshit," he reassured.

"I'm sure there will be some residual feelings there, on her part and yours," Ellie said. "That would need to be completely over before I made a permanent move. My divorce would need to be finalized before we do whatever it is we call ourselves doing. I like you, Loyal. My heart might even be begging me to say it's a little more, but I'm not reckless with my life. I can't afford to be. Where we go next depends on what you do next," Ellie said.

"Right now, I just want to decorate a tree with li'l mama and get around these guards you got. That's my next move," he said.

He was so damn cute, so cool, and calm, and collected. He wanted her to go hard or go home and he wasn't afraid at all to move all his pieces around on the Chess board to make it happen. Ellie was terrified to give in to Loyal.

She had grown complacent in the dysfunction of her marriage. It was a terrible relationship, but it was the devil she knew. She was used to Cairo's abandonment, and she knew exactly how bad his worst got. She could anticipate the threshold for pain with Cairo, and although it hurt, it had already scabbed over. Cairo didn't have the power to make her bleed out. Loyal brought the spark back to a dormant heart, and the picture of love he painted was so enticing that it gave her hope. She didn't want to be let down again. The vulnerability he exposed in her was dangerous.

"Thank you for coming to check on us and for making it better. I know you're busy, and there were probably much better things you could have been doing today," Ellie leaned her head on his shoulder. She knew he had paused his entire day to fix a heart he didn't break, and it counted even more because the heart he had repaired was Tessa's. His compassion and empathy revealed an emotional maturity that most men didn't possess.

"I'm where I want to be right now; don't sweat it," Loyal replied.

"We should head back," she proposed.

The drive back was quiet. Tessa was worn out and slept the entire way, and Ellie was in her head. Still, there was a peace in the car that she appreciated. Loyal allowed her to be with her thoughts as he listened to the Pistons game play-by-play on XM.

"You're probably the only Pistons fan left," Ellie mumbled. "You and Papa."

"Don't do my niggas dirty like that. Look at the Lions. Thirty years of losses, and almost to the Super Bowl last year. It ain't never too late to make a comeback, and I'm riding when they down. I ain't like the bandwagon jumpers," Loyal defended.

"I am impressed by your loyalty," she stated sarcastically. "No pun intended."

He chuckled. "The Pistons was my dad's team. Can't give up on 'em. I remember the Ben Wallace era," he gloated.

"Oh my god, that was like 20 years ago!" she shouted, laughing. "Robert gon' have to choose a new team."

"Not Robert, my biological dad," Loyal corrected.

Ellie paused, noticing the inflection in his voice. "Oh," she whispered. "Is he still alive?"

"I don't know," Loyal stated. "He suffers from schizophrenia, which led to addiction. He's been on the streets my whole life. Robert adopted me when I was seven, but he's been around since before I could remember. He was my mother's social worker. Saw how we were living, saw the struggles she was going through with my dad, and saved us. He even tried to get my dad help, but that didn't last long. He thinks the medication is someone trying to poison him. He's homeless. I used to ride my bike down to this hole-in-the-wall bar where he used to sweep up in the wintertime. They used to let him sleep in the basement if he worked for free. It kept him warm, and it gave me a place to go watch the Pistons games with him. Giving up on the Pistons feels like giving up on him, so I'm riding for the long haul."

"How long has it been since you've seen him?" Ellie asked.

"Three years is the last time he was seen at the bar," Loyal stated. "He's a'ight, though. I know it. It's just taking him a minute to get his mind to come back to him. When he remembers, he'll turn up in the right place." She could tell it bothered him, but he was too strong to put his weakness on display.

They pulled up to her father's house, and Loyal idled the car.

"How about we take this tree inside, let Tess spend some time with her papa, and we go catch the end of the game at that bar?" Ellie said.

He looked over at her in shock. "Nah, that ain't necessary, E. This an old game, anyway. Pistons don't play 'til later tonight, but it's not even that serious. I'm cool."

"It's Christmastime," Ellie reasoned. "And he's your dad. The least we can do is try, and if he's not there, you try to get me drunk so you can take advantage of me at the end of the night." She shrugged.

"That second part sound like a move," Loyal said as he leaned back against the headrest and looked over at her.

"You helped me with something that hurts me. I'd like to try and return the favor," she said gently.

"Yeah, a'ight," Loyal agreed reluctantly. "Let me get this tree set up first, though."

Ellie grabbed Tessa from the backseat and then went to get her father so that he could help Loyal get the tree inside the house.

She kissed Tessa's cheeks as she lay lazily on her shoulder.

"Wake up, baby girl. Time to decorate your tree," Ellie whispered.

She stood back on the porch as she watched her 65-year-old father try to lift his end of the tree.

"Well damn, Ellie, what y'all do, pick the biggest tree on the whole farm?" Bishop complained.

"You should see the one your granddaughter wanted to get at first," Ellie laughed. "Come on, old man. You're the strongest guy in the world," she cheered, smiling. "Do it for your girls."

"This mu'fucka is heavy than a bitch," Loyal said, gritting his teeth as he backed into the house.

Both men were winded when they finally got it put on the stand.

"Go thank your papa." Ellie placed Tessa down, and she ran, hugging Papa first.

"Thank you, Papa!" she yelled. Then she rushed Loyal. "Thank you, OG!"

"Papa, do you mind if we skip out on the decorating part?" Ellie asked.

"Me and my baby girl can handle it," Papa stated. "There's some chili and cornbread in there. Take some of that with you."

"Not you think I ain't coming back tonight!" Ellie exclaimed. "You ain't raise no easy daughter, Papa!"

Loyal smirked and scratched the tip of his nose with his thumb as his brow raised in amusement. "She ain't lying, School. Your daughter difficult as hell."

Ellie went to the kitchen and set out four bowls. "Now I got to eat it here just to prove a point!"

She fixed everyone a warm bowl and placed all the fixings in the middle of the table. The only person missing was her oldest baby, and although she knew Cairo wouldn't hurt his child, she was desperately ready for Brooklyn to come home. They sat and ate together like a real family, no television going, no cell phones in their hands, no one rushing to finish, just good, old-fashioned quality time. Seeing Loyal there, with her father and her child, so comfortable, made her wonder if he really could be the man for her. He seemed not to be able to get enough of her. She couldn't believe that a man like him would be this intrigued with a woman like her. It wasn't that she felt unattractive. She had always been pretty, and when she put in the effort with makeup and hair and the whole nine, she was a downright bombshell. Life had made her feel like she wasn't a contender for a man like Loyal. He was bossed up. A seven-figure earner, probably eight, if she had to guess. He was the perfect amount of rough. He was attractive, without being a pretty boy, independent, honest, and carried an authority that came with getting it out the mud. Men like him didn't normally go for difficult women. They didn't go for women with children or even women her age. They wanted young, impressionable, easy girls with perfect bodies and no attachments. From the moment Loyal laid eyes on her, he made her feel like a prize. He wanted to win her, and she wanted to let him.

# CHAPTER 14

They ended up decorating the tree and then sliding out to head to the bar. They pulled up to the seediest part of town, and Ellie glanced nervously out her window. Her heart broke as they passed an alley with encampments made from cardboard boxes, grocery store shopping carts, milk crates, and any other random material that could be found. Her eyes watered as he parked the car.

"How can they stay warm like this?" she gasped. Michigan wasn't a place where you could survive outside overnight in the wintertime. The temperatures dropped to below freezing all the time. "There are kids out here, Loyal. When did it get this bad?" Ellie grew up in Flint. She remembered a neighborhood bum or two. She didn't ever remember seeing anything like this.

"We don't have to do this," Loyal said.

"To see this, and not try, feels wrong. We have to," Ellie stated, eyes filled to the brim with tears. "This is fucked up."

She couldn't understand how he was unaffected. "This doesn't make you feel bad?" she asked.

"When I was a kid, it would fuck me up. I've been down here and seen this shit so many times I don't feel shit about it anymore. People make their choices," Loyal stated.

"They didn't choose this," Ellie whispered. "Nobody chooses this." He opened the door and came around on her side of the car to clear her path so she could step out of the car. Bums saw the expensive car and swarmed them instantly, but Loyal waved them off and they walked the half block to the bar.

The inside was dark and smoky. 92.7 WDZZ played in the background. The regulars sat at the tables along the wall, sparsely decorating the place.

Loyal led her to the wood top bar and pulled out her stool before seating himself. He reached into his back pocket and pulled out a picture of his father, along with a hundred-dollar bill.

"Yo, my man." He called the bartender over and placed the picture on top of the money before sliding it into the center of the bar.

"Have you seen him?" Loyal asked.

"Come on, man, you know we don't do that here," the bartender stated. "I don't know shit. I ain't seen shit."

"I ain't the police, nigga, this is my dad. He used to sweep up here for a warm cot in exchange. I'm just trying to see if he's been here lately," Loyal stated.

"I'm new here, man. Been here about a month. I ain't heard nobody mention no arrangements like that, though.

You might want to check with the other bartenders on the other nights, though. I only work Tuesday and Thursday. The owner is here on Friday nights," the man informed.

Loyal nodded, slightly perturbed. "Yeah, a'ight, man," he shot back. "Let me get three shots each of..."

He let the words linger and then looked at her, implying that it was her choice.

"Do you have Casamigos? Anejo?" she asked.

"No Anejo; I got Reposado," the bartender offered.

"That's fine. Chilled with a sugar rim, please," she added. "Three shots. Your mission is to get drunk, huh?"

"You don't want to know my mission," he said mischievously. "Are you satisfied? He's not here." He reached for her chair and pulled the entire thing closer.

"I'm sorry he isn't here."

"You're here," he answered as the bartender delivered the shots. "That's enough."

"I really could love you so much," she admitted.

"Take the could out," Loyal stated.

She picked up the first shot, and he followed suit.

"To love belonging to us one day," she said.

He tapped her shot glass, and they tossed it back.

"Double up," he said, taking the second one immediately after. She struggled to get that one down, but she took it like a big girl as the third shot lingered.

"If I take this third shot, I'ma want some dick," she said bluntly.

He finessed his goatee, unable to contain the look of shock on his face as he blushed.

209

"What?" she asked, laughing. "You can press go on the love, but I can't press go on the sex?" Ellie asked. The tequila had her hot and a little daring. Okay… a lot daring.

"What happened to Daddy's good girl?" Loyal asked.

"My daddy ain't here." She stood and grabbed the third shot, taking it by herself before she stepped in between his legs and whispered in his ear. He put one hand around her waist and gripped her ass. "And I'm really, really trying to see something."

He picked up the third shot.

"You got to drive," Ellie protested.

"The car drives itself," Loyal stated. The mischievous smirk that crossed his handsome face stirred adrenaline inside Ellie. His arrogance was natural. His wealth was apparent, and he operated at a higher level than every other man in every room. He wasn't braggadocios, however. The man just lived at a certain level, and tonight that level involved a car that could drive him home while he got a piece of pussy on the way. Ellie was so turned on that she didn't care how wild the notion seemed. He wanted her, here and now, so he would have her.

"Good," she answered. "Time for you to show me your place."

Loyal gripped Ellie's thigh as they drove down 75. He moved his hand to his lap, slightly gripping his dick, and Ellie knew he was feeling the sexual tension that was coursing through her entire body.

She leaned over and turned his face to hers. "Let the car drive." She fed him her tongue as he put the car on autopilot. Ellie leaned over his seat and unzipped his denim. She was glad he didn't ruin the moment with protests, but instead, placed his hand behind her head, fisting her hair as she took his dick into her mouth. Ellie hadn't sucked dick in four years, and rarely, even when she and Cairo were on good terms. But Loyal's arousal motivated her own. The power to make a man like Loyal crave her so badly that his dick got hard thinking about it on the ride home made her want to pleasure him. He tensed into her mouth slowly as she took thick dick, relaxing her throat so that she didn't choke. The size of him made it hard not to gag, but every time she did, her mouth got wetter, and he pumped into her mouth deeper. Ellie wasn't this girl. She hadn't sucked dick in a car, ever, and it blew her mind that she wanted to for him. Loyal brought a side of femininity out of her that included an empowerment that made her feel like it was okay to go with the flow of the moment. He had been turning up the heat on her since the day they bumped into each other at the bar. It had been a non-stop seduction. He made her want him in a way that lingered beyond his presence. When he left, thoughts of him remained. She was so turned on by his every word and, more importantly, every action that followed. After the way he connected with her child today, the way he was always so patient with her father, and the way he seemed to be concerned about conflicts that bothered her, he had earned a little head in the car. He was a grown-ass man. Sometimes, the nut couldn't wait until they got home. His dick was so pretty and big, it felt like she had unwrapped a new toy. She moaned like crazy as she swallowed him. Her mouth was extra wet.

"Damn, E," he moaned.

The spontaneity in this moment made it that much greater.

"I got to have you in my bed, E. You can't foul me out the game in the first quarter like this. Damn, baby, you ain't playing fair," Loyal groaned.

Ellie was going hard, paying extra attention to the head of his dick because she loved how thick and wide it was. Her body trembled just thinking about the moment he entered her body. She had been reduced to porn and vibrators for years because she was too traumatized to even want to deal with a man after Cairo. He had her trapped in a state of perpetuity, bound by vows that Cairo refused to keep, but somehow, they kept her imprisoned in one-way faithfulness. She was someone's wife. What if they ended up working it out? She would just end up explaining all these random dicks she had taken along their way to healing. That had been her rationale. Before today, that had been her logic. As she pumped this glorious dick in her hand while spitting on it and swallowing him down to his balls, she knew she wasn't justifying or explaining shit. She was long overdue for this, and she felt like a fucking lady even while she was doing some ho shit.

"Wait, E. I got to get through the gate," he said as they pulled up to his building.

"Your security guard ain't never seen you getting head in the car?" she asked.

Loyal looked down at her while she kept going. "Oh, you on your fucking level," he groaned, amazed that she even had this type of sexual prowess in her.

She drowned her head in his lap and Loyal damn near lifted out his seat.

"What the fuck you on, E," he groaned.

He showed the parking pass to the gate attendee, trying to keep the window up as much as possible to avoid exposing her. It was obvious what was taking place in the car, however, and the Black dude at the gate smirked.

"Y'all enjoy that," he said, almost with pride as he buzzed Loyal through the gate.

"Slow the fuck down, E. Fuck," he moaned as he parked. She came up, kissing his body as she pulled her sweater off.

"Let me get you upstairs, at least. I need a bed, E. Damn, I want to see you in my bed," he stated.

"I'm on fire, Loyal. I won't make it," she whispered.

The realization that she was on ten made his dick jump. She pulled off her jeans and climbed over the seat, straddling him. There was barely room, but she lowered onto that dick, and her mouth fell open. "Oh my god, Loyal," she whispered.

He pulled her face down to his and kissed her as she rode him. This wasn't love making. It was raw, desperate, and sweaty. Her ankle was smashed against the door, and her knees were aching, but this dick was phenomenal. She didn't even want to come this fast, but when he pushed her back against the steering wheel and used his thumb to play with her clit, she couldn't stop herself.

"Aghh!" she screamed, head falling back in defeat as her pussy pulsated around him. Her pussy frothed, and her cum coated his dick. The visual alone was enough to bring him to the finish line. She climbed out of his lap just in time as he erupted.

"Nah, baby. The way you wetting this dick, we about to take this upstairs for round two," Loyal stated.

She laughed, panting as she retreated to her side of the car, and he re-adjusted himself.

"Wet my whole fucking shit up," he stated in disbelief. He was glad it was late, and that they could make it to his condo without many people seeing them.

She dressed and he went around to her car door to let her out before tucking her under his arm and escorting her inside.

"I can't believe I just did that," she said, leaning into him, laughing.

"Don't get shy now," Loyal stated. "I want all that shit you hiding behind that ladylike persona."

They stepped onto the elevator, and he backed her into the corner. "I don't even love to kiss like that, E," he said. He tilted her chin and bit his bottom lip. "But these lips," he tasted them with a soft peck. "That's all I look at when you talk," he said, obsessed as he bent down to indulge in them once more, then her neck, as his hands caressed her breasts. Every place he touched tingled.

"Why am I this desperate for you? I've never been this horny before," she panted. Ellie was in heat.

The elevator let them off on the top floor, and they stepped out into the hallway. There was only one unit on this floor. The penthouse.

"Your place is really nice," she admired as she stepped inside. The floor-to-ceiling windows had nothing to cover them, and they were the best part. The entire city seemed to sparkle beneath them. She felt like she was on top of the world as she walked over and stared out.

"It's a'ight," he stated, coming up behind her and wrapping his arms around her before burying his face in her neck. He slipped one hand down the front of her jeans and trapped her clit between two fingers. He shouldn't know how to rub a woman like that. He applied the perfect pressure, the same pressure she applied when she masturbated at night, and Ellie's eyes closed. She noticed a condo across the parking lot, and she could see a group of people congregating inside.

"Can they see us, too?" she asked.

"Probably," he whispered as he rolled her pants down her legs, kissing the skin he uncovered on the way down. She removed her sweater; her panties and bra had been left in the car.

"Giving niggas a perfect view," he mumbled as he bit into one of her asscheeks. "Put your hands on the glass."

She did and leaned over. The way he spread her labia open and sucked on her pussy from the back ruined Ellie. He didn't care that she hadn't cleaned up from the first orgasm. He took ahold of her clit and sucked on it with aggression while moaning like it was the rarest fruit.

He slurped and sucked and flicked and spread her open against that glass window as she made ugly faces.

"Oh my fucking god!" she moaned. "Loyal, stop, Loyal, God!" She was clawing at that glass, but there was nothing to hold onto. Her nails just slid down the smoothness as she made the ugliest faces.

He slowed down but kept licking, pushing his tongue deep into her folds but relieving her of the pressure he used when he sucked. "You want me to stop?"

"No," she groaned, "But I can't take it. It feels too good."

"I need to suck it, baby," Loyal groaned. "I'll go light."

"Okayyyy," she screamed as he took her clit hostage again. It was lighter, but damn if it didn't cause a different sensation. "They can see us," she whispered as she noticed the crowd in the adjacent building gathering at their window.

"Fuck 'em," Loyal stated. He stood and she didn't even move. She leaned against that window, gasping for air, enjoying the break, as her legs shook, and he stepped out of his clothes. The way his dick pressed into her was so erotic that all she could do was cooperate as he took one leg and lifted it as he slid in from behind.

"I love you," she whispered.

He paused, panting in her ear, surprised at her confession. Then, he kissed the back of her neck and replied, "I know." He beat that pussy up so good that Ellie felt her cum and his leaking down her inner thigh all the way to her ankle when they were done. She had never gotten this nasty for a man, and she had no regrets.

"They're giving you a round of applause," Loyal said when

he glanced at their voyeurs and noticed the group cheering.

Ellie laughed as he scooped her, carrying her over his shoulder as he gave the onlookers a salute and then slapped her ass as he carried her to his bedroom.

She wasn't even embarrassed. She was surprised at the level of comfort she had with him.

"It's been four years since I've let a man touch me like that, and that's not even a fair statement because I've never been touched like that," Ellie admitted as Loyal guided her into the shower.

He turned on the shower, and four shower heads turned on.

"Cuz that lame-ass nigga don't know how to handle you," Loyal spat. "It's a fucking shame that pussy been going to waste."

She blushed as he pulled her close, grabbing a loofah and lathering it before taking it to her body.

"You don't belong to him no more, Elliot. Hear me clearly," Loyal stated. "I will put your baby daddy in a grave if he ever disrespects what's mine again."

"You just claiming I'm yours, huh?" she asked playfully.

He pinched her chin and lifted her gaze to his. "It's a courtesy warning," Loyal stated. "You're mine, E. Be mine, baby."

Her heart shouldn't even be capable of beating so fast. He had her in a whirlwind.

"What if..."

"Fuck the what ifs," he interrupted. "We only fucking with what is. So don't get on your bullshit."

"But what is it?" she asked, genuinely confused. "Because all of this is sudden, but you make me forget everything I've been through before you. Love has never felt like this for me, Loyal. It was never this good, never this flattering, never this fun, this safe." She was panicking. She felt it, trying to put rationale to her emotions. "Sex was never this good. Laughter never this joyful. His arms were never this safe. This can't be real after a few days. It feels like I've known you forever."

"Maybe you have, E," Loyal stated. "These bodies are just a version of us in this lifetime. What if the one before this, you were my wife? Or the one before that, you were a queen, and I was your soldier? Or the one before that, we were on a plantation making shit work the best we could while finding freedom in each other? My soul knows you. I don't know how, but I ain't questioning it either. I know that I love you, and that I'm supposed to have you, so I'ma have you. It's us or nothing," he answered. She nodded, heart fluttering, stomach hollowing, and soul crying. "In every lifetime, I'ma find you."

"In every lifetime," she whispered. She prayed she wasn't making the biggest mistake of her life because the way Loyal made her feel, if they ended, she would never bounce back the same.

# CHAPTER 15

**December 22ⁿᵈ**

Courtney closed the laptop and wiped her tears as she finished her first counseling session. She had never even considered going to therapy before, and she had been intimidated to go. She thought it would be strange to divulge the things she was ashamed of to a stranger, but oddly, it was a release that freed her from suffering alone. It was the safest she had felt in a long time, and knowing that the woman would never share her secrets with anyone gave her the confidence to speak up on things she had silenced for years.

It was the best gift she had ever received, and she had Sloan to thank for that. Ten thousand dollars, and a year of paid therapy was her Christmas present from Sloan. It was better than anything she could have unwrapped.

"Court! You have a delivery!" Shy shouted.

Courtney dapped her eyes and replied, "Coming!"

She made her way out to the living room, where Shy was sitting with baby Christian. She motioned toward the bouquet of flowers, and the white gift box that sat on the kitchen island.

"I'll come take him. Thanks for watching him while I took my appointment," Courtney stated.

"Girl, he's fine. He's not bothering nobody. Auntie Shy got to get her time in," Shy cooed as she covered him with kisses.

Courtney really did have a tribe of women around her who loved her. They didn't count favors, and she appreciated them beyond words. "You need rest. Go do nothing, Court. But first, let's see who sent them fucking flowers."

Courtney plucked the card from the bouquet. "It's from James," Courtney said. She was a little shook. All they had done was argue and text battle. "He asked me out on a date. He wants to take me to the company Christmas party at his job."

"Didn't you say he was being hella shitty about you leaving?" Shy asked.

"Yeah, it's been bad," Courtney stated.

"I promise you that nigga bipolar," Shy said. "The flowers are beautiful, though. What's in the box?"

Courtney opened the box and pulled out a Macy's garment bag. She held it up, unzipping it to reveal a black cocktail dress.

"It's a pretty dress," Shy said casually. "I'm more of a Neiman's and Saks girl myself, but he gets an A for effort. Are you going?"

"I don't know, maybe I should. I mean, he's trying," Courtney said. "It's a nice gesture."

"He's a 50-year-old man. He needs to do better than just try," Shy said. "But I'll watch the baby if you want to go."

"Or you, Ellie and Sloan can come as my backup in case I need to get out of there quick," Courtney proposed.

"I can get Lola to watch the baby," Shy said, getting hyped. "I love a good corporate party, and my glam team can do everybody's hair and makeup. I can hit some stylists I know and have them pull dresses because that little Macy's getup ain't gon' work."

"The dress is fine, Shy," Courtney shot back. "But I will take the glam. Okay, now I'm excited."

"James don't even have to be your focus. It'll just be girls' night out, and you can save him a dance," Shy stated. "That way, you set some boundaries, and he don't think he back in from some flowers and a hundred-dollar dress."

"Okay, you really got to stop doing that," Courtney said. "Your digs. They ain't cool. Everybody can't live like this, Shy. A hundred-dollar dress is big money to me and my family."

Shy stood up in shock. "I'm sorry, Court, my bad. I didn't mean anything by it. I was only joking."

"The jokes aren't funny when they're always at my expense," Courtney admitted. "Like, damn, bitch, are you my friend, or am I just around to make you feel bigger?"

"You're my friend, Courtney! Of course, you're my friend!" Shy defended.

"Then don't act like your money makes you better than me," Courtney said. It was a conversation that was long overdue, and from the shocked look on Shy's face, she wasn't prepared for it at all.

"I never said it made me better," Shy said. "You make it seem like I got to turn down my light…"

"Oh, bitch, everybody sees your light. Ain't nobody asking you to dim your shine, Shy, but you're fucking obtuse to everybody else in the room sometimes! You're my bitch, and I want you to be the biggest. Bitch, you are the biggest! You're the baddest. Car the nicest! But don't flex on us, ho! We cheering you on. You deserve everything you got! I know where you came from. It just seems like you're forgetting," Courtney said.

Shy had been slapped in the face, and Courtney was holding a mirror up to her.

"If you feel like that, maybe we not as close as I thought, Court." Shy was in her feelings, and Courtney knew she would be, which is why she had never said anything, but she couldn't take the little snipes and jabs. Courtney was going through enough. She didn't need to be torn down by her friends at the same time.

"Yeah, Shy, I'ma go home," Courtney stated.

"I didn't say you had to go home, Court," Shy shot back. "I don't trust James."

"I don't like feeling like your charity case! Like your little, poor friend!" Courtney shouted.

Baby Christian felt the energy in the room, and he started wailing.

"I knowwww, nephew. I'm sorry," Shy soothed as she walked him around the room. "Your ugly-ass mama getting on my nerves."

Courtney couldn't help but laugh. "Bitch, have my glam ready with your rich ass," Courtney shouted as she turned to walk back to her room. "And you better not say shit about my damn dress later!"

The two had argued plenty of times over the years, and there would be plenty of arguments to come going forward. They were friends who had become sisters, not by blood, but by loyalty and love. Arguments came with the territory.

The smell of coffee roused Ellie out of her slumber. Her entire body hummed with satisfaction. All the stress she had been carrying in her body for years had been worked out last night. She could hear Loyal on the phone, and she climbed out of bed, wrapping the white sheet around her body before following his voice to the kitchen. She stood at the edge of the counter, watching him move around the kitchen as he handled business. He was fully dressed in denim, a white, slim-fitted t-shirt, and Alexander McQueen sneakers.

"I'll confirm the final guest list this afternoon," he informed. "Are Christmas bonuses set to go out today?"

Whoever was on the other end of the phone confirmed, and he replied, "Good." He looked to Ellie and walked over to her, pulling her in by the waist, and planting a kiss on her neck. "I might have one more change to that guest list, but

I got to talk to my lady before I can let you know. Give me a minute. I'll hit you back."

He hung up the phone and gave Ellie his full attention.

"Good morning," he said, tilting her chin and kissing her lips before picking her up and placing her on the kitchen island.

"Why didn't you wake me?" she asked. "You seem busy. I can be dressed and out your way. I know you missed a whole day of business for me yesterday."

"Wake you for what? You were sleeping, E. Just because I got to handle some shit don't mean you got to leave. Stay if you want. I put the spare key by your bag and sent you a text with the door code and the alarm info," he stated.

"Loyal, I can just leave…"

"You can just relax and make yourself comfortable in your man crib," Loyal stated sternly.

She sighed because she knew she had no wins in this argument, so she gave in.

"Okay," she complied.

"I've got this thing tonight," he said. "A company Christmas thing. It's kind of a big deal. We do it every year. I've got to be upfront with you about something."

She tensed, and he leaned into her. "This ain't no bullshit, E, you don't got to brace yourself. I'm bringing it to you because I want you to tell me how you're comfortable with me handling it. If I was on some bullshit, I wouldn't even tell you."

"Why am I not liking how this is starting?" she asked.

"I invited Tisa to my company Christmas party before I met you. I can uninvite her, but I think it would land a lot better if I handled her with some grace. For the sake of us, my son, and her, I think honoring the invitation is better than pulling the rug from under her feet. I can tell her it's over tonight, after the event."

"You're telling me you're going on a date with your baby mama?" she asked.

"I'm asking you to let me keep my word so that I can keep a civil relationship with the woman I raise a child with," he stated. "I'll let her know before I drop her off that it's over, but I want to handle this as respectfully as possible."

"Okay," she whispered unsurely. She didn't love it, but what could she say? He was raising a whole human with this woman. His intentions seemed pure, but she wondered if she was playing the fool.

He could see her overthinking, and he feathered her arm with one finger. "Why don't you and your homegirls get dressed up and come? I can put you on the list at your own table. Cassidy's supposed to pull up."

"Yeah, okay," she said, forcing a smile. She didn't want to start a situation with him with insecurity in her heart. *If he was on bullshit, he just wouldn't have told you. Girl, relax,* she thought. "Why not?" she answered aloud. He pulled his wallet from his back pocket and removed a platinum American Express. "For whatever you and your girls need to get ready. The keys to my Benz are hanging by the door. I'll have a driver arrange to pick you up for the party. I take it you're leaving from Bishop's?" he asked.

"Yeah, probably so," she answered.

"It starts at eight o'clock. I'll have the car come at around 7:30," he said.

Already she was forcing smiles and going along with shit she wasn't comfortable with. She didn't want to be the woman who let her past relationship influence her present one, but she had trust issues. She didn't expect a man Loyal's age to be completely available. A man with kids just came with the territory after you hit 35, but it was never easy to handle. She knew that seeing him with Tisa tonight would tell her all she needed to know about what she was dealing with.

"What are you doing here, Dr. Martin? I thought you were out on vacation?"

Sloan looked up from her desk and gave a polite smile because her nurses were used to her being polite.

"I'm just catching up on some work. That's all," she replied. All Sloan knew was work. It was how she coped with everything. Science was something that had never failed her. It was predictable. It was dependable. It was black and white. When the world confused her. When stress wore her down. When her emotions were out of control, she indulged in the beauty of science, her work, and her life's mission. She was working on her next medical trial. She wanted to eradicate fibroids in women, especially Black women, and she knew it would take hundreds, if not thousands, of hours of research.

It was the perfect distraction from the pain she felt. It didn't cure the loneliness, but it left little room to dwell on it. Her job was the one area in her life where she excelled. It was the one thing that no one could sabotage. Her accomplishments were vast, and when the world went to hell around her, she found solace in helping other women. Whether she was delivering babies, counseling, and educating young girls, or contributing to the evolution of reproductive medicine, it all made her feel like she had a purpose. People failed her every time. Science never did.

"Any big Christmas plans?" her nurse asked.

"No, no plans. Just work," Sloan answered. "Can you close the door, please?"

Friendsmas break was supposed to be fun. It was supposed to be a reunion filled with love and laughter. She hadn't foreseen the heartbreak that had come along with it. She didn't know if Cassidy had tried to call or not because she had blocked him. She knew it was for the best. She just couldn't understand why she couldn't stop herself from aching inside. She knew that she would have to come clean to Ellie one day. There was no way she could keep this a secret from her now that Courtney and Shy knew. She prayed that Ellie didn't overreact. The last thing she wanted to do was fall out with her best friend. Ellie had always had a "don't even think about it" mentality when it came to Cassidy. Sloan had broken that rule, and she knew that it would come to light eventually.

Her phone rang, and a foreign number popped up on her phone. She didn't want any distractions, so she silenced it and continued working. When the same number called her right back, she frowned in irritation. She hated when people called her back-to-back like that, and she answered it with every intention to put someone in their place. Whoever it was didn't respect the boundary of voicemail; they were imposing themselves on her time, and it pissed Sloan clean off.

"Dr. Martin; how can I help you?" Sloan answered while scrolling down the laptop as she read the article in front of her.

"Auntie Sloan, can you come get me, please?"

Sloan gave the phone her full attention as she picked it up and took it off speakerphone.

"Brooklyn? Is everything okay? Where are you?" Sloan asked. It wasn't uncharacteristic for Brooklyn to call Sloan. Sloan was her Godmother. Despite their physical distance, Sloan made sure to impact her life in a positive way. They spoke every week, twice a week, no matter what, and it was a ritual they had done ever since she was born. Before Brooklyn could even talk, Sloan would be cooing to Ellie over the phone and flying in once a month for visits. Their bond was strong, but this phone call felt odd, considering she was supposed to be spending time with her dad.

"I'm at my dad's, but I really want to come home," Brooklyn said. "I want to call my mom, but he won't let me."

"What do you mean he won't let you?" Sloan asked, her voice elevating as instant anger built in her chest.

"He took my phone because he says I'm ungrateful, and

when I asked to go home, he said no. My mom must have his number blocked because my calls won't go through from his phone. This is his phone I'm calling you from."

"And you have to sneak to call me?" Sloan asked. She was already gathering her things.

"I just want to come home, Auntie. He hasn't even spent any time with me. He works all day and leaves me here with his girlfriend. She doesn't say two words to me. I don't even think she wants me here. I feel uncomfortable, Auntie Sloan. Plus, there's no room. I'm sleeping on the couch because her brother is staying here, and he was in the guest room first, and the other room is being used for storage. She said it didn't make sense for him to give up his room for someone who is only staying a week. Can you please just call my mom for me?"

"Her brother? How old is this brother?" Sloan snapped. She grabbed her laptop, some thick medical books she needed for research, her bag, and her keys before storming out the door and to her car.

"I don't know. He's like 30 or something," Brooklyn said. "I got to go, Auntie. Somebody's coming." Brooklyn rushed out the words so frantically that Sloan didn't even have time to respond.

Click.

"Oh, Cairo has lost his mind," Sloan mumbled as she threw her things in the car. She immediately called Ellie. Voicemail. "Girlll," Sloan sang. "Answer your phone." She tried Ellie again, to no avail, before sending a text.

## Sloan

*Call me as soon as you get this. It's important.*

Sloan didn't wait to get the return call from Ellie. She headed over to Cairo's house. She was almost positive that Ellie would be going to get her child if she knew what was going on. She cleared the expressway, pushing 95mph the entire way. The day was as dreary as her mood. Michigan winters came with gray skies, and the dusting of snow that was falling from the sky forced Sloan to turn on her wipers to get a clear view. She was grateful that she and Shy had done a stakeout for Ellie a few years back. They had done some things for each other over the years. When Cairo had first abandoned Ellie, her friend had desperately wanted to know if Cairo was living with another woman. She couldn't make the trip to Michigan to go on the opps mission herself, so Sloan and Shy had done it for her. They had stalked that man all night until some heffa had done the walk of shame the next morning. They slut-shamed the poor lady all the way to her car, hooting and hollering out the window and shouting, "He's a married, cheating-ass man!" at the top of their lungs. Cairo had always despised their friend group, but he absolutely hated them after that. She hadn't been back to his house since, but instant directions popped up in her memory now that she needed to get to her Goddaughter.

She arrived and called Ellie one more time. When she Didn't answer, Sloan made the executive decision to go get Brooklyn out of that house. She prayed she didn't have to snap on Cairo or his girlfriend. She was in no position to fight. She wore closed-toe Pigalle's and her doctor's coat. She'd look a fool trying to pop off on anybody, but she wasn't against it if somebody got stupid. She rang the doorbell, and when Cairo opened it, a look of disgust crossed his face.

"What the hell are you doing here?" he asked.

"I'm here to pick Brooklyn up. She called. She's ready to go back to her mom," Sloan said sternly.

His girlfriend stepped up behind him. "Baby, is everything okay?"

"Brook is fine. She's being a brat because I'm putting down some rules in my house. This don't concern you, Sloan. I'd appreciate it if you leave my house," Cairo stated. He was acting like he had some sense, so Sloan wasn't completely thrown off, but she wasn't backing down.

"Look, Cairo, you and Ellie chose me because you trusted me to love your daughter like she's my own. She doesn't want to be here right now, and I don't know what that's about. Four years is a lot of time to let go by without seeing your daughter. There are some things that need to be worked out, it sounds like..."

"This is not her place, Cairo," the girlfriend piped up.

Sloan deadpanned on Cairo and gave him a warning look. "You better get your fucking girlfriend, nigga, because you know how I get down. If anybody is out of place, it's her and her fucking thirty-year-old brother that's sleeping in this house while my niece is here. Why is Brook on the couch while that grown-ass man is sleeping comfortably in a bed? Why is he in there with her at all while you at work? Come on, Cairo! You got more sense than this," Sloan hissed. "But if you don't, and you want to make this a thing, I can call Cassidy to come settle this. It's easier to deal with me than him or even Ellie. You and Ellie can work out the details later, but my Goddaughter called me, so let me take her."

Cairo was steaming mad. She could see it, but she could also see that he understood the reason.

"I got this, baby, go back in the house."

The girlfriend sucked her teeth, but she turned and walked back in the house.

"Don't let your ego ruin your relationship with your daughter. You want her to want to come visit you, negro, and at the very least, be home when she's here. Take the time off work so your daughter can get reacquainted with you —outside of the toxic bullshit you got going on with Ellie. You did her wrong. You got some repairing to do. Don't just pick her up and think spending the night under your roof is enough!" Sloan fussed.

Cairo's nostrils flared, and he sighed as he glanced behind Sloan, avoiding her convicting stare.

"Brooklyn!" His voice boomed so loudly that Sloan felt her heart jump.

"Yeah, Daddy?" Brooklyn shouted back.

"Come here for a minute!" Cairo yelled.

Brooklyn appeared at the door moments later, and Sloan could see the instant relief fill her Goddaughter's eyes when Brooklyn saw that she had come.

"You want to go back to your grandpa, Bishop's, house and bring Christmas in with your mama? Or you want to stay here?"

"I want to go to Papa's, please," Brooklyn stated, eyes watering.

"Go get your things then," Cairo stated.

Brooklyn practically ran for her bag, and Sloan sighed in relief. It had been easier than she expected it to be. She could see the hurt on Cairo.

"What are you thinking? With all this? The way you've handled Ellie? And Tessa," she whispered, lowering her tone. "Cairo, I don't like your ass, but come on. Those girls don't deserve this. Can you imagine how guilty Brooklyn feels even being here with you, knowing how her sister feels at home? How her mom feels? You're going to lose her too if you don't get your shit together," Sloan stated. Brooklyn came back to the door, and Cairo moved aside so that his daughter could exit. He pulled her phone from his jacket pocket.

He handed it to Brooklyn. "I'm sorry you couldn't stay longer and that I had to work," Cairo said, clearing his throat. "Call me on Christmas, okay?" There were tears trying to form in his eyes. He cleared his throat and avoided eye contact with Brooklyn.

"Okay, Daddy," Brooklyn replied with a disappointed tone. She truly was a daddy's girl, but she was beginning to see him through the lens of a teenage girl, not the little girl he remembered.

Brooklyn headed down the walkway, and Sloan gave Cairo one final piece of advice. "She's the kid. You call her on Christmas. You come to her on Christmas and don't come with gifts for one. Get your shit together." And with that, she was gone.

When she got to the car, Brooklyn practically jumped over the passenger seat to hug her neck.

"Thank you, Auntie," Brooklyn whispered.

"Did that bitch or her brother touch you?" Sloan asked.

Brooklyn shook her head. "No, ma'am."

Sloan grabbed her niece's chin and looked her in the eye. "Did he touch you?"

Brooklyn shook her head, and Sloan sighed. "Okay,"

She reversed out of the driveway, and then put the car in drive, and sped away from the house.

By the time Ellie returned her call, she was pulling onto Bishop's street.

"Hey, girl, sorry. My phone was on Do Not Disturb," Ellie explained. "I'm just now getting home, and bitch, I have to catch you up! You good?"

"I'm almost at your papa's house; open the door," Sloan said, answering the question.

"Oh!" Ellie exclaimed. "Okay, cool."

Sloan's heart stopped when she noticed Cassidy's car sitting on the curb. "Fuck," she whispered as a sudden nervousness crept into her chest.

She pulled into the driveway and turned off her car. Before she and Brooklyn got out, she said, "I need you to take it a lot easier on your mom, Brook. I know you're going through your own thing with your dad being gone, but so is she. She loves you. Stop making all these bad decisions. The smoking, the grades," Sloan stated. "Now, I understand the boys because, baby, Auntie Sloan had them niggas lined up when I was your age," Sloan gloated, snickering.

234

ASHLEY ANTOINETTE

Brooklyn blushed and smiled widely. "But she can't trust you with no little boy if you can't show her that you make good decisions with other things. You're smarter than the choices you've been making," Sloan said gently. "And if you need help with something, or you feeling a way and you can't talk to her, you know you can talk to me. Or your auntie, Shy, or your auntie, Court. We are your village. We will keep your secrets and help you through anything you feel like your mom won't understand, baby girl. We've been in your life since before you were thought of. You were a name in a notebook when Ellie thought she would marry Greg Dawson in 8th grade," Sloan laughed at the thought. "We are here for you."

Brooklyn nodded and dropped a tear. "Can we maybe talk before we leave town, Auntie? Can I spend a night with you one of these days? You're just always so busy."

Sloan knew that her job got in the way of a lot. Brooklyn wasn't lying. Maybe Sloan needed to be more available to her niece. "How about this? When you guys leave to go back home, I'll come with you and stay through the New Year. I have more vacation time. I'll spend New Year's Eve with you guys."

"Really?" Brooklyn perked up.

"Yeah, really. You can introduce me to your friends and show me around, and I'll even show you how to check your vape and weed to make sure it ain't laced," Sloan said.

Brooklyn's eyes widened as if she wanted to deny that she smoked at all.

"I'm not your mama. Can't lie to me. I can see that you're high just by looking at you. I'm a doctor, Brook.

But this shit is killing people out here. It's not the same as it used to be when me and your mom were experimenting. You're being stupid," Sloan said. "And I want you alive. Of course, I'd prefer if you didn't smoke at all, but I'm not naive enough to think you never will again. So, yeah, I'm coming to town to get you together before something bad happens to you."

"I wish my mom was more like you. I can talk to you," Brooklyn said.

"Your mom is so much better than me. Your mom is the best woman I know. So, respect my friend. If you give her a chance, she will be your very best friend, but you're her daughter. You're her cub. You grew inside her body, Brooklyn. That's hard work. That's the hardest work a woman ever has to do, and a mother is going to protect that work. If you make her feel like she got to protect you from yourself, then you will never get the side of your mother that doesn't have to worry. You taking it easy on her makes her take it easier on you," Sloan preached.

"I understand," Brooklyn nodded.

"Okay, now let's get in here," Sloan said.

Sloan climbed from the car and walked behind her niece. They didn't knock. They walked in because Sloan had been walking in unannounced her entire life. She was a fixture in the Whitlock home, so their doors were always open to her.

"Brook!" Tessa screamed at the top of her lungs as soon as she saw Brooklyn.

Brooklyn laughed as Tessa ran into her at full speed.

Ellie shot Sloan a confused look but opened her arms wide

for her daughter. "Oh my god, baby, I didn't know you were coming home. I'm so glad you're back!" Ellie exclaimed.

Brooklyn hadn't been too keen on hugging Ellie lately, so Ellie was shocked when Brooklyn wrapped her arms around her tightly.

"I'm glad I'm back too, Mommy," Brooklyn said. "I'm sorry." Brooklyn broke down on her apology, and Ellie's eyes watered. She held her daughter, her own eyes misting as she looked over Brooklyn's shoulders at Sloan.

"Thank you," Ellie mouthed. She was unsure of what had occurred, but she recognized Sloan's magic when she saw it. She felt it all in Brooklyn's hug.

Papa was in the kitchen, and he stepped out to greet Sloan. "Hey, beautiful," Papa greeted.

"Hey, Papa," Sloan said, moving around Ellie to hug the old man.

"Are you okay?" Ellie asked Brooklyn. Brooklyn nodded.

Ellie looked to Sloan, who nodded in confirmation.

"She's fine," Sloan said. "We'll talk later."

Ellie nodded and released Brooklyn.

"Okay, get settled in, I guess," Ellie said, grabbing her belt loops with her thumbs and then shrugging.

Brooklyn headed for the stairs, and Ellie called her name. "Brook?"

"Yeah, Ma?" Brooklyn turned back.

"I love you," Ellie said.

"I love you, too, Ma," Brooklyn stated.

"Come on, Brook! Let me tell you about OG! You missed the Christmas Tree Farm!" Tessa exclaimed as she pulled her big sister up the stairs. Papa hugged Brooklyn and then made his exit.

"I'ma be in the back with Cass; give this boy a hand. There are homemade catfish Po Boys in the oven for everybody when y'all ready to eat," Papa said. "There's more than enough for you, daughter," he said, talking to Sloan. "You know I always cook more than enough."

"Thanks, Papa," Sloan smiled, kissing his cheek. Sloan was relieved that Cassidy was too tied up to notice her presence.

Ellie turned back to Sloan. "Am I going to need a drink for this conversation?" Ellie asked.

"Probably," Sloan said. "You want to step out for a minute to grab one? I'll fill you in." Sloan was looking for an excuse to duck out of there before she ran into Cassidy.

"Nah, you know it's some liquor here, and Papa just cooked. Come on. Take that coat off," Ellie led her to the kitchen table, and Sloan pulled off her coat, revealing her doctor's jacket and work outfit underneath.

"Are you coming from work? I thought you were off for the week?" Ellie asked.

"I went in to catch up. Brook called me while I was at the office. Said she wanted to come home. That nigga took her phone, Ellie. Had her sleeping on the couch, and his girlfriend's brother is living there," Sloan informed.

"Wait, girl, what?" Ellie's heart sank. "I will kill him." An instant panic filled her as the worst-case scenarios played through her mind.

"Brooklyn!" Ellie shouted.

"Ellie, she's fine. I asked all the right questions, nothing happened. I went and got her immediately," Sloan said, calming her friend's nerves.

"Why the fuck would he put my child on the couch? Why would he even take her there with another grown-ass man she's not related to living under that fucking roof?!" Ellie hissed in a whisper. "I am going to murder that nigga."

"Honestly, Ellie, I think you need to force that divorce. It's time. Get some structure in the girls' lives. Get a formal visitation schedule set up with some rules in place. Nothing happened, thank God, but it could have," Sloan stated.

"Yeah, you're right," Ellie said.

"I'll get the names of some attorneys and set up some meetings for you after the holidays," Sloan stated.

The sound of a chainsaw erupted, and Sloan frowned.

"What are they doing back there?" Sloan asked.

"You remember the tree house?" Ellie asked.

Sloan snickered as she shook her head. "Of course, I remember the tree house. That's where we did all our damn dirt. Remember, we thought your parents were going to the casino and would be gone all day and we snuck those boys in the house? I think Cass had a tournament or some shit, so we had the house to ourselves. They came home early on our asses, and them niggas had to climb up there and hide out."

Ellie cracked up. "They were up there alllll fucking dayyyyy!"

"We were low-key bad as hell," Sloan said.

"Bitch, high-key," Ellie agreed. "It's all rotted out. Tessa saw it up there and Cassidy told her what it was, now she got him rebuilding it for her for Christmas, chile."

"Oh, wow," Sloan exclaimed. "She's going to love that." Sloan stood and went to the window. Her heart wrenched in her chest as soon as she laid eyes on him. She knew she needed to tell Ellie about what had happened between them but now didn't seem like the time.

"Where were you the other day? We missed you when we went shopping," Sloan asked as she turned away from the window and reclaimed her seat at the table. Ellie stood and grabbed two plates and then fixed them lunch.

"Yeah, umm, so you remember Loyal?" Ellie asked. Ellie placed a plate of food in front of Sloan and then turned back to make them a quick drink.

"Bitch, stop! You Didn't !" Sloan whispered excitedly.

"And did," Ellie confirmed.

"Bitchhhh!" Sloan died from the shock of it all. Ellie wasn't the type to sleep with a man casually. This was completely out of character for her. "Wait...you got to start from the beginning because how did I miss all this?"

Ellie sat and handed Sloan her drink.

"I don't know, girl. I just..." Ellie sighed as she thought about what she wanted to say. "I like him. He's assertive and understanding, and he's so good with Tess. Girl, like he's unbelievable with her."

"He's been around Tess? Ellie!" Sloan gasped.

"I know, I know," Ellie groaned. "It just happened so organically. He stopped by to check on me, and him and Papa started kicking it. He knew about the shit with Cairo, and he just made her feel better. He just has a presence that makes you feel safe."

"And he talked you out your panties," Sloan snickered.

"Clean up out them bitches," Ellie confirmed.

Sloan lifted her eyebrows in satisfaction because she wasn't mad at it at all. "Was it good?"

"Bitch, the best," Ellie bragged, lowering her voice to a whisper. Sloan and Ellie giggled like they were teenaged girls, sharing their secrets, and Sloan gave Ellie a high-five. "The motherfucking best, do you hear me?"

"Like the best you ever had?" Sloan asked.

"I mean, it wasn't better than that basketball player I was knocking off in college. That nigga was hung different. He wasn't circumcised either, so he was hella vocal when he was in it…"

"Pause, bitch; you had a turtleneck papi?" Sloan asked in shock. "How you leave that detail out before?"

Ellie cackled. "I did, girl, and it was good too. A little ugly, but that turtleneck dick did what it was supposed to do! And he was here from overseas, so it was just a different vibe."

Sloan smirked and nodded her head. "And Mr. Loyal is in second place with the good drug dealer dick," Sloan said.

Ellie nodded. "Real Estate Developer, but he fuck like one of them niggas out them books, bitch," Ellie confirmed.

Sloan squealed, the tea was so hot. It was times like this that she missed. There was nothing like girl talk with her best friend.

"I'm happy for you, girl. You deserve some good dick after that damn four-year drought," Sloan said, only half joking.

"He wants me to move here," Ellie added.

Sloan bit into her sandwich and paused, grabbing a napkin as she chewed. "Oh!" she exclaimed. "Wait, this is more than just a friendly fuck?"

"I think so," Ellie stated. "I don't know. It feels like it could be, but he has this baby mama, and I'm whole-ass married and..."

"Timing is a cruel bitch," Sloan interjected.

"He invited us to come to his company Christmas party tonight. It's like this formal thing. He said I can bring my girls. He's holding a table for me."

"Why would you bring us? Wouldn't you be his date?" Sloan asked. She bit into her sandwich again.

"Girl, you fucking that sandwich up!" Ellie teased, biting her own.

"You know your daddy can cook," Sloan defended, laughing guiltily. "My ass ain't ate all day! Don't try to change the subject. Why aren't you going with him?"

"He invited his baby mama before he met me, and he doesn't want to go back on his word. He's supposed to make it clear that they're over, and I'm supposed to be working out my shit with Cairo. We agreed that we needed to close those chapters before we could really explore what this is."

"Oh, that's complicated," Sloan grimaced. "Are they still together?"

"He says they aren't, but they still fuck around from time to time. He's been hella upfront about everything else. I don't know why he would lie about it. He didn't even have to tell me about the party, so he technically could have taken her, and I would have been none the wiser, but something about it just feels…"

"Like he's running game," Sloan finished for her.

"Okay, so it's not just me?" Ellie asked. "Okay, now I feel better. He just seems too good to be true, and this baby mama situation is problematic."

"Shit, your situation is worse, Ellie. You got a whole bitch-ass nigga for a husband."

Ellie sighed.

"Should I even be going to this event?"

"Oh, bitch, we are definitely going," Sloan said. "Ain't nothing gon' tell you more than seeing the shit for yourself."

The back door opened, and Cassidy walked into the room. Sloan lost air as he halted in his tracks.

"My bad, I ain't know you had company, E," Cassidy said as he stared at Sloan. "I ain't mean to interrupt. Let me get out y'all way."

Sloan couldn't even look at him without becoming emotional.

"Don't worry about it. I've got to go. I got to get back to work. Send me the details, Ellie. I'll be there." Sloan stood from the table.

"Mommy! We need you!" Tessa's voice carried through the whole house.

Ellie hopped up in a hurry because it sounded urgent.

"Better check on that," Cassidy said.

"Have kids they said," Ellie joked. Sloan smiled, and Ellie rushed upstairs, leaving Sloan and Cassidy alone.

"Can we talk?" Cassidy asked.

Sloan was already headed for the door. She stopped at the door, collecting her shoes as she struggled to get them on her feet. Cassidy followed her. He got down on one knee and took her foot into his hand. He slid both shoes on her feet. Just his touch sent chills through her body. He stood, looming over her. "Sloan," he whispered, taking her chin between his fingertips.

"Ellie's upstairs," Sloan whispered.

"I don't give a fuck about, E," Cassidy replied. "Look at me."

Sloan's eyes flooded. "Cassidy, please."

"I know what we felt the other night," Cassidy said. "Behind all your doubts, all the fear, I know what you felt, Sloan." They had spent twenty-three years apart from each other, and after one night together, separation was unbearable. "If I'm reading shit wrong, let me know."

Her eyes were so damn full of emotion that she couldn't even blink. He wasn't reading anything wrong. She felt all of what he felt, and it wasn't something you could have once without craving it again. Allowing herself to have him one time would make her want him forever. He reached for her, and she exhaled. There was so much release in that breath as he held her face in his hands.

Her medical pager went off loudly. Sloan gasped as if she was coming up for air as she swiped her tears and snatched the pager off her purse strap. "Oh, no," she whispered to herself as sudden dread consumed her. "I can't do this right now. This is a patient, and it's 911. I've got to go."

Cassidy caressed the side of her face and the look on his face was so conflicted as she clung to him, gripping his jacket as she closed her eyes. There was so much hurt between them. She felt it. Their souls were tearing in opposite directions.

"I've got to go," she insisted. He took a step back, and she rushed out of the house, headed to the hospital. This was why she couldn't keep a man. Moments just like this interrupted pivotal instances in her personal life, but it was what she had signed up for. It came with the job, and as much as she wanted to stay and have this conversation with Cassidy, she had to put her feelings on the back burner and put her career first.

# CHAPTER 16

Sloan hated this part of her job. Most of the time, childbirth was beautiful. It was full of happy moments and grateful parents. She got so much fulfillment in being the one to bring life into the world, but on days like this, her job felt like a burden. She rushed through the hallways of the hospital, peeling out of her street clothes as she passed them off to one of her interns. "Where is she?" Sloan asked.

"She's in emergency room 3. Fetal heartbeat is faint. Her blood pressure is 141/98." The intern ran off the stats, and Sloan knew she didn't have time to spare.

"Let the operating nurse know I need OR 5 prepped and ready for an emergency cesarean; now!" Sloan shouted. She kicked off her heels, leaving them in the hallway as she ran to the doctor's locker room. She came out of her clothes as quickly as she could and was barely in scrubs as she rushed to see her patient. She was terrified, but she was trained to steady her voice and present a confident front to keep her patient calm.

"Hey, girl, hey. I thought we had an agreement. That baby

wants to make his debut for Christmas, I see," Sloan said, smiling as she walked into the room.

"I'm scared, Dr. Sloan. There's so much pain, and I... aghh."

Sloan washed her hands and then pumped hand sanitizer in them for good measure before she gloved up.

"Let's see what's going on," she said. "Don't be afraid, Monica. I'm right here with you." She sounded more confident than she was. She pulled the stirrups up, and as soon as she inserted her fingers for a vaginal exam, she knew something was wrong. She snapped the glove off and spoke to the nurse.

"Hand me the ultrasound gel," she said.

Within thirty seconds, Sloan identified a deadly problem. "This is a placental abruption," Sloan announced. "Monica, we're going to be delivering this baby today via C-section."

"Wait! But we had a birthing plan! My husband isn't here. I wanted to do this naturally!"

Sloan grabbed her patient's hand and looked her in the eyes. "We must detour from the plan, Monica. The plan can only happen under the very best of circumstances. These aren't the best of circumstances, and we cannot wait for your husband." Sloan didn't want to scare her patient, but time was of the essence.

"Is my baby going to be okay?"

Sloan knew that there was no way she could make any promises to this woman. There were no guarantees when it came to surgery. She had years of experience in this field, and she had to rely on her dedication, knowledge, and commitment to her skills to try to deliver this baby safely.

"I am going to do my very best in that operating room, Monica, and I am the absolute best in my field," Sloan stated. She meant that shit. She was confident in her abilities. There was no other OBGYN in the state who could trump her professionally. She knew that God would have the final say, however, but she was going to do her part. If it was humanly possible, Sloan was going to bring this woman and her child through this surgery.

She ran ahead of the gurney so that she could make it in time to scrub into surgery properly. There was never a time that she stepped in the operating room that nerves didn't fill her, but today she was distracted. Today, she felt Cassidy in the back of her mind. She felt his kiss on her lips, his hand on her cheek. He was infiltrating her soul, and she couldn't walk into this woman's surgery anything less than focused. She needed her heart settled. A surgical intern stood next to her scrubbing as well.

"Stop scrubbing and pull out my phone," Sloan said.

"But Dr. Martin, I won't be able to scrub back in, in time to participate in this surgery," the intern said.

"And I won't be able to focus on this surgery the way I need to if you don't make this call," Sloan stated. "Get the phone."

The intern reached into Sloan's pocket and pulled out the phone.

"Siri, call Cassidy Whitlock," Sloan announced. "Put it on speaker."

Sloan was scrubbing her hands, under her nails, and her

forearms to death as her gut tightened, and she listened to the phone ring.

"Hello?" Cassidy answered.

"I'm about to cut into this woman's body, Cass, and I can't focus," she said, panicking. "I can't focus because my entire body is aching over you. I can't stop thinking about you. I know how to do this. My hands are the best surgical hands in the state, but I'm distracted, Cassidy. I keep playing the look on your face back in my mind, and the words of our argument keep ringing back in my head. I can't operate with that being the last thing on my mind. Please say something to calm my nerves. Please tell me that I can do this because my patient's baby is in trouble, and she's expecting me to enter this operating room and save her child. Cass, please calm my nerves."

She had never felt a love that consumed her this way, and she didn't like it. She was sick to her stomach.

"I love you, Sloan. That's all you need to know. That's enough to get us through any argument, any misunderstanding, any obstacle that keeps us apart." Sloan closed her eyes and swallowed the lump in her throat as he spoke. "That's what Papa used to say when he would fight with my mama. My mom would be ready to pack her shit, she would be cussing his ass out, hell, cussing me and E out too, just cuz we was in the house looking like his ass. E would cry and tell Papa to fix it, and he would say, 'When you love a woman like I love your mother, God fixes it.' He said all he had to do was wait. And I love you like that, Sloan. I've always loved you. Meet me at the party after you're done," he said.

"Cass," she replied, hesitantly. The C-section she was about to perform would only take her about an hour tops.

"Just think about it. If you don't show, I'll fall back, Sloan, and respect your boundaries, but I really hope you give me a chance to explain away the shit that scares you."

"Okay," she answered. She exhaled, and the weight that lifted off her shoulders was insanity to her. To love a man so much that he could heal or harm you with just his words was terrifying. Cassidy was in control of her soul. He had relieved her of whatever was stopping her from doing her job.

"Go be great, Dr. Martin," he answered, and then he hung up.

The intern stood there, mouth agape, as she said, "Wow. Totally worth not scrubbing in."

Sloan smiled, and then rinsed her hands, lifting them in the air as she walked through the door that led to the surgical floor. "God, operate through me and bless my hands," she whispered to herself as she walked through the door. She looked at the other surgeons and nurses in the room. "Let's get this baby out of there," Sloan said confidently.

# CHAPTER 17

s Sloan coming?" Shy asked as she sat in the makeup chair, getting her face done.

"I haven't heard from her since earlier. She had a patient, but I did send her the details, and she said she would be there," Ellie said.

"Thank you so much for bringing the girls by to watch the baby while we go," Courtney added.

"You don't have to thank me for that, Court," Ellie said,

"We want to," Brooklyn stated.

"He's so cute," Tessa added.

"Lola! Can you grab my shoes out my closet? And grab my keys because you're driving. Oh, and make sure you get whatever lipstick she's using and keep some in your purse in case I need a touch-up through the night," Shy said.

"Got it," Lola answered. Even she was dressed to perfection. She couldn't attend as Shy's assistant without following the dress code.

All four women were beautiful.

"I haven't been this dressed up, besides my wedding, of

course, since prom," Ellie said as she looked in the floor-length mirror.

She had done some damage to Loyal's credit card. The Alaia dress she wore was black and form-fitting with puffy feathered sleeves and a puffy feathered skirt that showed off her toned thighs and legs. Thank God for Pilates. It fit her body like a glove. She wore her hair middle-parted and bone-straight in a short, full, bob. Four-inch Alaia heels graced her feet.

"Lola, put some body butter on her legs, please," Shy instructed. Lola went to move, but Ellie held up a hand.

"I've got it, Lola, thank you," she said, taking the butter from Lola's hands.

Courtney's dress was gold and strapless, with beading that covered the entire floor-length gown. The lace portions of the dress gave it a sex appeal that Courtney hadn't felt since before having the baby.

"You look beautiful, Court," Ellie said. "Especially with the updo. It's giving all the things."

Courtney smiled.

"Not gonna lie. Your rich ass came through with the glam team," Courtney said to Shy.

"Yeah, they did their jobs," Ellie said, admiring her brown and smoldering look.

"All of you guys look good," Brooklyn smiled. "Especially you, Auntie Shy, in that red."

Shy showed the most skin with a red bralette and long, satin, skintight skirt that had a split that went up to her hip. The tall red gloves she wore finished out her look. Good thing skin was in because Shy was showing it.

"Okay, my driver is here. Are you sure you don't want to just ride with me?" Ellie asked Shy.

"No, Lola can drive my car. We'll follow behind you. You like to call it an early night. We might want to keep the party going afterward," Shy said.

"Oh yeah, well, definitely drive your shit then because I'm going home after this. Girls, come give y'all mama a kiss. I'll be back in the morning to pick y'all up!" Ellie shouted.

Brooklyn and Tessa came and kissed her goodbye.

"I love y'all. Brook, if you need anything, call my phone. Are you sure you can handle the baby?" Ellie asked.

"I'm positive, Mom. He sleeps most of the time. All I'm doing is changing diapers and feeding him on a schedule. I got it," Brooklyn reassured.

Ellie looked skeptically. "Maybe I should just..."

"You should get your ass out the door before we're late. She's got it, girl, now go'n," Shy fussed.

Ellie and Courtney hopped in one car and Shy hopped in the backseat of her S-Class as Lola took the driver's seat.

"Girl, who the fuck Shy think she is?" Ellie snickered.

"Chile, you know she always gave rich bitch, main character, energy. Let her live."

The girls shared a laugh because their friend had always been that bitch, even in middle school when she used to wear her two-inch heels from Payless. She had graduated to Red Bottoms and Birkin bags, and you couldn't tell her shit.

"The best part is raiding her closet because she had the perfect purse to go with this dress," Ellie said. "What is the plan for James? Does you accepting this invitation mean you're going to go back?"

Courtney sighed.

"It means I'm willing to go out tonight. I just feel like we need to work on it day by day. Today might be yes, tomorrow might be no. It depends on him and his progress and his actions. It also depends on me and mine. That first therapy session made me realize I'm not really ready to be a partner for anyone. I've got some healing to do."

"I'm so damn proud of you, Court. Like, for real," Ellie said. "You're so strong."

"I don't feel like it, but thanks, Ellie," Courtney responded.

Ellie's stomach twisted nervously as they arrived at the venue.

"Wow," she muttered as the valet opened her door and she stepped out. Shy and Lola pulled in right behind them, and they all walked up the red-carpeted staircase. It reminded her of the Met Gala. Loyal had rented out the Flint Institute of Arts for the evening, and it was beautifully decorated. The event's photographers and the local newspapers were out, taking pictures of everyone as they arrived. Ellie posed alone and then with Courtney and Shy before they all made their way inside.

"Where is Sloan?" Ellie asked herself as she stepped into the room. She pulled out her phone.

**Ellie**
*Hey, we just arrived. Are you on your way?*

She slid the phone into her small clutch and then found her way to her seat.

"It's beautiful in here," Shy said, amazed at the transformation of the arts institute. The live band played R&B classics as waiters in black pants and white shirts and black ties, served champagne from crystal trays. The speakeasy theme was dark and moody, and a casino royale was the running activity. There was gaming tables set up around the room. At each seat was a gift bag for each attendee with fake chips inside. She picked up the note.

"The player with the most chips at the end of the night gets to donate the pot to the charity of their choice. Remember, you have to bet big to win big. Good luck!" she said, reading it aloud. She laughed because it was a cute concept, and it instantly excited her.

"Your boy knows how to throw a party," Shy complimented, digging through her gift bag and pulling out the expensive items inside.

"*Essential Body Love, Boujee Hippie* supplements, *Boss Locs* hair products, *Hairapy* by Enjoli, *Marty's Kitchen* spices, *Dipped by Toni* cupcakes, *Euphoric Collections* candle, *Sweat Freak* t-shirt, *B-Edits* affirmation cards, and a motherfucking Ashley Marie autographed book? All these are top-tier Black-owned businesses. Plus, *Foundation Health Care* is the platinum sponsor! The partnerships are intentional and lit," Shy exclaimed. It was an elevated experience without question.

Ellie nodded her head smoothly to the music as she looked around the room for Loyal. When she spotted Cassidy instead, she smiled. Her brother was dapper in a cranberry JW Anderson suit. "That boy is clean," Ellie teased as she watched the women in the room clamor over one another for his time. His only accessory was the gold presidential Rolex on his wrist. It was perfect for the occasion, and he wore it like the designer had made it specifically for his frame.

"Yeah, he is," Lola admired.

Ellie snapped her neck back in shock as Lola lifted from the table. "Excuse me," Lola said. Courtney snickered as Lola crossed the room, looking like a million bucks, interrupting all the women who were surrounding Cass.

"Umm, not your assistant trying to shoot her shot at my brother," Ellie noticed. "I mean, she is cute, though." She watched as Cassidy accepted the glass of champagne that Lola had picked up along the way. Ellie jerked her head back even further and put a hand on her breast. "Oop, and not he like her."

"Lola better pump her brakes before Sloan walk through the door," Shy mumbled.

"Wait, what?" Ellie shot back, turning in her seat to face her friends.

Courtney pinched Shy underneath the table.

"Ouch, bitch, quit pinching me!" Shy exclaimed.

"What are you talking about? Why would Sloan care about what Cass and Lola got going on?" Ellie asked.

Shy sipped her champagne, and Courtney opted for silence, but the shady essence between them told Ellie they were keeping secrets.

"Unt uh, bitches. What the fuck?" Ellie said, moving a seat closer to narrow the space between them. She leaned into her friends. "What is going on?"

Shy rolled her eyes. "I don't know why you and Sloan like to play stupid when it comes to this," Shy sighed. "You gonna sit there and tell me you don't know that Sloan is in love with your brother?"

Ellie jerked her head back. "Eww, no. He's like her brother, too. She don't want Cassidy's ass."

Shy rolled her eyes. "Okay, girl."

Ellie held up her hands innocently. "Come on, Court. Back me up here. They are literally like brother and sister."

Courtney gave a sour smile and leaned her head to the side as she said, "Ehh. I mean, their chemistry is kind of undeniable," Courtney added. "Think about it. Whenever they're in a room together, you feel that they're in the room together. And they always end up next to one another."

Ellie shook her head in denial.

"Yeah, nah. Y'all reading too much into this. Sloan knows how I feel about my brother and my friends. She literally wouldn't go there, and they're practically related," Ellie said. "Sloan is a second daughter to my parents. She always has been."

"Okay," Shy said, shrugging. "If you say so."

Ellie glanced back at Cassidy, who was conversing with Lola intimately. Ellie had always been the little sister who had to beat the girls off her brother. He had always been handsome, always rough, always alluring, always a ladies' man, and Ellie didn't play. She had never liked any of his little teenage girlfriends, and was always on guard when girls would want to befriend her because it was often to get to him. She had never had to worry about Sloan. Sloan never short-changed Ellie with false interest just to be in proximity to Cassidy. She never overloaded the conversation with questions about Cassidy's whereabouts or tried to milk her for information about him. If anything, they all hung out. They'd all play a game of Monopoly with real money that Cassidy funded. They would all go to the skating parties back in the day. Cassidy would be their ride back and forth to the movies before they could drive. Sometimes, Sloan and Cassidy would argue each other down, fighting like cats and dogs, similar to the way she, herself, would fight with Cassidy. Sloan was her sister; she was family. Ellie just couldn't see it.

"There goes your boy," Shy said. Ellie's eyes drifted from Cassidy to Loyal, and her stomach hollowed. He was just effortlessly fine in classic, tailored Ralph Lauren. She loved a man who wore a suit well. Wasn't shit worse than a baggy-ass suit or pants that were too tight and too short. Loyal was fitted to perfection. The black tuxedo looked like money against his rich skin. He was regal. He exuded power, and Ellie felt giddy at the sight of him. He greeted every person who stood in his path, giving them each a moment of his time. Everyone wanted a piece of him, and Ellie didn't want to crowd him, so she remained where she was. He got to the end of the entryway and paused, looking back as Tisa walked in. He held out his hand for her, and as Ellie took them in, her intuition went haywire. Tisa was just as beautiful as she had been at the charity event, only today she was formal, in a pearl-colored, silk, floor-length dress that complimented Loyal flawlessly. The dress was backless, and while most women relied on hips, ass, and titties to create their sex appeal, it was Tisa's back that made Ellie take pause. She was model-esque, with the most beautiful and sexy back Ellie had ever seen. *Not a damn back roll in sight*, Ellie thought in disgust. *Bitch.*

She was hating, and rightfully so, because Tisa was on the arm of her man. It was the way they moved in unison that tore Ellie's gut out. The way Tisa smiled and greeted his guests right along with him as if they were a power couple and this entire crowd was there to kiss the rings of the king and queen gave Ellie the damn bubble guts. He hadn't even panned the room with his eyes to search for her yet.

"Fix your face, bitch," Courtney said, giving Ellie the heads up that she was wearing her heart on her sleeve.

"And he said they're not together?" Shy leaned into her ear and whispered. "Look like they together to me."

Ellie wondered if she would stay or leave. She didn't want to seem childish or insecure, nor did she want to overreact. Even though inside, she was doing all three. She felt like she was watching another woman with her man, but she wondered if she had the roles misconstrued. Tisa had been there first. They shared a child. In fact, where was their child? Ellie hadn't met anyone of any significance in Loyal's life. Was his son being babysat by a doting grandmother? Were their sisters and brothers on standby for this lovely couple? Did they have an entire life together? Was there a village of love that supported them on occasions when they had to step out on the town? No one even knew about her. *I don't even know his son's name*, she thought.

As she watched Loyal escort Tisa around the room, she realized that Tisa wasn't the one in the way. His son's mother wasn't being let down gracefully, nor was he fulfilling one last promise. Loyal was flaunting Tisa like she was the completion of his missing puzzle, and she felt slighted because he had personally invited her to come watch. He was wearing her proudly like he couldn't possibly do this without her. It was known to be said that a man's best accessory was the woman he chose to put on his arm, and Loyal had blatantly chosen Tisa. Ellie was his best-kept secret. She was a good secret, too. The type of woman who left his bed and then attended his event and sat quietly in her place in the back. Humiliation filled her. *I really don't belong here*, she thought, feeling out of place. She thought she could handle this. She thought Loyal would be less connected to Tisa. She had assumed that he would make a point to lessen the affection. He knew that she was somewhere in this room, watching him, struggling with the sight of him being so intimate with another woman. Just from the glow on Tisa's face, Ellie knew that the girl was under Loyal's spell. She knew how easy it was to fall victim to his reveries because she was also under a trance. She wanted to be angry at him, but at her big, grown age, all she could do was be mad at herself.

"I'll be right back," Ellie said as she excused herself from the table. She couldn't get to the restroom quickly enough.

She rushed to the sink and gripped the porcelain edges as she sucked in a deep breath. In through her nose, out through her mouth. Stupid-ass shit didn't calm one fucking nerve. Shy walked into the bathroom moments later.

"Are you good?" Shy asked.

"I can't believe I fell for this shit," Ellie said, ashamed.

"Of course you did. You ain't been in the dating game as a grown woman. These niggas giving out dick and damage. Women aren't falling for that shit anymore, sis. He fine, he paid, you're vulnerable, and he clearly has a roster. He added you to it."

"I am too old to be in this bathroom, crying over a man," Ellie whispered. "The last time somebody's nappy-headed son had me holed up in a bathroom embarrassed was..."

"In 11th grade when Jeffrey Foster got caught two-timing yo' ass with Tamika Smith behind the bleachers at the homecoming dance. You tucked your tail then and let him and that ugly bitch win."

"She wasn't ugly, though," Ellie snickered.

"Bitch, let me add some razzle dazzle to my story to hype you up," Shy stated.

Ellie lifted her hands, giving Shy the floor. "My bad, girl, carry on."

Shy stepped behind Ellie and put her hands on her shoulders, forcing Ellie to look in the mirror.

"Now, look at yourself. You're freaking gorgeous. Much prettier than that long neck, big foot, fatback baby mama of his."

"But she's not any of those things," Ellie said, confused and frowning.

"You know what?" Shy said in frustration. "Fine, ho. Go out there and act like she's better than you then."

"Okay, okay, wait, hype me up again. You right. I'ma get it right this time. Fuck that bitch," Ellie stated half-heartedly.

Shy shook her head because Ellie wasn't giving the confidence she needed to give.

"Nah, say it with your chest, girl; put your whole titty in that shit. Fuck that bitch."

Ellie nodded, feeling a little more brazen.

"Fuck that bitch!" She smiled and shook her head because no matter the circumstance, Shy always had a way to make her girls smile.

"That's right. Fuck him and who?" Shy asked, waving her finger with attitude.

"Fuck him and his duck ass baby mama," Ellie snapped. "Lying-ass nigga."

Shy had gotten Ellie started.

"Let me get my shit together. He wants to play. Let's play." Ellie gave herself a once-over in the mirror, reaching inside the top of her dress to adjust her titties. She had been letting Loyal treat her like he was the prize. "Fuck all this sad shit. Nigga got me fucked up."

Shy smiled and snatched open the door.

"That's my bitch!" she cheered, whispering as they walked out of the bathroom.

Ellie walked back onto the main museum floor, and her resolve was dissolving by the second. He was so damn fine, and she was so jealous she almost couldn't contain it.

She walked over to the bar for a little liquid courage. "Lychee martini, please, with a sugar rim," she ordered.

"You mind if I squeeze in here?"

She smelled the gentleman behind her before he spoke. Whatever he wore was intoxicating, and she turned to take him in. He was the perfect distraction. He was a little light skin, but he had an edge to him that gave dominant energy. She moved her clutch from the space beside her and he eased in next to her.

"Thanks," he said. "You're lovely, by the way."

It was such a gentle compliment that Ellie smiled genuinely. She blushed.

"Thank you," she said.

"I'm Rich," the man introduced.

"Elliot," she returned. "So, do you work for Loyal?"

"With Loyal, on a few projects. I own a bank. We finance a lot of the projects Loyal does. We just broke ground on a 100-million-dollar apartment community in downtown Ann Arbor," Rich informed.

"Wow, that's impressive," Ellie replied.

"We do alright," Rich smiled. "What charity you playing for?"

"You know what? I am the wrong person to even indulge in this little game because I have no idea how to play any of this stuff. I don't gamble, so..."

"That means you'll have beginner's luck then," Rich proposed. "Let's spin the block a little, and I'll teach you."

The bartender delivered her drink, and she picked it up. "Why not?"

Two could play the game Loyal had started. They walked side by side, and Ellie allowed him to guide her to the blackjack table.

"Doesn't this include counting? I'm not the girl who can add numbers up in her head at the drop of a dime and calculate the probability of the next card. I went to Vegas once and lost all my money," Ellie said, grimacing in shame. "This requires skill."

"I'm very skilled with numbers. I've got you covered, I promise," he chuckled.

She sat, and he stood behind her chair, reaching over her to place her wager. Ellie sipped her drink, long and hard because she felt the pressure as he placed a large stack of chips in front of her.

"Rich, are you sure?" she asked.

"I think you're lady luck," he whispered in her ear.

Five other players sat beside her, and the dealer began.

"Why am I so nervous?" Ellie asked.

"That's natural. Everybody else is just playing it cool," he chuckled, leaning over her. "You can't let the house intimidate you."

"But I'm so intimidated," she exclaimed, giggling as she sipped her drink. The alcohol was an instant anxiety reliever. She noticed his hands were tattooed as he reached over her to stack more chips in front of her.

*Oh yeah, he's sexy*, she thought.

"Good luck on your Ace," the dealer told her as he flipped the first card over in front of her.

Rich leaned down and whispered in her ear, "I'd hit that."

Ellie blushed, and then her heart galloped as Loyal stepped up in place of the dealer and said, "It'll be the last card you ever play, my boy. Nice try, though. She's taken."

"Of course she is. I thought I'd gotten lucky. No disrespect," Rich said, laughing as he stepped back. "Let me get that chair, beautiful."

Ellie didn't move. She looked at Loyal in challenge.

"I mean, how would he know? You're pretty preoccupied, and from the looks of things, you have your hands full," Ellie shot back.

"Yo, E, you supposed to be risking chips, not lives," he stated. "Come dance with me, gorgeous, so I can make it clear for you."

Ellie sipped her drink and then took it with her as she lifted from the table.

She sipped it once more, and he took it from her hands, placing it on the tray of a passing waiter. He led her to the heated glass atrium.

Christmas lights illuminated the space, and she looked up at the stars through the glass ceiling.

"Nice event," she said curtly.

"It was about to get ugly if you kept flirting with my mans," Loyal said, brow bent. She reached for his forehead and smoothed the lines from it with soft hands.

"I'm surprised you noticed," she said. "You seem happy with the date you came with. You didn't even come speak to me."

"I didn't see you, E," Loyal said, honestly.

"You didn't come looking either," Ellie shot back. "And the hand on the small of her back? Can we not do that again?" They stood in the middle of the room. They were supposed to be dancing, but he just stood there, in front of her, body to body, staring down at her.

Loyal wrapped one arm around her body and placed his hand on the small of her back. He pulled her into him, and she felt his natural affinity to her presence.

"Yes, ma'am, it won't happen again," Loyal stated. "You in that dress. It's..." He shook his head as if he had no words. "...a problem."

She smiled.

"It makes niggas think about what's under the dress, E. I been doing business with Rich for ten years, and tomorrow, I'ma find a new bank. You can't be flirting with niggas in here. Your jealousy leads to pouted lips. My jealousy leads to much, much worse," he stated. "Nigga thinking about fucking you, and I ain't feeling it."

"It's just a dress," Ellie snickered, taking her pointer finger and touching his lips. The pressure of her body against his—the way his dick reacted to her and the way he made sure she felt it. "It doesn't have that much power."

"It's the body in the dress..." He shook his head again. He backed her against the wall and devoured her lips. "You taste so fucking good, E," he whispered as he raised one thigh.

"What's going on with you and Tisa? It feels like we're sneaking away in empty rooms, so we don't get caught," Ellie said.

"I'm just being respectful, E," he said.

"To her," Ellie said, eyes narrowing in disbelief as she eased from beneath him and began to walk away. He pulled her hand, forcing her back to him.

"Loyal, just go back to your party." She was disappointed as she rubbed her arms.

"Loyal? Baby, are you back here?"

Ellie was mortified as Tisa walked into the secluded room, eyeing them suspiciously.

"There you are," Tisa said, looking back and forth. "What's back here?" Tisa asked, eyes never leaving Ellie.

"Tis, this is Elliot. We've been spending some time together," Loyal introduced, taking a neutral step away from Ellie. "E, this is my son's mother, Tisa."

"I'm sorry, I don't mean to be rude, but I just sweet-talked the building commissioner of Macomb County for you. I know you've been trying to get a meeting with him. He wants to meet you. I sat him at our table. You need to stop hiding in corners and get in there," Tisa suggested.

"Nah, I'm good right here," Loyal stated. "I'll catch up with him another time." Loyal answered, looking at Ellie. "I'm busy. I'm trying to enjoy my night. Tell that nigga to grab a shrimp cocktail or something and enjoy his, too," Loyal said.

"Loyal, if you impress him tonight, that's hundreds of millions of dollars in construction jobs secured," Tisa said under her breath.

Ellie interjected, "No, please. I'm a big girl. Go handle your business. I'll be here."

She wanted him to stay, but she didn't want to make it seem like he had to babysit her all night. Loyal walked off with Tisa, and Ellie lingered in the private room to admire the art. She wasn't too thrilled to watch Tisa work the room on Loyal's behalf, so she opted for the more private experience. When Tisa reappeared, she caught Ellie by surprise.

"You're Cassidy's sister, right?" Tisa asked as she passed Ellie a champagne flute. There was a smile on Tisa's face that Ellie couldn't decipher. She didn't know if Tisa was being nice nasty or willfully obtuse.

Ellie wanted to bite back, "No, Loyal's girlfriend," but they hadn't decided on titles, and girlfriend sounded childish when speaking to the woman who had given him a son. She wanted to follow Loyal's lead and keep this thing between her and Tisa positive. She respected him enough to not blow up his relationship with his baby mama— at least she was trying to. She wasn't a young girl anymore. In her 20s, she would have been ready to take it wherever it needed to go over that man, but she was supposed to be grown. She was supposed to come into his life and bring peace, not spark a war. For lack of a better introduction, Ellie responded, "Yeah, Cass is my brother."

"I'm sorry about everything you've got going on. That little thing with your husband. Yikes," Tisa said, gritting her perfect veneers. "Loyal is always in a charitable mood. Glad he was able to give away those tickets to your daughters to make them feel better. I wasn't feeling too well. He knows I hate those games. Glad they went to good use."

Ellie frowned. *Here we go*, she thought, knowing that Loyal had been too optimistic about how this night would go.

"Yeah, it was great. My girls loved sitting courtside, but I didn't see much of the game. Loyal was so nice that he showed me the suite. Robert and Tracy were nice enough to keep the girls on the floor. Everybody had a memorable night," Ellie's subtle jab landed with precision. She didn't have to say too much. One thing a woman was going to do was fill in her own blanks. Ellie hadn't even slept with Loyal that night, but Tisa was running a movie in her head.

Tisa sipped from her champagne glass.

"He's a gentleman that way," Tisa said affectionately, giggling. "I remember the first time he asked me for a threesome. I was so nervous to try something new. Scared he would like it too much. I asked myself a hundred questions." She smiled sheepishly as she listed them off. "What if he sleeps with this girl behind my back? What if I'm expected to go down on her?" She shrugged. "Although, I quickly got over that. I truly overthought it. He's found girl after girl; we've done this many times. He's never doubled back for any of them, and the orgasm is top-tier. Give a man a fantasy, and he'll maintain your dream."

Ellie played it cool on the outside, but her mind was going haywire. Was Loyal grooming her for an indecent proposal? *He's met my kids. He knows this can't be casual for me. He wouldn't do that.*

"We even kept one around for almost six months. Took vacations and all, but at the end of the day, he and I only need one another. We're just having fun before baby number two arrives, and I'll need someone to relieve my stress when those hormones are going crazy."

Ellie felt like Tisa had wrapped her hands around her neck.

"You're pregnant?"

"Not yet, but actively trying. That's why we were late. Something about Loyal and car sex before a big event," Tisa said giggling. The revelation made Ellie sick to her stomach. "We want to be pregnant within the next few months."

It was the actively trying that fucked Ellie up. She knew that Loyal had been intimate with Tisa, but she had just given her body to him the night before. She had assumed his intentions with her were pure, but to hop out of bed with her and inside another woman was hurtful, to say the least. It was fucking nasty and irresponsible, to say the most. Ellie was sick to her stomach, and everything in her wanted to cuss this bitch out.

"Men are cool, but I promise you there is nothing like getting your body catered to by a woman, and let's face it, I'm not going to want to have sex all the time when I'm in my second and third trimester, so he'll have needs. He wants my approval with you, and I approve. You're pretty enough, but I see stars in your eyes, so let me have this conversation with you now. This can be enjoyable for everyone involved, but don't forget, you're replaceable." Tisa lifted her flute to Ellie. "Salud," she said before walking away.

"You look...wow..."

Courtney sat at the bar, waiting impatiently as she scrolled through her social media timeline. Shy had quickly become a social butterfly in this room, but Courtney was more reserved. James hadn't arrived yet, and she was beginning to wonder if he was going to show up at all. She turned toward the man beside her. The compliment was rare. She was the friend in the friend group who never took center stage. Her self-esteem had always been an issue. She had come up when people thought, "Oh, she's pretty for a dark-skinned girl," was a compliment and not an insult. Everyone around her had always commented about her appearance. Her grandmother had given her a complex about her hyper-pigmented skin. Her elbows and knees were always too dark. Her hair was always too short and nappy, and her body was always too thin. It wasn't even society that had ingrained unrealistic beauty standards on her, her complex for what was deemed beautiful came from the hood. The phrase, "It be your own folks," had never rang truer. Courtney had made some very damaging decisions in her formative years, chasing love and acceptance. It was how she had fallen for James in the first place. While boys her age had called her ugly her whole life while praising all the light-skinned girls on the block, James had come into her life and told her she was beautiful. He had showered her with attention, but as a teen, she didn't recognize that he was sexualizing her before her time. He always told her she looked sweet. "The darker the berry, the sweeter the juice," he would say. She remembered him spending the first three months of their relationship, sneaking her to hotel rooms and going down on her. She was fourteen years old when they met. He was 24, and the things he exposed her to made her feel a mixture of power, dirtiness, euphoria, and shame. The first time he went down on her, she remembered the orgasm had blown her mind, but she had gone a week avoiding his calls afterward out of pure confusion and embarrassment. He caught her on her way to school one morning and convinced her to get in the car with him so he could apologize. His form of apology was oral sex.

He turned Courtney out before she was even old enough to understand why it felt so good, and her virginity was given freely. She was pregnant before she hit tenth grade. James got a job in construction, and it paid more than either of them were used to. He took care of her and their son, upgraded her wardrobe, sent her to the hair salon weekly, and bought her gold rings and necklaces. Suddenly, the dark-skinned girl who nobody saw as beautiful was the most popular chick her age on the block. Having her first son at a young age thickened her out, and she had been known as "that bad-ass young chick James got pregnant." Those moments stuck to her like glue. She revisited the history of their relationship in her mind often. Sometimes, it brought her to tears. Sometimes, it brought laughter. Today, as this random man stood next to her in his fancy suit and hopeful eyes as he shot his shot, it made her feel resentful. Courtney didn't have a history of dating. She had only experienced one man. She had given up her entire youth to commit to James and their family, only for them to end up miserable together. She didn't necessarily see herself as a victim. Sure, he was older than her, but she justified it in her mind that it was just how things were back in the day. *I was a willing participant*, she thought. She hadn't grasped the fact that she was groomed. So many women couldn't see their own victimization at the hands of men who had plucked them from the vine too early.

"You care to finish that sentence?" she asked, giving a half-hearted smile.

"I was going to say beautiful, but it doesn't even describe you. I saw you all the way across the room, and it took me ten minutes to work up the nerve to come speak."

She frowned.

"Laying it on kind of thick, aren't you?"

"Not even a little," the man replied. He pushed his glasses up on the bridge of his nose. "I would shake your hand, but my palms are sweaty. I'm Harlow."

"Courtney," she replied shortly.

"You work for the company?" Harlow asked.

She shook her head. "No, I was invited by an employee, but it looks like I've been stood up," she replied, shrugging.

"It's crazy that someone who looks like you would even assume that," Harlow said, chuckling. "The poor guy probably caught a flat tire or something."

"Yeah, poor guy," Courtney replied sarcastically.

"Can I buy you a drink?" Harlow asked.

"It's an open bar," Courtney answered, smiling.

"See, I'm nervous," Harlow chuckled, wiping his sweaty palms against his designer slacks. She smiled. "Okay, how about this? Can I join you and have a few minutes of your time? Maybe after a freaking drink, I might be able to form a sentence that doesn't come out all fucked up and weird."

Courtney laughed and nodded her head in compliance.

"Let's give it a try."

"Thanks for cutting me a break," Harlow answered. "I'm afraid my brother got all the luck with the girls. I've always been his geeky sidekick."

"Who's your brother?" Courtney asked, laughing.

"Loyal Brier. He owns the company," Harlow stated. "That guy right there." Harlow pointed to Loyal, and Courtney nodded.

"He invited my friend, Ellie. Small world," Courtney shot back. Courtney took Harlow in. His presence was easy, a little quirky, but enjoyable still. His tree bark-colored skin made Courtney want to see his mother because she had birthed two different shades of melanin, and she couldn't help but wonder what their creator looked like. The one thing that matched were those signature dimples. When he smiled, they pushed into his cheeks deeply.

"What can I get you?" he asked.

"French 75," she replied.

He motioned for the bartender, and Courtney watched curiously.

"Hey, my man, what's your name?" Harlow asked.

"Jake," the bartender replied.

"Good to meet you, Jake. Can I get a French 75 and a Coke for me," he ordered.

"Right away, sir," the bartender spoke.

"No sir necessary. That's for Loyal. Just Harlow is fine," he said, smiling graciously as he removed a money clip from his pocket and placed a generous tip on the bar top.

His confidence was loud but not overwhelming. He handled people with authority but also with respect. Courtney took notes in her head.

"Just a Coke?" she asked.

"Yeah, I don't drink," Harlow stated.

"Like ever?" she asked.

His eyes lit up in amusement at the judgment in her tone. "Is that a bad thing?"

Courtney shook her head. "I mean, no, I just didn't expect that."

"I mean, I'll have one every now and again, but I drove, so you know...it's the law and all," he said.

She was tickled, and it showed.

"Law-abiding citizen. That's good to know." He nodded proudly, making her smile more. "Do you work for Brier Investments too?" Courtney asked.

Harlow shook his head. "No, I'm in Tech. Mostly, software and app design at the moment," he said. "How about you? How do you spend your days?"

Courtney hesitated because she was almost embarrassed to say. She had no success story, no real accomplishments that were impressive enough to throw out over casual conversation.

"A little of this and a little of that," she said, keeping it light.

"You're going to make me work for the good stuff, huh?" he asked.

"Absolutely," she returned. It was an easy conversation, and she was grateful for the company. It distracted her from the disappointment that filled her as every second ticked by.

"I'm trying to figure out the most intriguing three questions I can ask you before your late date arrives and I miss my shot," Harlow said as Jake came back with their drinks. She accepted hers and looked out over the room once more. She sipped her drink as she thought of James. Her disappointment was palpable.

The band played a classic 90's cut, and Courtney nodded, tapping her red-painted nails against the champagne glass in unison to the beat.

"You like this song?" He noticed, observing her.

"Can't go wrong with a little Mint Condition," she said.

"You want to dance?" he asked.

Courtney glanced around once more.

"I mean, you can wait, or you can dance?" Harlow invited.

Courtney sighed, releasing the anxiety that had built in her all night. Dancing beat looking pathetic at the bar. She felt like everyone could tell she had been stood up.

"I'd love to dance."

She stood from the barstool and downed the rest of her drink before he took her hand and led her to the floor. He was huge. Height and stature, he dwarfed her. He had some weight on him like he was supposed to be on someone's offensive line instead of behind a computer.

"Is this too close?" he asked as he put his hand on the small of her back and pulled her in. Whatever he wore instantly enveloped her in a hug. He smelled divine, and his arms were strong. He was so big he felt like a fortress, like he could hide her behind his hold of protection and grant access as she deemed fit.

"No," she said. She placed her hands on his lapel as they swayed to the music.

"I'm trying to think of the most interesting questions I can ask you before I miss my shot," Harlow said as he looked down at her.

"Oh Lord," she replied, a bit nervous.

"This might be my only chance to get to know you. Can't ask the wrong thing. The questions are important," he joked.

"You right, they are," she agreed. He was pulling easy smiles out of her. This was the most carefree time she had experienced in years. There was something about a man flirting innocently with a woman that felt natural. The way he looked at her. The effort in the way he chose his words. The exhibition of the best version of himself. Courtney hadn't experienced this, well, ever. She was a grown-ass woman who had never dated. She had never even allowed a man to pursue her because she had an old head at home who she never wanted to upset. She had always tried to prove to James she was good enough. She had always chased him. She had always earned him. Usually, with sex. Her currency to the relationship was keeping him pleased. She had never felt this dynamic, and it was so carefree and fun that it made her feel something she hadn't felt before. The power of femininity. He desired her, and not just her body. He wanted her conversation. He wanted to learn her. It felt organic.

"What's your favorite movie?" he asked.

"Really? That's the question you came up with?" she asked, hollering in amusement.

"Dawg, that's one of the most important questions a man needs to know! That can establish a lot out the gate. Two people who like totally different movies can lead to a lifetime of miserable-ass movie dates," he reasoned.

She nodded.

"True, true," she agreed, tickled. "Okayyy, so I got a few. Can I give you top three?"

"The fact that you need to pick three is a plus," he shot back as he spun her on beat to the music and then pulled her right back to safety.

"*The Devil Wears Prada*..." she answered, looking to the sky as she thought of the other two.

"A chick flick, but Meryl Streep can never be a wrong answer," he commented.

"Hmm, let's see... *Titanic*," she continued.

"I'm seeing a painful pattern here," he said, gritting his teeth.

"What?" she exclaimed. "*Titanic* is a classic!"

"Long-ass romance where my boy got the short end of the stick at the end. She could have shared the damn door," Harlow criticized.

Courtney hadn't smiled this much in her entire life.

"Okay, okay, my final choice," she said, thinking hard. "Denzel; *Remember the Titans*."

"There she go," he said in approval. "You saved it with that one. We might be able to catch a movie or two."

"Yeah, maybe," she said, whimsically as she stared up at him.

Courtney blushed as he bent down to whisper in her ear. "I'd really like the opportunity to take you out. I think you're beautiful. Way too beautiful to be waiting on anyone to show up. If there is a ring, I'd like to throw my hat in, even if it's just casual, like friends enjoying a bad romance."

Courtney inhaled sharply, and before she could answer, she felt a tap on her shoulder. She turned to find Shy standing there.

"I'm sorry to interrupt," she said. Shy stepped closer to her and whispered, "Bitch, James is here. He's by the bar."

Courtney's body stiffened and she came back to reality as she took a step back from Harlow.

"Thanks for the dance, Harlow," she said.

"Anytime," he said, nodding as he placed a hand over his heart.

Courtney walked away and there was a sense of urgency pushing her high heels across the dance floor. She felt like she had been caught cheating, and from the look on James' face, he felt like she had, too.

"Hey," she greeted. "I didn't think you were coming."

She hated how nervous she felt, how sour her stomach was. Her entire nervous system activated at the anticipation of his reaction.

"Yeah, I can see that," James replied dryly as he swallowed the stiff drink he had in his hand. "Who the fuck is that nigga?"

"He's nobody. I just met him. He just asked me to dance, that's all," Courtney said.

James didn't rush to respond, and she knew his silence was purposeful. He always weaponized his engagement with her, and it always worked. Her worry over what he might be thinking sent her body into overdrive. He was angry.

"James?" she whispered.

"You lucky I ain't slapped the shit out you yet," James said, without looking at her.

"Why are you mad? You were late. It was innocent," she defended. She was in distress, so she was naturally louder than she intended to be.

"Lower your motherfucking voice," James sneered, grabbing her waist, and digging his fingers into it painfully as he discreetly pulled her closer.

"Are you drunk? Did you come here drunk? What is wrong with you?" she cried, eyes watering.

"Bring your ass outside, let me talk to you," he said. It was the way he spoke to her that revealed his disdain.

"I'm not going outside," she said.

"Oh, you not?" he asked, challenging her.

"No, I'm not going outside with you," Courtney hissed. "I'm done with this shit. I should have never even accepted this invitation. I thought you would try. I thought we would both try." Her eyes were betraying her, and she didn't want to cry in the middle of this event.

"Bitch, you ain't trying, you in here hoeing," James said. It was sinister the way he could undo her without raising his tone.

"Because of a dance? I'm a ho now? Okay," she said, scoffing. "I can't talk to you when you're on this level." She knew she needed to be the one to keep a level head because engaging would only add fuel to his fire. He had decided her intent the moment he laid eyes on her on that dance floor. They would have a blowout fight, and he wouldn't come out of this vengeful rage until after it had already gone too far. It was the cycle of their entire relationship. She didn't want to do it here. She was tired of doing it at all.

"Probably sucked that nigga off in the bathroom," James said. He was going lower and lower, and Courtney was on the verge of tears.

"Everything good over here?"

Courtney was so grateful when Loyal stepped between them and motioned for the bartender.

"Let's get my guy here a ginger ale," Loyal ordered.

"Everything's good, man. Thanks for inviting me and my girl. This is…"

"Courtney. Yeah, we've met," Loyal said.

"Met when?" James asked, unable to holster his jealousy.

Loyal turned sharp eyes to James because he heard the undertone of unreasonable jealousy. "Yo, my nigga. You coming in here with too much heat on your chest. That's a mistake," Loyal said, holding out his hand for a shake. James reluctantly took his hand and Loyal squeezed that hand so tightly that it felt like James' bones were breaking. "I know you said you getting some things together up top, my nigga. Don't let your mind get too lost that you forget where you at and who you talking to," Loyal whispered. Loyal took a step back and turned to Courtney. "James is going to let you enjoy the rest of the night with your girls. I need him to handle something for me. I'm not sure if he told you, but he's the new general foreman of one of my construction sites."

Courtney was uneasy as she replied, "No, I didn't know that. That's amazing. Congrats, babe."

James' nostrils flared, but he replied, "Yeah, that's what I invited you here to tell you. That I'm working on some stuff."

"You got a lot of work to do," Loyal stated in a tone that implied so much more. "Hard work. Let me walk you out and let you know what I need you to do. Court, I'm sorry to have to end y'all night early, but if he gon' be the boss, this can't wait. I think Ellie's looking for you."

Courtney nodded as she watched James and Loyal exit.

Ellie browsed through the room, admiring the art as she called Sloan for the third time.

"Girl, where are you? This nigga's baby mama just said some shit to me that fucked my mind up! I need youuu. I'm so confused," Ellie hissed into the phone. She hadn't worked up the nerve to return to the main ballroom, instead, she gave Loyal the space to be the boss as she processed Tisa's words.

A threesome? It was so far out of bounds for a woman like Ellie. She loved good dick, but she didn't want to share it. She wanted to confront Loyal, but she didn't want to bring drama to this classy event. Opting to stay out of the way felt like the right move. She kept waiting for him to come back and check on her, but after half an hour of solitude, she figured that he would be monopolized for most of the evening.

"Ellie!" she turned to find Courtney yelling her name frantically.

She rushed to the hallway. "What? What's wrong?" Ellie asked. She could hear the panic in her friend's voice, and without even knowing what was wrong, she knew something was off.

"Ellie, I think Loyal is putting James out," Courtney panted frantically.

"What happened?" Ellie exclaimed.

"He's tripping. He showed up over an hour late and walked in on some jealous shit because I was dancing with Loyal's brother."

"His brother?" Ellie shot back, trying to follow the chain of events. Ellie didn't even know Loyal had a brother.

"James is drunk, and he was a little aggressive, but…"

Ellie's face twisted up. "Aggressive? But nothing. He got aggressive with you?" Ellie asked.

"He wasn't going to do anything. He just gets like this. He gets mean, and he makes threats, but…"

"Bitch, if you excuse his bullshit one more time," Ellie fussed. "Where is he?" Ellie demanded.

Ellie went storming off for the front door as Courtney trailed after her, trying to explain away the situation.

"Ellie, you don't understand. You and Loyal getting involved only makes it worse; please, just get Loyal. I can handle James," Courtney pleaded.

Ellie pushed through the front doors and caught Loyal just as he was putting James inside a car.

"James! You threatened her, nigga?" Ellie shouted.

"Ellie!" Courtney shouted. "Please!"

"Whoa, whoa, whoa, whoa," Loyal said, intercepting Ellie and all her rage. He turned back to the car. "Close the door and get him out of here," Loyal instructed the driver.

Courtney was mortified.

"Courtney, baby, can we just go home? We doing this in

front of all these people. Just come home. I'm drunk. You took my baby and just left. I'm going crazy," James said.

Courtney looked at Ellie in confusion.

"Maybe I should just go home with him. This is embarrassing. Y'all shouldn't have to be involved in this."

"You're not going anywhere with him. She's not coming. Courtney protects your ass, James. She keeps a lot of shit to herself, and I know she do. We're all over the place, so we miss a lot of bullshit that you take her through, but we're all right here this time. We not letting her miss shit. We not taking no excuses as to why she can't show up. One missed phone call, and we're coming to wherever she is. You touch another hair on her head, and I'ma kill you myself, you piece of fucking shit!"

Loyal pulled her hand aggressively and forced her to turn to him.

"You've made your point, E. You ain't wrong, but that's enough," he said. Loyal closed the door and hit the roof of the truck with one hand. "Get him home." He turned to the valet and handed one of the men James' ticket. "Get his car and follow the truck to his address. Ride back with my driver."

Ellie was on fire. She pulled her hand from his and shook her head. "Why are you protecting him?"

"I'm not protecting him. He's going through a rough time, E. Let that nigga sleep it off. Cooler heads will prevail in the morning." Loyal was a leader. He was a thinker, and right now, he was her enemy.

"Fuck what he's going through," she whispered. Ellie turned back to Courtney and wrapped an arm around Courtney's shoulder before they walked back inside together.

As soon as they stepped inside the warm building, Shy was coming out the ballroom. "I've been looking everywhere for y'all. What the hell happened?" Shy asked.

"You don't want to know. Go line up the shots, y'all. We deserve them. I'll be right in," Ellie said.

"I'll fill you in, girl," Courtney stated as the pair walked off.

Ellie felt Loyal's hand on the small of her back, and she turned to him.

"We need to talk," she said.

Loyal shook his head. "You look like you got a lot to say, and I'm almost certain I'ma hear it all, but can we table it, E? I just want to enjoy the rest of my night with my girl."

Ellie scoffed and shook her head. "Which is who, Loyal? Because right now, I'm feeling like you're trying to play me, and I'm not feeling it." She walked away, entering the ballroom, and his voice halted her.

"Elliot!"

She turned around. His baritone echoed through the room, and everyone gave him their full attention as uncertainty clung to the air.

*I know this nigga is not making a scene*, she thought, embarrassed but standing her ground.

"What, Loyal? What do you want from me?" She shouted back. Yup, they were making a scene. Lights, camera, action in this bitch.

The way he took his time crossing the floor to get to her drove Ellie insane. He was so damn arrogant. It was like he knew she wouldn't dare move until he released her. The entire room was watching, and she was annoyed because the way she felt, she wanted to cuss his ass out. The notion of being propositioned for a threesome kept playing in her head.

"I don't know what I did to piss you off," he said as he stood toe to toe with her.

"Why don't you ask Tisa?" Ellie asked.

"I'm asking you. Ain't nobody in this but me and you, so if you listening to anybody else, that's your first mistake," he said.

"Yeah, well, your actions speak volumes too. Nobody in this room even knows I belong to you," she said.

The band returned to playing at a reduced volume to try to shift the attention away from the bickering couple. Ellie was grateful because the partygoers went back to their own business once they realized nothing explosive was going to occur.

"We're fighting in the middle of my party. I think it's pretty clear who you belong to," Loyal replied, annoyed as he rubbed one hand down his wavy head.

"Is it? Because I'm so fucking confused," Ellie retorted, shaking her head.

Loyal tilted her chin toward the ceiling, and she noticed the mistletoe that was hanging from the ceiling around the chandelier. She didn't even know how she had missed it before. It was hanging from every chandelier in the room.

When he finessed her chin back down, his lips were there.

She forgot why she was fucking mad. The band increased their volume as Loyal kissed her under the mistletoe. She had never understood the hype around this Christmas tradition, but the way her heart fluttered in this moment, she got it now. It was the most romantic and simple kiss she had ever experienced. *You can't fall in love with this man. YOU CAN NOT FALL IN LOVE WITH THIS MAN. BITCH, TAKE YOUR LIPS BACK.*

Ellie was fighting a losing battle in her head. His dominance was all over her. He commanded her mind and body. It was in the way he held her to his body. It was in the way they exchanged breaths. It was in the way that he held onto her neck like he was the ruler who decided when and where he would have her, and she was his willing subject. He wanted her here. He wanted her now. He was clearing shit up. Baby mama or no baby mama, Loyal Brier had his sights set on Ellie. She was trapped.

*All I do is think of you…day and nightttt*

"Whatever she told you, unhear that shit," he whispered. He only pulled back long enough to speak the words. Ellie was floating. She absolutely hated how new this felt. It was illogical. It was young bitch shit. It was so irresponsible, and still, she was allowing it to happen. She could see the red flags from the backseat of the car. They were waving in the wind in the distance and Ellie was anticipating it like the carnival. She wanted all parts of this man. He gave her a feeling she hadn't had since she was a young girl. The feeling of possibility. She was sure if she were in high school, his name would be all over her notebooks with hearts around it by now. Ellie told herself she could handle him, that she could control this thing, whatever it was. Just have fun. This can be fun. No strings. No expectations. Stop listening to the promises. Just enjoy it for what it is. "It's clear now," he said. Only it wasn't. It so wasn't.

# CHAPTER 18

Sloan heard her phone going off and she couldn't bring herself to check it. She knew she was supposed to be at the Christmas party with her girls, but facing anyone besides God right now felt impossible. She held onto the shower wall in front of her as she lowered her head, sobbing. She had scrubbed all the blood from her hands, but she just didn't feel clean. In all her career, she had never lost a patient. There had been miscarriages. There had been ectopic pregnancies. There had even been some close calls during deliveries, and she acknowledged those traumas in women, but this was her first time losing a patient that she had grown close to. She had begun this journey with Monica and her husband, John, from egg retrieval until Monica's very last breath. Sloan had performed a flawless C-section and brought a beautiful baby boy into the world, but the mother to this new soul hadn't survived. Sloan was sick. It was a feeling she couldn't quite describe. She hadn't done anything wrong. She had done her job to perfection— if there ever was such a thing. Sometimes, modern medicine just wasn't enough. It seemed so unfair more Black women lost their lives during childbirth than any other group of women. She was like a zombie as she grabbed her towel and exited the community shower. She dressed slowly, putting on fresh scrubs before she walked out. She couldn't go home. Being alone would make it worse. There was only one person who could make it better, and although there were a thousand reasons why she should stay away from him, she just couldn't, not today, not after this loss. She knew it wasn't fair to treat him like an emotional buffet. She came and went as she pleased, choosing the parts of him that she wanted most, but leaving the rest behind. He would have every right to send her away, but she prayed he wouldn't. She drove to the party in scrubs because she didn't have time to change, and she didn't have time to overthink this. She needed him. When she arrived, she felt foolish. The red carpet set the tone, and here she was in medical scrubs, a doctor's coat, a bare face, and a curly, wet ponytail. "Damn it," she muttered as she picked up her phone and called Cassidy's number. It rang to voicemail, and she immediately tried Ellie. Voicemail. "Come on, somebody, answer the phone," she fussed. When she discovered Courtney and Shy were dead ends, too, she knew she was going to have to go inside. She looked so out of place as she climbed out of her car.

"Ma'am, are you in the right place? This is the Brier Annual Christmas party," the attendant informed as he looked at her skeptically.

She nodded and stared up at the large museum then walked inside.

She felt like a fool as people stared at her as she entered. Her eyes bounced around the room for Cassidy, and the pangs of emotions dinging in her chest caused a nausea that was almost crippling. She found Ellie first, and she rushed over to her, interrupting what appeared like an intimate dance.

"I'm so sorry to interrupt," Sloan whispered, eyes tearing up. "Ellie, I need you."

Ellie frowned in confusion as she took in her friend's sudden appearance. Ellie looked at Loyal apologetically and said, "I'm sorry, give me a minute."

Ellie took Sloan's hand, and Sloan laced her fingers inside her friend's. Cass might not be there, but Ellie was, and she was nobody's substitute, the love was soothing in a different way. Sloan followed her to the hallway where there were less people, and she broke down. She was a mess. She covered her eyes and cried as Ellie stood, confused, but available to her friend. Ellie wrapped her arms around Sloan.

"Sloan," Ellie whispered. "What's wrong?"

Sloan was so distraught that Ellie led her to a portion of the museum that was roped off. She knew she would need backup for this. Sloan wasn't the friend who showed her weaknesses. She could only remember a few instances where Sloan had revealed this much emotion, and it was only under the most extreme circumstances. Whenever Sloan had a breakdown like this, it was usually related to her mother. Ellie texted Loyal to send her friends out, and within minutes, Courtney and Shy were at her side. Sloan sat on a bench and sobbed as they gathered around her. They were speechless, and they knew not to say a word until Sloan got it all out. If they spoke too soon, Sloan would try to bottle it all up to appear strong, and she deserved this release. Every woman deserves to take their cape off sometimes. Sloan had been carrying a lot ever since her mother died, and finally, she had decided to lean on her friends for help.

Sloan struggled to pull her shit together. She sat there a full ten minutes, crying until she was able to breathe through it.

"I'm so embarrassed," she whispered.

"Don't be," Courtney encouraged, rubbing her back.

"What happened?" Shy asked.

"So much has happened. I don't even know where to start. I lost a patient a few hours ago, and it just cracked my chest wide opennnn," Sloan cried, losing control again. "I just needed one person. He can take it all away, and he told me to come, and I missed him. He's gone, and it's too late,"

"Who, Sloan?" Ellie asked.

"Ohhh my goodness, Elliot!" Shy shouted in exasperation.

"She came here for Cass," Courtney said softly.

Ellie looked at Sloan, stunned as Sloan's jaw quivered.

"You're here for Cassidy?" Ellie asked. Ellie turned in her seat so that she was facing Sloan. Sloan couldn't even deny it. She wore her guilt all over her. "You're fucking my brother? So what? This friendship has been fake all this time? You get close to me to get close to him? How long has this been going on?" Ellie asked. She looked around at Shy and Courtney. "And of course, I'm the last one to know."

"I love him," Sloan admitted in an exhausted tone. "I'm completely in love with him, Ellie. I want to tell you it just started when I saw him this week again for the first time, but I don't want to lie to you. I've loved him since we were in middle school."

"You're unbelievable," Ellie stated. "I thought you were my friend."

"I am!" Sloan defended. "I am your friend, Ellie. Why does it have to be one or the other?"

"It just does, Sloan! You used me to get close to Cass, just like all those other girls. They didn't see value in me! They didn't want real friendship with me. They just wanted him. You're no different," Ellie stated as she stood.

Sloan knew she would react poorly; it was why she had hidden her feelings all these years.

"I'ma do you a favor. You don't have to worry about a friendship, sis, because I can't trust you. You're in the clear. You can choose Cass like you been wanting to all this time," Ellie spat.

"Ellie!" Courtney called after her as she stormed off.

Shy and Courtney sat around Sloan, and Sloan shook her head. She was distraught.

"This shit is a disaster," she whispered, wiping her nose with her sleeve.

"Yeah, pretty much, but she'll be alright. You know how Ellie is. Let her calm down and come to her senses," Courtney said.

"But about you and Cass..."

Sloan shook her head. "I had my reasons before why me

and Cassidy shouldn't do this. This is just one more reason. I was right, y'all. I should have just followed my first mind. If I have to choose between Ellie and Cassidy, I'm going to always choose my friend. She's my sister. I need her," Sloan cried, getting emotional all over again.

"He left here with Lola, Sloan," Shy whispered. Sloan's reaction was pure devastation. Of course, he did. Lola made it easy for him. Lola didn't push him away. Lola hadn't left him waiting on her. Lola hadn't insulted him. She damn sure wasn't afraid of him, because logically, what was there to fear? He was fine. He was accomplished. He was reformed. He was attentive. He was patient. He was everything. He was also a trigger for Sloan, and the idea of giving second chances made her fear that it would be a generational curse that would repeat itself. Second chances led to regret in her family. She had watched it happen with her mother. She would be so foolish to chance the same happening to her. She knew it was emotion and not logic driving her decisions, but she couldn't ignore her intuition. She also couldn't ignore the aching of knowing another woman was tending to a man who was supposed to be hers. A man she loved beyond comprehension. "Do you want me to put a call in and put a stop to that shit?"

Sloan shook her head. "No. Cass don't belong to me." Even as she said the words, she didn't believe them. She choked on her own words. "I've got to get out of here." She stood and rushed out, leaving her friends feeling helpless.

"Is your friend, okay?" Loyal asked.

Ellie shook her head. "She's not my friend," Ellie replied as her eyes stung.

"As fucked up as you are about whatever happened, I find that hard to believe," Loyal stated as he stared across the backseat of the Maybach. He lifted the partition to separate them from the driver and then pulled her across the seat.

"I don't want to think about her or talk about her." Ellie crossed her arms and stared out the window. She didn't even realize she was pouting until he leaned over and grabbed her chin.

"The pouted lips when you're upset is sexy as fuck." He pulled her to his face and planted soft kisses to those lips. "Come here," he directed as he patted his lap, giving her a cue that he wanted her there. Ellie straddled him, arching her back as his hands rested on her ass.

"Tell me what's on your mind," Loyal coached.

Thoughts of Sloan brought tears to her eyes. "My friends are my world. They have literally been the constant in my life since I met them at 13. Sloan is my best friend. Like, she's the one I would save if I had to make a choice. She knows everything. I've trusted her with every chamber of my heart, and she knows how I feel about my brother. She knows my rules. She knows how people have always stepped over me to get to him, and she does the same thing. It's hurtful, and I feel betrayed."

Loyal rubbed circles into her shoulder as she settled into his lap. She clung to his collar, pouring her heart out, and the comfort he brought was so settling.

"Before I answer, I need to know what kind of response you want in this moment. Are you coming to me for my opinion, or are you coming to me so you can vent? Those are two very different responses."

"For now, just let me vent. I don't want my feelings to be discredited just yet," she admitted.

"Okay," he replied.

She loved that he was such a man. If only all men knew to assess the need in that way, the world would be a much better place. Loyal knew when to be dominant and when to fall back. It made him easy to follow in times when leadership was non-negotiable.

"Anything else on your mind?" he asked.

"You and Tisa," she admitted. His hand stopped moving once he realized he was in the hot seat.

"Care to elaborate?" he asked.

"For one, she said she fucked you tonight in this car," Ellie snapped.

"You don't even believe that shit, or you wouldn't be in my lap right now," Loyal said.

"I mean, you do like car sex," Ellie mumbled, rolling her eyes like a brat as she pouted. "She might have been telling the truth."

"She was trying to scare you off, and it looks like you're letting her," Loyal replied. "Stop." His answer was simple, and Ellie sighed in uncertainty.

"I was jealous of her tonight," Ellie admitted.

"You don't ever have to be jealous of anyone or anything," Loyal stated firmly.

"It just felt so intimate between you two, and I felt out of place," she admitted.

"She has my child, E," Loyal stated. There was sympathy in his tone but also a firmness that told her he didn't really negotiate about the reality of his situation. He had love for Tisa. He would always have love for Tisa. Ellie would have to deal with that, and if she was honest, she respected a man who acknowledged a woman who had given him children. She wished Cairo had operated under the same code. It was still hard being the new woman in the situation, trying to decipher the dynamic. "It's always going to be a little intimate between us. We share something. I can't erase that. You're who I want, though."

"It feels like a competition. She basically told me she wasn't coming up off you," Ellie whispered.

"And where is she now? Where are you? She's in a car on her way home, alone. You'll be in my bed," he said, resting his head against the headrest, as he feathered her cheek.

"She said you're grooming me for a threesome. That this is what you do. You finesse women, and then y'all have them for a while, you get bored, and then you move on to the next," Ellie said, her stomach tightening in anticipation of his response. "Is that what I'm here for?"

"Just because something has been true in the past doesn't mean it's true now," Loyal responded.

Her heart sank. She hadn't expected him to admit this. She would have preferred it not to be true.

"So, she's not lying?"

Loyal shook his head and he sighed. "This is the type of night we're about to have?" he asked, impatiently. His irritation was not to be missed.

She sat up in his lap so that she could see his eyes. "I just need to know what this is. You're persistent and direct and passionate, and this is moving so fast. I don't want to be another notch on your belt. I have too much at stake to play games and to fall victim to false promises all so you and your baby mama can make me your new toy of the month."

"She's not lying about the threesomes." His words deflated her, and she shook her head, scoffing.

"I knew this wasn't real," she mumbled, trying to move out of his lap. He placed his hands on her hips, keeping her in place.

"Tisa and I have threesomes. Every woman don't get the same version of a man, E. That's not what I'm trying to do with you," he clarified. "But I won't lie. You got the visual of her eating your pussy in my head, so you might want to stop bringing it up." He snickered.

"It's not funny," Ellie whispered. She was worried. This new revelation bothered her. "I'm not into that, and if that's what it takes to keep you satisfied..."

"Tisa loves women, E. She loves every part of a woman. She enjoys courting women. She enjoys spoiling women, tasting women, fucking women. It's her thing. Hell, Tisa liked you until I told her how I was moving with it. The threesome thing was her need. I'm a man, so I'm with it, but she initiated them. I don't need that from you. Now, if you ever want it, I've seen her do some things with that tongue that I'd love to watch her do to you, but it's not required. I don't require much at all from you. Just you. Don't let anybody play with your head."

"I'm trying not to," she said. "But it feels like that's exactly what you're doing."

Loyal lifted the center console and pulled out a black box.

"How's this for playing with your head?" he asked. He flipped open the box and a brilliant VVS square-cut diamond ring rested inside.

"Loyal," she gasped. "I cannot accept…"

"Before you get on your soapbox, know I ain't returning it. It can mean as much or as little as you want it to," he answered. He was so damn cool as he stared up at her with hooded eyes. The effects of the champagne relaxed him. He smiled a lazy smile, dimples pinning his cheeks as he took the ring out of the box. He took her dainty hand and slid it onto her left ring finger.

"To replace the other one," he said simply. "You don't have to decide what it means now. Take a month, take a year, take five years. Either way, it's yours."

"I'm so scared of what the next chapter of my life looks like," she said.

"I can tell," he answered. "That's why you've been stuck. Can't go backward. Afraid to move forward, so you holding in place. If you gon' hold, at least get your pussy ate in the meantime."

He ran a finger along the edge of her panties, and she tensed as he reminded her of the power a man could yield over a woman. She was made to react to him, and she did. His thumb found her clit, and she looked down at herself as he pushed up and then down. Loyal drove her mad. He was the type of man to say the sky was green and she would believe him. His ability to completely persuade her into bending to his will was scary. It removed the control from her hands and forced her to exist at his mercy.

"Loyalll," she moaned. She was out of control. She was out of her body. She was his. To play with. To tease. To love. To fuck. To hurt. To please. To reward. To punish. To attend to. To ignore. To hinder. To fulfill. He had all the cards; all the options, and she was in a state of anxiety, trying to guess which one he would play. That was the thing about love and relationships. They required a vulnerability that allowed someone the space and opportunity to ruin you.

"I ain't gon' do too much, E, we ain't alone. I just want to see how wet she gets for me," he whispered. He took his thumb to his mouth like he had a little barbecue sauce on it, and he was cleaning it off. He slid her panties back in place, leaving her flustered and bothered.

She leaned forward and kissed him. "I wasn't sure if this was real because it's happening so fast, but the way I felt when I saw you with someone else…" She shook her head. "I'm falling in love with you."

"That ain't a bad thing, E," Loyal stated. "If the bond is this strong at first sight, imagine what it will be like in six months, or a year, or three, or when I change your last name, or when you give me a baby."

She knew her head was gone when she didn't correct him because having another baby at her age was unfathomable, but if the love remained, in due time, she wouldn't tell a man like Loyal no.

"Is that something you want? A wife? More kids?" she asked. "These are the things you learn over time, and we're just hitting fast forward."

"I do," Loyal stated. "With you. Nobody but you, E."

"How can you know this already?" Ellie asked, befuddled by his certainty.

"I told you we been here before," Loyal answered, reaching for the champagne bottle that sat in the ice bucket. She followed suit and grabbed the glasses as the rock on her finger sparkled flawlessly.

"This is a whirlwind," she sighed as he popped the top on the bubbly and filled one glass. He took his straight out of the bottle and then sat it back in the ice bucket as she sipped hers slowly. "I can't believe I'll have to say goodbye to you in a few days," she whispered.

"I thought we settled this." He said it so simply, but he didn't realize that it was easier said than done. "I did my part. I ended things with my baby mama. The rest is on you."

"I know, I know," she sang. "My part is just going to take a little more time and planning. I've got to hire a lawyer..."

"That's already done; what next?" Plain and simple. No delaying, no excuses. He was handling business, and Ellie's mouth fell open in shock.

"What do you mean? You hired a lawyer for me?" she asked.

"Best divorce lawyer in the state," he informed. "She'll make sure you come out on top."

"When did you have time to do that?" she asked, stunned.

"She received a 3 a.m. call this morning after you went to sleep," Loyal revealed. He was just a man of means who made whatever moves he wanted to. He didn't ask permission. He was dead set on having her, and she couldn't belong to two men at once.

She was speechless.

"Now, what's the next problem?" he repeated.

"The girls' schools," she stammered. "I…I can't move them mid-year."

"Sure, you can. Headmistress at one of the best K-12 private schools in Bloomfield Hills is awaiting your call after the holiday. Their spots are held, tuition paid. I didn't know their information and all that, so you still got to register them, transfer records, and all that shit, but the spots are theirs if you want them. Whatever judge decides your divorce agreement is going to put a joint custody plan in place anyway. It'll be easier if you're in the same state. Blame it on that; either way, it's done."

"Loyal!" she protested. "You can't make moves without consulting me."

"We consulted. We decided. Ain't no backtracking," he said, already losing interest in the back and forth as he pulled out his cell phone.

"I'm overwhelmed," Ellie admitted.

"And I'm certain," Loyal said.

Ellie wanted to protest, but her phone rang, and Brooklyn's picture illuminated her screen. She held up a finger. "You just wait because we're not done discussing this."

He chuckled as she moved out of his lap, but he had already moved on from the conversation.

"Man, check on them babies, and quit worrying about something that you ain't changing," Loyal stated. He was standing firm.

"Brook? Hey, baby, is everything-" Before she could even get her full sentence out, Brooklyn was screaming in panic.

"Ma! The police are here! They said we're trespassing. They have us in the back of a police car!"

"Wait, what?" Ellie asked. "I'm on my way, baby. Is there an officer in the car with you?"

"No, they're talking to some woman on the porch. They didn't tell me anything. They just stormed in with their guns pointed. They were yelling, and Tess was crying, and the baby was screaming. They put us in the car, and now they're searching the house and talking to this white lady. She told them we refuse to leave."

"I'm on my way," Ellie shouted, anger boiling at the thought of her children having an interaction with the police. "Stay on this phone, Brooklyn, do not hang up!"

Loyal sat up. "What's going on?"

"I need you to go to Shy's. The police are there and have my daughters in the back of a police car," Ellie informed.

"Have them in the back of a fucking car, for what? Are they in cuffs? Did somebody call the police on them?" He fired off questions and lowered the partition at the same time. "Yo, my man, I need you to go back to the address you picked her up from earlier this evening. And put some speed on it."

"Baby, are you cuffed?" Ellie asked, putting Brooklyn on speakerphone.

"No, I'm holding the baby, but I'm scared, Ma," Brooklyn said. "They said we aren't supposed to be here."

"I'm coming, baby. Your aunties are probably already on their way there. Just stay on the phone," Ellie said. She opened her texts and went directly to the group chat.

### Ellie

*Shy, the police are at your house.*
*They have the kids. They're saying they're trespassing.*

*WTF?*

*How far are y'all from the house?*

*GET TO MY BABIES NOW!*
*I'M EN ROUTE!*

The thirty minutes to Shy's house were cut down to twenty, and when Ellie arrived, she and Loyal climbed out of the back of the car. She rushed over to the police car where her daughters were trapped in the backseat, and she pulled on the door, freeing them.

"Ma'am! Step away from the police cruiser!" an officer shouted. The officer made sure to put his hand on his holster, and Loyal's rage clicked on without hesitation.

"Put your hand down, bitch-ass nigga," Loyal barked. "Fuck you gon' do? Shoot a mother for checking on her kids? Fuck is wrong with you? You acting like them, and your skin darker than ours!

Ellie didn't have to say another word. Loyal took over the situation.

The officer lowered his hand off his weapon. "We're just responding to a complaint, man. We're just trying to clear the confusion and do our jobs."

"They're kids, man. Should have never put them babies in the backseat of that car, anyway," Loyal demanded.

"Where are your coats? The baby's blanket? Your shoes?" Ellie asked, taking off her mother's mink coat and handing it to Brooklyn. "Hold Christian to your chest. I'm gonna button you up. Keep him warm, Brook."

Loyal removed his suit jacket and wrapped Tessa in it. She was crying, and he picked her up. "It's okay, baby girl," he whispered as she held on tightly to his neck. "OG, got you."

Shy and Courtney pulled up to the home, and Courtney rushed over to check on the kids.

"They're fine, girl," Ellie said. "We just trying to figure out what's going on." Ellie turned to Shy.

"Officer, this is her house! Here's the homeowner. I'm sure this is just a misunderstanding," Ellie shouted.

"I've got it, Ellie. Let me go clear this up," Shy said in a low tone as she eased by their group and walked up to the officer and the white woman giving the statement on the front porch.

Shy disappeared inside the house with the white woman and the supervising officer.

"I'll be right back," Loyal said, walking toward the officer.

"Yo, my man, let me holler at you for a second," Loyal said. He rubbed Tessa's back as he stepped out of earshot of Ellie and Courtney. "Fuck is going on here?" Loyal asked. "Be straight up because putting these kids out in the middle of the night in this weather ain't making sense."

"Look, man. We didn't want to put them out, but the white lady insisted. She showed us the title of the home. She says they're trespassing and refusing to leave. Apparently, it's a property that she's put up for sale. No one is supposed to be living here. She got a water bill that was higher than it should be because it's vacant and only open for showings. When she came over here to check on it, she found it's being lived in."

"Look, I need to get these kids and my lady in the car. Nobody's running off. I'ma square everything, don't matter how much it cost, but it's freezing fucking cold out here. They ain't even got on shoes," Loyal stated.

The officer looked sympathetically at the group and said, "Women and kids in the car is fine."

Loyal trudged back over to Ellie. "Get in the car. Everybody get in and get some heat," he instructed.

"What's happening? What did he say?" Ellie asked.

"Don't worry about it. I'ma go inside and handle it. Just get warm," he said. They all climbed inside the Maybach, and Ellie looked at Loyal curiously before she closed the door. His anger was apparent. His handsome facial features were set in a deadly grimace.

"Should I come?" she asked.

"No," he answered. No elaborating, no nothing. He kissed her forehead. "Everything's going to be fine. I'll be right back," he announced to the entire car.

"Girl, what the fuck?" Courtney said as they all watched Loyal head toward the house.

"Is OG going to be okay, Mommy?" Tessa asked.

"He's going to be fine," Ellie reassured. "He's going to figure all this out."

"OG?" Courtney questioned.

"That's the name they came up with together," Ellie smiled.

"Oh, girl!" Courtney smiled back, shaking her head, and raising her brows knowingly. "You're in over your fucking head, cuz, chileeee. Well played, sir."

Ellie blushed as she watched Loyal assert himself over the situation. "Yeah, I think I am."

"I didn't break in here. I'm renting this place from my realtor," Shy argued. She couldn't believe this was happening. She had always kept her image intact. She was the popular friend. Shy was the one with influence and with money. She was the one who wore designers the others couldn't pronounce and who flew in private jets to exotic places. She was living a lavish lifestyle. Shy posted everything and bragged endlessly, making all the bitches who talked about how raggedy her clothes were and how poor her family was as a child sick. The only problem was her posts didn't match her reality. Her entire life was smoke and mirrors. She had been squatting in this place for two weeks, just to have somewhere to host Christmas. She had the hook up with a realtor, who would let her use brand-new show homes to film content. All she had to do was throw the realtor a few hundred dollars, and she'd let her keep the keys for 48 hours. She had only needed this one for two weeks to make it through the holidays. Only, this one wasn't a new build. It was for sale, and the family who owned it was supposed to be in Switzerland for the holidays. It had been a perfect plan. She Didn't know how it had blown up in her face.

"This place isn't for rent. That's a lie. She's trespassing, and I want her arrested!" The homeowner was vehement about pressing charges.

Loyal walked through the door, and Shy knew she really had to save face.

"It's late; my realtor isn't available tonight, but I can easily clear this up in the morning with a phone call," Shy stated. She was calm on the outside. She had grown used to the art of fronting. Her car was a rental for the month. This home was borrowed. Her clothes were purchased and returned as soon as she shot them and posted pics online, and her shoes were purchased second-hand. Everything else was attained through influencer contracts. Wigs, makeup, and boutiques flooded her P.O. Box with merch in exchange for posts, so she was never short on looks. It was easy to find a man to spend money on her and cover a few months of living expenses. They gained clout when they dealt with her anyway, so it was a fair exchange. Even Lola was an intern. She was working for product and under the promise that Shy would eventually help her build her own influencer brand. She was going through life on the barter and beg system, and this hiccup was humiliating.

"I'm not waiting until the morning, and it doesn't matter what your realtor says, they weren't authorized to lease my home. Here is my deed. Here is my listing, proving that my home is for sale, not rent. She's trespassing, arrest her, now."

"I think we can work this out without making a bad situation worse," Loyal said. "She's clearly living here, and you haven't been paid, is that right?"

"I don't know who's being paid, but it isn't me," the woman stated adamantly.

"How long have you been here?" Loyal asked.

"This really isn't necessary. I've already paid…"

The look of impatience Loyal hit her with shut her up mid-sentence. He knew she was lying. She refused to answer, however.

"I checked on this house after Thanksgiving, so it had to be after that," the woman said. "She's been here almost a month."

"So, how about I pay you for the time she's been here, and for the rest of the month to give her time to get the place back to its original condition? I'll pay you two times the rental rate in the area, which should be about $5000 per month. I'm in real estate, I should be accurate, but you can verify if you'd like. That's $10,000; plus, a cleaning fee of $2500, so you can have it professionally assessed after the end of the month. It's much easier for us to take care of with money, than to send these officers out of here with hours of paperwork over a misunderstanding. Don't you agree?"

The woman wanted to be stubborn, but the $12,500 was sounding like quick cash for her. "I want her out of here by the 31st."

"You have my word, and I'll leave my contact information so you can get in touch if there are any issues," Loyal stated as he opened the banking app on his phone. He handed it to the woman. "Enter your account info here," he instructed. Within sixty seconds, the wire was sent. "Sorry for the inconvenience, gentlemen." Loyal stated to the officers. He waited for the officers and the woman to walk out of the door before he deadpanned on Shy. "You're welcome." The words sent a chill down her spine because she could tell he was not pleased to have to get involved at all. He walked out, and she watched as he went back to his chauffeured car.

Everyone exited and walked back toward the house.

"We're going to stay here with you tonight," Ellie announced.

"I'll send the car back for you in the morning," Loyal said, pulling Ellie into him.

"Thank you… for everything," she replied.

"Stop thanking me. Come home to me in the a.m., a'ight?" he proposed.

Ellie nodded, and he kissed her neck. "I'm serious," he whispered.

Ellie melted, and Shy stood there in awe. Courtney, too, because Ellie didn't even show this much affection to her husband. Now, their friend was standing in the doorway, unabashedly loving on this king of a man, allowing him to whisper sweet nothings in her ear in front of her kids.

Ellie curled up close to him and whispered, "I know you're serious, sir. That's all you know how to be is serious." It was a joke, but it carried a tone of truth beneath the laughter.

Loyal licked his lips as a humble smirk revealed a bit of embarrassment. Ellie was hypnotized by his every move, giggling as Loyal gave her a chin-up with his finger before making his exit. He didn't even acknowledge anyone else. It was like all he saw was Ellie.

Loyal turned Ellie into a mushy girl. He allowed Ellie to be the girl who sighed and placed her hands on her heart as she looked to the skies in amazement when he left the room. That turned Ellie into the happy girl who blushed at the scent of masculinity he left behind.

"Oh, I freaking love that for you," Courtney snickered. "Bitch, his nose is wide open. Rough-ass, rich-ass man just eating like a dog out the palm of your hand."

"He's just different," Ellie said, but when she focused on Shy, her smile disappeared.

Shy braced herself as Ellie put the happy girl away. "Bitch, now back to you. What the fuck is going on?"

"Wait," Courtney intervened. "Let me feed him and get all the kids put down. Then, we'll have a come-to-Jesus meeting."

"Girlllll," Shy groaned.

"Courttt, man, ain't nobody trying to pray and calm down and all that," Ellie added, joining the protest.

"Your mama taught us how to come to Jesus about this girl tribe when we were in 9th grade. When everybody is…"

"…Misaligned, let Jesus do the straightening," Shy and Ellie echoed her word for word because it was a lesson they had heard many times from Ellie's mom before she died. They hadn't brought their arguments to Jesus many times, but today, it was needed."

"Fine; we better bring it to the Lord because after my kids were put at risk, ain't no telling what might fly out my mouth," Ellie said.

"And she ain't the only one on bullshit tonight," Courtney added. "Don't climb too high up on that horse. Your ass needs to be told about yourself too."

"Me?" Ellie feigned innocence as she scrunched her face in confusion.

"Yeah, ho, you," Courtney stated. "PJs in the living room in thirty."

# CHAPTER 19

N ice place," Lola complimented as she walked around Cassidy's townhome. It wasn't much. A little three-bedroom spot he was renting. It had taken a full year to get on his feet. His father had saved his portion of his mother's life insurance, and Cassidy had met freedom with fire under his feet. He had built a million-dollar business in a year's time, and he was so busy building that he hadn't had time to spend the fruits of his labor. The partnership he and Loyal had established would only expand his business further and build his wealth. Getting money had never been a problem. When he was young and dumb, he had risked his freedom to acquire it; now, he knew better. Nothing was worth his freedom, but some men just attracted paper. His mentality wouldn't allow him to stay down long. He established something legal, and it was flourishing. Still, he remained modest to avoid attention. Modest but modern crib in a middle-class neighborhood. No new car. No flashy jewels, besides his Rolex, and even that he kept classic, no bust downs, no added faces. Cassidy wanted to move smart so he could have longevity. He had no desire to attract the wolves because then he would have to tap into a side of himself that had sent him away for 23 years just to defend his kingdom. He was low-key by choice. He was a 42-year-old man who knew exactly how to move. Wealth was silent. Cassidy wasn't trying to make too much noise.

"It's just a place to rest my head," he answered. "Can I get you a drink or something?"

"Or something," Lola answered seductively.

She was a beautiful girl. Body for days. Pretty face. Beautiful smile. And she was willing. Oh, was she willing. She played sweet, and that baby face portrayed good girl, but he knew her type. She was trying to secure a position. She fit the aesthetic well enough, and he was certain she would try her very best to please him, but his mind was miles away. He hated the way Sloan controlled his emotions. He had missed a lot. He had just been getting started when he was locked up, so the ups and downs a woman could take him through were foreign to him. Sloan made him physically sick. He hadn't slept right since their fight, and focusing on anything except her was a joke. Having sex with Sloan had been a mistake because, ever since, he had felt her all over him. He was losing his mind without her. Even now, as Lola stood in front of him, waiting for him to make a move, he hesitated off the strength of Sloan. Lola put her hands on his chest and looked up at him with pure lust in her eyes.

"Cass, I really, really want you to fuck me." She ran her hands down to his manhood, and she smirked. "And it looks like you really want that too."

*She didn't fucking come. You don't owe her shit. She don't want you,* he thought, as he tried to justify the decision he was about to make. Rejection was a harsh consequence of his actions, and it stung to know that Sloan thought so low of him. He had waited all night for her to walk through the door, and the realization that she wasn't coming was a blow to his ego. No matter how much he grew, or how successful he became, Sloan would never see him past the day he had been sentenced. She had him like a little-ass boy out here, pining over his first heartbreak. Most men went through this earlier in life. Sloan had a grown man paralyzed. He was out of sorts, so much so that he was about to send good pussy home. He trapped Lola's hands, but she pulled them loose and reached for his face, planting her lips against his.

"This is a bad idea," he said, pulling his head away. His heart and mind were at war. Emotions versus ego. He knew Lola was just filling space, substituting for the absence of another, and repairing an ego that was fragile and looking for redemption. His dick pressed into her, lust-filled, seeking pleasure. She would be good for the night, but in the morning, his longing for a woman he couldn't have would still be there. Sloan confused him. She was a puzzle he couldn't construct. He could feel her attraction but couldn't understand her will to deny herself of something this potent. It was torture. She was a drug, and he needed to be high on her. He was glad that he hadn't indulged in Sloan before he had gone to prison. To crave something like he craved her but be locked away from it for a lifetime would have killed him.

"It's the best idea you've ever had," Lola whispered as she got on her knees. He took a step back, but she reached for his belt, undoing it with expertise. Cassidy's dick grew as she rubbed him through his tuxedo pants. "I'm going to suck your dick so good, boy," she teased as she got her on her hands and knees for her prize.

"Damn, man," he whispered as he looked down at her. She was gorgeous. That mouth was available and ready, and her pretty stiletto nails were wrapped around his dick, stroking him like this was her profession. Cassidy just needed to release his stress. It would be so easy to let Lola top him off and then fuck her good before sending her on her way, but he couldn't. He stepped back out of her reach and gathered himself, zipping his pants.

"Get up, man. I'ma put you in a car," Cassidy grumbled, swiping a hand of frustration down his face. His body was screaming one thing; his mind was screaming another.

Why the fuck hadn't she shown up? He had waited most of the night before calling it, and the thought of being so close to having her as his own haunted him. Sloan's phone call had given him hope. Seeing her at his father's house had poured gasoline on a fire he had been trying his hardest to snuff out. The burning in his soul was out of control. It had spread like the winds of San Andreas had blown the blaze everywhere. Sloan was on his mind, heavy on his heart, and she had burrowed deeply into his soul. He was here with this beautiful woman. She was young, she was sexy, she was willing to please him in every kind of way, and he couldn't do it. Sloan wasn't even his girl, and she had his conscience in a chokehold. It was like she enjoyed the string she had tied around his heart. She told him no, but then pleaded with him for reassurance. A part of him wanted to fuck with Lola just off GP to show Sloan he had options, to make her watch while he loved another woman to perfection. But his devotion wasn't created for all. His options were fuckable. His options were physical. His desire to love a woman from the top of her head to the soles of her feet wasn't universal. It was reserved for one. He didn't know if his sentiments regarding Sloan were locked in his mind because of the way he had memorialized her while he was locked in that cell or if this was real. His father had warned him of this, of being trapped in a time and space that represented his days of freedom before he went to prison. Pretty-ass Sloan, his sister's best friend, the one he had mashed niggas out over because they were his age checking her out. Sloan, the girl he made sure he bought an extra pizza for on Friday nights because she didn't eat what his family ate, and she would have to pick the toppings off. Sloan was just Sloan, and no amount of pussy, no matter how top-tier it was, would shift his focus. He was just a man who wanted to love a woman. One woman, but she was playing with him.

"Or you can put me in your bed? We both know you want to." Lola was young and persistent, after dick that she knew would change her life if she plotted on it right.

"Yeah, I really, really fuckin' do," he groaned, fighting the lust coursing through his veins. "But I'ma pass," he said. He walked over to the door, held it open for her, and removed his phone from his slacks. "Your ride will be waiting for you downstairs. Type your shit in."

Lola couldn't believe he was turning her down. "You're serious?" she asked.

"It ain't you, trust," Cassidy stated, blowing out a breath of overwhelm.

Lola grabbed the phone, typed in her address, and then stared up at him, confused.

"Cassidy?" she said. "I'm right here in your face. I promise you I'll make you forget everything that's on your mind. I'll be everything you need me to be in that bed, on these counters, in the shower, on the floor, whenever you need it, however you need it. There isn't a place on my body I won't let you enter. Slide down my throat, Cassidy," she damn near moaned the words, and his dick swelled. "I will milk that dick so good, baby, all you got to do is let me." She stood on her tiptoes and kissed his lips. Cassidy believed every word. If she sucked dick half as good as she was sucking on his tongue, she would take his soul.

He picked her up and pushed her back against the door, closing it.

"Give me all that," she whispered as she felt how hard he was. "I'm so wet." He kissed her, and flashes of his night with Sloan rushed his mind. He went to Lola's neck, and she cried out, but he heard Sloan's voice. He turned Lola around roughly, and she lifted her hands to the wall, willing, ready. So ready, and he couldn't.

"Fuck," he whispered. He took a step back, placing one hand on his dick.

"She's not here, Cass," Lola panted, turning around to face him.

"Who?" he asked.

"You know who," Lola said. "Sloan isn't here. I'd never not be here for you." Lola was almost begging. Cassidy held his chin up and flicked his nose, sniffing away frustration and willing discipline to send her pretty ass away. He knew she was telling the truth. Lola would be there. She would be loyal. She would be available. She would worship the ground he walked on. She would never tell him no. He could have his way with her, and still, he turned her down.

"Your car's probably here," he said.

"For the record, if Sloan doesn't realize what she has, she's a fool. Call me if you ever change your mind. You're a good man, Cass. When you're ready, hit me up."

Lola walked over to him and put her hand to the side of his face. He moved it out of her grasp. "You have a good night."

She scoffed and then walked out, sticking her middle finger up and leaving the door open as she made her exit. Cassidy went to close the door, and then he looked around at the empty space.

"Fuck, man," Cassidy said, flopping down on his couch as he gripped his phone. "Damn girl gon' drive me fucking crazy." He wanted to press Sloan, but how could he show any sort of conviction without it looking like aggression to her? He wasn't a passive-ass nigga. She was already terrified of him. As much as he wanted to force her to see him, force her to talk to him, he had to wait for her to come to him. It seemed she had made her decision, however, and as much as it hurt, as much as he wanted to fight for her, he couldn't do anything but respect it.

"Sloan isn't answering the phone," Shy said. "Do we really want to do this without her?"

"Just let her be," Ellie said.

"She's a part of this girl tribe. You know the rules. When we come to Jesus, we got to come together in prayer," Courtney stated.

"We can't make her disloyal ass answer," Ellie snapped.

"Let's just record the prayer and send it to her," Shy suggested. She was never not in content mode. She set her phone up on a tripod and pressed record.

"This bet not go up on your social media," Ellie sniped.

"It's just for Sloan," Shy promised.

They stood in a circle and took hold of one another's hands. Ellie noticed that Courtney's hands were shaking, and she gave her a reassuring squeeze.

"God, I'm so triggered right now," Courtney whispered. "My life is falling apart. It feels like every single brick I've laid in my life so far is crashing down around me, and I feel the weight of being buried beneath the mess. I'm so embarrassed. I've hidden how James has treated me for so long that I feel like I have to protect him now that the secret is coming out. I've been lying for so long that I've convinced myself that this is normal. It's not okay, and I'm not okay. I'm afraid of him, God. I don't know when it happened, or maybe I've always been, but my heart sinks when he walks into a room. I feel like I'm walking through a field of land mines when he's around. I just don't want to set him off. I love him, but God, I'm desperate for detachment, and at the same time, I'm terrified to let go. I don't know what to do. I just know I need help. I know if I stay, I'll drown. Help me, Lord. Help me allow my friends to help me. Help me allow myself to walk free. I'm in chains, mentally. I'm so stuck, and I just need You to save me. I don't even need a sign. The signs have been there. I just need the courage to choose me. And I need You to remove my pride, so that I can hear my friends in this moment. We come to You when we need You to guide us as a group. Whatever we say to each other, please place it in Your love. Let it be free of judgment. Let our hearts be open to receive it and strengthen our friendship, God. You didn't bring us into each other's lives by mistake. Make sure we are honoring the design You made for this sisterhood. In Your name, I pray, Amen."

Tears ran down Ellie's face as she embraced Courtney tightly.

"Come on, Sarah Jakes!" Shy shouted in excitement.

They shared a laugh as they held onto one another, and Ellie was moved to speak next. "I don't have a whole prayer. I just want to ask God to order my steps. Order them in every aspect of my life, from my friendship with Sloan to every move I'm making with Loyal. To the way I'm raising my girls. I need courage and motion, God. I've been in the same spot for so long that I feel like I've grown roots. Help push me forward. Help me forgive Sloan."

"Oh my godddd," Shy shouted. "Pause, God, cuz I'm about to gather Your spoiled daughter right quick. Ellie!"

"What?" Ellie defended.

"You're wrong, friend," Courtney interjected. "The whole argument tonight with Sloan. You could have handled that better."

"She lied to me. She broke my rule! She's sleeping with my brother!"

"Bitch, your brother! Not your man! And you came up with that rule in 6th grade, heffa, let it the fuck go. We get it, but this ain't no schoolyard crush. These are two grown people with a clear connection. You can feel it between them. Like, these two mu'fuckas can be sitting at a table and there is just so much chemistry it's sickening. Them hooking up don't leave you out. You're still important, Ellie, but to stop Sloan from having this with Cassidy is wrong. To make her feel bad about it is dead-ass wrong. Our girl doesn't fall easily. She's guarded and stubborn and mean and anxious, and she's dead set on following those damn vision boards. She don't leave no room for spontaneity. She's detouring for Cassidy, Ellie, and you have to let her. Shit, let them figure it out because as far as I can tell, that nigga loves her right the fuck back."

Ellie wanted to be mad, but hearing this made her feel a bit of joy for both her friend and her brother. "Fine," Ellie said simply.

"All that and all you got to say is fine?" Courtney asked, tickled.

"Bitches, I said fine, they ugly selves can have one another," Ellie stated, rolling her eyes. "They bet not say shit when they break each other's hearts."

"And now I guess it's my turn," Shy sighed. The girls bowed their heads. "God, give me the courage to live in my truth. I'm creating a whole persona for the world to see because I'm afraid to show who I really am. I don't have anything figured out. All this stuff is just stuff. It was begged for, borrowed, or stolen. I'm broke. I've made so many financial mistakes that it feels like I'm in too deep of a hole to climb out of. My life is all smoke and mirrors. It's all fake, and I'm praying for self-discovery. I'm praying for self-love. I'm praying for discernment so that I can figure out why I've always felt the need to hide who I really am. Give my friends the type of hearts that accept me no matter what. Give my following the empathy to understand why I felt the need to hide. If I strip down and take off this makeup, these clothes, this façade, please let people accept me for who I am. I'm not quite sure what my relationship with You even looks like, if I reveal myself, because my parents threw me away when they found out, and I've been hiding who I am ever since. I'm seeking acceptance, God. I'm seeking unconditional love. I'm praying for support. I'm praying for forgiveness."

"Forgiveness for what, Shy?" Ellie asked. Shy's confession felt weighted, and Ellie almost guessed Shy's next words.

"I'm a lesbian," Shy admitted. "And I'm broke, and the white lady who accused me of squatting in this house was telling the truth. I got it on a hook up from one of my homegirls who is a realtor at the company who's listing it. God, take these crazy looks off my friends' faces. Amen."

"Amen."

Shy ended the recording and then turned to face her friends. Ellie was stunned to speechlessness.

"Say something, bitches," Shy said. She was so embarrassed that she was turning red.

"I've got so many questions," Courtney blurted.

"I know," Shy responded.

"So, are you like gay gay, or are you pop a Molly in the strip club and you're gay on occasion type gay?" Courtney asked.

"I don't know," Shy whispered, eyes misting.

"How long have you known?" Courtney asked.

"I've always felt different. Don't get me wrong, I like dick. I'll take it, but I love women," Shy admitted, with a bit of shame in her voice. "I've just lived my life so long one way. Like, the world has seen me with rappers and ball players and all these elite men. How do I pop out with a woman?"

"You live in your truth. There's no shame in loving who you love. We don't feel no differently about you. I just feel bad that you were carrying this by yourself for so many years. I'm more shocked that your ass is walking around here fronting on me for wearing a Macy's dress when you broke like I'm broke, ho!" Courtney snapped.

Shy had never felt a larger burden lifted from her shoulders. "I've been insufferable. I know, sis. I'm so sorry." Shy looked over to Ellie. "Ellie, say something."

"So, I just have one question." Ellie was perplexed. She had seen Shy rotate men like panties. This new revelation was mind-blowing. She wouldn't have put a threesome past Shy; in fact, the proposition from Tisa would be just Shy's style, but to be attracted to women only was wild. Shy had hidden it well, and that saddened Ellie a bit. Still, Shy was one of her best friends, so she had to ask.

"Ask me anything, sis. I just want to be honest with y'all. For once in my life, I can let all this off my chest," Shy cried out.

Ellie looked at Shy curiously and lowered her voice. "So, bitch, you be scissoring and humping coochies and shit, and you ain't told us shit! Spill the fucking tea! I can't believe you been holding out on us!"

"Girlllllllll!" Shy exclaimed. "Best motherfucking orgasm in life!"

The girls fell out in giddy laughter as they listened to Shy's freaky lesbian tales over wine. It never failed. Their come-to-Jesus meetings were always healing. Their friendship had survived many phases of their lives, and their bonds had only strengthened over the years. It was rare that Black women maintained healthy relationships with one another, but they were committed to friendship. Most women valued men over every other relationship in their lives, but Ellie, Sloan, Courtney, and Shy realized very early that this foursome would be the bond that sustained them through all seasons of their lives. Men came and men went. Through breakups, makeups, parents passing, children being birthed, and even children being buried, this friendship had remained, and it had held each of them when they needed it most. They would always come to Jesus when they felt like their bond was being tested, and they would always make sure that their friendship came out intact.

Ellie pulled back from their circle, and Shy went into the kitchen to grab wine. Ellie turned to Courtney and took her hand, gripping it extra tight.

"Ellie, what's wrong?" Courtney asked.

"I heard you, sis," she said. "And I see you. You and Christian are never going back to him. Ever. It's not normal how you've been living and it's over now. We've got you."

She saw relief flood Courtney's eyes, and she pulled her in for a hug. Ellie could only imagine the shit that Courtney wasn't saying. She had a feeling that James had done much worse, but she'd be damned if he ever touched her again.

"I've got you."

# CHAPTER 20

### December 23rd

The covers swallowed Sloan. She cried so hard that she was hyperventilating. Sometimes a bitch just had to cry. She had been strong for a long time, and it felt like everything she had ever suppressed was pouring from her. She had lost her favorite patient. A little boy was motherless at her hands. That one event had been the move to bring the house of cards she had built tumbling.

She was thankful for the solitude because there were no witnesses to this sorrow. It was pitiful to cry over a man the way she was. It was unhinged to be a doctor and expect not to experience losses. Neither event should send her in a tailspin the way they were, but she knew at the root of it all was unhealed trauma. It was the little girl mourning the death of a mother taken too soon. The scars of that were causing her to miss out on what felt like the love of her life. The motherless child in her identified with that baby she had delivered. Oh, how she ached for him. She had never felt so lonely. She had always had her friends' shoulders to cry on, especially Ellie's. Ellie knew things that only existed inside her mind. That's how close they were. Sometimes Ellie could look at Sloan and pull a thought right into reality. The notion of their friendship changing behind this was tragic. She wished she could take back everything with Cassidy, even the night when they were kids because it had started there. Seeing him again as an adult had only convoluted things. If she never knew what it felt like to feel his heartbeat against hers, she couldn't need it. If he had never been inside her, she couldn't miss it. He lived rent-free inside her head. One night together had exposed a vulnerability she had worked hard to cover. Absence was the solution. She couldn't be around him. Not now. Not ever. Because after 23 years, all it had taken was him happening upon her, sitting in front of a fireplace, to breathe life into dormant emotions. She had thought it had been just a teenage crush on her sister's older brother. She had thought it was innocent and one-sided. She had been his mental anchor in a tumultuous sea. For so long, he had thought of her behind those bars, and nothing about that was casual. She wished he had never told her because her ears couldn't unhear confessions of love that deep.

*"I'm in love with you. I been on that type of time with you, Sloan."*

She heard it clear as day. The moment had been theirs for the taking. All she had to do was take a chance on Cassidy, and she had fumbled. Sloan couldn't cope. The shit ached in a place deep down in her belly, and the only cure was time—

even that would only dull it. It would never truly go away. That's why she hated love. It was why she had never allowed herself to feel it before him. When the right type of man loved you, the end would break you. He would break you so bad that it would send you into the abyss to chase any type of relief. Be it dick, drugs, liquor, or prayer. A woman would just go searching for something to ease the pain. Whatever gave her relief first became her addiction. Sloan was in dangerous territory. The grief was strong. She had tried to find him before she developed an unhealthy attachment to something or someone else, but Lola had taken him first.

Now, Sloan was left to her own devices to find the remedy. She didn't even know where to begin searching. She was stuck between love and loss. It was a lonely place to visit— twice— over the same man. She was too old to be going through bullshit like this. Cassidy was pulling her back in time with him. These were tent poles of trauma she had grown past. Her mother's death, his imprisonment, those were things that had been cauterized and sterilized so that they didn't break her. She was reinjuring some of the most painful things she had ever felt, and she hated it. Sloan wondered if there was a way she could get past Cassidy's violent history.

*I just don't understand how the same person who loves me like that could be so violent that he killed that poor, old man with his bare hands*, she thought. Her heart raced just thinking about it. She remembered the day the police had come to arrest him. She had been asleep in Ellie's room when an entire SWAT team kicked in the door and carted him off to jail. He didn't say one word as they manhandled him, forcing his hands behind his back, and slamming him to the ground. She remembered the sound of his body as it hit the wood floor. There had been so much screaming, so much crying that day, and as he lay on that floor with their knees in his back, she had thought they would kill him. She had run out onto the porch, behind his parents, behind Ellie. His entire family had been frantic. She had been desperate to remember everything about him because in her gut she knew he would be different the next time she laid eyes on him. It was the second worst day of her life, only trumped by the day she lost her mom.

Before Sloan could stop herself, she was pulling her laptop from her nightstand drawer. She opened it and typed his name into a search bar.

It wasn't the first time she had looked him up, but it had been years. His case had made national news, so article after article popped up and she read them. One after another, she searched for anything, something, that would make this make sense. The old stories only reaffirmed her fears, and when she got to the crime scene photos, her stomach turned. She slammed the computer shut and kicked out of the covers in frustration as she fought her way out of the bed. She was driving herself crazy.

Her room was funky and nasty. Used Kleenex was everywhere. Sloan had been bawling.

"Bitch, get your ass the fuck up," she scolded aloud. "Not over no nigga, especially not over no nigga that is literally out fucking with the next bitch at this very moment. He's not crying. He's not bothered. He's not worried about you. Pull it together." Tough talk for a tough girl, but the tears were still falling. She hated being weak. Sloan snatched the sheets from the bed and carried them to the laundry room. She started a load of laundry and then went back to her room to clean up. She opened her window, not caring that the freezing winter air was getting inside, and then she spent the next hour resetting her space. Her peace was impacted. Love had robbed her of it, and she would have to fight with all her might to restore it. How a reunion with the women she loved most had turned her life upside down, she didn't know, but she no longer wanted to participate. She needed to escape. A mental reset was overdue. She couldn't be strong for anyone if she was pouring from an empty cup, and Sloan was depleted. She decided then and there that she needed to take some time for herself. A suitcase and a flight somewhere warm would do the trick. She took out her phone and opened the group chat. The first thing she saw was the video they had sent. Her lip quivered as she read the words.

*Our come-to-Jesus meeting. We couldn't leave you out.*

Sloan played the video, and she cried even harder at the revelations she heard. She desperately wished she had been there to pour into her circle and to empty some burden off her own heart, but she hadn't, and right now, she just wanted to be alone. Her heart was too shattered to face anyone at the moment.

## Sloan

*I love y'all, so I didn't want to leave without letting y'all know.*
*I'm not in a good head space.*
*If I'm honest, I'm heartbroken.*
*It's been a long time since I've felt like this.*
*I can't let it get bad this time.*
*I need to take care of me.*
*I'm taking a few days to reset and find peace.*
*I won't be taking calls.*
*I probably won't speak to you guys until after Christmas, but my heart is there.*
*Your gifts will be under my tree.*
*You are my best friends, and I love y'all so much.*
*I don't want you to worry. I'll be fine eventually.*
*But I need a few days away from everybody and everything.*
*Merry Friendsmas, ladies.*

*-xoxo-*

# CHAPTER 21

### December 24th
### Christmas Eve

Ellie read the message, and tears came to her eyes. This was her first time coming home for Christmas in years, and a huge piece of her heart would be missing. Nobody ever discussed the ways friends broke your heart. They could be worse than the destruction of a romantic relationship. Every woman expected men to fuck up eventually. Even the best man didn't get the complete benefit of the doubt. Women just braced themselves for men to mess up, so when it hit, it didn't come from out of nowhere. When a friendship failed, you realized how much you relied on other women. Friends were your secret keepers, your hitters, your moral advisors, your spirit lifters, your insecurity destroyer, your worry mitigator, and your intuition confirmer. Friends were there at rock bottom, wiping your tears. Friends were there when you lost your virginity. Friends were there without judgment, holding your hair out of the way when you overindulged. Friends were there when you were on some crazy shit, riding past a nigga crib to see if he was cheating. Friends were there when you gave birth to your first baby. Friends were there when your parents left this earth. Through every single phase of life, your day-one friends were imprinted on every memory that mattered. Ellie felt incomplete, knowing that Sloan wouldn't be with her today. She knew calling her wouldn't change anything. When Sloan said she didn't want to be reached, it was a firm boundary. She would be surprised if her friend's phone was even powered on. Ellie wanted to try, but she was still so angry at Sloan. A conversation needed to take place, but today wasn't the day. She climbed out of bed and went to wake her girls, but their beds were already empty. She heard their infectious laughter, and she descended the steps of her parents' home to find her girls in the kitchen with her father, preparing for Christmas. Papa didn't play when it came to his holiday meals, so they were starting on Christmas Eve. Brooklyn was being taught how to clean greens, and Tessa was cracking eggs into the cornmeal. Ellie entered the room and placed her hands on Tessa's shoulders, leaning down to blow kisses on her cheeks.

"Good morning, my love," Ellie greeted. She reached down into the cornmeal and picked the shells out that Tessa was leaving behind.

"Morning, Mommy!" Tessa shouted.

"Hey, Ma, morning," Brooklyn added.

Ellie walked behind her daughter and hugged her from behind as she rested her head over Brooklyn's shoulder. "I love you, baby girl."

"Love you too."

"Hey, Papa," Ellie greeted her dad last as she bent down to kiss his cheek. He sat at the table, peeling sweet potatoes.

"Grab a seat; you can shred some cheese," Papa said, motioning for her.

Ellie smiled. She didn't mind helping. Some of her best memories were of her with her dad in this very kitchen. He was the reason why she could cook so well.

Cass walked into the house, carrying his father's fryer.

"Papa, let this be the last year you forget something and send me out to get it on Christmas Eve," Cassidy joked.

"Good luck with that. Daddy gon' forget something every year," Ellie stated.

"I went to three stores to find this," Cass shot back. "That's what took me so long."

"You're a good son, Cass. You won't be talking all that shit when I drop my famous turkey in that there," Bishop bragged.

Cassidy and Ellie laughed at the pride in Bishop's voice. He fried turkeys for the whole neighborhood— it seemed like. Every Christmas, their neighbors would drop off their coolers and get in line, starting two days before the holiday, to pay him to season and fry their big bird. He had taught Cassidy the recipe when he was a teenager, and while Cassidy's skill was a close second, Bishop was the undeniable king. This was Cassidy's first Christmas home in years, and Ellie felt a sense of completion being able to spend the holiday with her entire family. The only person missing was Sloan.

"I'ma get you set up in the backyard," Cassidy stated.

"I'll help you," Ellie said.

She grabbed the peanut oil from the pantry and followed Cassidy out of the sliding glass door that led to the deck.

She watched him unbox the new turkey fryer as he set it up next to the other three Papa planned to use.

"What you hovering for, E?" Cassidy asked.

"Ain't nobody hovering," Ellie replied, rolling her eyes because he knew her too well.

Cassidy looked up at her. She was twin. They carried their mother's features so similarly.

"What's going on with you and Sloan?" Ellie asked.

She saw a flash of hurt cross his face before he looked back down and continued with his task. Ellie instantly wanted to beat Sloan's ass.

*See, this is why they don't need to be involved with each other because if she hurts him, I'm going to kill her, and if he hurts her, I'm going to skin him alive,* she thought.

"Hand me that oil," Cassidy said. She didn't know if he was avoiding her question or thinking about what he wanted to say, but it was clear that he was affected by it. She felt her brother's heart. She knew him so well, even after all these years. This was a heavy topic for him. He wore his heart right on his sleeve. Sloan had pinned it there and signed her name to it in permanent ink, just in case he got lost. "Cass!"

"It ain't your business, E. Leave it alone," Cassidy said. He poured the oil inside the fryer.

"What do you mean it ain't my business? Sloan shouldn't

be your business!" Ellie exclaimed. "So, y'all are messing around?"

Cassidy stood and blew out a sigh of frustration.

"Sigh all you want, negro, but get to talking," Ellie demanded.

"I don't know what you want me to say," Cassidy stated. His guilt was evident. His shoulders hung low, and his eyes held no joy. Her brother was carrying sadness in his soul, and it hollowed her stomach.

"Cass! She's my best friend! How could you?" Ellie asked.

"How could I not, E?" He scoffed and looked out over the backyard. He asked the question like the thought of not having Sloan was absurd. His passion was palpable, and Ellie was stunned. "She's beautiful and smart and funny and driven and independent and..." Cassidy stopped talking and clenched his jaw as he gritted his teeth. His nostrils flared as he thought of Sloan, and Ellie stood there enraged. "How could I not?"

"And what about me? Neither of you cared to think of me? She knows my rules about my friends and my brother, and I know you. What happens when you become disinterested? When somebody prettier comes along? You just came home; you got two decades of coochie to catch up on. You not trying to settle down and stick to one woman. You gon' do something stupid. Then, I'ma have to choose between you and my friend, and of course, I'ma choose you, but I lose her," Ellie argued.

"I was a kid, E. You're judging me off shit I did as a teenager, man. I'm not out here hopping from woman to woman no more, trying to smash everything moving. It's different with Sloan."

"Oh, yeah? What about Lola? Cuz you left the party with her," Ellie stated. "You saying it's different with Sloan, but you sliding with Shy's assistant? Somebody Sloan will have to see and interact with?"

"Nothing happened with Lola," Cassidy answered.

"Nothing happened?" Ellie challenged. "You didn't fuck that girl?"

"No," Cassidy answered resolutely.

"You Didn't kiss her?" Ellie asked.

Cassidy sighed in exasperation.

"A kiss is something, Cassidy. Sloan will cut that damn girl's lips off over a kiss. Any misstep with Sloan matters!" Ellie argued.

"I know, man," Cassidy sighed.

Ellie shook her head. "Sloan is family, Cassidy! There are certain boundaries you just shouldn't cross! Especially for no stupid-ass casual hook-up!"

"It ain't casual, E," Cassidy declared. "It's so far from casual, it's crazy."

It was the second time she had heard this admission, and Ellie fought the urge to yell at him some more.

"And yeah, I thought about you. I've always considered your friendship with Sloan. I know what she means to you. I thought two things could be true at once. I thought I could have her, and she could still have you, but it doesn't even matter because it's over. It was over before it even started," Cassidy said. "Don't be mad at her. This ain't her fault. It was on me. I'm the one who complicated shit. I opened that door, and she shut it down. She's too good for me."

Ellie had never seen Cassidy this affected. Her brother usually presented a strong front, no matter the circumstances. He was trying, but she could see that Sloan hit differently for him.

"Do you love her, Cass?" Ellie asked. His silence was loud as he tapped on the window to get their father's attention. "You all set up out here, old man!" he shouted.

"You do, don't you?" Ellie pushed.

"It's all good, E," Cassidy said, playing cool.

"But, Cass…"

Cassidy's exasperation had a limit. He loved his little sister, but he didn't want to discuss this with her. "She's afraid of me, E! And I ain't talking about no metaphorical bullshit; like, she's afraid I'ma break her heart. She thinks I will harm her. She thinks I'm violent. She sees a murderer when she looks at me."

Ellie's eyes watered. He was so much more. The measurement of his manhood was so much greater than his biggest sin.

"So just leave it alone," Cassidy said, as he disappeared inside the house.

341

The smell of sweet potato pie warmed the air, and the sound of laughter bounced from wall to wall as the Whitlock family gathered for Christmas Eve.

"Ellie, girl, you skin and bones. You need to move back home so Auntie can teach you some of these family recipes. All that gluten-free, vegan, no meat Mondays mess you be posting got you rail thin."

Leave it up to an elder to talk about a bitch weight. Ellie took it in stride, smiling. "I know the recipes, Auntie. I just try to make better choices. You know high blood pressure run all up and through this family," Ellie replied.

"Well, one plate ain't gon' hurt you," Bishop said, handing her a piping hot plate.

She laughed, and her mouth watered because she was going to tear this plate down and regret it later.

There were so many people in the house that there weren't enough places to sit, so Ellie sat on the living room floor. She missed this so much. The rambunctiousness of family. The feel of home. Her cousins were playing Spades in the dining room. The kids were in the backyard enjoying Tessa's new tree house. The teenagers were in the den making TikTok videos. Cassidy chopped it up with his father and the old heads. She was sure at least one argument would break out over dominos or Spades, the teenagers would be trying to get dropped off somewhere, and one of the babies would hurt themselves before the end of the night, but it was all a part of a family holiday. It was a good, ghetto time. She couldn't believe she had allowed her shame to keep her from her roots for so long. This was the one place where she felt like she belonged. It was full of memories. Her mother's spirit dwelled within these walls, and as she looked around, she could almost hear her mom's laughter. The doorbell rang, and Bishop summoned her from the table.

"Baby girl, can you get that? I'm about to whoop on your old-ass uncle over here," Bishop called out.

Ellie climbed from the floor, balancing the plate in one hand. "I know you ain't gon' take that, Unc?"

"Your daddy all talk," her uncle defended. Ellie made her way to the front door, not even bothering to check the peephole because anyone knocking on this door on Christmas Eve was family. Except him.

"What are you doing here?" Ellie asked, face souring at the sight of Cairo. He ruined her appetite instantly.

"Can we talk?" Cairo asked.

"What do we have to talk about?" Ellie asked.

"Please, Ellie," Cairo said. "The girls here? Can I see them?"

"Nigga, no," Ellie stated. She pulled the first coat she saw off the coat rack and set the plate down on the hutch by the door before sliding out into the cold night air. "You've got five minutes."

Cairo blew out a breath, and the cold air formed a cloud in front of his mouth. He looked stressed, pained even, as he scratched the top of his head, searching for words.

"Four minutes," Ellie said, counting down.

"Your attorney sent a letter of representation. You hired a divorce attorney?" Cairo asked. The audacity behind his question was comical. She didn't even answer. She just stood there, staring at him. She couldn't even recall what she had ever seen in him. The shit she had accepted from him felt idiotic now. She was disgusted at herself for even participating.

"You don't think that's a little drastic? Why the sudden rush to file?" Cairo asked.

"You left me four years ago. What's rushed about it?" Ellie asked, disinterested.

"Ellie, come on. It's our marriage," Cairo stated.

Ellie laughed. She cackled. An insulting, deep down in her gut, brought tears to her eyes hoot. This shit had to be a fucking joke.

"I'm serious, Ellie. I want to come home. I'm sorry about the way I've moved in this marriage. I'm sorry about the hurt I've caused you. I want to be a father to Brook. I want to be the father Tessa deserves. I fucked up, bad, Ellie, and I just kept digging the hole deeper. It felt easier to just start over instead of trying to fix it with you, but you being here, this close... Sloan said some things when she picked Brook up the other day, and I just...I don't know...it got me to thinking. I was wrong. I just want to fix my family. I want you, and I want our girls."

It was the apology Ellie had waited years to hear.

"You really want to give up our entire family? You want to put the nail in the coffin without at least trying to make it work?"

She was speechless. A sickness built in her stomach that made her dizzy. She was hyperventilating, choking on emotion. Why would he do this? Why now? She was finally accepting the fact that it was time to pull the trigger on a divorce. She could finally see over the clouds of grief that clung to her after he left. She had prayed to God so many nights to fix her marriage. Was this a manifestation of her prayers or something else? Was this an example of the adage "Be careful what you pray for"? Ellie was filled with conflict. Cairo's presence in their lives would heal so many wounds for her daughters, but she wondered what it would do for her. And would it last? Was this newfound revelation an act of desperation to keep her from running his pockets in a divorce, or was it genuine repentance?

"You need to leave, Cairo," she whispered as she shook her head. "It's Christmas Eve. I can't even…" she scoffed. "You're unbelievable!" she shouted. Her brain was in overdrive. "You abandoned us!"

"I know," Cairo said. "But, Ellie, please let me fix this. Let me try. Before you give up on our family, let me prove to you that I can be a better man and a better father."

"Go home," Ellie whispered, pained.

"Please think about it. Think about our girls."

Ellie disappeared inside the house. She didn't even bother with the plate she had left behind. She rushed upstairs to her bedroom and locked the door before she bawled her eyes out. Christmas Eve with her family had been ruined. Cairo had turned her world upside down, for a second time, and she had no idea what she was going to do.

# CHAPTER 22

**Christmas Day**
**December 25th**

**M**erry Friendsmas!" Ellie shouted as she walked through the front door of Sloan's home. Sloan's home was beautiful. It was modern and bright. It was sterile and spotless. It presented perfectly, just like Sloan. It saddened Ellie that Sloan was MIA, but she understood. A lot had happened. The two best friends needed a little space to process.

"We're in the dining room!" Courtney called.

Ellie carried four gift bags in her hands. She couldn't wait to show her girls what she had chosen. The rule of Friendsmas was you had to buy your friends your favorite thing and then explain the significance behind it at the exchange. She only wished that they were all together, but she would leave Sloan's gift under her tree. They all would. The spirit of Friendsmas would be waiting for Sloan when she returned.

She found them in the formal dining room at the elaborately set table.

"Leave it to Sloan to save the day," Shy said.

"It's what she does." Courtney shrugged.

Ellie's heart was heavy. She pulled out her phone to FaceTime Sloan, but she got no answer.

"What if this time she's the one that needs the saving?" Ellie whispered.

The Friendsmas brunch menu was amazing. Everything from lamb chops to salmon and lobster grits was served. The trio sat, being served by the chef Sloan had hired.

"Even when she's not here, sis got everything under control," Shy stated.

"Have you thought about what you're going to say to her when she gets back?" Shy asked.

Ellie picked at her food. Her mind was all over the place. Between Cairo and Loyal, she had enough of her own drama. She didn't have the capacity to manage Sloan and Cassidy, too.

"I think they really love each other," Ellie revealed.

"I think they've loved each other for a long time, sis," Courtney added.

Ellie sighed. "I just want them to be happy. I love them both too much to stop them from being happy. They could have told me, though."

"Girl!" Shy exclaimed. "They ain't tell you because they knew how you would react, and when you found out, what did you do? Prove them right. Let grown people hunch on who they want."

Ellie laughed and rolled her eyes at the thought of her best friend and brother hunching on one another. "Y'all right. I'm out of it."

"Nah, they got you right in the middle of it. You're the closest person to them both, so you will always be their referee, but from what I can tell, what they have is worth making sure they fight fair," Courtney added.

"Okay, gift time!" Shy announced, lifting from the table. "Because if I keep sitting in front of this food, I'ma keep eating, and nobody has time for that."

They took their dishes to the sink, where the hired chef and Sloan's housekeeper cleaned. The trio made their way to the living room where the gifts sat beautifully under the tree.

"I'll go first," Shy said, stepping in front of the tree as Ellie and Courtney took a seat, grabbing throw blankets, making themselves comfortable. Shy grabbed two boxes and handed them to her girls.

"Sooo, going into the new year, I want to focus on becoming the most authentic version of myself. Ellie, it really hit me when you told me I don't know who I am. I wanted to be offended, but you were right. I don't know who I am, and a large part of that is because I don't know where I came from. Open your gifts."

Ellie and Courtney unwrapped the box and revealed a heritage history kit inside.

"What's this? Like, one of those ancestral DNA things?" Courtney asked.

"That's exactly what it is," Shy stated. "I know my mom is living in Ghana. My grandmother gave me her address, but I'm terrified to go alone. I want y'all to trace your ancestry and take a trip to the Motherland with me to discover our roots. Keep digging," Shy said. "I got Delta Airlines to sponsor first-class round-trip tickets to Africa. They're willing to cover four legs of a trip, which means we can visit each country our DNA traces back to. I can get the hotels covered if I cover the trip on social media. We can choose whatever dates we want."

Ellie was speechless. "Shy, wow. I don't even know what to say. This is a once-in-a-lifetime trip. Thank you!"

"I'm in my rebranding era. That's what we gon' call this next year!" Shy said, fanning her eyes emotionally. "I don't want to be the shallow friend anymore who cares about what's on me more than what's in me. I'm sorry for ever making y'all feel like I thought I was better. I just needed to feel worth something, and I was covering up all of who I am with Chanel."

"Feel free to slide some of that Chanel over here during your rebranding era," Ellie joked.

Courtney laughed. "Yeah, I'll take a bag or two to help you out. We got to be supportive friends; you know?"

The trio laughed, lightening the moment, and Shy shrugged her shoulders. "Okay, that's it from me."

"How the hell am I supposed to top that? Ellie, you go next," Courtney said.

"Nobody's topping that, Court, no worries. We all lost," Ellie snickered as she lifted from her seat. She had kept it simple, but she was sure the girls would love it. Spa passes that include five hours of services plus a catered lunch. It wasn't Africa, but it was something she knew they could all use. Women rarely took the time to cater to themselves and this gift would force them to treat themselves.

"Cash it in whenever you need it," Ellie said. "Should I do Sloan's?" Ellie asked.

Courtney nodded. "Yeah, I'll go last."

Ellie pulled the bright orange Louis Vuitton boxes from under the tree.

"Big Sloan, never the little one!" Shy exclaimed, laughing as the girls grew giddy from the anticipation of what was inside.

They opened their boxes, and each woman pulled out a brand-new leather handbag from their Winter collection. Each bag fit their personal styles flawlessly. The note read:

*A little luxury for my favorite girls. Merry Christmas.*
*–S*

Courtney finally stood and grabbed two presents from underneath the tree and passed them to Ellie and Shy.

"So, for one, I'm not working right now, so don't hate me that it's not super expensive. It ain't fancy, but I think y'all will like it," she said. "Open it."

Both girls opened their gifts, and Ellie's eyes instantly watered.

"Before the Streetlights Come on," she whispered as she ran her hand over the embossed quote on the front of the leather Bible. "Courtney, it's perfect."

"I can hear Mrs. Whitlock clear as day, too," Shy said. "She taught us to always make sure each other made it home before the streetlights came on. It didn't matter where we were, or what we were doing, she put it in our heads like clockwork."

"Remember we used to walk all the way across town to get to one another in the summertime and your mama used to be like, 'If y'all not at somebody's house safe and sound before the streetlights come on, I'ma put leather to some asses'?"

Ellie laughed as Shy mocked her late mother. "Mama Whitlock was always threatening to whoop somebody else's kids," Shy laughed.

"We were all her girls, that's why," Courtney smiled, reminiscing. "Remember when Sloan was dating that boy, and she told her mama she was spending the night at your house, Ellie, when she was really trying to stay the night with a boy? Girllll, she called Sloan little Cricket phone and told her to have her ass home before the streetlights come on or she was going to send Cassidy to bust that boy's ass."

"She sent his ass too!" Shy cackled. "Cassidy couldn't wait to beat niggas up over Sloan's ass! How did you not know they were in love? Do you remember that?"

"I remember," Ellie sniffled as memories of her mom made her emotional, while making her laugh at the same time. "Making it home at night is a blessing that people forget to count," Ellie recited by memory, going deeper into the lesson they had been taught.

Before the streetlights came on was a phrase that represented safety. As teen girls, it had represented a curfew. Naturally, as they grew from girls to women, that curfew had been removed. But the habit of checking in and being accountable to their girl tribe had been instilled. The symbolic curfew that had remained urged them to send that text that read: HOME to their group chat. Mrs. Whitlock was no longer around to remind them, but her spirit still governed them through the lessons that had been taught. It was a perfect gift.

Ellie and the girls stood and hugged each other. "You won, Court," Ellie whispered. "Merry Christmas. You reminded us of our responsibility to one another. I really love y'all."

"Awww, Ellie," Shy cooed.

"We really love you, too, girl," Court said.

Ellie was a ball of nerves as she stood in front of Loyal's door. She hated that Cairo had cast this confusion over her life. If there was only one heart on the table, she would choose her wants every time, but her daughters held first consideration over her life. Their needs would always trump her wants. Cairo's revelation had blown her mind. She had wished for this so many times that now that it had come true, it felt like a curse. Ellie was walking around, opening presents, and exchanging pleasantries with loved ones, when deep down, there was a war going on in her soul. She didn't know what to do. She didn't know what the right decision was. She knew what to expect from Cairo. Staying would be comfortable. It would be familiar. If she moved on with Loyal, she would be in unchartered territory. Taking that risk was petrifying. She was intimidated by the unknown. Loyal opened the door, and she was stunned to find a little boy in his arms. It was such a conviction of love.

"Merry Christmas, E. I want you to meet my son, Zion," Loyal said as he looked down lovingly at the toddler in his arms.

Her heart was storming. This was good faith. This was effort. This introduction was him including her in the most important role he served in his life. She had wondered when she would meet his son. He had met her children. He had bonded with her father and was in business with her brother. Meeting his son made her feel special, like he was adding some meat and potatoes to their emotional bond.

"Hi, Zion, Merry Christmas," she sang, smiling half-heartedly because she was aching inside.

"Come on in," he invited.

"Is Tisa here?" she asked.

"Nah, she left after we opened presents with him. We agreed that she gets him Christmas Eve. I get Christmas Day," he informed.

"Oh," was all she had to offer.

"Can you say hi to Ellie, man?" Loyal asked. He grabbed her hand and pulled her closer, kissing her lips. He felt so carefree. Daddy mode was extremely attractive on Loyal. He was typically assertive and calculating, but just the presence of Zion softened him. "Where are the girls? I got gifts for them."

"They stayed home. I had to do the Friendsmas exchange with the girls, so I went there first," Ellie informed.

Zion reached for her, and she beamed as she took him from Loyal's arms.

"You want to play with my toys?" Zion's little voice tap danced on her ovaries. It was the sweetest sound.

She looked at Loyal in shock. "Wow, he's a big boy. He speaks so well."

Loyal grinned like the proud papa he was. "Yeah, I never talked to him like he was a baby. Tisa and I agreed on that. We read to him from the time he was born, we don't fuck with the screen time, lots of interaction. He's so smart, and I enjoy teaching him. My mom said I was non-verbal until I was three, so I wanted to make sure my son could speak. I caught up eventually, but it was a fear of mine when Tisa had him."

"Well, I am too in love to speak to him like a grown man. He's just too cute not to get a little baby talk," Ellie cooed as she tickled Zion's tummy. The little brown baby was the spitting image of his father, and he giggled endlessly as Ellie played with him. His little chubby cheeks, and bright, inquisitive eyes were so adorable, and the curly hair on his head was tamed by two braids.

"He likes you," Loyal said.

"I like him too," Ellie replied. She was a bit emotional because love was supposed to feel just like this. Loyal had mastered it. It was so easy that she sometimes had to stop herself from waiting for catastrophe. She was on pins and needles with him, waiting for the other shoe to drop, but she was slowly realizing that he simply was who he said he was.

Zion wiggled out of her arms, and she freed him, placing him on his feet. "Come over here!" Zion yelled. She followed him to the tree where he sat. Open wrapping paper was strewn everywhere, and more toys than one child could play with were all over the place. She sat and played with Loyal's son while he watched them from the couch.

"Confirmation like a mu'fucka," Loyal mumbled, barely audible, as he shook his head.

"What are you talking about over there?" Ellie asked, without taking her focus from Zion.

She glanced up at him. "What?" she asked.

"Nothing, man," he replied, still shaking his head with a ghost of a smile on his lips. "How long I got you for? Robert and Mom Dukes are hosting dinner. My family will be there. Is it too much, too fast, to ask you to join me?"

"Maybe that might be a little fast," Ellie stammered. "Can we start here? With Zion? I don't want to keep you from your family. You and Zion should go. Papa does Chinese food and Christmas movies on Christmas Day. We sit around in pajamas and watch the classics. *Christmas Story, Home Alone*... I really shouldn't miss that. I haven't been home in four years, so I owe him a few movies," Ellie chuckled. "I didn't want to not see you, though. I really needed to feel you."

Something in her tone made him take a deeper look, and he got down on the floor with her and his son. "I ain't made you feel nothing yet, so it's definitely not time to leave," Loyal whispered in her ear, while kissing the side of her face discreetly. "What you need to feel, E?"

She was breathless. His emotional intelligence was magnificent, but their physical connection was like a pulse that filled every room they both occupied.

"I tried so hard to ration my feelings for you, Loyal," she confessed. "This is damn dangerous. We're doing 100 mph in a 35-mph zone, and I'm like, gripping the door handles from the passenger seat."

"If I'm in the driver seat, you can rest easy, E," Loyal said. This power of a human being was so loving to her. He knew the strength of his dominance enough to know when not to use it. The intimacy of these sweet nothings in her ear, of the subtle nudges and kisses. Ellie loved it here. "Zion, hand Daddy the red box under the tree," Loyal said, pointing to its location.

Zion's little body climbed under the branches and retrieved the box. "This one?" He asked.

"That's the one. You want to give it to Ellie? That's her gift from Santa," Loyal said.

Zion's little legs carried him over to her, and he handed her the box. "What is it? What is inside of there, Ellie?" The way he said her name was too cute not to laugh.

"We working on them Ls," Loyal snickered.

Ellie laughed and reluctantly accepted the box. "I didn't know we were exchanging gifts, Loyal. I'm not prepared for this."

Loyal rubbed his lips. "I only want one thing; you ain't even got to wrap it," he flirted.

She blushed, and her body reacted to him. The power of a man when a woman actually liked him was miraculous. All it took was one word, a simple look, hell, sometimes just a thought, and her body turned on. It was something she had struggled with in her relationship with Cairo. He never took the time to heat her oven. He just wanted to put the dish in with the touch of one button. He was a lazy and unprepared cook. Loyal was a sous chef.

"Do you want to help me open it?" Ellie asked.

"Yes, please," Zion answered. She pulled him into her lap and allowed Zion to snatch the intricately wrapped paper and bow off.

She opened the box and frowned at the key that sat on top of a QR code.

"What is this?" she asked.

"It's a key, silly," Zion answered. She rubbed the top of his head and then reached inside her purse to retrieve her cell phone. When she scanned the code, a home listing popped up, only it was marked: SOLD. Her eyes fluttered up at him in disbelief.

"It's a five-bedroom. I got it in Bloomfield because I figured you'd want a suburban feel. If I'm wrong, you can sell it, and you can choose a different area. It should be enough space for you and the girls," he said. "Everything's updated. It's not a new build because I'm a contractor who loves the quality of homes built before the year 2000, but it's been completely redone inside. Old bones, new guts."

Ellie was washed in a sense of overwhelm. This was too much for her. He was too good for her. He was so sure, and she was everything but certain.

"There's one more thing," he informed. He stood and walked over to the mantle to retrieve a manila envelope. He handed it to her. Tears were imminent, but she was fighting them off tooth and nail.

"It's ten percent of the partnership that Cass and I are starting. I'm gifting you ten of my shares," he stated.

"I can't accept this," Ellie whispered, eyes brimming with disbelief, but most of all with sorrow. "Loyal!"

"E, we ain't got to do this dance. Let me give you what you deserve," Loyal said. "Ain't no strings. Your name is on everything."

Ellie shook her head, moving Zion from her lap gently, and then standing to her feet. "I can't..." She felt wetness hit her cheeks and saw Loyal's confusion all over his face.

"Elliot, talk to me," Loyal said, following her to the kitchen, out of earshot from his son, but within eyesight. He was calm. Every time she was a different version of her neurotic self, he was patient. She appreciated his ability to stay levelheaded even when she was being insane. Cairo had never done that. Their arguments would escalate every time because Cairo matched her energy instead of allaying it. "Whatever you're telling yourself we can't have, I promise you, we can. It don't matter what I got to do to make it happen. You don't like the house? The location? What?"

"The house is beautiful," Ellie sighed. "It's perfect. You're... you showed up in my life too early, Loyal. I'm not ready for you. I'm damaged, and you aren't the one who broke me. I've got to deal with the person who broke me before I can go into something like this with you. It's not fair to you."

"Fuck we talking about here, E?" Loyal asked, brow bent. "What you mean you got to deal with that nigga?" Loyal didn't mince words. He wanted to be clear, and she couldn't lie to him. He didn't deserve anything less than the truth.

Ellie held onto the edge of the counter and bowed her head. Her chin quivered. *I just met this man. This can't be this hard,* she thought. Only it was this hard. It was impossible. She was about to throw her life off course. She felt it. The possibility of what life could look like with Loyal was beautiful. It sat just on the horizon; all she had to do was keep putting one foot in front of the other. She had to grow. She had to move forward. But her past was calling her. She had time invested with Cairo, and what if…What if they could really repair and make things work? It was too much invested to not try. Right?

"Cairo came by the house last night. He wants to work things out," Ellie could barely choke out the words. She saw them land viciously, and his entire body stiffened. He went from caring to indifferent in seconds.

He looked down at his son and then up at her. This was hurting him. She could tell. He was too stubborn to show it, but his eyes gave him away.

"What do you want?" Loyal demanded. Patience gone. He was angry, and she couldn't even blame him.

"I don't know," she whispered. "But I do know that my girls need their father. They deserve parents who fight to make it work for them. If I can give that to them…" She couldn't even finish the sentence because it hurt.

Loyal nodded. "I can't have this conversation in front of my son," Loyal stated.

He wanted to yell. He wanted to escalate the shit. Ellie wished he could feel her heart right now. This wasn't easy for her. It was breaking her inside.

"I'm sorry." If her sorrow was a measure of her regret, then it was infinite. Her heart shattered more and more as every second passed. His silence was punishment. She hated it. Finally, he said,

"Yeah, me too." He turned his back to her and went back to Zion. "You should get back to your family."

"Please don't hate me," she whispered.

He looked at her with the eyes of a stranger. It was like he was bumping into her at the mall. "How can I hate you? I don't even fucking know you, Elliot." Not E. Not even Ellie. Just Elliot. Damn.

She stifled the sob that tried to escape from her lips because she didn't want to alarm his son. She couldn't get out of there fast enough. Ellie barely made it to the hallway before she broke down. She knew that she was giving up something special with Loyal, but she also knew if she didn't, her daughters would be giving up something greater. They needed Cairo more than she needed Loyal. If anyone had to sacrifice, it would be her. She and Loyal had just crossed paths at the wrong time, but in the short time she had known him, he had completely transformed her expectation of love. Now, she had a standard. She just wasn't sure anyone else would be able to live up to it.

# CHAPTER 23

### December 26th

Sloan pulled up to the address Ellie had sent. She hated that she was nervous. They had never gone this long without speaking, and the knot in her stomach made her feel like she would throw up. She hated the discord. Christmas had been spent on the most glorious beach, but the sun did nothing to melt away the feeling of disconnection that she felt. She had gone away hoping to heal, but she had only isolated herself and intensified her pain. Relief had filled her when Ellie had waved the white flag. To think of bringing in the New Year without fixing things with her friend was heavy. Ellie was her constant. Ellie was her sister. She felt obligated to make amends. Soul mates came in many forms, and hers was Elliot Whitlock-Campbell. The traditional home was picture-perfect. It looked like something out of a *Home Alone* movie. The snow-covered lawn framed the bricked colonial with the three-car garage.

She bent her neck to look out her passenger window as she parked curbside. Ellie's mother's car was parked in the driveway. Sloan climbed out of the car and walked to the door. She rang the bell, and Ellie pulled open the door.

"Come on in," Ellie welcomed before leading Sloan to the living room.

"Whose house is this?" Sloan asked as she turned in a circle while giving the place a once-over. It was beautifully renovated inside. Everything was new, updated with the highest finishes.

"It's mine," Ellie answered.

Sloan turned to Ellie in surprise.

"A Christmas gift from Loyal. I guess I'm moving back home," Ellie said, shrugging.

Sloan gave Ellie a small smile. It was all her soul could offer right now. She nodded.

"Wow, this is a big gift. You're living here with him?" Sloan asked.

Ellie shook her head. "No, alone. I told Loyal I need time. I need to settle my divorce, give the girls time to adjust, and give myself time to process the end of a marriage and a relocation back home before I let Loyal whisk me off my feet. I tried to give the house back, but he said it was an insult. So, I guess this is our new home."

"Is it in your name?" Sloan asked.

"Bitch, you know I ain't Boo Boo the fucking fool. Absolutely," Ellie replied.

"That's a good move, Ellie," Sloan said. "We all wanted you closer. I know your dad is happy, and I'm really happy you decided to pull the trigger on your divorce. You deserve so

ASHLEY ANTOINETTE

much better. I know it'll hurt. It's grieving a person that's still alive, but I think it's for the best."

"Yeah, me too. He pulled up to Papa's house on Christmas, after he got wind that I was filing, and tried to talk about a reconciliation," Ellie informed.

Sloan jerked her neck back in shock.

"Exactly my reaction," Ellie stated, not even needing words from Sloan. "I considered it too. I wanted to do what's best for the girls, and I felt like I should stick it out so that their father could come home, but nah. Fuck that and fuck him. What's best for my kids is showing them how to walk away from something that doesn't serve them."

"You're absolutely teaching them what they should and should not accept in a relationship, Ellie. Just because it's their dad doesn't make the lesson go away. You showed them how to stand up for themselves. You're doing what's best for you, which means it's what's best for them. A healthy and happy mother matters." It was such a generic response from her best friend, and Ellie felt the tension in the room. Sloan was hurt, and so was Ellie. They couldn't just move on like their disagreement had never happened.

Ellie looked at her, frowning, and Sloan felt an insecurity fill her. "What?"

"Bitch, I can't stand here and play pretend with you. This is awkward, and we're being all cute and nice when we know it's an elephant in the room. Let's just put it on the floor. I'm fucking mad as hell at you, but I love you too much to stay mad. I was wrong, and I'm sorry."

Sloan sighed, pushing out a breath of relief. "No, girl, I'm sorry. I should have never entertained your brother, Ellie. I knew how you felt, and I did it anyway, and now everything is all awkward and fucked up. It was selfish, and I'm so sorry. You're my best friend. I don't want to lose you. I don't want to change our dynamic, and I don't want you to think I was using our friendship to get to Cassidy. I wasn't. It wasn't like that."

"The dynamic has changed, though," Ellie replied. "You're my friend, Sloan, but I've always wanted a sister. My brother is crazy about you, Sloan. I don't want to stand in the way of the two people I love most in the world loving each other."

"You're not the only thing standing in the way," Sloan admitted.

"I know," Ellie replied. "But Cassidy isn't who you think he is. He did his crime, and he paid for it, but it wasn't a random act of violence. This isn't the same circumstance that your mom went through. He would never hurt you. He's not crazy. He's not going to black out on you one day, Sloan. He's Cass. He's the same guy he's always been to you."

"How can he be? Killing someone with your bare hands got to change a man," Sloan whispered. "That's terrifying, Ellie. Every time I think of it…" Sloan felt the fear creep into her soul, and she shivered.

"I have something for you. I stole them from Cass, but you need to read them," Ellie stated. She went to the pantry door and disappeared inside. She emerged with a shoebox and placed it on the table. Sloan followed her and took a seat.

"What is this?"

"It's my mom's letters to him while he was in jail. I haven't read them because I don't need to. I know who Cass is. You should," Ellie urged.

"Ellie!" Sloan hissed. "This is personal! These are your mom's words. They're meant for Cass. I can't invade his privacy like that. I won't. If there is something in these letters that I should know, he is going to have to be the one to tell me."

The doorbell rang, and Sloan's eyes shot to the door as Cassidy came waltzing in.

"Well, here is his chance," Ellie stated as she stood from the table.

The shock that took over Cassidy's face when he landed eyes on Sloan told her that he hadn't been expecting her.

"Ellie, you shouldn't have done this," Sloan whispered. "This ain't cool." Sloan stood, preparing to leave.

"Sloan, please," Ellie begged. "I know you're afraid, and I understand why, but he's not who you think he is."

"E, it's cool," Cassidy stated.

"No, Cass! It's not cool! She doesn't even know-"

"It doesn't matter, E," Cassidy dismissed.

"What doesn't matter?" Sloan whispered. "What aren't you saying? Please, just tell me, Cassidy. Tell me anything because I don't want to have to sneak and read letters from your mom to try to figure you out!"

Cassidy walked over to the table, discovering the shoebox. There were over a hundred letters inside, all from his mother. He turned to Ellie, knowing she was responsible for this.

"This what we doing? These don't belong to you, E. You're out of fucking line," he spat sharply. "Did you read them?" he asked Ellie.

"No, Cass, but she should!" Ellie shouted.

He turned to her, face bent in anguish.

"I don't know what you want from me," Cassidy drawled.

"I want you to tell me you regret it! I want you to tell me that I have nothing to be afraid of. That you're sorry. Tell me why you did it! Tell me something, Cassidy!"

"Fuck no. I don't feel bad about shit, and I'll never regret it," Cassidy stated in a low tone. "If I had to make the same decision again, I would. I'd beat the life out that nigga." It was his certainty that made him menacing. It was the peace in his eyes when he said it that told her he meant every word. He was so unremorseful, and it made him seem heartless. She couldn't fathom this level of violence. It was cruel and inhumane. Goosebumps formed on her arms because she didn't know how not to fear a man this ruthless.

Sloan's eyes teared, and she had to clench her fists to stop herself from shaking. "Who are you?" she whispered, shaking her head.

Sloan stormed for the door, and Ellie pinched the bridge of her nose.

"Damn, Cass! A little gentler; do you want her to walk out the door?" Ellie whispered, chastising her brother.

"She's looking for answers I can't give her," Cassidy stated solemnly.

"Sloan, please, just stay. Both of you, just listen to me! Y'all are giving up on each other!" Ellie shouted at the top of her lungs, exasperated. They were like two freight trains headed toward one another on the same track. "I was wrong. I don't know how I missed the bond y'all have all these years, but I see it now. Sloan, Cassidy loves you. He loves you so much, and I know why you're afraid to trust him, but I also know that you trust me with your life. I'm telling you that he will not hurt you. Everything that you think you know, you don't. Cassidy, please say something! Fight for her!" Ellie looked to Cassidy, who stood, rubbing the back of his neck in distress. She walked over to him and placed a hand to his forearm and gave it a gentle squeeze. "You have to tell her everything. I know you're hurt by what she thinks of you. I know you made a promise all those years ago, but it's time to break that promise. It's time to tell the truth. Because if you don't, you're going to let the love of your life walk out that door, and you'll lose her. You deserve her, Cassidy. I'm going to go to Papa's and give y'all some time to talk. Say something that matters, Cass." Ellie grabbed her purse and her keys and then walked out.

Sloan stood with her arms folded, swaying impatiently, defensively as she willed herself not to cry.

Cassidy walked over to the table and sat, legs wide, leaning elbows to his knees as he bowed his head. He steepled his fingertips under his chin.

"I'm sorry she ambushed you like this. I didn't know you would be here." Cassidy's stress was evident. "She asked me to come move some shit in. This whole shit was a setup."

"Yeah, she Didn't mention you'd be here either," Sloan responded.

They were both so stubborn. Mad at the world because they were choosing to be mad at one another.

"You ain't got to steer clear of me, Sloan," Cassidy said. "I know you've spent every Christmas at Papa's since your mom passed. He missed you this year. Ellie missed you. My nieces missed you."

"You were there. I couldn't be," she answered.

"You hate me that much?" Cassidy accused.

"I love you that much," she corrected. "And it hurts me to breathe the same air as you if I can't have you."

"I made my mama a promise twenty-three years ago, Sloan," Cassidy revealed. Sloan turned and leaned against the wall, giving him her full attention. "I've never broken that promise for anyone."

"I'm not asking you to…"

"Only, you are, because if I don't, I'm going to lose you," Cassidy stated. He put his hand on the shoebox and spun it around on the table. "This is all I got left of her."

Sloan stepped closer to him, and he rested his face against her stomach, closing his eyes. She sighed and placed her hands on top of his head. There was so much rest in these seconds when they allowed this connection to exist.

"Read the letters."

Sloan lowered into the seat next to his, facing him as he tapped one finger on top of the shoebox.

"I'm giving you permission to read the letters," he whispered.

ASHLEY ANTOINETTE

She lost air. He was trusting her with something he treasured. A mother's words to her son were sacred, and he was sharing those words with her. It was a great privilege to be trusted so much. A bit of her resolve melted. "I don't think I should, Cassidy," she answered.

"If you want the answers to your questions, they're in these letters," Cassidy revealed. "They're dated and organized from the very first one. The first letter came a week after I was sentenced."

"This feels intrusive. This wasn't my idea. Ellie gave them to me. I would never..."

"I know," he reassured. He stood. "It'll take you some time to find the answers you're searching for, but when you're done, you know how to find me if you want to talk."

Sloan nodded and reached for Cassidy's hand.

"You didn't come to the Christmas party." His voice was somber.

"I came, Cass. I lost my patient that day, so I was late, but I showed up, and you were gone. You left with another woman," Sloan scoffed, shaking her head.

The realization that she had shown up washed over him, loosening the Vise-Grip that had been on his chest ever since.

"I'm sorry about your patient," Cassidy said.

"Me too." Her chin quivered, and she lowered her face in embarrassment. "This is just a really hard time for me."

They grew quiet, and Sloan looked down at her hands. "Nigga, you sorry about the wrong thing," Sloan snapped.

Cassidy chuckled and rubbed the back of his neck. "So, is this a you-don't-want-a-nigga, but I-can't-fuck-with-nobody-else typ'a thing?"

371

"I don't know what it is, Cass, but did you sleep with Lola?" she asked.

"I thought about it." At least he was truthful. "But I sent her home before shit went too far."

Sloan's relief was audible.

"I'm losing with you, either way, baby…"

Sloan's heart fluttered at the sentiment, but she didn't interrupt.

"If I force the issue with you, I scare you; if I pull back, you're jealous…"

"Ain't nobody jealous," Sloan interrupted. "You're just not supposed to move on from me that fast."

"I don't want to move on at all," Cassidy admitted. He leaned forward and took ahold of her hands. "You're shaking, Sloan."

"My heart is racing," she murmured. She squeezed his hands harder as if she was bracing herself for the drop of a steep roller coaster, and maybe she was. Maybe all these hard moments after they decided to have sex were the ascent that came with choosing to be intimate with another human being. People rushed so quickly into sex that they didn't realize the portals inside themselves were opened during that act. She was completely exposed, and so was he, and all they seemed to be doing was hurting each other because they hadn't stopped to think of the responsibility that came with having each other in that way. She gazed into his eyes and got lost. This hurt so good. Cassidy was the first person in a long time that made her feel weak. It was almost a relief to know that she was capable of something other than strength.

"Don't cry, baby," Cassidy whispered.

"I just want to feel safe," Sloan's words were almost a whisper. They were a plea, revealing her desperation. Her sorrow was a reflection of all that she had lost when her mother had been taken from her. When he brought her clenched fists to his lips and kissed them, she panicked because she knew he was about to let go.

"Take some time with the letters. I respect your decision to say no, Sloan. But you've been in my life a long time. Even if we ain't supposed to be more, I don't want to be less. I don't want us to not exist to one another. You've always been family. I don't want to lose more than I've already lost. My freedom, my time, my mother. Adding you to that list…"

Cassidy shook his head and flicked his nose as he stood. "How much more punishment do I need to take for it to be enough? For me to be free of it? You're keeping me tied to it, Sloan. So, please, just read them."

She nodded. "Can I read them with Ellie? I don't want to be alone."

Cassidy sighed. "You can process them however you need to if it helps you know me better." And then he was gone.

"I think you should read these alone, Sloan," Ellie said as she sat in the middle of Sloan's bed, Indian-style the way they used to as teenagers.

BEFORE THE STREET LIGHTS COME ON

"You don't want to know what they say?" Sloan asked.

Ellie shook her head. "I don't need to know what they say," Ellie replied. "I know Cassidy, and I think the part that hurts him most is that he thought you knew him, too."

Sloan closed her eyes and lifted her head to the sky. "God, help me with this," she whispered.

Ellie reached out and hugged Sloan. "I'll be here, just hanging out until you're done. Just holler if you need me." Ellie frowned in disgust suddenly.

"What?" Sloan asked in confusion.

"Wait, bitch, did you fuck my brother in this bed?" Ellie asked, truly repulsed as she stood.

"Girl!" Sloan laughed. She picked up one of the pillows and tossed it at Ellie. "Get out so I can read."

Ellie winked at her, knowing she had lightened the mood. "I'll be in the living room."

"I did fuck him on that couch, though!" Sloan shouted after her, snickering.

"Gross!" Ellie shouted back.

Sloan pulled out the first letter, and as soon as she read the words, My Sweet Son, Cassidy, her chest locked. She could hear Mrs. Whitlock's voice as clear as day.

*My Sweet Son, Cassidy,*

*What did you do, son? My God, how I have failed you. It is a mother's job to protect her children, and here I am, watching you be punished for protecting me. I will never be able*

*to rest knowing my baby is locked up. That
man was an animal who should have been
locked up a long time ago. They punished the
wrong one, Cassidy, and I am heartbroken
that my ghosts have come back to haunt you. I
am so sorry, baby. My heart is broken because
the gift of relief was given to me in the form
of your sacrifice. You should be free, my love,
but instead, you set me free. The ultimate
expression of love is sacrifice, and you have
given me your life, son. I am not worthy of you.
A jury of your peers can see your spirit, son.
You'll never be guilty in my eyes. God knows
the demon you slayed. It wasn't yours to defeat,
though, son, and it is my burden to bear to
know that I am the reason you're in there. I
love you. No matter the time or distance, my
love will be with you. When you're afraid, know
that I am with you. My sweet boy.*

*Love Mama*

It was only the first letter, and Sloan was already a mess. She went through letter after letter, and box of Kleenex after box of Kleenex as she pieced together the tragedy that had occurred. Before she knew it, the sun was rising.

The knock at the door caused her to gaze up as Ellie peeked her head inside.

"You haven't slept all night?" Ellie asked.

BEFORE THE STREET LIGHTS COME ON

Sloan shook her head and tried to speak, but nothing came out but emotion. "Why did this have to happen?" she choked out. "This is trauma, Ellie. How is he supposed to be okay after this?"

Ellie's own eyes watered, and she answered, "Love will heal him, Sloan. He deserves all the love he can get, and if that's not from you, the least you can do is not judge him. He cares a great deal about what you think."

Sloan rolled her eyes to the heavens and then removed her reading glasses, pinching the bridge of her nose before putting them back on and grabbing the next letter.

"You can't possibly read them all," Ellie said, frowning. "That's over a decade worth of letters!"

"I have to," Sloan whispered. "Before I talk to Cassidy again, I need to."

Ellie nodded. "I'm going to head home. If you need me, I'm only a phone call away."

"Thanks, Ellie," Sloan sighed.

"And, Sloan?"

Sloan looked up one more time.

"Don't break my brother's heart," Ellie said. "I will still fight you about him." Ellie warned.

"I think I'm the one at risk for that. Make sure you tell him you'll beat his ass if he hurts me," Sloan scoffed.

"The threat has already been issued," Ellie said softly with a wink. Ellie departed, and Sloan was compelled to continue. Through heavy, burning eyes, and with anxiety filling her to the brim, she dove back in.

# CHAPTER 24

**December 27<sup>th</sup>**

The letters sent her down a rabbit hole of research. The trial was public record, so she accessed everything. The crime scene photos, the statements that had been acquired by the police, even the witness transcripts for both attorneys. When she was younger, she had wanted Cassidy to be innocent. She had prayed every night for the jury to free him. As a grown woman, she realized that innocence was irrelevant. She wanted him to be justified. It took Sloan four days to read all the letters. She carried them everywhere with her. To work, to the grocery store, to the hair salon. It was all she could think of. She asked Ellie questions, but she quickly realized that Ellie didn't have the answers herself. Ellie trusted her instincts and rode with Cassidy no matter what. The details were in these letters, and the only person who could complete the picture for her was Cassidy. She hadn't heard from him, and she knew he was being respectful and giving her space, but it was time that she faced him. When she finished the final letter,

377

she felt like she had witnessed love in its purest form.

She had flipped through envelopes, drowning in a sea of handwritten emotion. Now that she was done, it felt odd. It felt incomplete, and she knew why. She had heard his mother's reactions. She needed his transparency, his accountability. She picked up her phone. She knew it was rude to call him this late. She still dialed his number.

"Yeah." His baritone bombarded her ear. She could tell he had been asleep. She was sure he hadn't even looked at the phone before answering. She was silent, unsure of how or where to begin.

"Yo, who is this?" he asked. A beat of silence. She knew he checked the screen this time because her name followed. "Sloan?"

"I finished the letters."

She heard motion. If he had been asleep before, he was wide awake now.

"You were defending your mom. She never said what he did. Please tell me your side," she whispered. "I have to know the full story."

It was his turn to be silent. She feared he would tell her no.

"I'm no longer judging. I just want to know you," she pleaded.

"I took my mama to the grocery store every Saturday afternoon so she could get her groceries for Sunday dinner..."

Sloan sighed in relief as she settled in.

"I can remember what was on her menu like it was yesterday. Meatloaf, mashed potatoes and gravy, cabbage, and homemade sweet rolls. It was the last meal I ate before I got locked up."

Sloan's forehead bent in concern at the road he was going down. Mrs. Whitlock had been the cornerstone of their family. She had been so loved. Sloan had adored her, and she remembered those Sunday meals well. She was a guest at that table more times than she could count.

"I remember we went to the store. She always took E because she wanted her to know how to put a meal together. Said a little girl that didn't know-"

"How to make groceries might as well be a little nappy-headed boy..."

Sloan finished his sentence with a soft laugh. "I remember." They both fell silent as their memories of her manifested in their spirit. "What happened at the store that day, Cass? Her letters are full of sorrow about what occurred, but she never mentioned what happened," Sloan said, urgently. "Her side is like one side of a puzzle. I need your side to complete the picture. Please, help me understand this."

"I feel like I'm dishonoring her, Sloan. Telling you this goes against her wishes. She kept this secret her entire life. She was embarrassed by it, ashamed. She was afraid to speak life to it," Cassidy said. "She trusted me with it."

What a burden for a first-born son. Sloan's empathy knew no bounds for this family. The Whitlocks, her second home, where her dearest friend lived, and her soulmate was torn from.

"I understand if it's too much for you to say. I can tell it's heavy on you. When you're ready for help carrying it, know I'm here," Sloan whispered.

She heard him sniff away emotions.

"Can I hit you back?"

He needed to get off the phone, and she understood.

"Okay."

He hung up, and Sloan climbed out of bed, rushing, a bit frantic as she stepped into leggings and a slouchy sweater. She dressed as quickly as she could and grabbed her bag and her keys. She was arousing his demons, and his past was picking at a wound she hadn't healed. She just wanted to see him. She called Ellie.

"Bitch, it's two o'clock in the morning, you better be dying," Ellie groaned sleepily in the phone.

"Text me Cass's address," Sloan said.

"Is everything okay?" Ellie asked, more alert.

"I finished the letters, Ellie. Please, just send it," Sloan pleaded.

"Do you even have a plan? Did you change your mind about him? Bitch, clue me in!" Ellie asked in excitement.

"I don't know, but I just need to see him. Thanks, sis," Sloan said, hanging up. Sloan drove 40 minutes to get to him. It was the middle of the night and freezing outside. She was sure she was unwelcome. She had done nothing but make him feel unworthy of her. She was making him face her anyway.

She pulled up to Cassidy's townhome and gripped the steering wheel as anxiety filled her.

"Fuck it." She climbed out and walked to the front door. She pressed on that doorbell repeatedly until he snatched open the door.

"Your mom trusted you with her truth. Trust me with yours, Cassidy," she said, eyes shining desperately.

He stepped aside to let her inside and then closed the door, turning the lock. She didn't know why that lock felt final, like, he was never letting her leave.

"I'm really trying to respect your boundaries, Sloan, but you keep coming around. What you want me to do? Earn you? I'll do that. I ain't afraid of that; but if you really don't want this, you got to respect your own boundaries and keep from around a nigga because it's only so much resisting I can do," Cassidy said. "You being here at three o'clock in the morning is begging me to do something. You ain't here to talk."

She was like a deer in headlights. He was right. Her heart was pounding, and her body craved connection. She was wound so tightly with anxiety and aching that could only be healed one way, by one man. This man was damaged. He was hurting. He had been for so long over a sacrifice he had made for his mother. A boy protecting his mother, when the roles were supposed to be naturally reversed. Sloan couldn't imagine what had pushed his back to the wall, but she knew it was unspeakable. She didn't need to know the full story to know that it weighed on him because even his half-truth was like a boulder tied to her ankle in a river of confusion. She was trying to tread water as best she could but only he could save her.

"We can talk in the morning," she heaved. Why couldn't she catch her breath? Cassidy advanced on her, picking her up and placing her on the kitchen island. So much tension had built up between them, it was like relief as he kissed her. She panted, squeezing her eyes shut as he stripped her of her coat and everything else underneath.

"I'm so sorry," she whispered between kisses. He pulled off his shirt, and the definition of his body took her breath away. "For everything I said, everything I assumed." He leaned into her, forehead to forehead as their noses touched. The strain between them wasn't just physical. It was psychological and emotional. It was all-consuming. Allowing themselves to have something once was like a hit of heroin. They couldn't just stop. They couldn't will themselves to quit. Sloan had become this man's medicine, and he would either be consumed to her detriment or her healing. She was trying to discern between the two. Her body didn't care. It rioted for him. His every breath she inhaled.

"I'd never hurt you, Sloan. Ever. Know that. Know me."

She nodded. "I know you," she confirmed. "I've always known you."

She wrapped her arms around his neck and her legs around his waist, and he carried her up the stairs to his bedroom.

He descended over her as he placed her in his bed. "I love you so much," she admitted.

He looked at her with a sincerity that made her eyes water, but his silence set off a panic she hadn't felt before. He didn't believe her, and she reached for him, pulling him down on top of her. "You don't love me anymore?" Her worry was so viable that it drained out her eyes, sliding down the side of her head until it hit his pillow.

"You know better," he replied. "Don't you?"

She nodded as he kissed her neck, awakening every nerve in her body as his tongue drew circles against her skin. He positioned himself between her legs and knocked down her every emotional wall as he entered her. Cassidy was amazing in bed. He had the type of dick that made women bust out car windows. He was so thick, and the perfect length, and his head was so wide that Sloan's mouth watered. Cassidy was a pinch hitter. He was the one to hit it out of the park when others who had tried failed. He stroked her slowly but with an aggression that told her he had some heat on his chest. He dove deep until he was rooted so deeply inside her that all she could do was suck in air. Was this punishment? Unrequited love? Had she denied him one too many times and now he was weary to give her what she needed? He was right. She did know better, but she still wanted to hear the words. She was desperate for reassurance. She was desperate for him; for this. Heavy breathing filled the space between their lips until he took those too.

It was in the way that he fucked Sloan that blew her mind. He was so grateful for her. He was patient but wanting at the same time. He was aggressive in a way that let her know he was in control, yet his stroke didn't come with an ounce of pain. All she could do was submit while he put in work. He lifted her legs over his shoulders and pulled her hips into him, and she cried out in ecstasy.

"Cassidy," she moaned. She couldn't not call his name. She wanted to scream that shit. Sign it. Write it in Braille. Tag that shit to a wall. She had thought the first time had been good because of the anticipation that had led up to the moment, but nah, the nigga was just magnificent. He tested her limitations and sexed her like he had read her body's manual. He understood that his size could be a bad thing if he went too hard. He was delivering pleasure, and he never took her past the threshold where pain existed. Hands everywhere. Mouth everywhere. Dick every fucking where. The hand to her neck was the sexiest shit she had ever experienced. She would have never trusted any other man to choke her. It was an immediate trigger, normally. With Cassidy, it was erotic and dominant. She was in love with this man, and she knew it now more than ever because of the level of trust she was extending. She didn't even know why she was acting like there was a choice in this matter. This man had her soul. He owned her body, and the heart that she was trying to keep control of was giving in. It was a complete takeover. Yes, she was terrified, and she still wanted this shit. All of it. All this love. He was hitting it so good that her legs trembled, and he lowered them, showing that he was merciful in these sheets.

Her back arched off the bed as she absorbed his stroke. He brought her to orgasm, then turned her to the side and stroked her there, dick so thick and long it was effortless for him to hit it until he came too. He held her from behind, playing in her hair as he bit gently on her ear.

She reached back and placed her hand on the side of his face, closing her eyes. How she had ever questioned whether he was safe was foolish. There was no place safer. She could feel love all over her body.

"That day at the store changed my life," Cassidy muttered. "It wouldn't have taken me 23 years to get here with you if it wasn't for that day." She didn't move. Didn't breathe because she didn't want him to stop talking. He wrapped one arm around Sloan and held her tight as he found his place in the groove of her neck. She stared at the wall and held onto his arms as he continued. "She bumped right into him when we were leaving. I've never seen my mother so afraid. He walked up on her, smiling. He called her Caramel, like that was her name. It was casual enough. He seemed friendly. He was happy to see her, but it was the look on her face that told me something was off. I remember her hands shaking as we got in the car, and she was quiet the entire way home, but her hands… they just kept shaking. I remember that part so well for some reason. When we pulled into the driveway, and I went to help her from the car, the entire seat was wet. She was so terrified that she peed herself. Papa was at work. I carried her into the house and up to her room. I tried to clean her up, and she gripped my hand so tight, and she said that she hadn't seen his face in 25 years. That man from the grocery store had raped her from the time she was five years old until she was 13. He lived across the street from her as a child, and she used to play with his daughter. My grandma used to send her over there for play dates. That nigga used to make his daughter take a nap and rape my mama while she was there. It only stopped because she moved to the other side of town when my grandmother got a job as a housekeeper for a white woman on the

Southside. She never said a word to anyone, until she told me, and she made me promise not to tell anyone, and I haven't— until now. Papa don't even know."

Sloan's heart tore in half.

"Oh, Cassidy," she whispered sympathetically.

"I found out where that nigga lived the same night, went over there strapped. I had used a gun before, hadn't killed nobody, but I had shot at niggas on some tough guy shit, so I thought it would be easy. The nigga had violated my mama. It was the heaviest trigger I had ever felt. He saw me hesitate, and he came at me, took my gun, put it point blank to my head, and the gun jammed. I was supposed to be dead right then and there. He was a big nigga, had a lot of weight on him. I remember thinking of my mom as a little girl under all that weight. He grabbed the pole first. I don't even know where it came from."

Sloan's hands moved to her throat. She felt like she was choking because she remembered this part of the story from the trial. She remembered the bruises on his neck. The defense had made the old man sound like a victim who had fought back and lost.

"He choked you with it," Sloan whispered. Her tears flowed, creating a salty river from her eyes to her mouth.

"The whole room was fading out. My shit was burning so bad. My lungs just needed air. He was a drunk, and I was grabbing for anything. The bottle on the floor beside me was what my hands found first. I hit him as hard as I could, and it was enough to get him up off me and get him to drop that pole. I grabbed that bitch, and I swung. I ain't let up off that nigga until I was sure he wouldn't get up. I swung what felt like a hundred times," Cassidy whispered. He sniffed and thumbed away a tear that had escaped. He cleared his throat, and she felt him stiffen behind her, restoring his strength. "The nigga violated my mama, so I handled that for her. Nobody protected her, so I did, and no, Sloan, you, or nobody else will ever make me regret that. I gave up half my life. They buried my mama while I was in there, wouldn't even let me out to come to the funeral. I missed birthdays, holidays. My sister became a grown woman, and my dad aged and got sick. Friends forgot about me. You outgrew me and became Superwoman. It was all a sacrifice, but it was worth it because my mama got to know what protection felt like before she died. She felt safe. She visited me every week, until she was too sick to come, and even then, she wrote me letters, and she never judged me. She thanked me. She was proud of me, and that's enough. I'll eat those years every time for her. You're the first person I've told."

"But Ellie knows," Sloan whispered.

"Ellie don't know," Cassidy said. "She's guessed pretty damn closely over the years, and she put a story together in her head based on what she heard at trial, and what she saw at the grocery store that day, but I've never come out and told her. I never had to. She knew that I killed him, and she knew I had a reason, and she never questioned if I was justified or not. She knew I was because she knew me."

Sloan had to fold her lips in to trap her emotion. That last part was for her. She had treated him like a stranger, like everything she knew about him didn't exist. He was right. She should have known. She turned to him, kissing his lips. "I don't deserve a second chance at this. I should have known."

"I understand why you have doubts. I watched niggas finesse women from prison for years. I watched dudes come and go with the worst of intentions. Niggas who hated women. Niggas who planned the ways they would hurt the very women who held them down while they were locked up. It was woman beaters, scammers, rapists, pedophiles, murderers of women. Prison is hell. It's a lot of devils in there. I went through a lot, especially being so young when I went in, but I held my own. I kept my head down, and I did my time as honorably as I could, Sloan. I've got my own demons I fight from being in that place. None of them will ever make me harm you. Not ever!" She snuggled her face into his chest, and he lifted her chin to force eye contact. "Not ever, Sloan," he stressed. "I'm not like the man who killed your mom."

She turned to him and snuggled close as she placed one hand to the side of his face. She breathed his air, she was so close.

"You're the man who saves women like my mom." She had always been attracted to Cassidy, but she was in awe of him, of his sacrifice, for the most important woman in his life... his mother. "Your mom always told me and Ellie that the way a boy loves his mama reflected the way he would love a woman. I'd be so lucky if you loved me that way." It was like she was discovering the depth of his heart for the first time. "I'm so sorry for ever disrespecting you with my fear. I was so wrong about you, and a part of me always knew that I was wrong, but I was too afraid to follow my heart. I'm so sorry, baby. I hurt you, and I don't want to do that. You've been hurt for too long. You were trapped for so long, Cassidy. I want to love you so well you feel free. You're free with me, Cassidy. I love you."

"I've loved you from the first time I put eyes on you, Sloan. I thought it would go away as I walked down those years, man. I thought I would forget you. I thought I would get out, and you would be married with a family or some shit. But none of that shit happened. I'm here and you're here. We finally in the same place and on the same page and a nigga just want you, Sloan. I don't give a fuck about the walls you got up, or the demanding job, or none of the other difficult shit you come with. I just want my girl. I'ma do my job with you. I'ma love you like I'm making up for lost time, Sloan. All you got to do is let me."

He kissed the top of her head, and she wrapped her arm around his waist, resting her head on his chest. For the first time since he had been snatched away from her life, Sloan didn't worry, she wasn't afraid. She was safe, and he was safe, and they were together. It was a young dream fulfilled.

# CHAPTER 25

New Year's Eve
Four Days Later

Ellie looked around her new home, and her soul felt full. Her friends and family scattered about, filling the walls with noise and love. Her home was big enough for everyone, and Loyal had spared no expense on the furnishings. It was the perfect place to bring in the New Year.

"Thank you so much, Ellie, for letting me and Christian stay here until I can get on my feet," Courtney stated as she walked up to Ellie, offering a hug.

"Don't even mention it, girl; we're happy to have you," Ellie said. "And it's no rush for you to get out. My home is your home. Have you spoken to James?"

"Not really. He sends me notes from his therapy sessions. I'm glad he's going, but I don't want to go back to that situation. Until he's better, I'm not comfortable with Christian being there without me, either, so Sloan's going to help me with a lawyer so I can file for full custody."

"I think that's smart, and how about you? You scheduled your next therapy session yet?" Ellie asked.

"It's January 2nd, actually. I want to start the year right. I've got a lot of healing to do."

"You're taking all the right steps, Court," Ellie said, cupping her friend's pretty face. "You're so beautiful and so deserving of good things. Never let another nigga play you small again." She put her forehead to Courtney's, and they shook their heads like they used to do in middle school. "I love you, my girl."

Courtney was emotional as she whispered, "Oh, Ellie, jumping your ass in the bathroom in 7th grade is the best thing that ever happened to this friend group," Courtney whispered.

"Jealous-ass bitches," Ellie snickered.

"Knock, knock!"


Ellie turned toward the door as Sloan announced her arrival. Ellie smiled when Cassidy walked in behind her. Seeing their shorthand with one another was amazing. They were a beautiful couple who radiated their love for one another wherever they went. *I really don't know how I didn't see the shit before*, she thought. They just fit, and if Ellie knew her brother at all, she knew it wouldn't be long before he asked Sloan to marry him. They were already spoiling one another. They had missed Christmas together but didn't hesitate to make up for it. Cassidy had purchased her a stunning diamond necklace and tennis bracelet, which she wore proudly. Ellie could see the matching ring coming from a mile away. He was just waiting for the right moment; she was sure of it. Sloan had forced him to put his classic car up for the winter, and they had gone car shopping. She forced him to join the Mercedes club by gifting him an S-Class AMG. They were a successful, sexy couple who exemplified Black love, and Ellie had gone from their biggest hater to their number-one cheerleader. She couldn't get one without the other, these days, because whenever she called Sloan, she was with Cassidy, and whenever she called Cassidy, Sloan picked up the damn phone. They were the annoying-ass couple, and Ellie loved it. She knew her mother would approve.

"Is that my daughter-in-law?" Papa called out.

"You know it is," Sloan replied as she kicked off her snow-covered boots and rushed to hug Bishop first.

"Not you over here sipping. What you got in that cup?" Sloan asked playfully while giving Ellie the eye.

"Not you over here snitching," Papa shot back. "Go'n back over there."

Cassidy chuckled and wrapped Ellie in a bear hug.

"Beautiful home, E," Cassidy stated.

Ellie beamed and replied, "Your boy did good."

"Where we posting up at?" Sloan asked, giving Ellie a warm hug with one arm because she was holding Cassidy's hand with the other. Ellie laughed at how connected at the hip they were. After all those years apart, she knew that they would be inseparable for a while. It was sickening but also adorable. Love had won. "Shy's pulling up now. She was trying to find a spot."

"Okay, cool," Ellie replied. "We can go in the den." She checked her watch. They still had an entire hour before the ball dropped.

"Hey, boo!" Shy shouted. She was her normal, bubbly self.

"Hey, girl, we're in the den, Ellie stated.

"How many shots am I down?" Shy asked.

"None; we just getting the party started," Ellie laughed. "You know I'm an old bitch. Can't turn up too early or I'ma be sleep before the ball drop."

"I'm already anticipating passing out in one of your guest rooms," Shy warned.

Ellie dodged little kids as she walked through the house. "Brooklyn! You and the other teenagers take these kids to the basement! They in grown folks' business up here!" Ellie stated.

She was grateful for the additional living space. When Loyal said renovated, he hadn't lied. The basement was finished to the highest of standards. Her home was beautiful, and as her loved ones filled it, she couldn't be more grateful. He had no clue the gift he had truly given her. The gift was reconnection. She couldn't remember the last holiday season that was filled with this kind of joy.

"You better than me. I would be going crazy with all this eating and drinking and spilling shit in my brand-new house," Shy stated.

"It really doesn't bother me," Ellie said, looking around at the happiness on all her family members' faces. "You buy a house like this to live in it. You fill it with memories. You put kids in every room. You host holidays and birthday parties. I want my house to always feel like this. I just wish…"

"You wish what?" Courtney asked.

Ellie's smile dwindled as she thought of Loyal. "Nothing," she said. The yearning she had for that man was real. She thought of him every day, but she never called. She hoped to hear from him, but it had been almost a week, and her phone never rang. She had gone back to her world, and he had gone back to his. It was like they had never even crossed paths at all— only they had. They had gotten to know each other over this Christmas holiday, and she couldn't un-know him. She took a deep breath. "Okay, let's take shots!" she said, clapping her hands together. Thinking of him would put her in a funk, and that wasn't how she wanted to bring in her New Year. She stood and went to the bar. "I have a full bar, so pick your own poison and drop your keys in the bucket if you having more than two shots. Won't drink and drive on my watch."

Everyone called out their preference, and Ellie started playing bartender. She passed out the drinks and then looked around the room.

"Everybody got a shot?" she asked. She looked at Sloan. "Sis, what you drinking? You want me to make you a drink instead of a shot?"

Sloan looked like a deer in headlights.

"Don't say you ain't drinking. It's New Year's Eve. You already know we're partying all night," Shy teased.

Sloan paused for an awkward beat, and Cassidy sat up in his chair. "You good, baby?" he asked.

Sloan sighed. "Yeah, I umm... Just don't feel like drinking tonight. We've got a drive, but you enjoy yourself. I'm chilling."

"Oh my god! Are you pregnant?!" Ellie blurted.

Cassidy's eyes scanned Sloan's entire body, and Ellie covered her mouth in excitement.

"Wait, what?" Shy asked, stunned.

"Sloan?" Courtney added.

Sloan was visibly uncomfortable as the entire room focused on her. Cassidy was on edge as he commanded her stare. He caressed one side of her face while staring at her curiously. "You got something to tell me?"

"You are, aren't you?" Ellie was so giddy she jumped up and down.

Sloan looked at Cassidy and said, "I wanted to be sure before I told you, but I'm four days late." The look of pure joy that took over his eyes made all Sloan's nerves dissipate. She was weary to announce this news prematurely because she knew how high risk her pregnancy would be, but his happiness brought her so much relief she didn't regret it at all.

"Oh my godddddddd!" The girls shrieked so loudly you could barely make out what they were saying. Sloan's girl tribe swarmed her, pushing Cassidy out of the way as they celebrated.

Cassidy shook his head and smiled. He knew their dynamic, and he laughed as they fawned over Sloan.

"You've wanted this for so long," Ellie crooned. "I'm so happy for you. I can't believe I'm going to be an aunt." She turned to Cassidy and hugged him so tightly. "Mama would be so proud of you. Are you going to tell Papa?"

Sloan stood, and Cassidy pulled her close.

"I wasn't even ready to tell Cass yet. I need to take a real test, Ellie. I need to take so many tests. I'm almost 40 years old. So much can go wrong. I don't want to get excited too fast. What if something happens? What if..."

"Nothing's going wrong, sis. This baby is a gift. Don't let fear take this moment away from you. You didn't have to find a donor. You didn't have to do IVF. No frozen embryos. None of that. I know you're a doctor and you put your belief in science, but I believe God. This baby was made from love. This is already happening for you. You don't have to pray for it anymore. You don't have to worry about it anymore." Ellie wrapped her arms around Sloan one more time, and Sloan broke down.

They had been through so much together. Through 27 years of friendship, to be exact, and it felt like life was just starting to get good. As Ellie, Shy, and Courtney made a circle of love around Sloan, Ellie realized no one could ever take these ladies places. They were the ones she trusted most. They were the ones she would do anything for. Cairo might have left her, and she might have fucked up things with Loyal, and who knows what other man was in her destiny, but one thing she knew for sure, her friends would be there through everything. As the New Year winded down and the countdown commenced, they all counted down together with joy, excitement, and tears in their eyes.

"Ten, Nine, Eight, Seven, Six, Five, Four, Three, Two, One..."

Before Ellie could scream her salutations, she felt a tug on her belt loop. She turned to find Loyal behind her. She wanted to pinch herself to see if this was real. She had wanted him here. She thought about inviting him, but he hadn't expressed the tiniest bit of interest since Christmas Day. He kissed her as the New Year rolled in. Ellie melted into him, and her heart exploded as he took his time with her. "Happy New Year, E," he whispered in her ear.

"What are you doing here?" she asked. She wanted answers, but she wanted his lips more as she held his chin in the palm of her hands and pulled him down toward her. Her friends whooped and hollered around them, hyping her up. Loyal wasn't shy, but he wasn't with this type of shit either. He pressed his forehead to hers, and she placed her hands on the sides of his face, shielding him. It didn't matter that they hadn't spoken. Their connection was just as potent as it had always been. A year could pass, and it wouldn't dilute.

"A friend told me I needed to figure out where I want to be before the streetlights come on," Loyal said.

Ellie's eyes watered, and she looked at Cassidy. There weren't too many people who knew the significance of those words. Her friends knew. Cassidy knew. And her father. Papa walked into the room, and Loyal greeted him like a long-lost son.

"My guy. You made it," Papa said jovially. He was so beguiled by Loyal, and Ellie loved it.

"Did you tell him mama's old saying, Papa?" Ellie asked.

"Let me tell you something. Your mama got that from me. I heard her in there telling y'all to make it home before them streetlights caught you, and she meant that shit. But let me tell y'all how that started. She used to tell me the same thing. Every morning when I would put on my steppers and walk out of that door, she would say those same words. *Bishop, 'be in my door before the streetlights come on'*, but when she said it to me, it meant to beat the moon home. Whatever I was doing that would keep my love out of her grasp had better be finished, and I better make it back home to my woman safe and accounted for before them lights flickered on. And I did. Every night, I'd race home to my wife because the hell I would catch if I didn't, woooweeee," Bishop yelled. Ellie smiled as she listened to her father recount the story. "She taught me responsibility. She taught me accountability. She taught me reliability. If I said I'd be home, then I'd better make it home. Home was safe. Home was love. Wasn't nothing out in them streets after dark but trouble and women. She was trying to keep you out of women, Cass, and she was trying to keep you girls out of trouble. I watched her teach y'all to make it home too. If you love somebody, you keep making it home, no matter how far you are, no matter how hard things are, no matter how busy you are in those streets…" Bishop focused on Loyal. "If you love my daughter, that's what you got to do. Fighting or not. You come home, and you work it out."

"Make it home," Ellie whispered. She turned to Loyal, and she reached for his face, rubbing the tension out of his forehead. "I'm so sorry. I love you. I thought I could sacrifice myself for what my girls needed until I realized that what they needed most was a mom who was happy. I told him no, Loyal. I moved forward with the divorce. I couldn't put my heart into my marriage because my heart is stuck on you."

"Then let a nigga make you his home," Loyal returned. She blushed and held onto him tightly as everyone yelled, "Happy New Year!"

"Aye, son! You and Loyal come have a shot with an old man," Bishop stated. "We got to toast to that new baby that's on the way."

Sloan's mouth dropped in stun.

"Papa, you weren't even in here when I announced that. How did you know?"

"I've known you since you were a little girl, baby girl. I knew then that you would end up with my boy, and I knew when you walked in here that you were carrying my grandchild. Your mother isn't here, and I know you don't know much about your father, but I will always love you like my own. You've always got your papa. You and my grandbaby."

Sloan was a mess, and Ellie was too. They were best friends, but sometimes your friends could be your soulmate too.

Ellie released Loyal and watched the three most important men in her life take a seat on her living room couch. Sloan stepped next to her and grabbed her hand. Courtney and Shy came up on each side of them and huddled close.

"Friendsmas was a success," Shy stated.

"The best one fucking yet," Ellie agreed.

**The End...For Now**

## BOOK CLUB QUESTIONS

1. Will Ellie and Loyal last? Do you think they're moving too fast?

2. Was Sloan justified in her fear of Cassidy?

3. Were Cass and Sloan meant to be or should they have let go of a childhood crush long ago?

4. Will Courtney go back to James? Was she a victim or was she a teenage girl being fast who lost control?

5. Did James love Courtney?

6. Did James' mental health and grief over losing their first son contribute to the way he treated Courtney?

7. Do you think Shy truly prefers women?

8. Why do you think Shy masks who she is behind a fake life for social media?

9. Will Brooklyn and Tessa adjust to the sudden move to Michigan?

10. Should Ellie and Cassidy tell Bishop about their mom's past?

Keep up with Ashley Antoinette on social media
and send her your feedback! She'd love to engage with you!


@ashleyantoinette on Instagram and TikTok
@novelista on X formerly known as Twitter
www.asharmy.com


Also, check out her entrepreneurial endeavors by visiting

www.boujeehippie.co

Printed in the USA
CPSIA information can be obtained
at www.ICGtesting.com
JSHW021917021224
74665JS00011B/16/J